D0983797

A Death in Bali

JENNA MURPHY MYSTERIES

A Head in Cambodia

A Death in Bali

A DEATH in
BALI

A JENNA MURPHY MYSTERY

Nancy Tingley

·Swallow Press | Athens, Ohio

Swallow Press
An imprint of Ohio University Press, Athens, Ohio 45701
ohioswallow.com

© 2018 by Nancy Tingley

Printed in the United States of America
Swallow Press / Ohio University Press books are printed on acid-free paper ⊗ ™

28 27 26 25 24 23 22 21 20 19 18   5 4 3 2 1

Library of Congress Cataloging-in-Publication Data
Names: Tingley, Nancy, 1948- author.
Title: A death in Bali : a Jenna Murphy mystery / Nancy Tingley.
Description: Athens, Ohio : Swallow Press, [2018] | Series: Jenna Murphy
  mysteries
Identifiers: LCCN 2017057487| ISBN 9780804011969 (hardback : acid-free paper)
  | ISBN 9780804040877 (pdf)
Subjects: LCSH: Women detectives--Fiction. | Museum curators--Fiction. |
  Murder--Investigation--Indonesia--Bali (Province)--Fiction. | Bali
  (Indonesia : Province)--Fiction. | BISAC: FICTION / Mystery & Detective /
  General. | FICTION / General. | GSAFD: Mystery fiction.
Classification: LCC PS3620.I537 D43 2017 | DDC 813/.6--dc23
LC record available at https://lccn.loc.gov/2017057487

To Joanna,

who taught me how to

read Borobudur

A Death in Bali

1

The dead man lay in a pool of blood at my feet, my gold sandals glittering in its viscous brilliance, I fought the bile rising to my throat, reached out my hand to steady myself, and encountered only air. So I pushed my feet farther apart, smearing his blood, leaving an arc like the slash of a brush on canvas. Gamelan music floated out of the speakers hanging in the corners of the room, gentle now, though they'd throbbed a hectic beat when I entered.

If I could just find a little distance, a place away from here, a place of safety, I would be okay. I closed my eyes and thought of my work as a curator at the Searles Museum, work that had brought me here to Ubud. I tried to push myself home, away from this carnage. I thought about my parents and brothers. I thought of the hell scenes carved on the Buddhist temple of Borobudur.

I shook myself and looked again at Flip Hendricks, the dead man. I had come to interview him, to study with him, and now I'd never know him. I averted my eyes. I'd known nothing of death until this year, when murder had invaded both my life and my dreams. But those deaths hadn't prepared me any more for this one than the battles fought on the walls of

Angkor Wat or the image of a Rajput painting that now burst into my thoughts, a body gushing brilliant, red blood in all its Technicolor glory.

I heard a sob and, startled, realized it had come from me.

When I entered the room, I'd stepped close to see if he was alive. Foolishly—a man with a spear run through him is certainly not alive. Now I didn't dare move away for fear the police would think my bloody footprints were those of the murderer. Nor did I want to move away. I wanted to find out who had done this. I wanted to take stock of the room and the man. I wanted to understand what had happened here.

He'd thrown his right arm across his face to protect himself. Yet there were no cuts nor scrapes, no bruises nor blood on his hands, no defensive wounds. He was a big man who looked like he would put up a fight. The blade had pierced flesh, then organs, and flesh again to finally stick out of his back a good five inches. Its damascened surface glistened and gleamed red, the blood pooling thick and thin in the rippled, layered metal.

I looked at the ceiling and took another deep breath. Sounds pulled me—chattering crescendos from Ubud's Monkey Forest. The keening that had begun when Flip's servant ran and left me with his ghost swelled up from the next room. Mourning had begun.

With effort, I returned my gaze to the blond hairs that had escaped from his ponytail and flew around his neck, his face. If I focused on the details, the full scene receded. I recalled the online photo of him, his hair down, the thick tresses arranged fanlike across his shoulders, his middle finger raised, flipping us all off. The hair already seemed to be losing its luster. His sensual full lips were parted in the hint of a smile.

Don't be dead, I thought, or maybe I said it. I wanted him to rise and get back to the easel lying on the floor beside him or to the table where our meal was to take place. I wanted the blood to be paint, the spear a joke.

His checkered *sarong*, tied tight around his waist, had fallen open to reveal flesh paler than the dark skin of his upper body and legs. He didn't wear underwear, and I looked away, but only for a moment. A small silk sack suspended from a string around his waist hung next to his genitals.

Outside, the dead man's servant called across the yard. The police. I took in the rest of the room, the overstuffed cushions on platforms and thrown to the floor. The lovely teak dining table set for our lunch. The bamboo-shaped handles of the silverware, small silver bowls atop heavy cream-colored plates. Tall, narrow glasses for iced drinks, batik napkins, and a small tray of *krupuk*, shrimp chips, in the midst of the three place settings. All so proper, so elegant, so at odds with the body.

I looked at the sack tied to his waist and wondered if he had been superstitious. If he, like his servants, would have run from a murdered man. What was in it? An amulet? A love token? An herbal concoction? The key to his murder? I dragged my eyes away and glanced at the paintings on the wall and the paintings and books and brushes and paints thrown to the floor.

A frond from a banana tree stuck through one window, the only window with a screen, a screen carefully cut to fit around the frond. At night, when the servants close the shutters against the mosquitoes, they must leave this window open, so that the tree can grow unhindered.

The voices grew nearer, competing with the women's keening.

I looked at Flip again, certain that the police would soon usher me out, a museum curator who no longer had a reason to be in Bali, a potential suspect, the person who found the body. I mentally catalogued the scene. I didn't seek meanings, just filed image after image, detail after detail. Surely standing here, taking in his posture, the room, the murder scene, meant the ghost would always be with me. The dead man would always be with me.

The dead man. The words produced an uneasy feeling in my mouth, at the back of my throat, in my gut. I looked at the spear and bile rose up. I fought to swallow.

The policeman's voice drowned out the servant's. I took a last look at the body. The arch of his back. The glistening of his blood. The mocking, sensuous lips, that hint beneath the arm of the broad features of a Dutchman, a reminder of Rembrandt's lumpy nose.

My eyes trailed down his body to the small sack, the orange silk, half exposed beneath his checkered *sarong*. I held my breath, reached down, and yanked at the sack, breaking the thread. With a single tug, I pulled open the strings to reveal a tiny bronze figure. Closing it again, I held it over the body, ready to drop it back. Then I hesitated. Maybe this was the reason he'd died. Maybe this was the clue that would tell me who had killed this man and why.

I wanted to know. I wanted to know about the moments before his death and those after. I squeezed the bag's hard contents and stood uncertain, his presence pushing, prodding, egging me on. The bag grew heavier in my hand, and when the policeman and the servant stopped at the door, I stuck it into my pocket, with a groan at the stupidity of what I was doing. I heard the sharp intake of the officer's breath and the sob that struggled from the servant's throat.

I waited for the policeman to tell me to get out, but he didn't. Then I heard him turn on his heel and retch at the side of the house. The servant continued her sobbing, turned away, and left me alone again with Flip.

Looking down at him, I felt queasy at what I'd done, dizzy from the vulnerability of that arm, that ineffective shield. I couldn't leave him on his own.

2

The policeman, finished retching, stood at the door and watched me; he didn't speak to me, tell me to leave. Nor did he come any closer.

The clack-clack of the monkeys' chatter had subsided, and now their jabbering mimicked the hum of a cocktail party, as the gamelan music rose and fell in counterpoint to them. The keening of the women, a pulse of sorrow, rose above all other sounds. The rich, sweet, fragrant aroma of cooking bananas, a particularly Indonesian smell, had filled the air when I arrived and continued unabated.

The single painting that still hung askew above the sitting platform invited my attention. The painting looked to be a Bonnet. Bonnet, a Dutch painter, came to Bali in 1929 and along with the German Walter Spies is said to have revolutionized Balinese art. This was the era that I had come to Bali to research. I squinted at the painting, trying to make out the signature. I thought briefly of walking to it, but my sandals felt glued to the floor.

I squeezed the bag and felt a surge of anger. At him for dying. At his murderer for killing him. At myself for plucking the sack from his waist. The policeman was staring at me, making it impossible to drop the sack back unnoticed. I concentrated on looking around the room for clues.

Absorbed, I didn't hear him coming until he stood beside me. A small man, his shoulder only a few inches higher than mine. He smelled of rice and peanuts. When the call came in, he must have been eating his lunch, a salad of *gado-gado* with peanut sauce, or skewers of *sate* with the same. I continued scanning the room. He looked at the body.

"*Selamat pagi*," I said, good morning, and turned again to the Bonnet. I dropped the silk sack into my pocket.

"*Selamat siang*," the policeman responded, his answer acknowledging the forward movement of time. My greeting a good morning, his, a good midday.

I glanced at him and, following his gaze, said, "It must have been a man."

"Yes. He was very strong."

"Not long before I got here. The blood was still glistening on the blade. It looks dry now. It dried fast in this heat."

"Ah."

"I arrived on time, right about noon. Maybe if I'd been early."

"No one is ever early in Bali."

"No." I pulled my hand out of my pocket, then stuck it back in. He was very still, this man. "If there was a struggle, I can't make out just how it happened. Where was he standing? Who attacked whom? Is his arm raised in defense, or has it just fallen that way? And if he didn't defend himself, why not? If the killer made a search, he was not very thorough. Unless he found what he was looking for and quit looking. Or my arrival interrupted him."

"That's possible," he said.

My thoughts tumbled out of me. "There's something vindictive about swiping the paintings off the wall. The ultimate insult for an artist, isn't it? And, he hasn't pulled off all of them. That Bonnet—I think it's a Bonnet—is still there. And the Spies over

there. Maybe it's only Flip's paintings that are now on the floor."
I looked into his eyes.

"Cruel," was all he said.

"Jenna Murphy." I extended my hand, realizing as I did that
I held my pen, which I shifted to my left hand.

His eyes flashed for a brief moment and he gave me a closer
look, scanning my face, slowing as he looked at my hair, and
frowning. "Wayan Tyo. Welcome back."

His name ruffled the surface of my consciousness, but Balinese names repeat, repeat, beginning with the indicator of birth
order—Wayan, Made, Nyoman, Ketut—followed by a seemingly limited choice of given names. "I came here to talk with
him about painting. To discuss the pre-war Balinese modernists.
My museum—I'm a curator—was given a collection. I know
that he had been pursuing serious research on the topic. Now . . .
What a loss."

We stood in silence, looking down on the man, the spear, the
mess of easel and paints at his side.

I looked again at the banana frond sticking through the window and felt the sweat run down my spine. The monkeys, the
cooking bananas, the jet lag, the dead body. I steadied myself.
From a nearby room the shrill keening had given way to soft
sobbing that shuddered a constant beat.

"Do you need to sit down?" he asked.

"I think the killer knew him and was very angry."

"He'd have to have been feeling some strong emotion to have
done this," he said.

"Beautiful weapon. Look at the damascening. Probably
quite old." The soft patina on the wooden shaft could only be
achieved over years, decades, of handling. "What does one use a
spear like that for?"

He didn't answer. Maybe he didn't know. Maybe he was too
busy making a mental inventory of everything in the room, just
as I had done. Maybe he had stopped looking and was listening

to the sounds of the house, the muffled footsteps as others joined the sobbing women. Maybe the person who had led me in was not a servant, but Flip's lover, or his wife.

Finally he said, "The *puputan* of the royal families in the early twentieth century."

"*Puputan?*"

"The finishing. The Dutch decided to conquer Bali, which they had previously largely ignored."

"Yes, I think, yes. I would like to sit down."

He led me to the dining table and pulled out a chair.

I tried to compose myself, to think of something other than the body that was now blocked by the chairs opposite me. "*Puputan.* Oh, I remember. Some of the regencies in the north fought, but the royal families in the south didn't resist."

"That is right. We came out of our palaces dressed in white, the color of purification and death. We carried lances—spears—though few of us used them on the enemy. Before committing suicide, we men and the older ones, men and women, killed the young women and children with our krises, so that the Dutch could not harm them. Two thousand people slaughtered in a single morning in Denpasar alone. Killed by the Dutch, outright or by suicide."

"This lance is from that time?"

"Maybe. The *puputan* is what comes to mind for me when I see a lance such as this. The weapons loose in our hands, unused."

The sobering tale caused me to ask about Flip, "Are there children?"

"No, not here."

"A wife? Was the woman who brought me in his wife?"

"No. He had women, but no wife."

That tallied with what I'd heard about Flip, that he was a womanizer.

"Are you in shock?"

I was startled by the question. "Shock? No, I don't think so."

He watched me carefully.

I thought for a moment. "I've been mentally cataloguing the room. Trying to imagine the event. Trying to understand what happened."

He nodded. "What have you touched?"

I flushed, the sack suddenly heavy in my pocket. "Touched?"

He pointed at the pen that I still gripped in my hand.

I felt my cheeks heat up. "I, well . . . I wanted to see what he'd been painting. I just lifted the edge of that board a little with the pen. Took a peek. That's all. I didn't move it."

"And?"

"Balinese modernist style, not his usual as far as I know."

"Nothing else?"

I shifted the subject. "Why did you just say 'Welcome back'? I haven't been here since I was a child."

His black eyes flashed as he held up his left pinky. I saw the long nail that Indonesian men favor and for a brief instant wondered what the gesture could possibly mean. Then I saw the thin, narrow scar running from the base of that finger to his wrist. I remembered the nausea I'd felt watching it being stitched. I looked again at his heart-shaped face, the delicate, feminine mouth and wide-set eyes.

"Oh, my god. It's not possible. Tyo?"

He smiled. "Big brother. When you left Ubud all those years ago, when you were eight, I told you that your big brother would always watch over you. This is why we both stand here. I have been awaiting your return. It took you a very long time."

We heard a commotion out in the garden, men's adamant voices and a woman's high, shrill words, yelling something in Balinese that I didn't understand.

Wayan Tyo said, "She wants to come in. I must go to stop her. Come with me."

When a man holds his hand out to you, there's nothing to remind you of him as a child. The palm is larger, the texture of the skin rougher. But the touch is the same. When Wayan Tyo grasped my hand, he used exactly the same pressure he had used when I was eight years old and he was twelve. When his fingers wrapped around mine, electricity ran through me, not a shock or a jolt, rather like a circuit being completed. Was this why I returned? Not my work, my passion for art, my curiosity, my research of these paintings, but a man?

"I need to—" I began to pull the sack out of my pocket to give to him.

"Come," he said, pulling me along, each step stripping my resolve to return the amulet. "We must hurry. She must not see him."

"But I want to—" He didn't listen, his attention on the sounds outside.

As he led me out of the living room, through the hall and out the antique carved front door, memories of that time twenty-odd years ago coursed through me, visceral and unformed. Tyo and his siblings. My brother and me. Tag, hide and go seek, kids strung together in a tug of war. My hand in his. A tear escaped my eye, muddying my vision so that I tripped over the bottom step. He steadied me without turning his eyes from the scene before us. He didn't acknowledge my distress in any other way.

She was thrashing and screaming violently while two young policemen held her arms and tried to calm her. Her words came out in short, venomous bursts of anger. I had no idea what she was saying, but guessed that she was cursing them. Her hair had fallen out of its fastener. It hung over her shoulders and across her eyes and fell down to her narrow waist. Dropping the sack into my pocket, I ran my free hand through my short hair.

She was very beautiful, as most Balinese women seem to be. Both her face and her thin, fragile body belied the strength she displayed as she struggled with the two policemen. She wore tra-ditional Balinese dress, sarong, sash, and the long-sleeved blouse called a *kebaya*. One of her rubber flip-flops had fallen off in the struggle. Her bag now lay on the ground at her feet. Suddenly she leaned back and looked toward us, her mouth opened for another burst of obscenity, but at the sight of me, or maybe of Wayan Tyo, no words came. She stared at me as if in a nightmare and sagged, so that now they didn't need to restrain her, but to support her.

"Ulih, Ulih. You must not go in there." Wayan Tyo let go of me and approached her. "He is gone."

The policemen released her and she fell to her knees. *"Tidak, tidak, tidak,"* was all she could say. No, no, no. She began to sob quietly, her head bent to the ground, all that beautiful glossy hair spilling around her and twining in the groundcover that wove through the stones of the path. Without her to support, the policemen no longer knew where to put their hands. Wayan Tyo knelt at her side.

Flip's death was a loss that shifted her life. Who were they to each other? If I had to guess, I would say he was her beloved.

Ulih's heartrending sobs joined those of the mourners inside the house, and I realized that though his death angered me and I would search for his killer, it was not personal. I'd stood over his body and tried to recreate the crime. I'd escaped from the reality of a dead body into the intellectual exercise, the whys and wherefores. I looked down at my hand; it was shaking. Maybe I was in shock.

Ulih unfolded herself from the ground and from Wayan Tyo's gentle words. She picked up her bag and asked, "Who is she?"

"She found him. She has just arrived and came to talk with him about business. She never met him."

She turned back to go down the gaily bordered path, welcoming and at odds with the surfeit of distraught emotion. She shifted the bag from her arm onto her head, steadying it as she walked. The lush grounds and the exotic woman created a scene right out of a glossy guidebook. To the right, in the northeast corner of the property, the household shrine was laden with offerings, sacred water, woven containers resting on textiles, flowers.

It was all very pretty. I'd arrived in paradise. Or had I?

Sirens were sounding. People were gathering at the gate.

"Tyo, I need to—" I fingered the sack.

"Not now, Jenna. I'm busy here. This officer will take you back to the station for questioning." He distractedly directed the arriving officers toward Flip's living room.

"Aren't you going to question me? And why do I need to be questioned? I arrived, the servant took me to the living room, and we found the body."

"Yes." He turned to a young man who was carrying two heavy bags. "Leave the one out here. There's no room for all that."

People were pressing up to the gate. An elderly woman the size of a child had entered and was toddling up the walk. "Get her out of here," Tyo yelled to the officer by the gate, who had been too respectful of his elders to do more than scold her gently as she entered.

I pulled the sack out of my pocket. "Tyo, I need to—"

"Really, Jenna. We can talk tomorrow. You will come to my mother's house for dinner, and we can talk then."

"I think it's better if . . ." I wanted to give him the sack. I wanted to turn back time and stop myself from taking it.

He said to one of the officers who had held up Ulih, "Take her down to the station and have Nyoman question her. Tell him that she was the one who found the body."

I was beginning to panic and tried to catch his eye. "I want you to question me." He didn't answer. "Please, Tyo."

Exasperated, he said, "Tomorrow. We'll talk tomorrow." And he turned and walked into the house.

"I need to speak with you in private," I called out and started to follow, but the officer who was to take me to the police station stepped belligerently between us.

I felt abandoned. Annoyed. I fingered the outline of the small figure in the sack. Angry. At Tyo for not listening to me.

But more at myself for taking the thing. As we walked toward the gate, I considered dropping the sack on the ground, but the thirty or forty people who had gathered to watch the excitement would see, and really, I wanted to give it to Tyo. To explain to Tyo what had been going through my mind when I'd taken it.

What had I been thinking?

I looked back at the chaos of the crime scene. At least a dozen people milled around the front yard. How many more were in the house, I didn't know. But they were walking everywhere, through the garden, around the pool.

The officer said, "Come," and tugged at my elbow, gently at first, but when I still didn't move, more forcefully.

"Just a minute. What are they doing? Why aren't they trying to find footprints? Trying to preserve the scene as it was when I arrived?"

He looked toward his colleagues and shrugged.

"They don't know what they're doing," I said.

"We do not have murders in Ubud," he said, as if that excused their behavior. They did have TV, and everyone who had TV knew what you should do at a crime scene. You should wear white booties on your feet, a mask on your face. "Come."

"Did she do it?" someone called out as we pushed through the crowd.

"No," he said.

But when I got to the police station, you would have thought otherwise. They took my prints and photographed and questioned me as if I were their number one suspect.

3

Walking numbly away from the police station, I tried to find balance. I'd been thrown by Flip's lifeless body. By meeting Tyo. By my own foolish action.

The one positive thing that had happened in the station was that they hadn't frisked me. If they'd found the sack, I would probably be in a cell. I wasn't a thief. I wasn't a criminal. But I was impulsive. I shook my head. I had to give the sack to Tyo—though after seeing the way the police were acting at the crime scene, I doubted they would ever find the killer.

What should I do? I tried to calm my racing mind, but the busy streets only heightened my anxiety. Cafés bore names like Lucky's Warung, their menus all alike, spiceless fried rice and fried noodles, pizza and ice cream. They had embraced the Western need for choice, though they called themselves *warung,* those individual stalls that traditionally served a single dish—fried fish, roast chicken, suckling pig.

If I could transport myself from the events of this day, get some distance . . . I stopped walking, closed my eyes, tried to visualize Ubud that summer twenty years ago when my family visited. The color green flashed before me—trees, rice—a lushness only intermittently interrupted by yellow or a splash of red. I didn't recall this busy scene.

I opened my eyes. Unable to hold the memory of Ubud a lifetime ago, I stopped and read one menu after another, my finger underlining the words, as if by this mundane act I could reverse time. As if I were on my way to Flip's, ready to eat. As if I would arrive early to find a living man. As if I didn't have this sack in my pocket.

My stomach roiled with hunger. Yet the hunger battled with a queasiness. The officer's abrupt, threatening questioning at the police station had done nothing to calm me. If only it had been Tyo.

I recalled his warmth when he'd explained who he was. But then he'd been abrupt as I left. I sighed, looking blindly into the café before me. "Come in, come in," said a waiter.

The cafés wanted me to eat, but I couldn't, so I moved on to a row of boutiques. They insisted I buy. Flowing garb, gaudy jewelry, carvings in multiples of twenty or forty. I stared in at a jewelry store window, not at the displays, but at my reflection. Me in Ubud, me alive. I held the image in my mind, but only for an instant. Flip with a spear through his chest, blood haloing his body, gazed back at me. I closed my eyes.

A stranger, I consoled myself. A man I never met. A man whose last moment was etched on my mind forever. The spear, the blood . . .

"Come in, come in," said a young shopkeeper. "Very pretty earrings for you."

"Taxi," said a man to my right.

"Taxi," said his friend.

I turned and walked on.

One day soon, when the world righted itself, I would go through the shops, searching for a bargain. I'd enjoy the back and forth, the foreplay and the consummation of making the deal, of the haggling. Not today. I needed to get back to my hotel. I needed to curl up on my bed. I needed to sleep. I concentrated on navigating a path through the throng of tourists. A man's elbow jabbed my ribs. A woman yammering to her husband collided with me, then glared.

I stopped to take my bearings. The distraction of stores and restaurants, the art galleries with their gaudy abstract paintings bursting with hints of Bali—half-visible sheaves of rice, Rangda the witch's bared teeth, the thatched roof of a temple—was not enough. Not enough to wipe Flip, the wisps of his hair, the arc of his arm, the arch of his back, from my eyes.

I stepped off the curb to avoid being run over by a group of jostling Australians.

I felt like Alice in some overwrought version of Wonderland. The roar of motor scooters and horns honking, the jostling of tourists and hawkers, a visual and aural onslaught. I reached my turnoff and was within five minutes of my hotel when I noticed a small building set back from the road, a little retreat from the madness. A discreet sign read "textiles," and in a bid to escape I turned down the short path. Tactile textiles were a soothing promise, a reprieve from that pool of blood.

"*Selamat siang*," the young shopgirl said.

"*Siang*," I answered, and automatically asked her how she was. "*Apa kabar?*"

She smiled. "*Baik.* Can I help you with anything?"

"Just looking." I knew a little Bahasa Indonesia, the national language, and to practice, I said, "*Lihat-lihat saja.*" I didn't know any Balinese, but knew she would understand the Bahasa.

She stepped back behind the small counter and sat, pulling out her cell phone.

Along the walls textiles hung on wooden rods that stuck out like tree limbs, haphazard and bristling. Piles of new textiles sorted by the island of production filled the center table. Batiks from Java, natural-colored *ikats* from Timor and Flores, and the *ikats* of Sawu and Roti, with their greater concentrations of blues and reds. I stared at a Roti sarong, so similar to one thrown over the back of Flip's couch that they could have been woven by the same hand. Red the color of dried blood. Shaking myself, I looked up to the old textiles hanging on the wall.

"Do you have other examples of old *tapis*?" I asked, turning from Roti and Flip and blood to a fine Sumatran piece framed and hanging above the others on the wall. I had always wanted one of these skirts, with its combination of *ikat* ground—the pattern dyed into the thread before weaving—and the entire field embellished with embroidery.

"Yes, we do," she said, but made no move to go to get the other *tapis*. I riffled a pile of cloths on the table, thinking she was just finishing a text, a game. The seconds became a minute, two. I had lost any interest, feigned or otherwise, in the textiles in the pile, and irritation bubbled up. "Can you show them to me?"

"No, madam. I am not able." She kept looking at her screen.

I waited for her to explain and when she didn't I said edgily, "And why is that?"

She looked up, but her fingers continued to move over her phone. "They are locked in the back and only my boss has the key. She is not here today."

I asked as calmly as I could, "When will she return?"

"Tomorrow afternoon, I think. Can you come back then?" She poked at the keys.

"Yes. Do you have a business card?"

"Yes, sorry, Bu." She handed me the card. She was addressing me as an older woman, though she didn't look any younger than me.

Outside on the step, woolly-headed from jet lag, disoriented by death, I determined not to make any more stops. Murder had made me angry.

A hundred yards down the road my determination dissolved. I was drawn by the familiar. Row upon row of bicycles, and at the back, a Giant ATX Pro, red and just my size. An entry-level mountain bike that couldn't compare to my bike at home, but it would work. I entered the shop. A young man, dressed in biking clothes, came around the counter to greet me. "Sorry, are you about to go out?" I asked.

He looked puzzled. "Out?"

I realized he wore his biking clothes around the shop. His prerogative. "I want to rent this bike." Together we walked outside, where I pointed at the Giant that I wanted.

"Sorry, we use that bike for our tours. You can rent any of those." He pointed to a row of inferior bikes.

"No. I want that bike. How much is it?" All the emotion that I'd felt, the distress at the murder, the anger at Flip for dying in that macabre fashion, my disgust at myself for taking the silk sack, welled up. For an instant, irritation surged at Ubud—at the Westernized cafés, the curio shops, men who wore their biking gear when they weren't biking, shopgirls who texted rather than paying attention to their customers.

"I can't rent you that one." He pointed at another one. "This is a very good bike. I think you will like it."

He didn't know me, so he didn't see me switch from irritation to determination, my jaw set, my feet become grounded. "Where's your boss?"

"He's out in the shop repairing a bike for a tour." He waved his arm in the direction of a building behind the small curio shop next door. "He does not want to be disturbed."

I felt the need for control, for something to happen as I wanted it to happen, and I headed in the direction he'd indicated. I needed a single transaction, a single event, to occur in a manner I understood. Not a murder. Not a dead man at my feet. I needed the security of having a bike I would enjoy riding, a touchstone that related to my life at home.

"Excuse me, Bu, I am afraid you cannot go out there." He tried to keep up, but I pointed to two people who were looking at the row of bikes nearest the road. He hesitated, and I put some distance between us.

Three men, hands on hips, consternation on brows, stood around an inverted bike. One was shaking his head. I stopped. They were just guys trying to fix a bike. None held a spear in his hand, or for that matter a phone. They were neither threatening nor dead. They had nothing to do with what had just happened in my life. They were familiar, bikers focused on the one thing that mattered, that bike.

The shopkeeper I'd been talking with caught up with me. He apologized to the one not wearing biking clothes, the boss, in Balinese, said something about the Giant ATX. All four of them scowled.

I took a deep breath. "Excuse me. You have a bike out here that I want to rent."

"I'm sorry, Bu," said the boss. "We need that bike for a tour that we are taking out tomorrow."

I spun the front wheel of the bike they were repairing, picked up a wrench, and fiddled with it until it was fixed. It wasn't a complicated repair, but they looked impressed, so I pushed my advantage. "It's nowhere near as good as my Safire Pro, but it would do."

I hated myself for bragging, but I had three brothers and I rode with men, so I knew that bikers respected one of their own. They looked stunned. I guessed they knew the stats for every bike in the world, even though the best ride they had here in Bali couldn't compare to what was available in the West. "So how much is the rental on the Giant for two weeks?"

"I'll be happy to help you," the boss said as he accompanied me back to the storefront. "What did you do?"

I explained, then asked him about his favorite rides on the island. By the time I left, he and the men who had been repairing the bike had given me a list of rides and invited me to accompany them on a lengthy one they'd been planning. We exchanged numbers.

As I walked away, the bike at my side, I had the sensation of someone watching. I looked around for Tyo. Tourists sheathed in sarongs, hats, and sunscreen busied the sidewalk. Tyo was nowhere in sight. I stumbled and caught myself, the bike's handlebars a strong horizontal keeping me upright. Crazy to think Tyo would follow to take care of me, then only watch from a distance. But he might follow unseen if he suspected me of murder. I couldn't think why he would. My interrogation had been relatively brief.

I climbed on the bike and headed back to my bungalow and a nap. As I rode, I thought of calling Alam. Talking with him would be calming. But it was the middle of the night in California, and we had decided to use this trip to consider our relationship. I had told him I needed to spend some time apart. He wanted a commitment, and I needed to think about that.

4

Loud splashing and hollering from the pool awakened me from my afternoon drowse. My first thought was that maybe I should have taken that quiet bungalow at the far end of the compound. My second contradicted the first, as any more sleep and I'd be awake all night. My third was of blood glistening on a lovely, sharp blade. Veering from that last thought, I let my ears take over, listening to men laughing, water lapping against the side of the pool. A swim sounded good.

As I rolled onto my side I felt the hard amulet press against me. Sitting up, I pulled the silk bag out of my pocket and looked at it for a long moment. I turned it over in my hand, tested the strings that opened it. I thought, if I don't open and examine it closely, it won't mean anything. But that was magical thinking.

It felt hot in my hand, like metal in the noonday sun. I must have been lying on it, though I'd awakened on my back, in the same position I'd fallen asleep. Strange. I ran my finger over the bag, then yanked at the strings.

The tiny sculpture dropped into my hand. I took a single long look before I put him back. I'd seen him before, or a figure like him. My hands trembled as I pulled the strings tight to rid myself of his accusing gaze.

Shaken, I put the silk bag in my toiletry kit and prepared for a swim.

Looking at myself in the mirror, I cursed bathing suit makers for the thousandth time. Why can't they make bikini tops to fit me? Not all large-breasted women wear a size 16; some of us are small-boned and petite. I readjusted the cups that were too far apart and revealed more than I wanted to reveal. No time to fix that now. No diving today.

By the time I got outside, the racket had died down and the men I'd heard lay dripping on lounge chairs. A French couple had taken over one end of the small pool, their chaises far from each other and their voices loud to cover the distance. The man's intonation reminded me of an old boyfriend. A French boyfriend dimmed by the men I had known since.

A single chair crowded the narrow side of the pool, and another was set close to the men. About my age, though moments before they had been acting like they were twelve. I had no problem with being twelve; sometimes I was twelve myself. I headed toward the chair near them, the fragrance of the plumeria tree a remembered scent.

"The water's great," the shorter, hirsute one said to me in an American accent.

"I heard," I said as I pulled the chaise so that it wasn't too close to them.

"Did we wake you?" asked the other. Another American. He was tall, lean, and very tanned, which suggested they'd been in the tropics a while. His short hair revealed a single pierced ear with a tiny lapis earring. I noted that he didn't have any visible tattoos, and probably none at all, given the size of his bathing suit. That was good. I don't like tattoos; too permanent. I've sworn never to sleep with a man with tattoos or more than three piercings. Alam had neither.

"Wake me?" I rubbed my face to erase any pillow creases on my cheek.

He pointed and laughed. "You still have an earplug in one ear."

"Ah. I thought you were making an insightful guess." I pulled out the plug and stuck it in my bag.

"Maybe you just arrived?"

"Yep, jet lag." And death, I thought as I arranged my towel on the chair. "Have you been here long?"

"No, got here a couple of days ago. Came from Thailand through Singapore. This is the finale of the trip. My name's Seth, by the way." He raised his hand.

"Randall," said his friend.

"I'm Jenna. What do you do when the trip ends?" I took off my sarong.

"We have to get back to the States, to jobs." Seth raised his beer bottle in a toast.

I held up the sunscreen in response, wondering if I needed it this late in the afternoon.

"We hope to jobs," Randall said, sitting up a little as he watched me. He ducked his head toward Seth. "He has more interviews."

The Frenchman burst out laughing, and his wife threw a towel at him.

"What kind of work do you do?"

"Just passed the bar."

"And a last trip before the grind?" I asked as I stretched out, the chair feeling a bit like a ship at sea. Jet lag wooze.

He nodded. "This is our celebration. You?"

"Here for work and I'm taking advantage of the free flight by adding on a two-week vacation. Seeing the sights, enjoying the sun."

"Your first time in Indonesia?"

"No, my family spent a summer in Bali when I was eight."

"I imagine a lot has changed. What do you do?"

"Museum curator."

"You're working here as a curator?" Randall brightened, clearly impressed.

"No, no, I work in California, in Marin. I'm here to research Balinese paintings. My museum has a large collection, and we're planning an exhibition." I was conscious of them looking at me. "I think I'll get into that water."

I WAS floating beneath the plumeria tree, its long, curving branches hanging over the pool to provide shade and an exotic, otherworldly ambiance. I imagined being driven backward by the force of a spear piercing me. If my arms were at my sides, the surprise, the shock of pain would probably keep them at my sides. If I had my arm out, trying to stop the person, then what?

I threw my arm across my eyes, twisted my head to the right, and curled my left leg upward beneath me. All very easy floating in the water. Holding my left shoulder in place proved harder. I thrust and twisted my abdomen, leaving imaginary space beneath me for a six-inch blade. Even in the water, the position wasn't comfortable. I removed my arm, opened my eyes, and saw Seth standing by the edge looking down at me.

I stood.

A slight smile flickered over his lips. "We're going to dinner in a bit, then to see a performance of the Rangda and Barong dance. Like to join us?"

I didn't hesitate. A distraction was just what I needed. "Sure, that would be nice. What time?"

"We're going to the 7:30 performance at the Royal Palace. There are lots of performances around town, but that promises to be a good one—as far as tourist performances go. See you at 6:30?"

As he walked away, I thought of the pros: nice body, not terribly muscled but not flabby, pleasant face, seemingly intelligent, bushy eyebrows with the one off at an angle giving him a rakish air. A charmer, though I wasn't sure if that was a pro or a con. Cons: work to do, Wayan Tyo's family to meet again, staying in the same hotel, his hirsute companion, here only part of my stay. No, the fact that he was here only a short time tallied on the pro side.

I leaned my head back and floated once again. I thought of home and Alam. Alam who called me regularly. Alam whom I'd avoided as best I could since our trip to Cambodia the previous fall. Alam who had said he was persistent and who hadn't been exaggerating.

We were now eight thousand miles apart, a distance made greater by the decision to reconsider whether or not we wanted to continue seeing each other. I glanced again at Seth, then went back to my floating.

5

"I've got this," said Seth, pulling out his wallet.

"No, I'll pay for mine."

"Really, it's nothing. A bargain."

We stood in front of a large covered pavilion near the entrance to Ubud Palace. "The museum covers my expenses." I handed him the money.

He acquiesced and the three of us found seats midway in the audience with a good view so Randall could photograph the performance. The gamelan orchestra sat to either side of the stage, all men and each wearing a vivid turquoise shirt and *udeng*, the traditional batik hat.

"I've been looking forward to seeing the Barong and Rangda dance in Bali. I saw a performance here when I was a child. I remember that it was terrifying. More recently I attended one at Zellerbach Auditorium at UC Berkeley, but contained indoors on a stage it lost some of its force."

"Terrifying? Why?" Seth asked.

"I can't remember exactly, but I recall dozens of Barongs swarming a wide street and performers with krises that they turned on themselves."

"And why was your family here?"

"My parents believed that you should subject your children to as much culture and difference as possible. Maybe 'difference' is the wrong word. My father's a teacher, and he's always teaching. Well, almost always." I thought of my father's drinking.

"Ah."

"So each summer we went on a vacation that was intended to teach us—about a new region, a culture, history, art. Whatever. This was our most exotic vacation." I thought for a moment. "One of our most exotic. I think they must have saved for years."

"No Europe?"

"To Washington, D.C., one year, the Four Corners a couple of times—cheap camping—Mexico once. That was a trip. We drove, which turned out to be a bad idea. Once they took us to Europe, to the Mediterranean, from Greece over to Turkey. They encouraged us to save our earnings and travel the continent during college vacations."

Randall interrupted. "We've seen the groups of men and boys in the costume of Barong. But who is Barong? He's fierce looking, but this program says he represents good."

"Yes, he's fierce—he looks something like a lion. But he fights endless battles with the evil witch Rangda. For the Balinese, the battle represents the struggle between good and evil," I said, fanning myself. I was thankful for the light breeze that blew through the open-air pavilion, but it wasn't enough.

The many pieces listed on the program suggested abbreviated versions of the battle between Barong and Rangda as well as shortened *legong* dances, unless we were going to be here for four hours. I realized how much I wanted the lengthy tense and primal battle between Barong and Rangda, especially now. Hadn't I seen evil win out just this afternoon? The murder of a man—a complicated man, not a good man according to all I'd heard, but could murder ever be for good? Still, there would be time for more dance and music during my stay; performance was an art form that permeated Balinese life.

"He has to be fierce to stand up to evil," Seth volunteered.

"I guess." Randall frowned.

"Quite an eclectic crowd," said Seth.

"Yes, it is," I replied. Around us I heard Chinese, Australian English, Spanish, Italian, but no other American accents, which surprised me, as everyone I knew back home seemed to have gone to Bali, to be in Bali, or was planning a trip.

As the music started, a man in the second row set up his tripod in the middle of the center aisle, blocking the view along either side. He raised the level of the tripod to a foot above everyone's head and began focusing his camera. "Honestly," I said.

"Tourists," said Randall smiling.

The woman in front of us asked him to move the tripod out of the aisle, which he did, but he didn't lower it. I asked him to do that, and he complied, grudgingly. Flashes went off right and left as a dancer appeared on the stage. At a performance at home, I thought, the first announcement would be to turn off your camera's flash.

The dancer, wearing richly brocaded textiles and a headdress with two bobbling pom-poms, met the rising and falling beat of the instruments with her hands, her feet. Her eyes widened in astonishment and joy. I would have found her expression exaggerated in other circumstances, but it now reflected my own gyrating emotions. Cameras flashed, people stood, photographed, sat down. It all felt a bit surreal, an impression driven by the gongs and drums of the gamelan.

Seth laid a hand on my knee and leaned toward me. "How does it compare to the performance in the States?"

"Good. The dance is a precise series of gestures and steps, so not so different. It feels more authentic than in the States, maybe because of the setting." I felt the warmth of his palm and his breath in my ear. I shifted my knee slightly and he withdrew.

"Can't imagine dancing in this humidity," Randall said. "Especially with those elaborate costumes."

I nodded, keeping my eyes on the dancers, not wanting to engage.

Tripod man raised his tripod, again blocking my view. I closed my eyes and let myself be carried along by the rhythmic gamelan, the percussive sounds so different from Western music. The drums beat, the gongs rang out, a flute cut in, and I felt as if I had arrived. The morning's woes receded. Tripod man was still there when I opened my eyes, but I didn't care. Someone would ask him to sit eventually, and the dancer was now to one side of the stage. I turned my attention to the people standing along the sides of the pavilion.

I tried to guess their nationality by their dress, their haircuts, the way their mouths moved when they spoke. A man near the front looked French, but when he bent over to speak to his wife, his mouth didn't have that little moue that the French language gives a person, and I put him down as German. The young girl next to him, with her Rasta hair, could have been from anywhere, but I guessed Australia because the two people with her clearly seemed Australian.

I looked to the opposite side of the pavilion. A man was staring at me. A tall, gangly, wild-looking man with deep-set eyes, hair run amok, and a mobile, twitching mouth. I stared back, and he abruptly turned away. I shivered, seeing that lance once again, this time imagined in this wild man's hands, moving forward, toward me rather than Flip. I shook my head. But this man hadn't killed anyone, he was just doing the same thing I was doing, looking at the people, guessing. It's what we do when we travel: gauge our surroundings, the strangers, try to find our place. I looked back to the performance.

Barong entered through the middle of three doorways that led onto the stage.

"Pretty silly, if you ask me," Randall said.

From a Western perspective, he was right. Barong's shuddering jaw, his inability to get through the door, and the fact that there was no threat in sight to bring on his exaggerated acting combined to make him seem silly, a silliness to us because of our different relationship to time. Barong's movement wasn't so different from one of those long rhythmic passages in the gamelan that, to a Western ear, sounds repetitive. We want to say, get on with it, what's the next note, the next dance step? While the Balinese is content to stay in the moment.

I tried to sink into it, to the tempo of the music, the simplicity of the action onstage, but maybe my day had been too filled with adrenaline. Maybe I just felt off-center, disoriented. "Too bad," I said to Randall as Barong left the stage.

"What is?" Seth leaned toward us.

"No battle. There's usually a terrific battle." Though you would think that I had had enough violence for the day. I was cranky and tired, wondering what had brought me to this performance with these men. If my intention had been to find escape, it wasn't working.

Seth's arm had found its way over the back of my chair, and I thought of Alam, his arm draped over my chair at a different performance. I leaned forward slightly, not really shrugging it away, but sending a signal. He didn't seem to get it.

Glancing back at the sidelines, I saw the Wild Man once more staring at me. Did I know him? Again he pretended to be perusing the crowd. "Is that man over there staying at our hotel?" I asked Randall.

He looked at him. "I haven't seen him, but we only got to the hotel a few hours before you."

"I thought you'd been in Bali a few days."

"We have, but Seth made us change hotels. He said the place we were in was too noisy. They made a big fuss because we were checking out ten minutes past checkout time. They wanted to charge us for the night." He shook his head in exasperation. "I didn't think it was particularly noisy."

I leaned back, wondering why Seth had suddenly wanted to change hotels. The music quieted. A *legong* dance based on the great Indian epic the *Mahabharata*, began. It was beautifully done, calming, the dancer's gestures reason enough to have come to the performance. Though her feet moved little, her hands and facial expressions told an elaborate tale, and I found myself relaxing, enjoying the soothing moment.

Then a man dressed in white appeared, flicking water out of a small pot with the tips of his fingers. Suddenly fifty men dressed in checkered sarongs rushed onto the stage, their shaking arms raised along with their voices as they grunted loudly. The grunting became the rat-a-tat chorus of the *kecak* dance, a drama developed in the early twentieth century as a scene from the *Ramayana*. The men sat in a circle and adopted casual poses, muting their voices until one of them shouted out a command and they began to jiggle their shoulders as their arms shot forward. The rat-a-tat-tat increased in speed and volume.

The *kecak* dance was brief but powerful, with its choreographed postures and stances and the aggressive chorus. Monkeys in the forest, machine guns, verbal violence. And there I was again, standing over Flip, the mourners keening, the monkeys' voices surging forth from the nearby Monkey Forest. I shivered.

I looked for the Wild Man, but he'd gone.

6

"Let's get a beer," Randall said as we walked out. "That place we went last night?"

"Good idea," said Seth. "You up for it, Jenna?"

I hesitated, but, with the picture of that spear in my mind, didn't want to walk to the hotel alone.

Seth reached for me. I stepped off the curb to avoid his reach and the hole in the sidewalk in front of me. I wasn't sure which offered a greater threat.

He smiled. "I was trying to steer you away from that hole. I wasn't sure if you saw it."

"Oh, thanks. I did." Embarrassed by my suspicious and libidinous mind, I answered the opposite of what I really wanted to say. "Sure, why not?"

The bar wasn't far, and as we entered I laughed at the cliché— the bamboo walls, rattan furniture, palm trees in the corners and separating tables. Christmas lights illuminated all, while a pulsing beat announced the dance floor at the back of the club. "Is this your kind of place?" I asked them.

"When in Bali . . ." Seth responded, smiling.

"I think I'm overdressed," I said. I was wearing a T-shirt and pants, but halter tops and skimpy shorts about the size of butt floss seemed to be the costume of choice.

Seth said, "If it makes you feel better about fitting in, you could—"

I cut him off, "Don't go there. You could, too." I pointed. A number of the men, clearly those who worked out, didn't wear shirts. Some had T-shirts thrown over their shoulders. Others had them tied around their waists. Some had clearly left their clothing behind in their hotels. The weather was hot, but not that hot.

"That looks pretty tasty," I said. Seth looked over his shoulder. I smiled. "Must be a margarita. What did you think I meant?"

He didn't respond, but said, "More likely a rum drink. Seems to be their specialty."

"What do you want?" Randall shouted over the noise.

"I'll have one of those," pointing at the blended, icy drink, "but without the rum."

"Better with the rum," Seth said.

"Not tonight."

"Maintaining control?" He had a twinkle in his eye, which I both liked and simultaneously wanted to quash.

"Trying to stay awake. Rough day."

"In Bali? How does one have a rough day in Bali?"

"You'd be surprised." I scanned the room, which was not quite packed. There were empty tables, but people were standing three deep at the bar—pickup time. I pointed to a table and we headed that way, while Randall went toward the bar. Two young women who appeared to have taken lessons from their hippie mothers were the only dancers, their sarongs psychedelic, their arms flung upward, their hips rotating at half-speed.

"He didn't ask you what you wanted."

"We've been traveling together for a few weeks already. He knows what I want."

I had a momentary thought that maybe they were a couple, though Seth's flirtation with me didn't seem to get a rise from Randall. I watched the people coming through the door, probably an influx from the performance. I suddenly remembered the bombing at the Balinese nightclub in 2002, and the thought made me place Flip here, rather than in his home.

"So, why a rough day?"

I ignored the question, watching Randall struggling to pick up the three drinks. Most of his troubles were caused by my oversized blended monstrosity. Practically an entire fruit bowl hung from the rim of the glass. I jumped up and ran over to help him. The glass in my hands was full, so I stopped to take a sip. As I raised my head I saw the Wild Man. He saw that I'd noticed him, but didn't turn away.

"That man is staring at me again. The one in the red shirt."

He looked over, "The one from the performance, standing on the sidelines."

"Yes, and he's still staring."

"There's a reason for that."

"What do you mean?" I tried to take another sip of the drink, but a spike of pineapple went up my nose.

"You're a looker, as my father would say."

I laughed. "Thanks, Randall."

Randall set down his and Seth's drinks. Seth, distracted by all that was going on behind us, paid no attention. He nodded to someone at the bar. I turned to look and saw half a dozen women in his line of vision as well as the Wild Man still looking our way.

"See someone you know?" I asked.

"No." He picked up his drink and, without meeting my eyes, took a sip.

I was beginning to realize that murder made a person skittish and suspicious. Being in a Balinese nightclub also made one a bit edgy. This bar was a bad idea, but the thought of walking home alone continued to spook me.

"At the bar they're talking about a murder," Randall said.

"Here? In Ubud?" Seth asked.

"Yep. A tourist, in his rented house."

"An expat," I said.

"How was he killed?" Seth watched me.

"No one seems to be sure. Probably shot, was the consensus." Randall wiped his wet hands on his pants.

"Spear," I said, having cleared a space between the pineapple, the kiwi, and an apple. I took a sip while they stared at me. "I found the body."

Randall's mouth dropped open, but it was Seth who asked, "You found a murdered body and you didn't say anything to us?"

"It's not exactly a great opener for someone you've just met. Oh, hi, I'm Jenna and I've just come from a murder scene. Or maybe I could have brought up Indonesian weaponry, or how blood congeals in the patterning on a damascened blade." I shivered.

"Would have been a rush for Seth. He studied criminal law." Randall sipped his beer.

"'Rush' might not be the right word, but I'm sure you would have caught my interest. Guess that's what you meant when you said you had a rough day." He leaned forward. "Are you okay?"

I took another sip so he wouldn't see the tears that welled up at his concern, and got ice on the tip of my nose. I wiped it away. "It's also the reason that that man over there, the one in the red shirt, is making me nervous staring at me."

Before I could say anything, Seth was halfway across the room, headed toward the Wild Man. The man's expression went from startled to smiling in an instant. He raised both hands palms forward in a gesture of pacification. Seth's back told me little.

"Was it awful?" Randall asked.

I thought for a moment, trying to condense the experience into words. "It was so unlikely. I'd gone to have lunch with him." I paused, searching. "Then finding him, seeing him like that. Disconcerting. Sad. Horrifying. Bloody. Awful, yeah, awful sums it up."

"You haven't processed it," he said matter-of-factly as he leaned forward and set down his glass.

"I'm avoiding processing it. Processing isn't really my thing. Pressing forward is more my modus operandi."

"Ah," Randall said.

We watched Seth and Wild Man chatting. Seth leaned on the bar. The man appeared to offer him a drink. Seth shook his head, motioning toward our table and his full glass.

As he slid back into his chair, he said, "He says you look like an old girlfriend."

I waited for more, but when it didn't come, I asked, "And?"

He took a sip of his drink. "Not much else. He's Australian. Friendly enough guy."

I should have confronted the man myself. Maybe Seth already knew him. Maybe it was the Wild Man he'd been nodding to a few minutes earlier. I tried to quell my suspicious brain. From Randall's reaction when I asked him about the man, it seemed clear that they hadn't met before. And since Randall and Seth were traveling together, you would assume if one knew him, the other would, too.

"Do you want to tell us about the murder?" Seth asked.

"Give her a break," Randall said protectively. "She's tired. She doesn't want to think about it."

"He's right. I'm tired. I need to finish this and get home to bed." I looked at the size of the drink in my hand. I thought I discerned rum, but I'd told Randall no alcohol. Maybe he'd ignored me.

Seth frowned at Randall before saying to me, "From your coming with us to the performance tonight, then here, I'd say you're avoiding thinking about it. It might do you good to talk."

He was right. It might be good. "I can give you an abbreviated version of what happened." And I did.

7

The French couple who had been at the pool the previous afternoon sat on the other side of the hotel's dining pavilion. They nodded at me as I entered. I considered speaking to them, but it was hard enough struggling with my minimal Bahasa Indonesia; digging up the French I knew was more than I could face.

The waitress came out of the kitchen and walked my way. "*Selamat pagi.*"

"*Selamat pagi,*" I answered.

"What would you like to drink?"

"Tea, please."

Pointing at the empty seat at the table, she asked, "One more?"

"No, I'm alone." I didn't add that I didn't have to be alone. That the night before Seth had made it clear that he would be happy to join me in my room. He'd been attentive in the bar, but still, I sensed he was a lady's man and a bad boy, which was why he drew me. Always the bad boy—one reason that I was inclined to hold Alam, the good boy, at bay.

As she cleared away the other place setting, I asked her her name.

"Ketut," she said.

In the garden an enormous mango tree arched over the exotic plantings. "Is that a shrine on the other side of the tree, Ketut?"

"Yes, madam," she said over her shoulder as she headed toward the kitchen. A tiny bird hung upside down from the orange bougainvillea that climbed the pink plumeria, their blossoms intermingled. The colorful bird, its long nectar-sucking beak piercing a flower, fit vividly with the pink and orange.

It was a peaceful scene overlaid by the sound of the activity beyond—cars, motorbikes, voices. A group of children walked by on their way to school. A vehicle hurtled down the road, its speed marked by the sound of gamelan music blasting from its radio. I could distinguish the conversation of some Italians, laughing and joking, one of them letting out a sudden whoop of fear. Then the ching-ching of bicycle bells merged with children's laughter, and I pictured a group of kids on bikes swerving to scare the tourists.

The garden and its border contained the hotel's sounds, including the clanking of dishes as the waitress put my teapot and cup on a tray. From the foliage of the mango tree a bird squawked, and as the abrasive sound died away, I saw a small white cat perched on a stone wall, hunting its prey.

My tea arrived. "Do you have *madu*?" I asked.

The girl walked over to the buffet and filled a small bowl from the honey that sat next to the yogurt. A profusion of pastries and fruit covered the table.

"Thanks," I said.

I would drink my tea and read my guidebook before serving myself. Flipping through the pages, I looked for the description of the judicial pavilion, the Tertha Gosa at Klungkung, with its paintings of Bima's quest, the son who travels to hell to obtain his father's release. I came across a photo of the cave of Goa Gajah with its fantastic carved entrance, a gigantic head alternately identified as Kala, who swallows time, an elephant, or Rangda. The thought of Rangda brought to mind dark forces. I thought of Flip. I saw the blood. I shook myself.

I'D agreed to sightseeing with Seth and Randall today, a decision I now regretted. I wanted to be alone. To wander. To think. The bird squawked. I wanted to stay away from men. I had time for a short walk before I met them.

I exited the dining pavilion through the lobby, nodding my hellos to the two receptionists, who cheerfully said good morning. At the entrance I started to turn right, but stopped myself. Better to go away from downtown, walk through the rice paddies, wander some quieter streets.

The streets were narrow, made narrower by the plants that graced every door and the occasional motorbike parked along the way. I could hear voices behind the compound walls, but few people were out walking, most having already found their way to work, to school.

I turned left, then right, admired a door painted a rainbow of colors, passed a sign identifying a homestay, glanced into a courtyard that seemed to contain a school. It was only when I came to the end of the block that it struck me what type of school I'd passed.

I walked back and stood in the doorway. Half a dozen young boys squatted on the ground or sat at tables, easels or tablets in front of them, paintbrushes or pencils in hand. An elderly man leaned over one boy, pointing at something on his page, then at the work he was copying. Without looking up, he waved me in.

The courtyard was spacious, the furniture haphazard, the boys quiet as they worked. One, who looked twelve but was probably quite a few years older, gripped a cigarette between his lips, the smoke that poured from the side of his mouth the only indication he'd just inhaled. I walked over to him, figuring he might be the least self-conscious of the group. He squatted on the concrete, his pad lying on a slanted construction of bricks. He was fine-tuning his drawing with rapid strokes of his pencil in preparation for the paint.

The scene was a typical Balinese painting of the type that had developed in the 1920s and '30s and that I'd come to Bali to study. The hero Bima battled demonic figures in the foreground, while the humans, arrayed in a forest above him, fled. Though two different places, two different worlds, were depicted, the only indication that they were not the same landscape lay in the figures—those at the bottom of the page, mythic, and those in the forest above, human. Only foliage demarcated distinct areas—the distant village toward which the humans fled was surrounded by trees of every imaginable type, distinguishable by their varying leaves.

"Very good," a voice beside me said. The teacher.

"Yes, it is," I said, not taking my eyes off the drawing.

"You must show the young lady your other work," he encouraged his student.

With a duck of his head, the boy reached behind him and pulled out a portfolio, which he handed me.

"No," said the teacher. "You can explain to her your work."

Embarrassed but obedient, he reached into the portfolio and riffled until he found the painting he wanted, then said in hesitant English, "This painting I copied from the great Lempad."

"Yes," I acknowledged, then realized I should take care in what I said, as any show of knowledge might intimidate him. I took the painting from his hand. Like most Balinese paintings it was small, the size of an average sheet of paper. The drawing was assured, with only a few slashes of color. Some of the ferocity of Lempad's work had been captured, but the freewheeling style of that artist, his demonic figure striding unhindered through space, wasn't quite there. From a teenager it showed great promise. "Very nice. Do you have more work in this style?"

"We learn by copying," he said.

I nodded.

"I have some that I have not copied."

"I'd like to see one of those, if I may." Two of the younger students had come over to us. Squatting behind him, they watched his every move, glancing surreptitiously at me. As he searched through his portfolio, one of the younger boys put his hand on his shoulder in a gentle, comforting gesture.

He hesitated, looking up at his teacher, who nodded and gave a quick flick of his hand, as if to say, that's right, you're doing fine. His warmth and encouragement made me sympathetic to him and his school, and I, too, nodded.

The painting he handed me was not what I'd expected. The forest foliage was, for it filled every inch that wasn't inhabited by figures. But the figures weren't doing what humans normally do in typical modernist paintings of village scenes. They weren't cooking, or bustling around their homes, or hunting in the forest, or shopping at the market. Instead, a road wound through the growth and figures riding bicycles filled it. Hunkered down over the handlebars, they skimmed past each other, the race uphill grueling and slow.

"Wonderful," I said, laughing. And it was true. It was wonderful. It was a painting with an eye to the present. "Completely unique! I love it."

He smiled shyly and glanced at his teacher, who nodded encouragement.

I sat down on the ground next to him, studying the work. The drawing was fine, the composition lively, with the curve of the road leading my eye up the page. Each of the figures was coping with the hard ride uphill in a different way. Leaning further over the handlebars, leaning back on the seat. One had given up and was pushing his bike up the hill.

"He is very talented," said his teacher.

The boy flushed.

"He certainly is. Excellent composition. Great tension in the smooth curves of the road and the sharp angles of the spiky grasses and palm fronds." I looked at the boy. "You should feel great pleasure from your accomplishment. May I see more?"

He pulled a pile of paintings from the portfolio and reached for the painting I held.

I shook my head and put it to one side on the small table behind him. I took the paintings he offered and settled in to look. The pleasure of examining something beautiful was the balm I needed. The work varied, as one would expect from a developing artist, but he had an eye for composition and a sense of humor. In one, a man dumped a bucket of water off a balcony, drenching two children. In another, a child pilfered a mango at the market as the shopkeeper lectured the child's friend.

I glanced at my watch. "This has been a marvelous way to begin my day. Thank you for sharing your talent with me. Do you sell your work?"

"I, yes, I do," he said uncertainly, looking to his teacher for help.

"May I ask what you would consider selling this painting for? I'm a bike rider, so it's particularly interesting to me."

He looked again to his teacher for help. The man said, "Fifty dollars U.S."

"Have you sold paintings before?"

"No," said the boy.

"Then I will buy this painting for the asking price. Normally I would bargain ruthlessly, but I'm happy to be your first client." I reached in my pocket, then realized that I hadn't brought my money. "I'm afraid I don't have money with me. Would you be willing to hold the painting for me? I promise that I'll come back." I looked from him to his teacher.

"Yes," he said, more confidently than he'd spoken before. As if the idea of a sale was enough to imbue him with self-assurance.

His teacher took the painting. "I will put it away for your return. May I ask your name?"

"Jenna Murphy. Do you have a card?" I asked the student.
He laughed and shook his head.

"I will give you one of my cards and will write his name," the old man said.

"Thank you. And when I come back, I'd like to see other students' work, if I may. And yours, of course." I looked around the courtyard at the smiling boys, all happy for their friend. An idea had come to me as I looked at his works, but I needed to run it by my museum's shop buyer before I acted on it. When I returned I'd bring my camera and hopefully greater opportunity for these children.

"Certainly."

8

"A good breakfast?" Seth asked as we passed, me on my way to my room and him toward the breakfast pavilion.

"Very. Quite a spread."

"We'll just grab a quick bite and be ready in about half an hour. Does that suit you?"

"Fine. See you in the lobby." I walked off the path toward the mango tree so that I could look at the offerings, then remembered I needed to call the Searles Museum as my deputy director had asked. Arthur Philen wanted to keep tabs on me. He wouldn't be happy that I'd stumbled onto a dead body. He seemed to think I looked for trouble.

"Report in," he'd said. A ridiculous notion, but I'd agreed. Even my mother didn't ask me to check in. I didn't want to have to communicate with Arthur about the murder. I wanted to speak with a friend. I'd call Brian, the curator of Western art and my closest friend, and have him tell Arthur that he'd heard from me.

I PULLED up Skype, clicked on Brian's direct line, and went into the bathroom to finish brushing my teeth. "Hello, hello," said Brian "Are you there? Jenna?"

"Just a minute," I said, putting away my toothbrush.

"Did you call me while you were in the bathroom? That's crude."

I held up my hands, palms forward. "I was only brushing my teeth."

"Sure you were. So did you meet the long-haired womanizer?" He was tearing open a letter as he spoke.

"Sort of."

"Sort of? What? He passed by in a car and waved? I thought you were having lunch with him. Or is that today?" He thought for a moment. "What time is it there, anyway?"

"No, it was yesterday. I went there and found him dead."

There was a pause, as if the connection delayed. "Dead? You're serious?"

I told him all that had happened.

"What will you do?"

"Try to find his killer. I have my doubts about the police department here. You should have seen them at the crime scene."

"No, I mean, what will you do about your research?" He put down the letter and leaned forward. "And really, it isn't a good idea for you to try to find his killer. Once a year is enough."

"My research will go fine. I'll try to get introductions to other people. I do know a family here."

"The detective you just mentioned?"

"Yes. I'm hoping that he can help."

"Jenna, seriously, I know you. You're curious to the point of recklessness. You should let this detective do his job and you can do yours, which is researching art. And you can take your vacation, do the things you want to do—the snorkeling, the bike riding, the sightseeing. All the pleasures you've been imagining."

"Right. Could you do me a favor?"

"Seriously, Jenna. Don't get involved."

"I am involved. I was the one who found the body. I feel . . ."

"What? You feel what?"

"I feel responsible in some strange way. As if finding him means I need to find his killer."

"You don't. Promise me. This could end up worse than the last trip to Southeast Asia. Didn't you learn anything from that experience? Stop meddling."

"I didn't meddle." I changed the subject. "The favor I have to ask?"

"Tell Philen you called?"

"Yes. I don't think I can bear talking with him today." I looked at the clock next to the bed. "Some people are waiting for me to go sightseeing. I better go."

"Sightseeing?"

"Yeh Puluh, Klungkung, Goa Gajah, some nearby sights. They're staying here at the hotel."

"A man, right? Really, Jenna. There is a perfectly agreeable man right here in Marin who wants you. A terrific man. Why can't you be satisfied with him?" Exasperation flooded his face.

"I've told you why."

"One man you couldn't trust does not make the rest of us lying, cheating womanizers."

"I was vulnerable."

"I know."

"I was young and it made an impression."

"I'll say. Jenna, you've got to move on. That was a dozen years ago."

"I'll talk with you soon," I said as I closed the connection, knowing he was right, but unable to do as he said.

As I entered the lobby, I heard Randall say, "Why don't we get a car? There are three of us and it won't cost much more than the motorbikes. Then we can leave our stuff in the car while we walk through the sights."

"Are we renting motorbikes?" I asked. We hadn't decided the night before what mode of transportation we might take. Though I prefer bicycling, the speed of a motorcycle almost makes up for the lack of sweat and muscle crunching. "Sounds good to me."

"But there are three of us," Randall repeated.

"The receptionist recommends getting motorbikes from the guy down the road."

"I'm in."

Randall groaned but stopped objecting, and we headed off.

"We need two," said Seth to the man lounging in front of a lean-to with a sign that said "Bykes Rental."

"Are you and Randall sharing a bike?" I asked innocently. I didn't like being appropriated. If I wanted to sit behind him, my boobs pressed against his back, my arms around his waist, my hand in his lap, I would say so.

Looking flustered, Seth said, "No, I thought that you could ride with me."

"Three motorbikes," I said to the man.

He pointed at two of the larger bikes and one slightly lower horsepower.

"I'll take that one." I pointed at one of the more powerful ones. At least it would propel me uphill at something greater than a snail's pace.

I gave the man my deposit and grabbed a red helmet. A girl had to think of fashion at all times. Seth headed for the other fast bike, and Randall stood hesitantly to one side. "I haven't driven a motorcycle before."

Ah, the reason for his objections. He should have said that in the lobby. There, we might have relented. Now, with the promise of speed, Seth and I weren't going to change our minds.

Seth said, "It's easy. You'll learn quickly. These are so small that it won't be much different from riding a bike."

Randall still looked uncertain and I added, "But you could always ride on the back of Seth's."

"Or . . ." he said, looking longingly at my motorbike. But before he could say more, I climbed on and started it.

Pleased to be renting three motorbikes, the man shoved a helmet at Randall, taking the decision out of his hands. He backed the motorbike out of the small stall and proceeded to give Randall unintelligible instructions in poor English. "Easy," he said.

Uh-oh, I thought, and called out over the sound of the bikes, "Seth, do you know the way?"

"I looked at a map, and I have directions on my phone," he said, struggling with the clasp on his helmet.

"It's okay," said the man. "Do not fasten." Though quite a few motorcyclists in Bali wore helmets, many didn't bother to fasten them.

Seth finally took it off and took another one. "It's not okay. But this one is." The fastener clicked in place.

"I'll see you there." I revved the engine and, without looking back, turned onto the road, easing into the traffic. I wondered if Flip's killer had ridden a motorbike to his murder. If he'd carried the spear as he rode. An image of Piero della Francesca's battle scene in San Francesco Cathedral in Arezzo, Italy, came to mind, horses cheek to jowl, spears piercing the sky.

9

Sightseeing had been fun, the motorbikes challenging in the uncertain traffic. Now I needed to use my muscles, to wear myself out, so that exhaustion would vanquish the bloody scenes of last night's dreams and today's imaginings. I said good-bye to Seth and Randall and traded in motorbike for bicycle. I wasn't due for dinner for another hour, so I took a roundabout route to Wayan Tyo's mother's house. I pedaled hard. The setting sun vanished as I flew down one hill, then re-appeared, playing peek-a-boo, as I topped the next.

The Balinese orient themselves mountain to sea, with the mountains the more auspicious direction. No island of sailors, the Balinese. Whether their antipathy to the sea is because their shore-line has few natural harbors or out of fear of the water is difficult to say. On the other hand, I thought as I tried to catch my breath, the mountains may be the reason few people in Bali ride bicycles.

Wayan Tyo had left Ani's address and directions at my hotel. He'd also left his mobile number in case I wanted a ride. Once in her neighborhood, I had to ask a couple of people directions, as the Balinese seem disinclined to number their homes.

Arriving, I was surprised to discover I didn't recognize the house. I thought that I had remembered it, but maybe I was recalling the bungalow where my family had stayed that summer years before. I zigzagged through the entrance into the compound, as there was the usual wall blocking direct access, a deterrent to malevolent forces. Demons only walk in straight lines.

As I came through the gate, children ran up to greet me yelling, Mimpi, Mimpi. Puzzled, I wondered if they mistook me for someone else, maybe another guest who was supposed to come to dinner tonight. The children waited for me to lock the bike by the central gate, and as soon as I took off my helmet, a small boy grabbed it and put it on his head. They screamed with glee.

A girl about seven grasped my right hand, and when her younger sister, a tiny clone of the older girl, saw her hand in mine, she clung to my left. When she looked up, her perfect face shimmered, the mouth slightly parted, the eyes wide and eager. I picked her up and planted her on my hip. My one-year-old nephew weighed more than this three-year-old girl.

A woman grasping a large handful of green leafy vegetables came around the side of the house toward me. "They are very excited to meet you," she said.

"Bu," I said.

"Ani, you always called me Ani," said Wayan Tyo's mother, grasping both my upper arms in greeting, the greens resting on my shoulder. She looked at my auburn hair with its lock of pink and gazed into my eyes for an instant before she smiled. "Come over here to the kitchen, then we will join the others."

"You look different than I remember."

"You look different too."

I laughed. "Twenty years will do that." The summer we'd stayed in Ubud, she had probably been about my age. Very beautiful, her long hair draped around her shoulders, her attention on young children, full of pleasure at their exuberance. Now, standing before me, the vague, idealized person of my imaginings slipped away. She had thickened and her hair was bound. Her slight limp when she walked and her gesture a moment before, grasping my arms, gave rise to a little burst of memory. No, not memory, a feeling of contentment difficult to correlate with the gesture, a contentment I'd felt when she'd looked into my eyes.

"What do you think?" I asked.

"The same. I believe you are the same."

"And what is that?" I laughed.

"Mischievous, quick in your mind and your actions, hurrying from this to that. Impulsive."

"That's how you remember me?" I smiled at the pleasure of being known.

She laughed. "That's how you were."

The kitchen was just to the right of the doorway, just as *bade*, pavilions for preparing offerings, stood just inside the entrance to temples. I assumed there was a correlation. It was a small kitchen, with a grill outside, and I waited while she put the greens on a table and said something in Balinese to a woman working at a burner. Then she led me to the main house, which lay at the back of the compound. Smaller buildings had blocked my view of it, and I wondered what each of them held as we walked across the tamped earth to a large, sheltering tree and the family who sat chatting or running around, depending on their ages. "I remember the tree," I blurted out.

"Why didn't you come to us as soon as you arrived? You and your family were our first guests in our bungalow. Our longest and happiest guests. You are welcome with us."

"My mother lost your address about ten years ago, along with some other important papers, when my parents moved. She tried writing to you using just your names, but never received a response, which I suppose means you never received the letters. All I had was your name. My plan was to try to find you, though I hadn't figured out how."

My mother had pressed their names on me and tried to describe the relationship of their house to the center of town. But I didn't know whether I would have followed through on the search. Even while talking to my parents about the trip, I had already been making mental excuses as to why I hadn't been able to track down Ani's family. My memories of them were dim, and after all these years I had no idea how they would greet me.

One of the young men seated on the far side of the courtyard rose at my entry. "Sister," he said. Thus began my introductions to the entire extended family. The group seemed to expand and shrink before my eyes, and consisted of at least fifteen people—children and grandchildren, a great-uncle. They greeted me, went in and out of the house, the children ran amok, all was lively. Ani's husband, Wayan Tyo's father, was nowhere to be seen, but his brothers and their wives and children had all congregated to meet me and to dine.

One young man hung back until Ani called him over. "This is Esa, Wayan Tyo's close friend."

I stretched out my hand, but he didn't take it, ducking his head slightly instead and taking an almost imperceptible step back.

"He is wary of foreigners. Don't worry, he will warm to you," said Ani, laughing.

"Why are you wary?" I asked him.

He seemed to consider the question. Finally he said, "Memory. History. The past."

Before I could think of how to respond, Ani bundled me over to the cluster of wives who had shyly moved in my direction. One asked, "Where is your husband?"

"I don't have a husband."

She and her sister-in-law exchanged glances.

"You have met my family," said Wayan Tyo as he came out of the largest of the buildings. He laughed as he saw the two young girls clinging to me. "And my daughters."

The older girl still grasped my hand. The younger had laid her head on my shoulder; a tiny hand caressed my neck. The electrical surge I had felt when Wayan Tyo touched me the previous day now jolted me through his children's hands. I tried to let go, but the older girl was permanently attached and the younger fitted me like a scarf. He came down the few steps, shooed the one away, and tried to take the other, but gave up.

"Oh, these are your children," I said. It hadn't occurred to me that he had children. Of course he had children. "I don't think I met your wife."

He hesitated, then said, "She is not here. Do you remember this place?"

"I'm not sure. Maybe what I remember is the bungalow we rented from you rather than this house. But this courtyard—I remember the courtyard and this tree. It all seems smaller, maybe because I'm bigger."

"Not much."

I scowled at him. "You don't have a lot of room to talk."

He grinned, and again tried unsuccessfully to disengage his daughter.

Ani reached past him, took her granddaughter, and set her on the ground. Then she led me across the courtyard and away from the others. "And here. What do you remember? About Bali, not just about our home or your bungalow. If we had known that you were coming, you could have stayed in the bungalow, but now a couple from Chile is there. We'll take you over after we eat so that you can see it."

"I told Wayan Tyo, I remember this courtyard. In the early morning, I think. It's not my most vivid memory. That took place at the bungalow where we stayed."

She nodded encouragement, and I saw that she was leading me away from the others back to her world, her kitchen, as if she wanted a private conversation with me. No one followed us or interrupted. The kids continued chasing each other around the tree. Wayan Tyo joined his friend, brothers, and uncle. The young women tended to a crying baby.

Just to be talking, I said, "I remember peddlers coming around in the evening to sell textiles and paintings, sculptures. And I remember one evening in particular. We came back from dinner or a walk to find a young man squatting at the bottom of the steps, smoking. He had the longest, straightest pinky finger-nail that I'd ever seen, longer than the cigarette. Not curved as they usually are. He held that little finger arched in such a way that I thought he was smoking two cigarettes."

Ani handed me a bowl of beans to snap.

"He preceded us up to the porch, opened his bag, and began to spread out paintings on the deck. All this without a word. My parents took chairs and my brother and I stood around looking down on the sheets of paper at our feet, those paintings with their masses of tiny people, the foliage arranged like wallpaper. I'd never seen anything like them. It must have been early in our time here, because we certainly saw many more young men with paintings. Didn't we?"

She was silent, peering into a pot on the stove that sent up a scent I couldn't identify. The rice cooker clicked to warm and I lifted the lid, letting out a cloud of steam and the comfort of the smell of rice.

"The peddler spread out sheet after sheet of paper, and we kids squatted down to look. The detail created patterns. People cooking, bathing, swimming, washing their clothes, all within a jungle that formed the ground, the backdrop of the everyday scenes. Trees consisted of identical leaves, flattened and pressed one against the other. Now I know that these paintings were in the style developed in the 1920s and '30s, the style of painting I'm here to research. Then I knew that they were paintings like I dreamed." Ani stirred whatever was in the pot.

"After looking for some time, my parents began speaking with the peddler, but he didn't have much English. He just nodded and smiled. Finally my mother said, 'Jenna, which one do you like the best?' My brother had jumped off the porch and was running around with a bunch of kids." Finished with the beans, I fanned the greens on the table into a pattern.

"My mother's question broke my reverie, so I began walking around the paintings, looking carefully at each one. This part might not be my memory. My parents still tell this story about me, so they may have filled in what I've lost. I looked and looked. It began growing dark and harder to see, and finally I pointed at one painting.

"The young man looked at me more closely and turned to someone who was standing on the ground below the deck. By then a group of people had gathered. He said something in Balinese. A woman translated for him." I snapped the stem off a bean I'd missed and pictured the arrangement of patterns on the bamboo deck. Most of the paintings were dark, but there was one that had a light background.

"Yes," she said.

"The woman was you? Ah. Well, you remember then, you translated for him and said that it was the one painting by his teacher. The best painting of all." I laughed. "It's the story that my family uses to illustrate why I became an art historian."

"Do you think it is the reason?"

"In part. My love of art, and the books, the words, the ideas that describe the art. The research."

She looked at me expectantly.

"They ground me. It's the place I go to slow my racing mind. And this story, well, I suppose it's the story that explains why I'm here. Researching the art."

"It is one reason you are here." Ani turned back to her cooking.

I looked at her. Was the other reason to discover the killer of the dead man? No, I thought. "Fate, is that what you mean?"

She sidestepped my question. "How does it make you feel being here?"

I thought for a moment. "I feel comfortable. I feel at home."

"How are you?"

"Very well, it's wonderful to be here."

"No, I mean how are you?"

"You mean the murder, finding the body?"

"Yes."

"Well, I'm . . ." I faltered. "I think I'm fine."

Ani looked at me steadily, and I took a breath and said, "I don't know. I don't know how I am. I feel confused. You know I came here to talk with Flip, to look at art and to talk with him. And now there's no Flip. So I guess I need to regroup and try to figure out a way to meet someone to help with my research." To my surprise, tears welled up in my eyes. Embarrassed, I turned away.

She waited.

"Then, also, violent death. It's not the first time." I saw her start at this bit of news. "Last year, I . . . But that was someone I knew, and my response was very different. I felt very sad. This time I felt physically ill."

"That seems normal."

"Yes. I began analyzing the room, the scene of the crime, to keep myself from getting sick. I wanted to know who killed him, more than, more than . . ."

She nodded and took my hand in hers, which only brought more tears. "Tyo has told me that when he has seen someone die badly, cruelly, he finds himself floating above them, a distance away, even if he is right there with the body. I think this is natural."

"Really? I know I didn't want to be there, but at the same time I did. I didn't make any attempt to leave. I rationalized that I shouldn't move my feet, that they might think my footprints were the killer's footprints. I tried to think of other things. I closed my eyes. I listened to the monkeys."

"You tried to find safety in your mind."

"Yes, but in retrospect my response was more disturbing than if I'd become hysterical or run screaming from the room. Do you understand?"

I took her silence as a judgment.

"What I felt. Well, actually that's it. It was not so much about emotions. It was about intellect, knowing. I want to know who killed him. I want to know what happened. As I stood there with the body, I felt as if I'd been there in that room when it happened. I could see the killer's anger, not just the way the spear was thrust through the dead man, but in the way things were pulled off the wall. The cushions on the floor."

"Tyo said you stayed. This is why you stayed. To try to solve the mystery."

"Someone needed to stay with him." I looked at my hand in hers and felt the comfort in it. "You're smiling."

"Yes, you think that you did not feel anything, yet you felt compassion for him. You felt that someone had to stay with him."

"You say compassion, and I did feel compassion. Then I would waver and worry about myself. I thought, I've just flown thousands of miles to speak to Flip and here he is, lying at my feet. I wondered, what am I doing here in Bali? And then it would come back to the biggest question." She looked at me questioningly, which made me think she hadn't heard all I'd said. "What I can do about his death."

"That is for Tyo to figure out." She spoke forcefully as she patted my hand. "This is not your job."

I shrugged off her words, knowing I couldn't argue with her about this. "I'm jet-lagged, too. When you're jet-lagged you feel so out of it. I couldn't anticipate this, a murder, an interrogation, my plans shot to hell."

"Was the interrogation difficult?"

"You know, I hardly remember it. They just asked me a series of questions. I suppose it was pretty obvious that I had just arrived at the house. I mean, after all, the girl met me at the door. I don't think they believe I did it."

"No."

I took that to mean that Tyo had told her I hadn't killed him, but I went on. "I don't know that a woman could have driven that spear through him. Someone needed a great deal of strength to kill him instantly, so that he didn't cry out." I pictured myself getting the spear halfway through him, unable to complete the thrust.

I said, "Maybe that was what Tyo thought when he saw the body. It didn't even occur to me that a woman would be able to do it. So why would the police suspect me? I suppose that they probably just had to question me."

"Probably," said Ani. I looked around the kitchen and felt a bit like those policemen when Ulih had fallen to the ground in front of Flip's house. Useless and not knowing where to put my hands. "They also wanted to make certain you had not disturbed the crime scene."

I looked down, hoping she couldn't spot a lie, my deflection, as easily as my father. "As I said, I didn't move my feet."

She looked at me closely. "You need to chop these beans. Small and thin, like this, and we will add coconut and sprouts. This is a side dish to the meat that we will grill. We will eat together tonight, though we usually each eat when we feel like eating. In the morning we cook a large amount of food, and whenever someone wants something, they come and get it. This is more common in Bali than the Western way of sitting down to a meal. Do you remember this?"

I shook my head and picked up a knife.

"Now tell me about your family. How are they?" She began to lead me away from death, back to normal.

"My mother and father are both fine. Still working. My father plans to retire from teaching; my mother continues with her job, though she could retire if she wanted. She's a bit of a workaholic." I didn't say that she wouldn't want to be around the house with my father day in and day out. His temper, the boredom that would surely paralyze and further anger him, his need.

"Do you see them often?"

"Pretty much every week. We live close enough to each other that either I drive over to the East Bay, where they live, or they come over to Marin for a hike or a visit to their favorite restaurant. They're both healthy now, though my mother has had some back problems."

"Yes, we are aging. And your brothers? Are they well, too?"

"Byron lives back east, in New York. We hardly see him— lucky if it's once a year. He's married, and his wife is pregnant with their second child. Sean lives very near my parents and sees a lot of them. I see quite a bit of him, too, even though he's the youngest, and we're nine years apart in age. We are very close."

"I do not know Sean. He had not been born when you were here."

"He's a sweetheart. He lives on a boat—he's crazy about boats and has been working for someone who designs them. It's what he wants to do. Eric." I hesitated. "Eric has some problems. He uses drugs, and we think that he deals drugs, though we aren't certain."

"He was only a baby, but he was a troubled baby."

"He was?"

"He made a good deal of noise."

I laughed. "He still does."

"We are ready to eat now. You will tell me more later."

I was happy that we were going to eat together. In the courtyard the men clustered under the tree, while the women chatted and ate around a table set a little apart. I sat with the women. Tyo's sisters-in-law included me, cheerfully putting up with my attempt at Indonesian until I discovered their English was far better. It shouldn't have surprised me, as everyone seemed to speak English. My attempts to communicate in Bahasa generally meant I said a word or two, then the conversation reverted to English. Still, I knew that the few words I spoke were appreciated.

10

At some point Tyo joined us, asking me, "How are you?"

The women gave each other a look I couldn't interpret. "Fine, they are putting up with my Bahasa. My very minimal Bahasa."

He said something to one of the women in Balinese and they all laughed.

I wanted to ask about his wife, but sensed that this was not a conversation that he wanted to have.

His brothers soon joined us. His friend Esa was the last, moving reluctantly in our direction. Wayan Tyo made a space between where he and I sat. Esa hesitated, then squeezed in, his shoulder against Tyo's older daughter, who sat to one side of me. He took her hand. She gave him a smile. The younger girl leaned against me on the other side.

"Do you live nearby?" I asked.

"No. I am on the other side of town."

"Do you work with Wayan Tyo?"

"No," he said, a master of brevity.

I felt the emotional push he was giving me, the unwillingness to talk with me. He turned to listen to one of Tyo's brothers, cutting me off, his shoulder a blade between us.

Everyone spoke English, even the children, though forgetting I was there, they began to chat in Balinese. I became aware Wayan Tyo was watching me, a questioning look on his face. I pushed my hair behind my ear, a nervous habit that drove my mother mad.

"How is it possible, in that house with numerous servants, that no one saw the killer?" I asked him. I had tried not to think about the murder, but now that I found him looking at me I could think of nothing else.

"We haven't found anything about Flip's killer. The only fingerprints at the scene are yours, those of the girls who do the cleaning and serving, and the gardener who waters the plants in that room. Well, there are also some prints at the table, but we can't identify those. He had many visitors dining with him, and his servants don't seem to know any of their names, other than the women that he entertained. That was all that interested them."

Esa leaned back, our conversation bouncing over him.

"There are no fences, so someone could walk in through the trees and remain invisible. A person who knows the household might well know their routine. Or, if they knew that Flip was having guests for lunch, the killer might have assumed that the women would be in the kitchen cooking. The killer might even have been the third person dining. You saw that the table was set for three?"

I nodded.

"The girls didn't know who was coming."

"I suppose. You would think that Flip would have called out, yelled, responded in some way when this person came into his living room with a vicious-looking weapon." I felt Wayan Tyo's younger daughter lean harder against my side, so I reached around and gathered her into my arms.

"It all suggests that Flip knew the killer and just didn't feel threatened."

"I suppose. So, since you have absolutely no idea who the killer is, you haven't any clue to a motive?"

Tyo didn't answer right away. The group had gone quiet, listening to what he had to say about the murder. Finally his youngest brother said, "Plenty of motive. No one liked the man. He pursued women, not just single women, so an angry husband might have killed him."

"That's not the only motive," the middle brother said. "There are plenty of rumors of him dealing in the illegal art trade, so an unhappy collector or dealer might have killed him. Or maybe he was not kind to his servants. One of them—or all of them—might have done it and are now covering up."

My ears pricked up at the mention of illegal art activity, but I said, "I think you can eliminate the servants. They began crying for him immediately."

"More likely crying for lost wages," said Esa.

Everyone nodded. I felt the strength of the community's dislike for Flip in this very courtyard, and by extension their disregard for the people who worked for him. "What do you think, Wayan Tyo?"

"I must rely on my intuition, though what my brothers say is correct. He was hated. He represented all that was bad in the expat community. Some foreigners who come here to live contribute to life on the island in a positive way. His contributions did include positive things—he gave work to people, he encouraged young artists—but his womanizing, his wild parties, his breaking down of local morals more than outbalanced the good that he did. We could do nothing to stop him, though we tried."

"Foreigners will destroy our culture," Esa said bitterly.

Before I could respond to that, one of Tyo's brothers spoke. "What did the police do?"

"We raided parties, but he always had watchers who saw us coming, and the drugs vanished before we got there, just as the music became quieter at our approach. There were rumors"—he nodded at his brother in acknowledgment—"that he dealt illicitly in art. But how? Theft? Fakes? Both were rumored, but we never caught him, though we tried. We even . . ."

All of us looked at him expectantly.

He set down his plate. "There is nothing. No clues in the room. No fingerprints on the spear. An old spear like that could have come from anywhere. Most of them have been sold to tourists as artifacts or taken by the Dutch as trophies, but some homes still have them. We visited the shopkeepers today who deal in this type of weapon, but none of them recognized it. We cannot find any information about either the weapon or who might have entered the compound, and I am very frustrated."

"Could it have to do with his painting?" I asked.

"Perhaps it could. But how?"

"Well, the painting that was on the floor by his easel at the time of his death was not his usual work. I only glimpsed a corner of it, but it was obviously in Balinese style. His work referenced that style, though his paintings weren't copies, as far as I know." I shrugged. "But, you might know more about that, Tyo."

"There are rumors that he did paint in the style of one Balinese artist, but I have never been able to get from the dealers any information as to who that artist is. So yes, you are right that it could have something to do with the paintings that he was creating. But I have never been able to discover any certain information about his forgery work. At this point that motive is no more likely than any other."

"But you assume that he forged?"

"I'm pretty certain. No proof." He shook his head, then clammed up. His girls, switching allegiance, went over to sit on their father. They snuggled up to him, sensing his unhappiness, and he asked about their day, pushed their hair away from their eyes, redid the younger one's hairclip, and hugged them.

His love for them was obvious. I, on the other hand, now felt a distance from him. At Flip's house he'd been attentive and greeted me warmly, then dismissed me as if we'd never met. Turned me over to a stranger for questioning. When I arrived at Ani's he was friendly, but now I felt him pulling away, and I heard restraint in his words.

He confused me. Of course, maybe he simply didn't like to talk about work at home, or murder in front of his daughters. I changed the subject. "With Flip gone, I don't know that I have much I can do here in regard to Balinese art."

Suddenly a little boy raced up to me, slapped my knee, shouted something, and dashed off again. The girls squealed and leapt after him. "What did he say?" I asked.

"You are to chase them," Ani laughed.

"You mean I'm it?" I stood, casually wiping off imaginary crumbs from my leg, pointedly ignoring the kids. I stretched, took a few steps, then yelled, "You better watch out!"

The girls squealed, the boys shouted in delight, and I had an opportunity to work off the enormous quantity of food I'd eaten.

"OH, my gosh. They've worn me out."

"I think you have worn them out." Tyo looked toward the kids, who lounged beneath the tree. "They will sleep well tonight."

"No wonder you are tired," Ani said. "You've run for half an hour, much of that time with the little one in your arms. You haven't changed."

I laughed.

"You were an energetic child, and now we see that you are an energetic adult."

"I remember you wanting to keep going when the rest of us wanted to stop," said Tyo's brother.

"Stop what?"

"Stop anything." They all laughed.

"Before you were distracted by the children," Tyo began, "you were saying that you don't know what work you can do now that Flip is dead. There are many others who know about Balinese painting. I will introduce you to one museum employee at a private museum here in town. You can meet him tomorrow."

"There are many Balinese who know more than Flip," Esa said. "You should not think a foreigner could know as much about Balinese painting as a Balinese."

Before I could answer that, Ani said, "Now she must go to her hotel to her bed." She must have seen my struggle to hold up my head, as well as to find the words to respond to Esa.

"You're right. It's still early, but I'm exhausted."

"You will come back later in the week to have dinner with us," she said with finality. "And you should feel that you can come here at any time. This is your home in Bali."

I nodded as I stood. "Thank you. Dinner was delicious, and it was wonderful to see everyone again." I looked down on Wayan Tyo's girls. "And to meet the new members of the family. Thank you so much."

"Come, I will walk you home." Tyo said something to his daughters and, nodding to his mother, led the way out of the courtyard. I followed, stopping by the gate to unlock my bike.

He waited for me. "A bicycle?" he asked.

"Yes. I ride a lot at home."

"I thought Americans always drove cars. Or jogged. You do not jog?"

"Not if I can help it."

"I will walk with you," Esa called from behind us.

I felt Wayan Tyo tense beside me. He nodded to his friend, but said nothing.

"Do you live near my hotel?" I asked Esa.

"No."

I waited for more, but it didn't come.

"He grew up in this neighborhood, but now lives on the other side of town," Tyo said.

"Closer to where I'm staying?"

"A different neighborhood, but that general direction. He has his smithy over there."

"You're a blacksmith?" I asked.

"Yes."

"May I come by some day to see you at work?"

He didn't answer, but I thought I saw him nod in the darkness.

Car lights lit the road.

"I feel that I am missing something. That there was something to see in that room that I didn't see," Tyo said, as much to himself as to Esa or me.

I wheeled my bike around a pothole. I thought of the sack and the small bronze guardian figure that it held. I didn't want to reveal myself in front of Esa, and I was feeling uncertain with Tyo. He might be furious, and it seemed possible he would arrest me. Though that might be a little extreme. "We could go back together and look, to see what we see together. I mean together and individually. Each time one looks at something one learns something new. At least in my line of work."

"Yes, tomorrow. Then I can take you to meet Made Badung at the museum. I'm sure he will be happy to help you. Especially when I take you there."

"He owes you?"

Wayan Tyo shrugged. "We were students together."

"He is our friend," said Esa.

I got the feeling that he didn't like the idea of Wayan Tyo thinking of me, a foreigner, as his friend. I wondered if Made Badung felt about foreigners the same way Esa did.

11

"Jenna. Well?" P.P. Bhattacharya stood away from his computer video cam so I could see him.

He always approximated a bouncing ball, with his round face, his globular upper body, and constant state of motion, even when standing in one place. I couldn't help but smile. "Hello, P.P. How are you?"

"Nehru said, 'Morning of the world.' About Bali. True?"

When I met him, it took me months to get used to his abbreviated conversation. Much of what he needed to say was spoken in his extravagant gestures. Now his arms drew a circle, like a child drawing the rising sun. How he injected color into the gesture was beyond me. "I haven't gotten far outside of Ubud, but aside from all the tourists, it's lovely. My hotel is charming, the food is good. Nice people."

"But?"

"Was there a 'but' in my voice?"

"Yes, yes." He began to walk away from the computer, then remembered that the range of the video cam wouldn't allow him to do his usual march around his office. He stayed put and bounced on the balls of his feet.

"You know I told you that I was going to meet that Dutchman, Flip? Well, he was dead when I got to his house."

"Dead? Heart attack?"

"No, murder. I found the body."

He stilled. "Tell me."

"He'd been run through with a spear." My voice cracked.

"All, tell me all."

I told him. I also told him about reconnecting with my Balinese family. At some point in the telling, I realized that he was getting impatient with the details, so I cut it short.

"Can't get involved. No Watson to your Holmes. Could come help. Be your Watson."

"No, no need for that," I said hurriedly.

"Do your work. See your friends."

I knew he was thinking about our trip to Cambodia the previous year. I changed the subject, which was easy enough to do. We could talk about his collecting. "So, tell me about this Indonesian bronze that you're considering buying. It looks to be ninth century and quite charming." My call was in response to his e-mail that morning about the bronze. I was happy for the excuse to talk with a friend; hotel rooms are lonely places.

"Here." He held the bronze up to the computer camera.

"Too close."

He pulled it away and slowly rotated it so that I could see it clearly.

"Manjushri, youthful bodhisattva of wisdom. I can't make out his necklace. Can you turn it that way?" I pointed.

"Tiger tooth."

"Good. Typical Javanese Manjushri, tiger-tooth amulet necklace for protection for a child. Almost pristine, only slight wear. But you know, P.P., I can't tell you anything without holding it in my hands. I'd have to take a close look at the patina. I'd need to do some comparative research—look to see what images are related. To find any anomalies, if there are any. To make certain that it fits into the Central Javanese ninth-century oeuvre. I don't see any problems when I look at it from afar, but I need to do some research. We both know that there are fakes in every area of Southeast Asian art."

"Yes. But your reaction?"

"What's the provenance?"

"Old Dutch collection. He says."

"Who's the dealer?"

P.P. ignored the question. He was often secretive about his buying. "I could bring it to you."

"I won't give you my final thoughts until I see it in person. You can wait a few weeks for that, surely? The dealer will let you have that long to make a decision." I didn't want P.P., patron of the Searles Museum, coming to Bali to interrupt my week of work and my two-week vacation. He'd become a friend, but a high-maintenance friend, and I didn't want to see him here. I knew he also wanted to be involved in the murder investigation. "You can't bring that into Bali, P.P. Customs would confiscate it. Plus it's a twenty-three-hour flight."

He shrugged and held the bronze up to his face, his glasses pushed up over his brow, the black frame filling in where his hair had once been. He brushed one hand over his shiny pate. "Going to Kolkata next week."

"Really, P.P., I will look at it when I get home. You'd have to pay the dealer for it if it got confiscated at the Denpasar airport. Pay for it, without having the possibility of enjoying it. Don't be so impatient."

"Right."

I breathed a sigh of relief.

He switched gears. "A miniature on the way. Indian."

P.P. epitomized the collector addict. He was always looking, always buying. Sometimes his impatience got the better of him and he bought impulsively. Fortunately for him, he had an excellent eye and the wherewithal to support his taste in South and Southeast Asian art. He'd come to rely on me as another set of eyes in the decision-making, a sounding board, which didn't necessarily mean he listened to my opinions.

A knock at my door interrupted me before I could ask about the miniature. "I'll be out in just a minute," I called. When I'd run into Randall and Seth at breakfast, they had invited me to join them sightseeing.

"Who?"

"Some people I met here at the hotel. We're going to Besakih, the most important temple here, a spectacular mountain temple. They're ready to go, so I'll sign off now. I promise I'll look at the bronze the second I get back." Wayan Tyo had left a message early that morning saying he'd arranged for me to visit his museum friend the following day.

"A man? Good." Before I could answer, he reached forward and signed off without a good-bye. P.P. and Brian. Making assumptions. I couldn't get angry. They were right. And of course P.P. thought it was good. He didn't like Alam—because of business differences, according to Alam.

I grabbed my backpack, double-checking that I had sunscreen, bug stuff, a bottle of water. When I opened the door, Seth was on the porch watching me, his arms crossed. "Sorry, a work phone call. Let's go get those motorcycles."

"No Harleys here."

"Isn't it too bad." I slung on my backpack and gave the door a second pull.

He laughed, turned, and led the way down the few steps from my room. His broad shoulders looked good in that tight T-shirt. At the bottom step, he put his arm around me. Buddies, his arm said, and I in turn began to melt, to sink my shoulder, to shift in his direction, to mold my collarbone to the angle of his elbow. We walked easily together.

"What do you think?" he whispered, his breath swirling in the whorl of my ear.

"Yes, what do I think?" My shoulder felt the warmth beneath the arch of his shoulder.

"It would be nice, don't you think?" He insisted, breaking the spell.

Alam's face flashed through my mind. His gentle smile. I edged myself from Seth, mentally chanting, enough of men, enough of men. I moved away, reconstructing my posture into my own, placing my feet so that they held me up—me, not us. My phone rang.

"Excuse me," I said, stopping. "I'll catch up."

He walked toward reception as I listened to what was most certainly a marketing call. An advertisement for what? I couldn't understand the Balinese. But I'd been saved by the bell. I let the foreign words roll over me as I thought of his arm, my shoulder.

They were waiting in reception.

"I'm sorry, but something's come up. I can't go today. We'll have to go another day to a different site, perhaps." I heard the stiffness in my voice.

Seth frowned. "Work?"

"Yes, afraid so. I'll see you both later. Have fun." With a wave, I turned away from them.

"We could go later today," Randall offered. "I was looking forward to you giving us a tour. I mean, since you know these temples and all."

I glanced back at them. Seth looked irritated, Randall disappointed. "No, no, that's okay. I have a couple of weeks to take it in. Your time is short. Better get there while the getting is good."

I gave a little wave and continued my chant all the way back to the bungalow, no men, no men. Still, I could feel the gentleness of his hand, the weight of his shoulder. I'd fit so snugly. I was drawn to him. There'd been safety in that arm. But then again, there hadn't been. I unlocked the door, looking back toward the lobby, empty now. Of course I didn't know if I could trust him. First of all, he'd nodded at someone at the bar, maybe that Wild Man who'd been watching me. Second of all, he was a man.

12

"What are you doing here?" Randall asked at the entrance to Besakih. "Thought you had to work."

"I did, finished early and thought an afternoon would be enough time to get up here and spend a few hours. You've been here a long time."

Seth looked at me darkly.

I realized what I had said suggested I'd hoped they would be finished and gone. I said weakly, "But I took my chances that you might still be here."

Seth looked skeptical.

Randall accepted what I said, and explained, "Motorbike trouble. It took hours to get it fixed in a village where everyone was a motorbike mechanic with an opinion. Then we got here and thought we'd have something to eat, and that took longer than we expected. Well, great you're here. We can walk through together."

"Yes," I said, kicking myself. I'd expected them to be gone, yet I'd looked for them once I'd arrived. I was like a magnet to the bad boy, or rather, the bad boy was a magnet to me.

Flustered under Seth's steady gaze, I pulled my phone out of my bag. Randall fell behind, snapping pictures. "The guidebooks give you so little information. You'd think for a large temple as important as Besakih, there would be a map of the site. Luckily I found a map online."

Seth finally spoke. "Much bigger than any other temple I've seen on the island." Our mutual discomfort, along with his anger, filled the space between us. He wanted to seduce, and I wanted to resist seduction.

I tried to defuse the moment. "As foreigners, we can't walk into sections of the temple compound, but we can view it from the outside as we climb Mount Agung."

"I see foreigners in there," Seth said, pointing.

"They paid. And I don't want to negotiate hawkers and pay-offs. We can see from outside the wall. Or feel free to pay and go in, if you want."

"I'm content looking over the wall," Seth said.

"It's difficult to find useful information about the temple, beyond the fact it's the Mother Temple of the island, established by the fifteenth century, maybe as early as the tenth. The guide-books focus on the 1963 hundred-year festival, during which Mount Agung erupted."

"You're joking," said Randall, who had caught up with us.

"The lava flow didn't reach the temple, but it threatened it. And it killed over a thousand people in nearby villages. Priests overseeing the festival argued whether to stop their rituals and get out of the way of the lava or to continue. Afterwards they argued over whether the eruption signaled the gods' approval or their displeasure."

"Wow," said Randall.

The exquisite siting of Besakih, with the volcanic Mount Agung rising above it, made the climb a pleasant one. "See those two smaller complexes off to either side?" I pointed to the other side of the compound, where we could see a tower rising above the others. "They're dedicated to Brahma and Vishnu. Along with Shiva they form the triad of Hindu gods that create, pro-tect, and destroy mankind."

They both nodded.

As we approached the upper end of the wall surrounding the Shiva compound, a group of buildings came into view.

"Look at that painting," said Randall, pointing up at one of the temple towers. "That's different."

"Sure is," I answered. "The style of those figures is based on *wayang* puppets. That's the traditional style of painting. See how they're flat—in silhouette like the puppets."

"They're very cool," Randall said.

"According to what I've read, the Pande clan—the blacksmiths' clan—built this corner temple," I said.

"Isn't this the most sacred section of the compound?" Seth asked. "Why would blacksmiths build here? Be allowed to build here, I mean. I would think there would be prohibitions against certain castes within the temple. It's a Hindu caste society, isn't it? Like India."

"It is a caste society, but without the constraints of India. All castes are allowed in the temple. Plus in Indonesia blacksmiths traditionally were very powerful, magical." I peered over the wall, trying to photograph details of the paintings. "I met a blacksmith yesterday. At my friends' house."

"Let's go look at that one," Randall said. "The Brahma temple. Or is it Vishnu?"

After we'd taken a quick look around the Brahma temple, Randall, looked toward the Vishnu temple and said, "That one looks like more of the same. I think I'll pass." Seth nodded in agreement.

"Okay, then. I'm going to walk up to Pura Gelap. I'll catch up with you back at the hotel."

"What's Gelap?" asked Seth.

"A temple higher up the slope—it marks the eastern form of Shiva."

"Can we join you? It must have a good view, and it's a clear day," said Randall.

"Up to you."

The view was fantastic. A soft-spoken priest invited us into the grounds, where we spent some time listening to his explanations. He made our time there special, he and the fact we were the only visitors.

On the way down, we took the path along the compound wall opposite the one we had walked up, passing many smaller temples parallel to the main complex.

"What's this one?" Seth asked. A festival was taking place. Gold-and-white textiles were draped around the many small structures within the compound.

I flipped through the pages in my hand. "Maybe Ratu Pasek. I've lost track of the number of temples we've passed. There are eighty-four of them in the compound." I stepped in to watch the women assembling offerings on a pavilion by the entrance.

An older, rather serious woman was pinning young, flexible coconut leaves into a shallow basket shape that she stapled together. The next woman would take the basket and put in flowers and rice and something else I couldn't identify. Another woman had tiny, already folded triangular leaves that she embellished with rice and a tinier triangular object.

The women had formed a regular production line. I realized as we stood watching them how much we had missed by not entering the Shiva temple. The practice. The active worship. The pulse of the temple. As tourists we had been held at arm's length, admiring the cluster of buildings, taking our photos. I suddenly felt impatient—with the place, the murder, my research, my vacation, and to top it off, this disquieting and attractive man.

"Let's go," I said.

13

"It's so nice to meet you, Made Badung," I said as I watched Tyo hurry off.

He shook my hand. "My friends call me Made. You know Made indicates that I'm the second born in my family. It's not uncommon, calling a person by this indicator rather than his given name."

"Yes, I do know that, though to a Westerner it's a little disconcerting. What happens when you are in a room filled with Mades?"

He laughed, but didn't answer.

"I do appreciate your taking the time to work with me."

"No problem. It is always nice to speak with a person who wants to discuss Balinese paintings in detail."

"I had arranged to meet with Flip because I'd read a couple of articles of his in English-language journals. Very little literature on the topic is available in the U.S." As I spoke I looked around the museum lobby. The grand open-air pavilion had no art, but was landscaped with lush plantings.

He surprised me by saying, "I did not know him," and turned toward the stairs, which led through a garden. "Shall we look at the photos that you have brought? We can discuss the paintings in your museum, and if we need, we can easily pull out comparative paintings from our storage."

I wanted to ask him what the different plants in the garden were, with their vivid flowers and spectacularly shaped leaves, but he was moving too quickly. "Does the museum get many visitors?"

"Not so many. And we are one of the larger private museums. I do not know how the smaller museums are able to continue. Even though wealthy men own them, they are expensive to run. It is not always clear why a collector builds a museum in Ubud."

I thought of the oversized bronze statue of the owner in the lobby of this museum. It suggested one reason why collectors built private museums, and it wasn't necessarily altruism.

I said, "Yes, tourists seem more interested in Monkey Forest Road and Jalan Hanuman, in food, shopping, and spas. Not to mention idyllic hotels."

I was still processing the fact he had not known Flip. In a town this small, you would think everyone who was interested in pre-modernist Balinese art would know each other. They would have attended the same openings, at the very least. He must have intentionally avoided Flip, since his wild reputation undoubtedly reflected badly on those around him. Local scholars would steer clear.

Made led me into another large building—this one enclosed—down a corridor to a small, neat, and very modern storage area with climate control, comfortable chairs, and a large table where we could work. A computer sat on an adjacent table.

I said, "I have my laptop with the photos of the Searles Museum collection, but I also have the file on a flash drive. It might be easier for us to look at them on your computer, if you don't mind. Your screen is so much larger."

"Excellent. While we set up, can you tell me about your museum?"

"Sure. Searles worked in Silicon Valley, but lived in Marin—that's north of San Francisco, while Silicon Valley is south. Unlike many of the tech people, he made his money when he was older. Forty-five or fifty."

"And bought paintings with it."

"Paintings and a good many other things. He was a serious collector—probably collected stamps or coins when he was a kid. He liked to travel and had a real interest in other cultures. Once he had money, he spent it. Fortunately for him—and for the Searles Museum—he had plenty and became a great philanthropist, giving money and art to the different museums in San Francisco. In particular, the modern museum. Then he had a falling out with the curator at that institution. I've been told that it bothered him enormously that there wasn't an art museum in Marin."

"You don't know him? Didn't know him?"

"Oh, no. He died about seven years ago. I know his widow. She's very active at the museum. At any rate, he decided that he would build a museum in Marin and purchased the land. Then he did the most surprising thing."

"What was that?"

"He hired a museum staff before he had the plans drawn up, and deferred to them regarding much of the planning."

"Ah, you are lucky."

"We are."

"Were you hired then?"

"No, not right away. They hired only one curator. His specialty is Western art, which makes up most of the collection, though it was always in their long-term plan to hire a non-Western curator."

"Is the collection very broad?"

"It's a collector's collection. His taste, his odd and eclectic collection. A bit of a hodge-podge. But enough non-Western art that at some point Brian, the Western curator, threw up his hands and said he needed help and he needed it right away. He couldn't wait until the museum opened. At the time, I had a summer internship at a museum on the East Coast. The Searles contacted the art history department at UC Berkeley to see if they had a graduate student who might be interested in interning at the Searles. I was lucky."

"Why is that?"

"My advisor answered the call and gave them my name. So for two years I interned at the museum, then as I came close to finishing my dissertation they hired me. As you can imagine, it took a few years just to catalogue and study the collection before putting it on display." I pulled up a photo of a painting on the screen. "Here you go," I said.

"Very nice," he said, looking over my shoulder.

"It is one of my favorites."

"No, I mean your story. But I do like that painting."

"It's lovely," I said, pointing at a detail. "The variation in the leaves, in color and shape. He's packed an entire forest into a three-inch square."

Made said, "Yes. Every time I look, I am surprised. Then I am surprised that I am surprised."

14

I leaned back in my chair, feeling the weariness of sitting in the same position for hours. "I sometimes wonder if it's my eyes that are thirsty, rather than my brain." Some people might think looking at twenty paintings over a four-hour period an exercise in tedium. Made and I were running on adrenaline.

"They fill up."

I laughed. "I say that. That my eyes are full, but it's true, isn't it? Like your stomach when you've eaten too much."

"Exactly." Made smiled as he pulled out another painting for comparison.

He was a wonderful teacher. As we looked at the paintings, he explained the genealogy of teachers and students, discussing the fine points of style. I hoped that he would have time over the upcoming days to continue looking at the art with me. Flip's death was a loss, but Wayan Tyo's friendship had brought me good fortune in introducing me to Made.

"How did you come to this?" I asked, gesturing toward the paintings that lay on the table.

"My father was an artist. So were my uncles, my grandfather, and before them their fathers and grandfathers. Painting was the food of my childhood and the vocabulary of our conversations.

If I try to picture myself as a child playing, I cannot. I see myself with a pencil or a pen in my hand.

"I began to paint when I was four. I don't remember being that young, or what I did then, but they tell me I was a prodigy. They were selling my paintings and drawings by the time I was five."

As he told me this story that he'd clearly repeated many times, all of his movements were self-contained, with little gesticulation. He tapped his finger to make a point, but barely moved his large eyes. Even his mouth seemed still as he spoke. And the story explained his reticence about Flip's knowledge on the subject, for Flip had not lived this painting as Made had.

"My early paintings were simple. Barong was my specialty, which makes sense. The tail end of the Galungan-Kuningan festival is happening this week. I'm sure you've seen the bands of boys and men marching through the streets playing music as Barong dances along with them, two people inside a costume with its giant head, snaky body."

I nodded.

"So Barong, the symbol of good, is very present for any young child, any boy who has walked the streets with the creature."

"You spent your childhood painting and drawing good as epitomized by Barong? No Rangda? No dark forces? No Darth Vader? I thought that the fearsome appealed to young boys. My brothers always drew monsters."

"Yes, rarely Rangda. To a Westerner Barong looks frightening. But we love our Barong; we love the conflict between Rangda and Barong." He took a painting out of the drawer and held it in his two hands, gently, as if he'd held paintings all his life. Which he was telling me that he had. He was a big man for a Balinese, broad-chested and strong. He wore a batik shirt that hung over his belt and the loosely fitted pants that a much older man might wear. His hair was long and pulled back in a pony-tail. His smile broadened as he thought of Barong.

"As you grew older, what did you paint?"

"Everything. I painted everything and in every style, because we were encouraged to copy the masters."

I thought of the school I'd visited the previous morning, reminding myself that I had to go back soon.

"I could paint all the famous 1930s painters. I'm not saying I was skilled at painting them, but if you took a quick glance at one of my paintings in a known artist's style, you would get the reference." He set down the painting.

"These painters, they were famous to us," he said. "Famous in a small circle, famous among the Balinese and the few Westerners who took interest. We all knew each other. Some, who lived outside of Ubud, would stay with my family when they came to town. Our family home was small, cramped, paints in every room. Each of us with the tools of the trade in hand.

"Sometimes they would paint with us. More often they would sit around and talk, discuss paintings they had brought. Critique each other. It was exciting. I'm too young to have met him, but my father told stories of Lempad visiting." He looked off, his eyes unfocused, evidently thinking about those times. "When I grew older, I realized that I liked the critiquing better than I liked the painting, the ideas around the paintings more than the creation of them." He returned a painting to a drawer.

"Also, you see, I was no longer a prodigy. I had outgrown my early greatness. I was an average painter, but a good critic, a connoisseur. The best painter in my family is my older sister, but she did not get the attention that the adults showered upon me. I received a scholarship to go to university. My family did not want me to go.

"I chose school. I did it for myself and for my sister. By my stepping away from painting, my sister had an opportunity that she would not have had otherwise. Now she is one of the best-known female painters here in Ubud." He spoke with pride.

"I would like to see her paintings. I hope to buy a painting for myself before I go home, and I would very much like to support a woman painter." Two paintings, once I bought the student's painting.

"I am happy to arrange for you to meet my sister and to see her painting."

I clicked a key to move on to the next work, and Made leaned toward the screen. "Ah," he said.

"Is that a good 'ah' or a bad 'ah'?"

"From your perspective it is probably a bad 'ah.' This painting is in the style of Ida Bagus Made, who, as you know, is one of the most famous of our painters."

"You've said the cursed words."

He laughed. "In the style of?"

"Yes." Every art historian knows that phrase as the beginning of a condemnation of a work of art."

"I have been trying to track down the person who paints so well in this style. I have found other examples of Ida Bagus Made forgeries. Not all of them are intended as forgeries. Young artists copy him as a way to learn. I can easily ignore those. But there are other, more sophisticated artists who mimic his work, as it is very profitable to sell an Ida Bagus Made, and he was prolific." He thought for a moment. "So sometimes one of his original paintings does turn up in a surprising place. These originals make us believe that it is possible to discover an unknown work."

"The newly discovered good one validates the fakes."

"Yes. In the past five years a large number of his paintings have been for sale. Some with private dealers. Some at auction. Now I am very suspicious of any painting that has his signature. Now I am more likely to condemn a painting than to say it is right, so I may be wrong about this one."

"What is the indicator?"

"In each and every one of them there is something slightly off. Not in the composition—no, a little in the composition—not in the detail or the brushwork, but where? I cannot put my finger on it. Maybe together we can figure it out." He stepped back.

"So this hits you immediately as a fake?" Intuition is particularly convincing for a specialist as knowledgeable as Made.

"I will get the two in our collection that I doubt, that I think may be fakes, and two that I do not doubt, one of which I know for certain is correct, and let you look at them and see if you can see the difference."

"Okay, a blind viewing. Don't tell me which is which."

"I will not."

When I began this project, Ida Bagus Made was one of the few 1920s and '30s Balinese painters I knew much about. Born into a Brahman artist family in 1915 in Ubud, he became one of the celebrated Pitamaha painters at twenty-one and was viewed by the Western artists living in Bali as one of the foremost painters of his time. He lived until 1999 and influenced generations of artists.

Made riffled through the flat work drawer.

Though I knew his bio and I could identify a painting as his, I wasn't sure I would be able to tell the forgeries from the real paintings. The past few hours had shown me the depth of Made's understanding, and if he couldn't sort out the problem, I doubted that I could. Yet it was the sort of exercise that I most enjoyed, the search for clues, the delving into the details of the visual, the eventual comprehension of something that I saw before me. That moment when the visceral, sensual experience coalesces with the intellectual understanding of a work of art. That's it for me.

I cleared away the books and papers that had accumulated on the table over the last few hours. "Wrong drawer," he said, and opened another. "Here they are." He laid four purportedly Ida Bagus Made paintings before us and stood back, giving me room to look.

Eventually I said, "Well, I would be inclined to put these two together and these two together. But honestly, Made, I can't tell you whether any of them are fakes, nor can I tell you in these two pairings which might be the fakes. I suppose I'm more inclined to guess this pair than that."

"Yes, I too have put these two pairs together. I believe these two are the originals and these two are modern as you have just said. All four have the correct type of paper, but in these two the paper seems fresher to me, even though it is 1920s European paper. Look here at the backs of the works."

I leaned over the painting. "You're right. These two sheets are very similar. No wear. The same slight discoloration. Straight out of the box, it would seem. Of course, if Ida Bagus Made had painted the two, the two sheets of paper might still be very similar. Fresher? Maybe. Any other reasons?"

"Just the feeling that there is something in this painting that should not be here."

I smiled as I looked at one of the works that he had said he was certain was by Ida Bagus Made. "There is so much going on in this painting, it would take days to go through every inch of it. It has the characteristic horror vacui, with every conceivable village event happening simultaneously. The lack of deep perspective, the abundant foliage, the itemization of one event after another—crossing the river, the cremation, the people cooking over here in this corner, children chasing each other—it's everything one expects a Balinese painting to be."

"Yes."

"It also has that emphasis on the center of the painting that Ida Bagus Made paintings seem to have—at least the ones I've seen—with this figure moved slightly forward and drawn a little larger than the others. Of course, that isn't unique to him."

"Exactly. These two that we each have put in a separate group do not have quite the same emphasis. Close, but not quite."

"Right. But he's painted works with a very different composition, hasn't he?" I jiggled my shoulders to loosen the tension that had built up sitting in the same position for hours.

"Yes, definitely. But, as you say, it is one of his typical compositional devices."

I bent over the work, searching one corner, looking at the diversity of the foliage, the small figures twisted and contorted, running and swaying in movement. The man was brilliant. "Have you gone over the entire painting inch by inch, beginning in one corner, going to the next?"

"No. I never seem to have the spare time to do that. I become interested in the problem, than some other idea or project or distraction carries me from it. But looking at these together has raised my interest again. I will make the time. Also, now I have you to talk with about this problem. I have been hesitant to bring it up with Balinese colleagues."

"Why is that?"

"I suppose the usual reasons. Fear of being wrong, of making a mountain out of a hill. Is that your expression?"

"Mountain out of a molehill."

He looked puzzled. Maybe they don't have moles in Bali. "Fear of angering people. Including my employer. He would not be happy if I were to say that two of his most important paintings had been painted by an artist other than Ida Bagus Made. He particularly likes this one." He pointed at one of the paintings that we felt uncertain was original.

"Also, once one raises worry it becomes a source of argument and a scholarly debate. I do not want to be . . ." He searched for the words.

"In the limelight?" I suggested.

"Yes, in the limelight. Looking together has given me courage. I will go over this painting first, because I am sure of it. Then I will look at the others. Inch by inch. But it might not be this week."

"I'll study the paintings as well. If we both take the time, we might be able to arrive at some conclusion. Do you have photographs of these four that I might put on my computer?" I picked up one of the paintings, sliding it between sheets of acid free paper.

He nodded agreement as he peered at another. "This original. It is exquisite. The drawing, the activity in the market, with these two women who are the focus of the scene haggling over the price of fruit. It is so detailed, you can see the fruit is jackfruit. The other areas of the market, with one woman cutting fish, another stacking mangoes, this third"—he pointed—"gazing at the foreigner who has wandered into the village scene and is sorting through fruits, trying to make a decision. We might not even see him if it was not for her looking at him."

I laughed at the delightful details, the cheerfulness of the work, and its fineness. "These are paintings that make you happy, aren't they? I didn't see the foreigner. He's tucked in there amidst so many people. And it's remarkable that we can actually tell that these two are haggling. It's more their postures than anything."

"He was adept at transmitting the meaning through postures."

"Yes. May I look at the back again?"

Made flipped over the painting, and we looked at the slight foxing of the edges of the paper, the discoloration in two of the corners.

"Not acid-free paper."

"No, none of it is. These paintings will not last forever."

"May I take photos of the backs of the two that you think are originals? I would like to be able to compare them to the back of the painting at the Searles. In fact, I should take photos of all four, shouldn't I? I'll see if I can get someone at the museum to photograph the backs of ours to e-mail to me, so that we can compare."

On the backs of two of the paintings we found the Pitamaha sticker that was applied when a painting had been in one of their exhibitions. "Have there been fakes of the sticker?"

"Probably," he said unhappily. "Where there is money involved . . ."

"Yes, it's true. I can't say that I'm happy that you think the Searles's painting is a fake, but I'd certainly rather know it now than after we publish a catalogue. Do you think you'll have time to go through the remainder of the paintings with me? This has been so incredibly helpful, I can't begin to thank you enough."

He looked at the clock on the computer screen. "I am afraid that I have a deadline. I am very busy this coming week. But I would like to continue to look at your paintings. How long will you be in Bali?"

"I'm in town for another two and a half weeks. I was afraid that you were about to tell me that you couldn't do any more with me. I've learned as much in these four hours as I've learned in many weeks of reading and researching at home." I gathered my laptop, pen, and notebook and put them in my backpack.

"Thank you. We are opening a new exhibition next weekend. After the opening I will have free time. I usually do not work on Sunday, but I will be happy to work with you on the weekend if we need to do that. This is very interesting, not just looking together, but also seeing what a Western collector values in the painting. It isn't necessarily what I as a Balinese would value."

"We'll talk about that more. And if it isn't too much trouble, I'm serious about wanting to meet your sister and see her work."

"I will arrange it after the opening." He reached over to a shelf. "Here is a copy of a catalogue for a small exhibition that I organized last year."

"Thank you. Can I help you tidy up here?"

"No, it's no bother. And I have a little more work to do."

We said our good-byes and I walked out of the museum into the dusk, I was happy not to be riding my bike. It had been an intense four hours huddled over a table, looking at finely drawn works, and I had a crick in my neck. Maybe I could get a massage, since I didn't have any plans for the evening. I needed to think of an excuse to avoid Seth and Randall.

As I turned down Hanuman Street, I thought I saw the Wild Man behind me. But when I turned back to confront him, he was no longer there. I was imagining things. And, even if he'd been there, Ubud is a small town and it's not unusual to see the same tourist day after day. It only meant he was staying nearby, or liked walking the same routes down the same streets. Still, I couldn't let go of the thought that he'd been following me.

Or the thought that Seth knew him, crazy as that thought was.

15

I hesitated inside the gate of Flip's compound as a feeling of revulsion swept over me. The emotion was at odds with the grounds before me. Lush landscaping encircled the expanse of lawn and shielded the pool, the large modern house, and the smaller buildings. To the left of the main house, the swimming pool; to the right, the small buildings.

Three days before, I had stood in the dead man's living room and looked down on his lifeless body. I'd maintained my composure then. More or less. I could do it now. I hoped that I would be viewing Flip's paintings in a room other than the living room. When I'd called last night to ask Wayan Tyo if I might look at Flip's painting collection, he hadn't asked why, nor hesitated in giving me permission.

He'd not only agreed but had asked me to create a list of the collection, so that they could keep track of Flip's property. He hadn't asked if I had suspicions about the paintings being significant in the murder case. I hadn't volunteered that I thought they were.

I tilted my head, looking at the upper story of the house, its balcony, the raw wood, worn and blending into the surroundings. Then I turned toward the garden with its shrine piled high with offerings, multiplied tenfold from the day I had first come, now offerings for the dead.

Like a foreigner, I was standing in the open, the hot sun beating down on me, but before I could break into a sweat, a woman of about my age came from the side of the house to greet me. "*Selamat pagi*," she said.

"*Pagi*," I answered, and fell into step beside her. She was tiny, inches shorter than me. "How are you all doing? It must be a difficult time."

"We do not know what our jobs will be. We are worried."

"I can see why that would worry you." I couldn't help but note that what bothered her was her job, not Flip's demise. "Was your boss well-liked?"

She hesitated. "He could be angry and yell, but he could also be fair." She was dressed in the uniform that the servants in Flip's house had worn the day he was murdered, a blue *ikat* sarong and a plain white T-shirt. The fact that the servants continued to behave as they had when he was alive suggested someone maintained charge of the property. Walking with the perfect posture that allowed Balinese women to carry meter-high offerings on their heads, she led me to the right of the main house toward the cluster of small buildings I had noted but not seen close up on my earlier visit.

I took a different tack. "Are you married?"

"Yes. I have two children."

"Girls or boys?"

"One girl and one boy." We passed two small children playing with toy trucks at the edge of a vegetable garden. A parrot sat on the older boy's shoulder, gently nibbling his ear. The boy scrunched up his neck, the bird's beak tickling him. Amid the beans and the tomatoes, the boys had created hillocks and valleys to dash the trucks up and down. The woman scolded them lightly, but didn't slow down to keep them from their play.

The bird looked up and said, "Hell yes, hell yes."

She said, "That is my son. With the bird."

"Very cute. Does your husband work here as well?"

"My husband is no longer in Ubud. He is living in Kuta."

"That's too bad."

"My husband did not like living here." She nodded toward Flip's house.

I took a guess. "He didn't like Flip?"

"Men often do not like my boss. Did not like my boss. Balinese men. I do not know about other men."

"Is that because he was inappropriate with his servants?"

She frowned. "I do not understand."

"I mean did he come on to his women servants?"

She stopped, her English failing her. "Come on?"

"Did he try to have sex with his women servants?"

"Sometimes. Sometimes he tried, but he did not rape us." She shrugged. "He was a man."

The small wooden buildings were randomly placed, a path weaving among them. Bougainvillea arched over one house; clematis clung to another. We stopped at the structure closest to the main house, and she climbed the three steps up to the front door. The wood of the little building had a lovely, rich patina suggesting decades of weathering. I wondered when it had been built. Surely before the main house. It had probably been moved from another location.

"But is that why your husband moved to Kuta?"

"Yes. He wants me to come to live in Kuta with him now that Flip has died." She pulled a cord with keys out of the waist of her sarong and unlocked the deadbolt on the door. "*Di sini*, it is here." She waved her arm toward the paintings stacked on shelves along the far wall, then switched on a dim overhead light and went over to a table that stood beneath a window. There she turned on a reading light. A wide, low eight-drawer file cabinet stood next to the table and promised works on paper.

I saw that there was a thermos of tea and a glass ready for me and that cushions had been placed on the uncomfortable-looking wood chair. "*Terimah kasih banyak*," I thanked her as she left.

Only the edges of the shelved paintings were visible, and I didn't see any labels to designate their arrangement, so I wouldn't know how they were organized until I began pulling each one out. Of course, there could be a list, but chances were it would be on Flip's computer or in his office. I kicked myself for not asking Wayan Tyo if he'd found any kind of list, though if he had he wouldn't have had me making one for him—unless he wanted to compare the two. If that was the case, he may also suspect the paintings played some role in the murder.

Deciding to begin with the works on paper, I pulled out my computer and set it on the table. I opened the top drawer of the flat file. Looking down on the contents, I reassessed the amount of time it was going to take me to go through the collection. Three piles of paintings and drawings filled the drawer, each work separated from the next by a sheet of acid-free paper. There appeared to be as many as thirty in one drawer alone, and there were eight drawers. So two hundred forty paintings if they were all as full as this one.

Compiling a list would require more than a cursory glance at each of the paintings, unless they were labeled. I sighed, as my vacation time shrank. This was turning into a working trip from beginning to end—not a sightseeing extravaganza. No snorkeling off Manjangan Island. No bike ride around the island or hiking in the mountains.

I looked again at the wall of paintings. All those paintings. All that information, that knowledge to be gleaned. I smiled. My vacation might not materialize, but I had this. Addictive, I thought. The paintings, the performances, the temples—Bali was an art historian's paradise.

Looking over at the canvases lined along the wall, I realized that I might only have time to count them, unless I could persuade Tyo I needed to study them. Still, the works on paper were what interested me most, as the 1930s Balinese painters generally worked on paper, not oil on canvas. If the key to Flip's death lay in fakes he was painting, then these drawers might provide the means to solving the case. Of course, if he was also creating forgeries of the Western artists who had been in Bali in the 1930s, then I did need to give the larger works a look. Le Mayeur, Bonnet, and Spies had worked on canvas. If he'd copied their styles, I would need to spend weeks in this room.

I took the thermos and glass off the table and set them on the floor by the door, poured myself a glass, then left the glass there too, so that it wasn't near any of the art. I took some cotton gloves Made had given me the day before from my bag and put them on. I pulled the first pile of works out of the drawer and set it on the sheet of clean paper that his servant had placed on the table for me. I lay my notebook and pencil next to the paintings and beside my computer. I was ready to go.

WAYAN Tyo simultaneously knocked and opened the door. He wore a white shirt and dark pants. Work clothes, I guessed, as he'd been more casually dressed when we had dinner at his family compound. I tried to remember what he'd worn the day I'd found Flip, but all I could get into focus was his face, the smell of peanuts, and the scar on his hand.

"They said you have not eaten any lunch. They have something prepared, and I can join you, though I cannot spend much time to eat." He rubbed his hands together as he spoke.

"Oh." I rotated my shoulders and passed the painting that I had been looking at onto the pile on my left. "I'm hungry. You won't believe what this guy was up to. Either that, or you won't believe what a collection of unknown 1930s paintings and drawings he had collected. It's impressive. You see this flat file? There are twenty to thirty paintings and drawings in each drawer.

That's a lot of art. It's worth a fortune. This building should have a guard on it. Who's going to inherit his estate?"

"They are putting the food on the table now."

"One more in this pile, then I can put it away. I wonder if we can find the key to these drawers. They should be locked, but they weren't, and I haven't found a key anywhere."

"Lunch first, then we can come back here to talk. Not in front of the servants, and anyway, eating time is a time to relax."

"Okay." I typed the artist's name into my computer, then placed the pile of paintings into the second drawer. "This is going to take longer than I thought. It might be good if . . ."

"After lunch. Do you know how to relax?

"I generally unwind by riding my bike ten or more miles as fast as I can possibly ride."

"Sounds very soothing," he said, shaking his head.

"We're not eating in the living room, are we?"

He nodded.

"WHEN the Pitamaha Art Guild was founded in 1936, that group of Westerners and Balinese formed a jury to evaluate the paintings artists brought to them. But I suppose you know that." I pulled a painting out of the drawer and adjusted the lamp on the small worktable. "Clearly they favored some artists over others—for good reason, since some of them were very talented. One has to assume others were not."

"You sound like a teacher."

"Sorry, I do get into pedantic mode at times. I teach the docents at the museum. You see this painting here? It's either an Ida Bagus Made or a copy of his work. I'm not a specialist, but if it's a copy, it's a good one." I didn't need to tell Wayan Tyo that Ida Bagus Made was one of the best-known of the Pitamaha painters and an artist whose work collectors covet.

He touched the corner of the painting with the tip of a finger and angled it toward himself.

"Made Badung told me yesterday that he'd seen a few paintings that he suspects are forgeries of Ida Bagus Made. Maybe we've found the culprit. We need to get Made over here to look at these. Once I've finished cataloguing, we might know what he needs to see."

"Yes." He picked up the painting and studied it.

"If he did paint this, he was extremely skilled. The painting lying next to Flip's easel when he was killed was in the style of Lempad, who worked in a radically different style. Lempad's quirky, elongated figures boldly placed in space bear little relationship to Ida Bagus Made's work. We should take a close look at that Lempad."

"Mmm. You know what this could mean?" said Wayan Tyo, more to himself than to me. He set down the painting on the table and turned toward the row of canvases. He walked over and pulled one out, pushed it back in, then pulled out another.

"Sure. For some reason he was killed because of his faking. That leaves an entire field of suspects. Collectors, dealers, middlemen, family members of the artists, and, last but not least, whoever inherits his estate." I fingered the amulet in my pocket. "That last person would benefit immediately, or have the option of selling all these paintings over time."

"Yes, but would they benefit more if he died now rather than ten years from now?"

"Maybe they needed money now." As we talked about the motive, I thought this might be the moment to give the amulet to Tyo.

He shrugged. "This is one possible motive for killing him."

"A good one." I took a deep breath as I built up my nerve.

Wayan Tyo held a small painting at arm's length and tilted his head as he looked at it. "As my brother pointed out, there were numerous reasons for killing Flip. Not least of which is jealousy."

"I'd put my money on forgeries."

He frowned, seeming to realize where the conversation had gone. "This is not for you to think about."

Not wanting to get into an argument with him about motive, I continued, "But it's hard to say, isn't it? Maybe it has to do with the inheritance. It's certainly a motive worth pursuing. From the stories I've heard about this guy, he would have been perfectly capable of changing his will at the drop of a hat. He was erratic, right? Did he even have a will?"

"We have not been able to sort that out. One of the reasons I came by today was to look more closely at the papers in his office and try to figure out who his most recent lawyer is and who inherits." He walked over to where I was standing and repeated, "This is not for you to think about. You need to think only about the paintings."

I ignored the last and said, "His most recent lawyer?"

"It seems he changed lawyers often and rewrote his will many times. But, as far as we know, he has no children, nor was he married." He was staring at me hard.

"Ah. What about Ulih?" I couldn't stop myself. My mind was racing through suspects. "That's her name, right? She did show up shortly after he was murdered, and she did seem truly upset. She's the one who's organizing his cremation, isn't that what you told me? Is this a case where the murderer returns to the scene of the crime?"

It took him some time to answer. "I find it difficult to believe she could drive that spear through him. I think it had to be someone very strong."

"Probably."

"Yes." He moved toward the door.

I pulled the sack from my pocket, but slid it back when he turned toward me. I saw the tightness in his face. "If you find a list of his paintings in his papers, could you give it to me? It would simplify my task."

"Of course." His hand on the doorknob, he opened his mouth, but I spoke first.

"You know, I was thinking about Flip's posture." I didn't tell him that I'd been practicing it in the pool. "The way his arm was thrown across his face. I think he had that arm extended when the killer drove the spear through him."

"He was probably trying to block it."

"Or he was reaching for the spear."

"Possible." Tyo looked skeptical. "Have you heard what I said to you?"

"Sure."

"Stay out of this, Jenna."

"I'd better get back to work." I pulled my empty hand from my pocket and picked up a pile of paintings from the next drawer.

He didn't leave right away, and I sensed he was considering whether to soften the harshness of his words or to say more. I didn't look at him.

Without another word, he was gone.

My taking the amulet was an act that grew heavier by the day. As did giving it back.

I looked down at the paintings. I was definitely in the right profession, looking at art all day long. He, on the other hand, looked at dead bodies and piles of potential evidence.

16

"That was a revelation." This time he didn't knock when he came in. He was looking a bit tousled, and I wondered if I looked as wilted.

"What was a revelation? This painting is superb. Come look."

He slipped off his shoes and came to stand behind me. He smelled of peanuts. Did the man keep a secret stash in his pocket? "Flip's will."

I looked up at him. "What did it say?"

"I should say, I found a will. Whether or not it is the latest will is a question. I have to make certain this is his most recent."

"And?"

"He left everything to his daughter."

"I thought you said that he didn't have any children?"

"We didn't think he did, but Ulih's daughter also happens to be his daughter."

"How could no one know that? Does the girl look like him?"

"No, she looks like her mother, though you get a hint of foreigner when you look at her. We all assumed that Ulih had slept with some tourist, who then went on his way. It happens." He looked down at the painting, a dance performance with Barong prominent in the foreground and the top of Rangda's head in the distance. "Another Ida Bagus Made."

"You know your Balinese painters," I said, surprised. "Yes, another. I think this"—I looked at my computer screen—"is number twenty-three by him. There's no doubt. I know Ida Bagus Made was prolific, but Flip couldn't have managed to put together this many of his paintings and drawings, even if he'd been collecting aggressively for twenty years. Not with all the other artists that he's managed to accumulate."

The painting, though radically different from the market scene that Made and I had studied, was similarly composed. Minor players actively moved around the central figure of Barong. "I'm sorry I didn't meet him."

"Ida Bagus Made?"

"No. Flip. I have the feeling he was a true master forger. Do you have information on what he was doing before he came to Bali? I mean, what kind of work he did? What his training was?"

"No. We'll have to try to find that out. I do know that he trained with some painters here when he first arrived. There is one older, well-respected painter that he studied with for a number of years." He paused. "But Jenna, don't get ahead of yourself. We don't know he was a forger."

I pushed ahead. "It would be worth talking with his teacher. I wonder if he has any idea what Flip was up to."

"I would be surprised. He's a well-respected member of our community, a priest at one of the local temples and an honorable man. The longer Flip was here, the wilder he became, and at some point his teacher dropped him. Or that's the rumor. Flip then studied with another artist, who painted in quite a different style." He pulled out a drawer of the flat file, slid the paper off the top painting, and quietly studied it. Then he put the paper back and closed the drawer.

"What is odd," he said, "is that no one talks about whether Flip became skilled at painting in the Balinese style. Nor does anyone say that he continued painting in that manner. Instead he is known for his oils, which a couple of the galleries in town sell."

"We can assume that he was keeping his talent quiet. If he wasn't and these works started turning up on the market, then the authorities, not to mention the dealers and collectors, might have guessed what he was up to. He must have been in cahoots with a dealer, or more than one dealer."

"Cahoots?"

I smiled. "It means when people conspire together. Good word, isn't it? Could he have had a falling out with a dealer? Maybe one who handles his oil paintings?"

Wayan Tyo was thoughtful. "I would be surprised if he was doing something with the main gallery that handles his painting. That dealer is an honest person. Also, he specializes in oils and works done by foreigners, or oils done by local Balinese who paint in a Western style, not this type of painting. It must be someone else." He began pacing.

I thought of my friend P.P., who often paced. I needed to contact him to make sure he wasn't coming to Bali. "Who else?" I asked.

"He could have had a falling out with anyone."

"Any candidates come to mind?" I placed the Ida Bagus Made painting on the finished pile and drew another out of the drawer onto the table in front of me. I had begun drawer three and hoped to finish it today.

"Sure. Both foreign and Balinese."

That stopped me. "You know, I hadn't thought about a foreigner driving a spear through him. Do you think that it might have been a foreigner? I somehow thought it was a Balinese."

"Run amok, so to speak?" He had a sly smile on his heart-shaped face.

I couldn't tell if the smile was amusement or annoyance at what he might see as racism. I would have to learn how to read him better, and be more thoughtful about what I said. "No, I guess it was the weapon. I was thinking that only a Balinese would have access to it, or would choose to use a spear rather than some more direct method. A gun or poison, a knife."

I looked down at the work before me. It was by an artist I didn't recognize. "You know, the thing that's confusing is that some of these paintings do seem to be authentic. They're by minor artists. It makes me wonder if some of the works by well-known artists might be real. If so, the valuation of these paintings is going to be a nightmare."

"No doubt." He looked over my shoulder. "That is by I Tomblos."

"You should have been an art historian."

"No. There is no value in it."

"Thanks a lot."

"I mean that one does not get paid enough. Not here in Bali, that is. Made struggles even though he works at a museum. A private museum where he is paid more than he would be at a national museum, and he still struggles. I have a family to support."

We both were silent, ignoring the elephant in the room, or rather the wife no longer at hand.

He looked uncomfortable. "Back to the question of what dealer he might have angered. I will think about this."

"You know, the other day I wandered into a textile shop. I noticed there were a couple of paintings on the wall by the register. I didn't look at them too long, but they looked good to me. I suppose anyone who gets his hands on an old painting might sell it. Which means it will be a long list."

I set down my camera, typed "I Tomblos" into my computer, put the painting on the finished pile, and picked up another. "It would be nice if Flip had some signature that he used. Some little clue that he was the artist. You might ask Ulih about that. Would you say that she's the one who knew him best?"

"I do not know, and it would not help her to tell me. If her daughter inherits all this, it would be better if the paintings were authentic.

"Yes, true. Who knows? Maybe she's honest."

"I think she is, but one must use caution."

"One thing." I turned around in the chair. "The paper."

"Yes."

"The paper that he used is 100 percent right. I mean, if these are fakes—and those in the museums' collections are fakes by him—he had gotten his hands on a cache of 1920s paper. It looks like the paper that was used for the works at Made's museum. You might try to track down where he got it. Won't necessarily solve the question of his murder, but it may lead the way to figuring out his forgeries. Maybe there's a box of it here in the house."

He nodded, raised his hand in a slight wave, and walked out the door. I watched him go, aware of the shifts that had occurred between us. One minute he'd been animated and sharing, the next he'd withdrawn. And I, I still had the damn amulet in my pocket, as I'd feared giving it to him.

17

I rode north, diverting to side roads when I could. The helmet was large on my head, and the wind whipping into it created an echo chamber. When I got to Desa Tamblang off the Ubud Singaraja road, I slowed my pedaling and turned. The road narrowed and tiny village replaced small village. Rice fields spread before me as I wound my way toward Sekumpul waterfall. Fields of red and green chilies alternated with groves of cacao trees, jackfruit, and clove that grew in hectic abandon alongside coffee plants.

I stopped to watch a crowd of men tie sharp spikes to their roosters' legs, then, holding the birds firmly, thrust them beak to beak in a circle of dirt. One of the roosters wanted to engage, while the other, its ruff lying flat against its neck, wasn't having it. The willing rooster escaped and the dust flew as it strutted around the area of tamped earth. I left before they found another rooster eager for battle.

At a sign that read Waterfall Parking, I locked the bike to a pole, left the helmet on the bike, and set off to climb the paved path to the waterfall, stopping at a *warung* to buy a soda. When the owner saw me prepare to walk away with the bottle, she rushed up and poured the liquid into a plastic bag, stuck a straw in, and wrapped a rubber band around the newly created neck. Ingenious, but all those discarded plastic bags were a nightmare for conservationists.

Forty minutes took me to the waterfalls that cascaded narrowly amidst a patchwork of plants. Spray prickled my arms and face, still hot and sweaty from my exertions. The hills, the coconut and areca palms, durian hanging in profusion from tree branches, and clove trees breathing out their fragrant spice—I felt free of Ubud and its worries.

Harsh Australian vowels cut through my solitude. I thought of the Wild Man, and my breath caught. Then a very young couple, he in micro shorts, she in a halter top and miniskirt, came round the bend. "G'day," said the boy as he stripped off his T-shirt.

"You're going under there?" the girl squealed.

"You are too," he said, and pulled her with him under the waterfall's edge.

Watching them, I thought of Alam. Of having someone to share all this with—the scenery, the bike ride, the performances and other arts. I needed to think long and hard about what I wanted.

ON my return I passed motorcycles with huge bunches of elephant grass, fodder for cows, lying across their backseats; trucks overladen with bags of rice piled six feet above the sides of the bed; a group of ten-year-olds riding motorbikes, their schoolbags on their backs, a few transporting younger children who stood in front of the driver while their friends sat behind. A huge red bus careened toward Kintamani, and I was tempted to follow it to the popular local market.

Tempted to ditch my responsibilities. To find a new beginning for this adventure in Bali that I'd looked forward to for months. Physical adventure, like snorkeling and bike riding, but also intellectual adventure, in all that I had hoped to learn from

Flip. I was learning, and even getting some bike riding in, but the fun was missing, the feeling of liberation. Everything was freighted with significance.

I swerved around a pig a young boy was leading on a leash and slowed for a row of women. In every town, large or small, women carried baskets with offerings on their heads as they walked to the temples. Ubiquitous the women, the temples, the tall, waving *penjor,* the flag-like offerings put up for the Galungan festival.

The road vanished as a stream of huge trucks negotiated the narrow two-lanes. I stopped and pulled up against a wall. Shaded, I looked up at the tall, empty stone seat for Sang Hyang Widhi that rose within the house compound. Like the women, the temples, the *penjor*, the god Sang Hyang Widhi was everywhere.

The trucks passed. "Hello," a woman called out. Her friends laughed.

I smiled. "Hello. How are you?"

One of the women pointed at the offering basket she carried on her head, then at me.

I leaned my bike against the wall and waited for her. Her slender arms rose and she plucked the heavy basket, with its pyramidal mound of fruit, from her head and placed it on mine. I felt the compression in my neck, a flattening of the top of my head. My spine straightened, my shoulders rose. "Don't let go," I said, but I doubted she understood me.

They were all laughing, and one of them pointed at the temple a hundred yards down the road.

"No way," I said, and tried to shake my head. Her hand still on the basket, she steadied it for me. "I couldn't walk a foot if I had to."

"Come," one said. Another took my hand.

I looked at the bike. A young boy who had run up to join the fun took the handlebars and said, "No problem," that universal English phrase spoken in every country of the world.

I reached up and steadied the basket with my hand as the woman took her hand away, and I walked hesitantly with the group past the walls, the laughing children, young men sitting outside a *warung*, to the temple. There she wrested the basket from my head and each of the women patted me, smiling and laughing. Punch-drunk, I thanked them, retrieved my bike from the boy, and began my return to Ubud, the wind blasting in my ears, my shirt flapping around me, replenished. Prepared to face the next catastrophe.

I left that village, but not civilization, as trucks, minivans, motorbikes passed me. A group of men yelled from the back of a truck. Standing, they fit like a jigsaw puzzle into its bed, their edges pressed hard against one another. A vehicle slowed behind me and I waved my arm for it to pass, as there was now no other car or truck in sight. A hill rose before me. I shifted gears and glanced back at a white van. Two trucks careened toward us and it fell back.

I turned my concentration toward the hill, my legs beginning to feel like jelly. The ride to the falls was a long one with way too many ups. If only one could arrange it so that there were more downs. I focused on the thought of the downhill when I breached the top. Cacao trees grew along the side of the road, and I could see the fruit, hanging in abundance.

I didn't coast on the downhill, since I wanted my momentum to carry me at least halfway up the next rise. I heard a car behind me and realized what a relief it was not to have a vehicle approaching as well, since the road was narrow. I glanced in my rearview, which I had been smart enough to bring with me—if only I'd brought my own properly fitting helmet—and saw a white van gaining speed and aimed right at me.

The world went into slow motion—me judging the terrain on the shoulder, the foot and a half between road and ditch, the ditch filled with muck, the cacao trees growing profuse and dense, and, twenty feet ahead, a side lane. I veered to the shoulder, rising high off my seat, braking, thinking of mountain biking in West Marin, of Pine Ridge, the Bolinas Trail, the time I'd totaled and had to be carried out. Shit, I thought. Shit, shit, shit.

Leaning, yanking the handlebars to the right, edging my rear wheel forward and turning parallel to the ground, I slid onto the lane, down the lane. Each motion, each twist of my wrist and turn of my body, every damn pebble that ground into my leg, my side, my bare arms, noted and filed. As if I could see it all happening. As if I were already up in the sky looking down, saying to myself, don't go down that tunnel. That would be death. Don't go down that tunnel.

I saw it. I saw myself, the van plummeting toward me and me veering away onto the shoulder, the smooth surface of tamped earth on the lane just ahead. The lane beneath me as I slid, the wheels of my bike continuing into the ditch and the muck. I was aware of the van slowing, traffic approaching, the van speeding away. My head pounding, my ears ringing, a hazy, slow truck followed by a string of vans, trucks, motorbikes, coming down the hill ahead. A minivan beeped, a motorcycle echoed the sound, all those vehicles wanting the truck to pull off the road so they could pass.

From the other direction, another truck as wide as the one approaching slowed and stopped. I didn't see it clearly, but heard it, and in my desire to get the picture complete, to embed the memory in my life, rather than my almost death, I imagined details of that truck. Only a few seconds, and no memories flashing before me, just me trying to control the bicycle.

As I lay on my side, my legs pulled up to my chest, I patted the front wheel, which was all I could reach. I love you, Giant, sturdy and tough, no expensive, flimsy road bike. Thank God.

"Okay? Okay?" a man shouted.

I nodded, slowly moving my legs, my arms, checking for what was broken. Nothing as far as I could tell, but I felt the sting of my scraped flesh, raw and red and thinned.

He reached down and took my hand to pull me up, but I waved him away. I wasn't ready for that yet, though I did shift to sit up. My ribs throbbed. Uh-oh, I thought, a broken rib. I shifted again, and decided just bruised. I reached up for his hand and added him to my picture of what had happened, then took in the crowd that was forming around me.

I had seen the front seat of the van as it passed, the driver tall, hair pulled back, no passenger. Was it the van that had been cruising so close behind only moments before? In any event, I had the impression that the driver was a Westerner.

18

"Lunch at one, Bu. Wayan Tyo called to say he would join you. Are you okay?"

Damn, I thought, I've just gotten here and he'll arrive in an hour. The trip to the waterfall had taken longer than I'd thought it would. The truck had dropped me at the bike shop, where the owner charged the cost of the bike on my credit card and promised the loan of another. I'd toyed with the idea of going back to the hotel, but resisted. I had work to do, and moving was probably the best medicine for my injuries. I'd been lucky. "Yes, thank you. No, actually. I should wash these." I gestured at my leg, my rib aching as I moved my arm.

She let out a little gasp of surprise, "I will bring a cloth and some medicine."

"*Terimah kasih.* I can find my way back there. Is it open?" I wondered if Tyo had arranged a guard for the paintings. I took the arnica I always carried with me out of my bag and popped three more tiny pills into my mouth. This should keep me from bruising too badly.

"Ya," she said nervously as we parted ways by the main house.

Hoisting my bag more comfortably over my good shoulder, I climbed the few steps and opened the door. I stopped short. "Who are you?"

"I might ask you the same," the tall, thin man responded as he turned. He had wild, unkempt hair and bright blue eyes that darted here and there as if he were trapped. The Wild Man.

"An old girlfriend? You followed me and told my friend this bullshit that I looked like an old girlfriend." I waited, not going any farther into the room. I'd seen Flip and what a spear could do. There was no spear in sight, but I was still wary.

He looked surprised and puzzled. "Your friend? Sorry I stared. I didn't mean you any harm. I was trying to figure out who you were. I saw you come out of the house shortly after the murder."

"You didn't mean me any harm, but here you are in a murdered man's storage shed. Your hand in the till, so to speak. And what were you doing here at the time of the murder, shortly after the murder?"

"Calm down. I'm a friend of Flip's. Or was a friend of his. I was just leaving."

"How did you get in?"

"One of the girls let me in." He slid the top drawer shut and picked up a shoulder bag.

"What are you doing here?"

Without hesitation, he said, "Flip's lawyer asked me to take a look at what was here—he thought maybe I should catalogue the collection for them. Do a valuation. For him and the police. I was just getting a general idea. I've been in the room many times, though."

Bullshit, I thought. He wasn't here for the police, and I doubted he'd ever been in this room. "You're a dealer?"

"Yes."

"And you've handled Flip's Balinese-style paintings? I mean, sold them?"

He sidestepped the question. "We were friends. I'm familiar with the collection. He liked to look at the works with others who were knowledgeable."

"What did you say your name is?"

"Eric Shelley. And you?" He tried to be jolly. "I feel as if I'm being interrogated."

"Jenna Murphy. Do you have a gallery here in Ubud?"

"No."

I waited for him to expand, but he didn't. "In Australia?"

"Yes. I have a gallery in Perth."

"Where you sell Balinese paintings?" I could tell that he wanted to leave, but I didn't move from the doorway. He'd have to mow me down or run me through with a spear to get me out of his way, and he seemed to be aware of that. Maybe if I could keep this conversation going long enough, Wayan Tyo would arrive early.

"Among other Balinese bric-a-brac. Things from Bali are popular in Australia. This is a destination for us, not too far away."

"Right. So what did you decide?"

"Decide?"

"Are you going to catalogue the collection?"

"I have to get back to the lawyer to discuss it." He adjusted his bag on his shoulder and took a step toward me.

I took one back, balancing on the edge of the doorframe. "Who's the lawyer, by the way? The police don't know, since Flip seems to have changed lawyers frequently."

He gave me a name.

"I'll have to tell the investigating officer that."

He paled, but regained his composure almost immediately. "Certainly. I'm sure they would appreciate the help. Can't be very good here, these police."

"Oh, I think they're very good. From what I've seen."

He seemed to be thinking about this as he asked, "Do you live here in Ubud?"

"No." I could be as brief as he.

Suddenly he brightened. "You're the one who found him?"

"Yes. You knew that."

He ignored the last. "The museum curator? Is that right? He told me that someone was coming to quiz him about Balinese painting."

"That's right. Unfortunately, I didn't get the chance."

"Yes, it's sad." He put on a sorrowful face entirely devoid of feeling. The guy was a lousy actor.

"Where are you staying?"

He hesitated. "Oh, I'm not. Just heading out of Bali this evening. Been up in the northwest snorkeling for the past couple of weeks. Flip was going to join me."

I noted his attempt at an alibi, "This evening? Hard to catalogue the collection from Perth, I imagine."

"Easy to return. Nice to meet you."

Someone came up behind me and I turned.

"Bu, here is the cloth and some medicine. I will help you."

Eric Shelley took the opportunity to squeeze past.

I opened my mouth to object, but then thought that there couldn't be too many evening flights to Perth. Surely Wayan Tyo would be able to track him down if he wanted to talk with him. Besides, the man was literally twice my size; I couldn't stop him without a spear, or at the least a kris. "If the police wanted to talk with you before you leave, where might they find you?" I asked as he walked away.

"Oh, I'll be around Ubud. Already checked out of my hotel." He picked up his pace. There was no doubt that he wanted to get as far away from me as possible.

And I wanted him to. I'd already been mowed down once today. I imagined Eric Shelley's hair pulled back in a ponytail. The girl had pulled the chair over to the door so that we would have better light and was gently pushing me into it. I didn't object. I wanted her to take care of me.

I watched as he went through the gate, then climbed into a white van and drove off. I cursed myself for not getting the license plate number, though I hadn't gotten it off the van that ran me down either, so there wasn't anything to compare. I gingerly stretched my leg. Very gingerly. Shelley had had plenty of time to beat me back to town after running me off the road. Plenty of time to steal some paintings.

She began washing my leg. "Yow," I said as I pulled out my phone and texted Wayan Tyo to hurry, that something had happened. Three things had happened, but I didn't need to tell him that. One, Eric Shelley had turned up and probably stolen paintings. Two, someone had run me off the road. I gritted my teeth as she scrubbed away the dirt. Would Tyo notice the scrapes? And three, Seth had lied to me. Shelley hadn't said I looked like an old girlfriend. That was clear from his confusion when I mentioned it. So what had he said? Why had Seth lied, and what had they talked about that night at the bar?

"Ouch," I groaned as she rubbed at the scrapes. I thought of the van, its speed, my luck.

I groaned again, at the thought that someone hadn't just tried to run me off the road. Someone had tried to kill me.

"Gentler, please," I said.

I had a lot to tell Tyo. I could tell him about Eric Shelley. I could tell him someone had tried to kill me. But I couldn't tell him that I suspected Eric Shelley of following me for the past few days. I couldn't tell him about the performance, the nightclub, the men from my hotel who I'd gone to a bar with my first night in Ubud just hours after I'd found a dead man.

The stolen paintings, yes. The white van, yes. But not the men and the bar and my previous sightings of the Wild Man.

19

"Lunch," but when I didn't look up, he said. "What happened?"

"He stole paintings," I said as I riffled through the pile in front of me. "Help me with this."

"Who stole paintings?"

"An Australian dealer named Eric Shelley. When I arrived this morning he was already here."

"Here? You mean in this building?"

"Yes, alone in this building. Help me figure out what he took." But Wayan Tyo was already gone.

Damn him.

Damn me. I should have numbered the paintings. Just a light number in pencil on the back of each painting would have done the trick, but I had been trying to save time. No, worse, I just hadn't thought of it. Damn, if only I'd gotten through all the drawers before Eric Shelley showed up. He could have easily taken paintings from any drawer, and if he took works from the lower five, I wouldn't have a clue what he'd taken.

I could hear Tyo's raised voice. I needed to calm down, eat lunch, then together he and I could look through the top three drawers to see what was missing. If Shelley was the one who had tried to run me off the road, he couldn't have been here long. But he had definitely rearranged things in this drawer.

Wayan Tyo continued chastising someone as they came my way. I looked up to see the girl who had greeted me, the girl with the keys, the girl who had tended to my scrapes, her head bowed and face pinched. He said to me, "I told them not to let anyone in but you. He tricked them, said that he was meeting you here."

I nodded. "This drawer is in disarray. He heard me coming and he had to go through it quickly. This may mean that he didn't get into the other drawers. He told me that he's leaving Bali this evening. Can you have him stopped at the airport? There can't be too many flights to Perth, can there?"

He pulled out his cell phone and placed a call, signaling me to follow him. When I motioned at the pile of paintings, he waved his arm and again waved me toward him. Lunch, it seemed, was our priority. The penitent girl locked the door behind us.

AT the table I moved the place setting so I didn't face the death room directly and so that my scraped arm was away from Tyo's seat. I wished once again that we were eating out on the patio or in the kitchen.

He said, "I have put someone on it. They are checking the airlines to see what flight he is taking. We can catch him—hopefully with paintings on him."

"He was big, thin, but tall. Probably strong enough. He could have done it."

Wayan Tyo was spooning rice into his mouth, his brow still furrowed. A servant came into the room and placed a platter of *gado-gado* on the table. She stood to one side staring fearfully at Tyo, who glared at his food.

"Is everyone afraid of you?"

"Only when I yell at them. I'm a cop, and people are naturally in awe of cops."

"Is that what you want, their fear?"

"In this instance, yes. I don't want them to let anyone else in. If I have to terrify them to make them do as I say, I will."

"What did you say?" I reached for the *gado-gado*, cringing with pain as I did. My shoulder ached. The girl jumped forward and spooned some onto my plate. Keeping my eyes on my food, I avoided looking around the room, looking at Tyo. I wasn't ready to tell him about the white van. Which made no sense, or perhaps it did. I was afraid he'd ban me from the murder investigation.

When I finally looked up, he was watching me. "What is the matter?"

"I don't want to look where the body was." I found it bizarre that we were eating in this room at all. When I'd objected the previous day, Wayan Tyo had just looked at me.

"There is no body," he said. "But that is not what I was asking."

"Someone forced me off the road."

He frowned. "I do not understand."

"On my bike ride this morning. A white van forced me off the road and I went down. Just a few bruises. What did you say to the servants?"

He debated whether to pursue the issue of my injuries or answer my question. "I told them that they were responsible for anything stolen from the house."

Startled, I said, "They aren't, are they? I mean, they couldn't afford to be responsible for the replacement of an expensive painting."

He looked pointedly at the girl, then raised his eyebrows at me.

Not wanting to undermine him, I changed the subject. "Did you have a good evening last night?"

"Very quiet. The girls were tired after a busy day of school and playing and we all went to bed early." He chewed thoughtfully. "Intentionally?"

We were having too many conversations at once. I wanted to ask about his everyday life to distract him—and myself—from my injuries. Did he get the girls ready for school in the morning, or did Ani? Did he bathe them, read them a story, do homework with them? Was he both father and mother, or was he absent father, pining for his absent wife? "Ah, they're darling, your girls. You must be very proud of them."

The furrow between his eyes flattened out and softened for a moment, but only for a moment. "Yes, I am. And? Did this person force you off the road intentionally?"

We were back to me and the road. "Yes, intentionally. I think," I said reluctantly.

"Was it planned? Or did they do it impulsively?"

I sighed. "They followed along slowly, and it wasn't until there were no other vehicles in sight and I was going fast downhill that they ran me off."

"They tried to kill you," he said flatly as he lay down his spoon and fork.

"Maybe. Yes, probably."

"Did you get the license plate number? Or a good look at the driver?"

"No, I was too busy lying on the ground." I took the last bite. "Some people helped me and I got a ride back to town. The bike was totaled. It was a white van. When Shelley left, he was driving a white van."

"And you don't think that anyone else saw this van run you down?"

"No, the person was careful and waited until the road was empty. I think they were behind me for a good long while."

"They. More than one person in the van?"

"I'm not sure. When I glanced back and realized that the van was headed right toward me, I only saw one. I think it was a foreigner."

"A foreigner?"

"Hair pulled back in a ponytail. Light hair."

"Shelley?"

"He has long hair, so it could be pulled back. Can we talk about something else? I don't think there's anything that we can do about that van." I was tearing up.

He took my wrist, which only made the tears stream down my face. I looked at my empty plate, willing food to appear so I would have something to do other than cry. The young woman gave me another serving of *gado-gado*, like a mother trying to calm me.

Tyo opened his mouth then shut it as he watched me thoughtfully. With a sigh, he started to talk about his older daughter's accomplishments in school. We spent the remainder of the lunch discussing the education system in Bali.

"Tradition bumps against the West," he said as he motioned toward the servant, dressed in sarong and T-shirt, her head bowed in subservience. "In every aspect of our lives."

"Yes, in all of Asia and elsewhere in the world. How will it reconcile?"

"That is what we do not know, isn't it?"

"The resolution will be complicated, though, here in Bali— even with all the tourists—it feels as if tradition will win out."

He shrugged and shook his head in bemusement as he rose from the table. "It is difficult to know what to want."

I thought, yes, very difficult. I looked toward the spot where Flip had lain, but before his image filled my eyes, Tyo took me by the elbow and led me out of the room.

20

"I haven't yet organized the list by artist. I wanted to finish going through all the files before doing that. I've started by first compiling the paintings in the order that I've looked at them, noting the drawer location. You can see here that I've written the drawer number next to each painting, which I list by artist and title if there was a title given on the back. Some have one, some don't."

Tyo was looking around the room, clearly distracted. I edged closer to him to get his attention.

"Some—many, in fact—have the Pitamaha sticker on the back. Seems that Flip not only got his hands on old paper, but he also found a cache of these red-and-white stickers, upon which he forged 'Pitamaha.'" The sticker increased the value, as it certified the painting had been passed and exhibited by the committee of Western and Balinese artists who dictated the economic side of the painting market in the 1930s.

"Yes." He fidgeted, his mind clearly elsewhere.

"I'll read you the artist's name or the title that I've given the painting, and you can mark it on the computer list. Does that sound okay? It will be much faster than if I do it alone."

"I have a lot of work."

"I know, but I need help." I took a step away, suddenly irritated at him. I needed his help, not just to speed things up, but because I was in pain and wanted to go back to the hotel and lie down.

He hesitated, his jaw set. "Yes, all right."

I listed one after another. There were four paintings missing from the top drawer. The four best paintings, by my reckoning. Three were gone from the second drawer.

"That's enough to stop him at the airport," said Wayan Tyo, standing.

"Let's finish this. Only one more drawer. That took us less than half an hour."

He sat back down. "I hate computers."

"Oh. Do you want me to do that? I thought it would be easier this way, since I just looked at the paintings yesterday and I can often recognize the artist without having to try to read the name, or I have an idea of the title that I've put on it."

"No. You're right. Makes me irritable. Let me just make another call." Before he punched in the number, he asked, "Why did you get here so late? Where did you ride to?"

"Is that what's irritating you? That I wasn't here to stop him? That I was busy being run off the road?" I was incredulous. I was compiling this list for him, and he was pissed at me for being late. I might never have arrived if that van had been successful.

His voice softened. "No, it's the computer. I was just wondering."

I sat stiffly, waiting for him to finish his call. Could a computer make a person this grumpy? I'd told him I thought the house needed a guard, but now I found he expected me to keep an eye on the paintings. I pulled open the third drawer. "There seem to be two missing here. We'd better figure out what they are."

After we'd worked for some time Wayan Tyo said, "Really, I wasn't suggesting that you should have been here to guard the paintings. I just wondered where you were."

"I told you, I went for a bike ride."

"Where?"

"Sekumpul waterfall."

"But that's far."

"True. It's a nice ride and I left early. Why do you look so surprised?"

He thought before answering. "I would not have guessed you would be up so early in the morning, and it is a strenuous ride—a grueling way to start the day. That you would go off to do that before you came here to work. Yes, that surprised me. I do not say that you have to do this."

I didn't feel that I needed to explain myself to him. To tell him that the ride to the waterfall had revived me, at least until my wipeout. Yes, the sweat poured from my body and my legs felt like jelly, but the cooling wind, the exhilaration of the downhills, the thumping of my heart as I climbed sated me both physically and mentally. If the van hadn't tried to run me over—if the driver of the van hadn't tried to run me over—I would have returned feeling complete. "Did I mention that I took photos of all of the paintings I went through yesterday?"

He laughed. "You are full of surprises. No. That will be extremely useful. Can you e-mail me photos of the stolen paintings?"

"Sure. I can't say I had any hint that I would need photos because the paintings might get stolen. I just thought it would be good to photograph them for an article or a talk. I wasn't sure when I started cataloguing what I might talk about, but now I think any reference to the collection will most likely be about forgeries." I paused. "And, of course, I figured you'd need them for the estate."

"Sounds like a good idea, giving a talk. If you will talk about fakes? We do not know yet."

The tension between us had receded. I wasn't sure why it had arisen. We'd begun a dance, Wayan Tyo and I. At moments it felt a bit like a waltz and at other times like a tango. I thought of

Rangda and Barong battling it out, good and evil. But between Wayan Tyo and me, who was evil? "True, but . . ."

"What?"

"Well, I'm not certain what percentage are fakes. A lot of them are real. It would be interesting to discover if he bought from any of the local dealers. Or if he had runners or middlemen searching for paintings for him."

"I think we can find out. I'll talk with the servants today while they are feeling contrite."

"Right. Let's finish so you can do that and I can get to work." I read the name on the painting I held in my hand, set it down, then continued with the remaining paintings in that drawer. We worked without speaking, both intent on moving on to the next task.

As we finished the third drawer, I said, "Maybe we could have Made come over to take a look at a few of the paintings tomorrow. Though he's busy, I bet we could lure him over here for an hour or so. He knows this work so much better than I."

"That sounds like a good idea. I'll see if he might be able to come by for half an hour." He rose to leave. At the door, he said without turning, "You're coming for dinner tonight?"

"Yes."

"We can compare notes then. I'm going to speak with Flip's servants, then head back to the office." He hesitated. "Do you need a doctor? There is a very good doctor here. I could take you there."

"No." I fingered the amulet, wondering. But the precarious balance of our relationship might not survive my ever returning it to him.

"Without a license plate number, I don't know what I can do about the van."

"Yes, I know."

"You will have to be careful."

"Yes, dad."

He scowled and walked out the door.

It would be nice, I thought, if he came back to tell me what he'd discovered from the servants, but I doubted he would. I opened drawer four and sighed. The sound of my sigh stopped me, and I wondered if I hoped he'd return because I wanted to learn what he'd found out or because I wanted to see him again. Falling for Tyo was not a good idea, especially with Alam waiting in the wings. I didn't need to be infatuated with two men at the same time. Seth, however, was a man without strings. Good-looking, smart, a man passing in the night. I shook my head, trying to rattle free my thoughts of men and focus on the subject at hand.

My inclination was to examine each painting in detail to try to figure out what was a fake and what was real, not to merely jot down the artist and title, then go on to the next. But I didn't have the time, and I was better off not looking too closely until Made and I had time to sit down together. After I'd put in more time with him, I would be better able to recognize a fake.

I turned a little too quickly, and a sharp pain stretched from my shoulder to my rib. I took the arnica pills from my purse. So far they'd kept me from visibly bruising, but I still felt the pain. I pulled up my pant leg and looked at my calf and the long, raw scrape that puckered from ankle to knee. Paintings, I thought, focus on the paintings.

What Flip painted. Which ones the pre-war modernist artists painted. What mystery might be resolved by the paintings. Forgery? Murder? So many choices.

21

Once inside the gate, I took off my helmet and parked my bike—the new bike I'd found waiting for me at the hotel. The owner of the bike shop had made good on his promise.

Ani was in the kitchen. "I remember this smell," I told her. "What is it?"

"Your favorite meal. I could not prepare it when you first arrived. I needed to make certain that it was still you." She looked at my arm. "Tyo said you had an accident."

"Yes." I didn't elaborate, since he apparently hadn't told her what really happened.

"Are you injured anywhere else?" She was looking at my arm.

I lifted my pant leg.

She gasped. "What were you wearing?"

"Pants, but they were thin and loose. Not to worry. I won't get an infection. I've put antibiotic cream on the cut and taken arnica for the bruises."

She waited.

"And a sore rib."

"Broken?"

"No."

"You rode here?" She frowned.

"Yes, not my best idea. I'm pretty stiff."

She opened her mouth to say something, but stopped herself. "Mimpi, come with me to the *kebun*."

"Mimpi? That's what the kids were calling me the other night."

"That's what we called you when you were small."

"Ah. Why is that?"

"Your father called you Imp and one of my children turned that into *mimpi*, the Bahasa word for 'dream.'"

Dream. Hardly seemed an appropriate nickname for me. "Where is the *kebun*? More importantly, what is the *kebun*?"

"The house garden. Here." She led me out and around the kitchen to a closely planted garden. "All Balinese homes used to have their own house garden, but in recent years, as real estate has become more valuable, many families have sold off part of their property, usually their gardens. We've managed to hang onto all of our land."

"What a delight," I said. A giant jackfruit clung to the trunk of the tree on my right, while the tree to my left was laden with mangoes. I recognized cassava, the source of tapioca. "What is that tree?"

"Rambutan."

"Ah." Other plants I didn't recognize grew randomly beneath the trees.

"This is sweet potato. I also have peas. They are not native here, but we all like them, so I planted some."

I picked a pod and popped it open. "I smell some spice. I don't know what it is."

Ani smiled as she leaned forward to pick some tomatoes.

"Can I help you?"

"Thank you, but you can walk around. Enjoy yourself."

At the far end of the garden, rocks girded a small pond overflowing with pink lotus. "Lovely," I said as I settled on one of the rocks and stuck my fingers into the water. A koi rushed up and hopefully nibbled my fingertips.

"What is bothering you, Mimpi?"

I hesitated. It didn't surprise me that she saw my worry. "Did you ever do something that you regretted but you couldn't figure out how to correct what you've done?"

She thought for a moment. "Yes."

"Were you able to make it right?"

"Right? No, not really. I was able to do as much as I could. I was able to face the consequences of what I had done."

"Ah, the consequences. That's what frightens me. Or one of the things that frightens me."

She put the last ripe tomato into her basket before asking, "Would these consequences be legal?"

Startled, I said, "I didn't kill him. It's nothing like that."

She nodded. Approaching the jackfruit tree, she pulled a knife out of her basket. "You have been impulsive."

"Yes."

"This is how you have always gotten into trouble, I think."

I laughed. "Too true."

"Now you need to think without impulse how to make it right."

"I don't think I can make it right." I knew I could give Tyo the amulet, but I feared I'd lose him in the giving.

"Do you want to tell me more?"

"No. Thank you, but no. It's something I have to work out on my own."

"Maybe you can talk with your mother."

Such a straightforward, traditional idea. When in trouble, one goes to one's mother. "No, I'm afraid not. She worries so much about my brother Sean that I can't add to her burden."

"And?"

"And she's always chastising me about being impulsive. I've been trying to convince her that I'm not any longer."

"But you are," she laughed.

"I should have said that I'm trying not to be so impulsive." I chose a small round pebble from the array at my feet and threw it into the pond. A swarm of hungry koi convened on the spot. "I'm not so successful."

Ani began to pick small red chilies from a low plant that bordered the rows of tomato plants. She changed the subject, something my own mother would not have done. "What else do you recall, other than food and the story of paintings?"

She asked the question so casually that I suspected it had greater import than it seemed.

"I remember some of the famous temples, probably because I've since seen photographs of them in books. Goa Gajah, with its huge face over the entrance to the cave, Gunung Kawi. Is it a long walk there, to the temples of Gunung Kawi? Downhill? I think my brother and I had a ball that we were rolling and throwing as we ran down the hill. Many steps, maybe?"

"Yes."

"I also remember a temple that I've never found in books. I haven't seen it so far on this trip. This temple was small and in a wooded area. I can't recall my family being with me. I only recall someone holding my one hand and that I had an offering in the other. And I remember the light, sort of misty, so it may well have been early morning. We walked up to the temple and placed our offerings. I had to reach up to put mine on the altar, and I set it down just as the other person reached out her hand and placed the identical offering next to mine. The symmetry of the moment remains with me more than anything else about the memory. Was it you?"

"Yes. I will take you there before you leave. It was early morning. Your parents were asleep. And the boys. You snuck out and came to my house and found me making the offerings. You made one, and we went to the temple. It was the morning I knew that you would return." She loosened and then rewrapped her sarong.

"Funny, I knew I would too. I can't say there was any special moment I realized it. I just knew I'd come back. Now that I'm here—" I searched for the words. "Now that I'm here, it feels so familiar. I can't say that I feel as if I've come home. That's how I always feel when I come to Southeast Asia. Anywhere in Southeast Asia. But there is something in Bali."

I thought for a bit. "I recall something else about that visit to the temple. I think that we were there quite some time, and I seem to remember that you were sitting down and people were coming up to talk to you. I listened, but didn't understand."

Ani smiled and said nothing.

"Is that right? Was that the same time?"

"Yes, it was."

"Oh, here you are. I thought the two of you had gone off and left preparing dinner to me." Wayan Tyo ran his thumb over a fuzzy leaf. "I'll go change, then come to help you."

Ani looked at me as he walked away. "Help me?"

We both laughed. "Does he cook?"

"Never. Not when he lived here as a child, nor when his wife was still with him."

"Tell me what happened."

"She vanished one day. She was a foolish girl." She rested her basket on her hip. "Even though her babies were still small, she worked in a shop. She wanted to buy clothes and jewelry, and she wore Tyo out. We don't know where she went. Maybe she is still on the island. She did not have a passport and Tyo placed her name on a watch list, so if she applied for one or left the island on an international flight, her name would have turned up.

"Perhaps she left or she took a boat to another island and lives there. If you know the right people you can get papers. Probably she met a man. There was a theft at the time she vanished. We don't think she was the thief, but maybe it was the man she had met. It is difficult to know."

She reached over to pick a green bean. "Tyo looked for her, afraid that something bad had happened. He looked for a year, then he stopped. It is sad for him and the girls. What is saddest is that he cannot move forward. He cannot marry another woman and give the girls a mother, so I have become their mother."

"They're lucky to have you. As is he." I set the sweet potatoes I carried down and tried to rotate my shoulder. "I remember Tyo. In my memory he's always holding my hand."

"Ah." She turned to watch me. "Tyo is worried about you. Because you have fallen from your bike."

"Yes. Feeling a little dinged up right now." I picked up the potatoes as we left the garden.

"It was an accident?"

I didn't want to lie to her. "No, it was intentional. Someone ran me off the road on purpose."

She nodded, but didn't say more.

We busied ourselves with the preparation of food. Ani was careful to show me what she was preparing, guiding me like a child, but not condescending. She was a good teacher.

"Okay, I am now ready to help," Wayan Tyo said, entering the kitchen. "To show the tourist that men in Bali can cook."

Ani gave me a look and we both stifled a laugh. "Good. You can begin by stirring the tofu."

"Tofu? No meat?"

"I SENT the customs people the photos, and I told you I already gave them Eric Shelley's name. We know the flight he is scheduled to take to Perth." He looked at his watch. "We should hear from the airport authorities and the Denpasar police shortly. Hopefully when they catch him, he will have the paintings on him." He accepted the plate that Ani offered.

"I'm surprised that you aren't there."

"The Denpasar police do not want an Ubud detective in their town."

"Do we have a motive for him killing Flip? Were you able to learn anything more from the servants?"

"They said that Eric came to Bali often. For many years he stayed with Flip when he was in town. That stopped about a year and a half ago. The servants said that they thought that he and Flip had argued about something. They had no idea what that would be. They also claimed that they didn't know anything about what Flip painted. Either he was very discreet around his servants or they have decided that it is best not to talk to the authorities."

"Did Flip buy paintings from Eric?"

"They didn't know. They said that Eric was always looking for paintings and that when he left he always carried a portfolio with him."

"Filled with paintings that he'd gotten from Flip?"

"Again, they didn't know. They did say that sometimes Eric came back to the house with paintings that he would then take home with him. They had the impression he was buying outside."

"Did Flip take him into the storage area?"

"They weren't sure, but they thought not. When he came today, he told them that he needed to get into the storage area, but he didn't seem to know exactly where it was. Just that it was off in that direction from the house."

"I would think that Flip wouldn't have let him know how many paintings he was creating. Having one Ida Bagus Made was one thing, but ten would have devalued them. Flip had to have been secretive with the dealers he sold paintings to. Whether they knew that he was painting them, or whether they turned a blind eye and pretended they didn't know, is something we can't answer now." I held up my fork. "This is really good tofu."

Wayan Tyo beamed and looked at Ani out of the corner of his eye, but said to me, "You are rushing to conclusions."

I ignored him and winced as I shifted my leg. "So Eric and Flip fought, but some time ago. Any recent arguments?"

Watching me, he said, "Not that the servants knew about. They thought that they were getting along better now than they were last year. Of course, Eric told you that he'd been in

Bali for a few weeks, and during that time it doesn't seem that he had contacted Flip. That doesn't suggest that they had become friends again."

I thought for a few moments. "If he'd been negotiating with a middleman or other dealer, he might not have gone by Flip's house. These dealers are very competitive and secretive. We may find that their argument was about Eric not taking any more of Flip's paintings. Or that Eric discovered they were fakes."

"If he didn't know."

"True, he may well have known."

Wayan Tyo said, "They could have been in cahoots."

I laughed. "Perfect use of the word. You're a quick study."

That got an embarrassed smile. "I think we can come up with multiple motives why Eric might have killed Flip. How are you?"

"Fine, I'm fine."

"Let me see your leg."

I pulled up my pant leg.

Ani said, "That is a bad scrape. It is not very safe to ride a bicycle in Bali."

"No, maybe not."

The sound of a quacking duck came from Wayan Tyo's pocket. His older daughter giggled. He pulled out his phone and responded to a series of comments with single words. "Yes. No. Interesting."

He hung up and shook his head. "He didn't show up for the plane." To his daughter he said as he tickled her, "You changed my phone ring. A duck? A duck?"

Ani volunteered, "Maybe he is guilty."

"It may be that he is guilty of theft and not murder," said Tyo.

"My showing up must have unnerved him. He may not be guilty of murder, but he is certainly our number one suspect."

Wayan Tyo gave me a look as he again pressed the phone against his ear. Then he stood and walked away from us. Just moments before he'd been talking about the case in detail with Ani and me. I'd assumed too much by saying "our number one suspect."

After he was off the phone, and after I had refused a third helping, I said, "I came across a couple of paintings purportedly by I Made Soekarja in one of the lower drawers. We have a similar painting in the Searles—a painting that Made told me he believes is a fake. I have a photo of the Searles painting, but I haven't had time to compare it to these works."

"Shouldn't you do that?" Tyo asked.

"If I looked at the paintings in detail, it would take me forever to compile the list. But you're right."

Ani asked, "What does that mean?"

"It either means that Flip copied an authentic painting by I Made Soekarja that he already had in his possession, or that he painted both paintings. Or that I Made Soekarja painted both paintings. I suspect it means Flip painted both, though Made can probably resolve that question.

"I don't think I've mentioned that when I e-mailed Flip to ask if I could speak with him when I came to Bali, he said that he'd heard of the Searles and knew that we had received a collection of Balinese paintings. I was surprised, as we hadn't yet put out any press about the collection. I know the collecting of Balinese pre-war modernist paintings is a small world, but still. Then, when I spoke with him a few days before I was coming here, he was absolutely gleeful.

"So this may explain his glee. His work, a fake, had made it into an American museum. That must be gratifying to a forger." I began to pile plates, but Ani stayed my hand.

"Don't worry about that. Tyo will be happy to do the cleaning up."

Tyo appeared not to hear her. "Tomorrow I'd like to look at those paintings. And I think we need to go back to take another look at the living room. I feel that I missed something."

I liked the part about taking another look, but I didn't like what followed. That he intuited something was missing unnerved me. I had to give the amulet a long hard look. In taking it, I'd rationalized that it was a clue. And now I had to treat it like a clue, not banish it to my pocket because I felt guilty.

Evidently reading my thoughts, he said, "Jenna, I know when I first asked you if you'd touched anything, you said no. And when my colleague interrogated you, you said that you hadn't touched a thing."

"The painting, with my pen. I told you."

"And nothing else?"

"I know I shouldn't have touched the painting," I said.

"Okay."

Ani looked at me. She'd heard me not answer. She knew I was holding something back. She probably knew that this was what I had been talking about in the garden. Damn that silk sack. Damn my hand. Damn Tyo's intuition and certainty that something was missing.

I got up to leave.

"I'll walk you home," said Tyo.

"I'm fine, thanks." I said my good-bye to Ani and headed out the gate.

LATE evening and few vehicles. Lights splashed onto the road from restaurant interiors or scattered randomly from tourists' bobbing flashlights. The town was much darker than an American town. After hitting the second pothole, invisible in the darkness, I dismounted and walked. Enough bumps and scrapes for the day, and my leg wasn't feeling too flexible at the moment. I was afraid the pedaling would open the scrape.

Women seemed to have vanished, except for a few shopkeepers, though men still frequented the small local *warung*. They sat in clusters, all facing the road, all making comments on my passing. Some spoke to me directly, friendly, welcoming. A few spoke lewdly. I ignored most but sometimes offered a smile or a good evening, a *selamat malam*.

Walking has its advantages. I saw things I would otherwise have missed—flower offerings distributed in the morning and now disturbed, rotten or squashed on the road, flowering plants, odd signs, carved doorways, a pothole in the sidewalk marked by a palm frond and an offering. The beat of gamelan was the background thrum that syncopated all other noise. As I passed one street, the rat-a-tat of *kecak* chanting sent a more urgent message, and as I walked further that battery of sound combined with the soft, melodic voice of Madeline Peyroux, singing songs from her first album, already obsolete.

The roads followed the contours of the hills, and I wound left, then right. I wanted to be lost, so that I could look at more *warung* with the young men sitting in the half light and so that I could smell more food cooking, the hint of flowers. I wondered that the Balinese who smiled and greeted me from their doorsteps could be bothered, given the number of tourists on the road. On the more congested streets I heard the cacophony of Italian, German, a Scandinavian language intermingled with Balinese. Ubud segued from its traditional, ritualistic core to an international city in an instant, then back again as I turned down a dirt lane.

Maybe I should get out of Ubud for a few days. Go to the countryside to a village specializing in painting where few tourists ventured. I could watch the artists at work, talk with the older painters. Or maybe go to Java for a few days to visit Borobudur and to Solo to the batik museum and the Eastern Javanese temple of Candi Sukuh. I'd had fantasies before leaving home about doing that.

"Jenna," a voice called from the road I'd just passed. "Wait up."

The voice came from darkness as I moved into the light of a string of lanterns hanging at the entrance to a small hotel. My heart pounded as I thought of the van, my slide across that lane. Then I realized it was Seth. Was he following me? And if he was, why?

"Oh, God, you scared me." My suspicions about him were farfetched. He and Randall had been at the hotel when I arrived; our meeting was pure coincidence.

"Sorry. I was just out taking a walk. Needed to escape Randall."

"Ah. An argument?" My heart was pounding.

"No, just constant proximity for the past few weeks. We're good friends, but traveling together for three weeks with anyone is a strain. I suggested we each get our own rooms here in Ubud, but he's short of money and I'm not about to pay for two rooms. It will be fine. I just needed to not be there. Here, let me take that." He took the handlebars. I hung on for an instant, then released them. "Nice that there are fewer cars. Evening is a good time to walk."

"Yes, it is."

Before Flip was killed, my life was uncomplicated. Relatively. I had this Balinese painting project. I had planned a lovely vacation in combination with my work here in Bali. Now what did I have, but the mystery of a dead body? The silk sack I'd impulsively ripped from his waist. And now men, too many of them. First Alam, then my old friend Tyo, and now this hunk walking at my side.

"Where were you tonight? I came by to see if you wanted to join us for dinner." His question seemed so casual that I immediately suspected him. But of what?

"I was eating with my friends."

"Friends?"

"The family we got to know when I was here as a child."

"Oh, forgot about that. Were you working today? We rode over to Amed."

"Yes, I was. Well, most of the day. I did get up early and ride to Sekumpul Waterfall."

"On a bicycle."

"You've got it."

"Is it worth the trip? I was thinking of going there tomorrow." We walked in and out of darkness, his silhouette fading to gray then sharply outlined in the lights that identified hotels, cafes, the occasional shop that remained open.

I was aware of his heat, his calmness, his certainty. I was also aware that someone was behind us, but when I turned to look, the man was in shadow and I could barely make him out. It wasn't Randall, nor was he tall enough to be Eric Shelley. "Yes. I was thinking of doing something similar tomorrow." I bit my tongue as I spoke.

"If you wouldn't mind company, I hired a motorbike today and kept it overnight. That is, if you don't mind being ferried. I know you like riding on your own."

I didn't respond, still trying to sort out Seth. Was he good Seth or evil Seth? Rangda or Barong? It was ludicrous to think he might be involved with Eric Shelley. Yet Shelley's expression when I suggested he'd said I looked like an old girlfriend indicated that Seth had lied. But why?

"I'll have to see. I crashed my bike today and I'm pretty stiff right now."

He stayed close to me, and I didn't veer from him. Uncertainty kept me close, though if you'd asked me what I was uncertain about, I wouldn't have been able to tell you. Uncertain if he was evil? Uncertain about cheating on Alam? I started as that thought rose to the fore. Could I cheat on a man I had been unwilling to consider a boyfriend? A man I'd avoided like the plague for the past year? A man who had patiently chipped away at my armor?

We arrived at our hotel, and as we turned into the entrance I glanced back again. "Oh, Esa. It's nice to see you. *Apa kabar?*"

Esa turned his eyes from Seth to me. "Fine, thank you."

"Were you behind us long?" Before he could respond, I said, "This is Seth. He's staying at the same hotel. We just ran into each other. I'm coming from dinner with Wayan Tyo and Ani."

Esa looked at us skeptically. It seemed that he was trying to understand our relationship. But he said nothing.

"Esa, I'm still planning to come by your smithy. Is that okay?"

Without answering me or showing any sign that he had even heard me, he turned down the street in the opposite direction, saying over his shoulder, "*Selamat malam.*"

"*Selamat malam,*" we both answered, then passed through the screen of plants that blocked our hotel from the road.

"He's an odd one," Seth said. "Who is he?"

"Friend of my friends."

Inside the gateway, the smell of jasmine enveloped us. One of the receptionists came from behind the reception desk and asked if Seth wanted to give him the bike. I told him no thanks. It was too expensive a bike to relinquish to anyone.

"Esa is an artist, or rather a blacksmith. I met him at my friends' home the other night. Quiet, didn't say much. I want to go to watch him at work."

Seth nodded.

I slowed as we neared Seth's bungalow, but he continued past it to mine, talking about plans for the morning. He carried the bike up the few steps, then locked it to the railing on the porch.

"May I come in?" he asked.

It was a simple request that asked much more. I hesitated, thinking of Alam waiting for me at home; thinking it unlikely that we would just run into each other the way we had this evening; thinking he would leave soon and if there was a fling it would be a short fling; thinking murder made one suspicious of everyone; thinking that I really couldn't commit to Alam. "Sure."

The room was large and sparsely decorated. A desk in the corner bore a single orchid and a phone. A rattan couch and rattan coffee table faced a window that looked out on a blossoming tree; not that I could see the tree at night, of course. My clothes hung from hooks spaced along one wall; my toiletries had been rearranged by the hotel staff in an orderly fashion along the back of the small dresser. I crossed the room to close the curtains. The housekeeper had lit a mosquito coil beneath the window, and a smoky haze enveloped me as I pulled the fabric over the glass.

I turned and looked at the mosquito net, all 90 degree angles, the seams of the netting equally dividing three sides of the canopy over the double bed. The fan fluttered the shiny, wrinkled, synthetic netting. The flat, firm pillows were like two bricks aligned with the edge of the top sheet, which had been neatly folded back to form a perfect isosceles triangle. The white bed with its shroud-like net dominated the room and our thoughts.

I watched Seth watch me as I crossed back toward the door and him.

22

In the morning I thought of the heat of his breathing as I looked at the ceiling, the dark wood, the light squeezing around the curtains' edges. I thought of Alam, then dashed the thought from my mind as quickly as it had come. Rising stiffly, I threw open the shutters and curtains, pulled the little silk bag from the bedside table, and climbed back into the cocoon, careful not to rub my sore leg against the sheet. I loved sleeping beneath a mosquito net.

I opened the bag and drew out Flip's small bronze sculpture. A mere two inches, the rigid male figure with arms angled away from his body and hands on his hips emanated power. The figure, frontal and iconic, bore a facial expression that suggested a strength of character, a determination. His sarong fell from the bare belly down to the ankles, the hanging front panel merely intimated in the carving. The fold at the waist was clearer because it pushed up his belly. I turned the sculpture over to look at the back. The detail was even finer. His hair was gathered in a chignon at the nape of his neck, and the hat, unclear on the front of the figure, was plainly described. It seemed to be the folded hat that Balinese men wear, and the overlapped fabric visible on one side of the head further indicated it was.

I ran my finger over the tiny kris handle that stuck out of the figure's belt at the back. The kris was the source of a man's power. This is what the sculptor wanted to capture, this dagger. Not the face, though the face and its gaze emitted a primal strength. It was the kris. The artist had invested it with such detail that one could see the tiny face and body that made up the hilt. I wrapped my hand around the object, feeling the warmth that I had imparted to it as I held it.

I flicked my finger at a mosquito that had settled on the outside of the netting, then I gazed at a palm tree through the haze of milky white gauze, the curtain beneath the curtain. A frond, silhouetted against the dawning sky, reminded me of a spine, each vertebra a tender leaf beneath my fingertips.

I reached out and ran my hand along Seth's back to his waist, then rested it on his hip. Was this the spine I'd been imagining? He stirred, turned to me, pulled me close, then quieted, his momentary hurried breath falling back into its sleepy rhythm.

I stayed very still, caught there in his arms, panic overcoming my moment of gushy breathlessness. I tried to wriggle, but his grip was strong and I didn't want my squirming to waken him. Look at me. I swore I wouldn't get involved with anyone. Of course, this wasn't involvement. This wasn't Alam or Tyo. This was some guy that I met on vacation. A fling, a moment's pleasure.

What would an outsider think? What would Seth's mother think? She'd think, oh, he's such a good-looking young man, he can get any woman he wants. But about me, she'd think, well, she'd think I was loose, not daughter-in-law material, wanton. Wanton, that's the word. Not a word anyone ever applies to a man. I wasn't certain I minded being wanton. It was a good word, though the implications were bad.

I tried to pull gently away. His hand slipped to my neck, two fingers pressing against one side, his thumb the other. A creepy kind of grip, a threatening hold on me. I'd moved an inch, but an inch wasn't enough.

"You're squirmy," he said, his breath warm as his lips slid across mine and his hand began doing things that any wanton woman might desire. "What's that little sculpture?"

My breath caught and I croaked, "What?"

"That intense-looking little guy in your hands? Where'd you get that? I wouldn't mind having a piece like that to take home as a souvenir."

"Oh, no, it's something I brought with me."

"Really? It looks like one of those fierce guardians you see at the temples. It's from Bali, right?"

"Yes, but . . . My dad gave it to me. He got it when we were here years ago."

Releasing me, he turned on his back. "Well, a conservative culture like this, I bet they're still making them. I'll have to look."

"Sure, maybe," I said as I slipped the bronze back into the bag, his kris glinting in the light.

Damn, I muttered as I nestled my head into his shoulder and adjusted my leg to avoid pressure on the scrape.

SINCE it was early for my meeting with Wayan Tyo at Flip's house and Seth had distracted me from my ride, I decided to stop in the textile shop that I'd visited the day of the murder. The door was open, and rather than the ubiquitous gamelan music that rhythmically throbbed from every other shop in town, I heard Dave Brubeck playing "Take Five." "That's a nice change," I said as I entered, shutting the door behind me.

The woman behind the counter turned toward me and we both stopped in surprise. Ulih quickly regained her composure and said, "What is?"

"Dave Brubeck." I fingered the coarse handspun Balinese *geringsing* that hung on the wall next to the door. The double-ikat pattern of the textile was perfectly aligned, no easy feat when the pattern has been dyed into the threads prior to weaving. "I'm sorry. About your friend. I never met him."

"Thanks." Her voice, deep and calm, was as hard as one of the sharp, high gongs that the gamelan players strike at significant moments. "Can I help you?"

Sounded as if we were keeping it all business. "Yes. I was in the other day and admired the *tapis* that was hanging on the wall there." I pointed in the direction of the Sawu cloth that had replaced the Sumatran one I'd liked. "I was wondering if you have any others that I might see. I have a small collection of mainland Southeast Asian textiles, and I've always lusted after Indonesian textiles, especially a *tapis*."

"Yes. One moment." She turned and went into the back room, where I heard her fitting a key into a lock. She returned with five or six carefully folded pieces, which she set on top of the table with its piles of modern textiles. She stepped back to allow me to handle them. The shop was small and not set up for comfortable viewing of large textiles. If she had any big-ticket customers, she probably took them elsewhere.

I lifted the first off the pile and set it aside, the second as well. Neither had much age, and even in their folded state I could see that they weren't that interesting. I opened the third and spread it out on the table. I was looking for clear patterning that the weaver achieved by carefully lining up the pre-dyed threads as she threw the shuttle across the warp. This weaver had been a nitpicker, the pattern organized to perfection, but the embroidered panels, two at the bottom of the skirt, had been recently reworked. I fingered one section that was particularly sloppy, then began to fold the *tapis*.

Ulih raised her eyebrows. "I'll do that," she said, taking it from me.

The fourth skirt looked promising. It had the squid-like motif that is one of the hallmarks of these textiles, but when I opened it I saw right away that it had had many repairs. Whatever had eaten through the cloth had chewed its way through each layer of its folds and left two-by-three-inch gaps that an unskilled darner had filled. "What a shame," I said. "How do you price a piece like this?" I didn't want it, but I wanted to get a sense of how much she would charge for a good one, the good one I suspected she had squirreled away.

"Two thousand."

"U.S.?"

"Yes."

"Ah." Two thousand for this damaged one meant five or ten times more for a pristine example. Way out of my price range. I handed it to her to fold as I picked up the fifth in the pile. Not a very interesting pattern, but the condition looked good. I confirmed that, then passed it to her. "I've been trying to get the museum where I work to buy Southeast Asian textiles. Not too successfully, I must admit. They have a narrow view of what art is. They don't seem to understand that textiles are more important in the context of Southeast Asian culture than the Hindu and Buddhist sculptures that they favor or the Balinese paintings that I'm here to study."

She watched me, not responding.

"I suppose the disadvantage of convincing them is that I wouldn't then be able to buy the few that I can afford."

"Why not?"

"It's considered unethical for a curator to collect in the area that they oversee, and since the Searles, my museum, has a rather broad collecting mission, it means that there aren't many areas where I can collect. I guess I should say that I neither have the money nor the inclination to collect much myself. But I do like textiles."

"And paintings?"

"I like Balinese painting, yes. We—the museum, that is— were given a large gift, about one hundred paintings and drawings, by the wife of the man who founded the museum. He had put together the collection, but hadn't donated or bequeathed it. That's why I wanted to speak with Flip, to pick his brain about painting. He's well-known among Balinese painting collectors in the West."

I handed her another textile and she folded it. "I saw the other day that you had an older painting hanging here in the shop. I don't see it today, though. Do you sell paintings?"

"Not usually. Sometimes one comes along and I handle it. Not often." She placed the folded cloth on the pile.

"I met with Made Badung at the museum the other day, and he was very helpful. I hope to have some more time with him." I wasn't sure if I should tell her that I'd been going through Flip's collection, then realized she probably already knew from his housekeeper or through village gossip. "I've been going through Flip's collection. Cataloguing it for Wayan Tyo."

"I have heard that you know his family. His mother is well-respected here, as is he."

"That's right. My family stayed in Ubud for a summer when I was eight. We were the first people to stay in the rental bungalow they had built, and we became close with the family. This is my first time back." I hesitated. "Have you seen Flip's painting collection?"

"Not really. Sometimes he showed me a painting or two. He had some good paintings by very famous Balinese painters. Also he showed me his own painting. Very proud. But he never took me in the storage area. He was secretive."

"Did he show you his painting in Balinese style?"

She frowned. "In Balinese style? He liked this style, but his paintings are more Western. I think maybe Walter Spies's paintings were more like his. Or rather, his like Spies."

I felt she was telling the truth. If she didn't know anything about his creation of Balinese paintings, then she could probably be eliminated from the investigation. I looked at my watch. "Uh-oh. I have to go. I'm supposed to meet Wayan Tyo. Thank you for showing me the *tapis*."

"You're welcome. You did not tell me your name."

"Sorry. Jenna Murphy."

"And I am Ulih. You are not interested in any of these *tapis*?"

"No, I don't think so." I didn't need to explain. She'd watched me as I'd looked at the textiles, and I hadn't been reticent about letting my hands drift over their flaws. She knew I knew about textiles.

"I have more *tapis* at my home. Maybe you can come to see them before you leave Ubud. Not this week, as I am planning the *kremasi* for Flip. After would be better."

"When will the cremation be?"

"Very quickly, as this is the Western way. But it will be a Balinese-style ceremony, and it will take place Monday."

"Maybe I can come to your home on Tuesday? Or is that too soon after the funeral?"

"That is fine. There are many preparations for the cremation, so it is before that there is a problem. Not after. And it is being difficult." She hesitated. "There are some people who do not think that I should have a Balinese *kremasi* for him."

"Why is that?"

"Because he was not born Balinese. They say that a Westerner cannot have this ceremony. It is not common. You know, he loved Bali and thought it his home for many years. He never went back to Holland."

"There is a precedent for it, isn't there? The Dutch painter Rudolph Bonnet was cremated at the same time as that famous Balinese prince, I think. In the late 1970s, wasn't it?"

"Yes, but he was a famous man and the time was different. Our religion has changed. It has been made stricter than it was in earlier times. Do you understand?"

"Codified?"

She thought for a moment. "Yes. Also, the numbers of tourists and foreign residents has increased since then."

"Will it be a problem? I mean, are there people who can keep you from having the cremation?"

"I don't think so, but it will make the preparations more difficult. Not only preparing the offerings and the tower, but having to talk and talk with the priests. The sarcophagus is a problem since the animal design of it is closely linked to caste in our traditional *kremasi*. Some priests argue he had no caste, so he cannot be in a proper sarcophagus, which will mean that the funeral will not be correct. How many roofs the tower should have is the same problem. Since he had no caste and the funeral cannot be correct, they say there is no reason to have a Balinese ceremony for him."

"It doesn't sound easy. Especially on top of your grief."

"Here we believe that a person reincarnates in his descendants."

"So you are thinking of your daughter and your grandchildren."

She paled. "What do you mean? How do you know? This is not known."

"No, maybe not. I apologize. I shouldn't have spoken. People will know soon, as I believe your daughter inherited from Flip. I was there when Wayan Tyo discovered the will. I promise you that I won't tell anyone." Secrets. I had acquired too many secrets. I fingered the amulet and wondered if I should show it to Ulih. Then I realized she must have seen it if she was intimate with him.

She frowned, absorbing this news from a stranger. Still, she said, "There were times he loved her and other times he did not want to remember that he had a daughter. He was difficult. Do you know what he has left her? I hope it is something from his heart. One of his paintings, something that had meaning for him."

I didn't want to say more. I imagined that she would hear soon enough that her daughter was now a wealthy little girl, at least by Balinese standards. "I've heard that he was complicated. Her inheriting from him will mean that everyone knows he was her father. Would that make a difference for his having a Balinese cremation?"

"I don't know. I will have to think about this."

"Speak with Wayan Tyo. He should be able to tell you when the will is going to be read. I'm sorry that I said anything. I just happened to be there when Tyo discovered this. I'm sure he isn't sharing the information with anyone else." I hesitated. "I'm happy for your daughter, that he was concerned for her."

She nodded and seemed to be reassured. "Yes, I will. I am glad that we have talked and look forward to your coming to my home. *Selamat jalan.*"

"Now I'm really late. I better hurry." I was sorry I hadn't brought my bike, but I was still too sore to be comfortable riding it. Hopefully Wayan Tyo functioned on *jam karet*, Indonesian rubber time, and would be as late as I.

"Thank you. I will probably see you before then."

"Yes. If you come by the shop when you have more time, I can show you more textiles here. If you are interested, though, I keep my best ones at home."

"Yes, I'm definitely interested." I was about to walk out when I thought to ask, "Do you know what Flip did in the Netherlands before he came to Bali?"

"He designed."

"Designed?"

"Yes. Books and advertisements. Other things as well."

"A graphic designer."

"Yes, that is it, a graphic designer."

As I turned, she touched my arm. "I am sorry for my behavior when I came to Flip's house."

"There's no problem. Don't worry. You were upset, and for very good reason. Wayan Tyo will find his killer." A thought occurred to me. "By the way, were you coming to have lunch that day?"

"No, I was in the neighborhood and saw that something was happening, something was wrong. Then I heard the crying and became afraid. Wayan Tyo has been very kind."

He hadn't told me he'd spoken with her. I wondered what else he hadn't told me. Of course, he didn't need to tell me anything. And maybe I didn't need to tell him anything either. I pulled my hand from my pocket, letting go of the amulet, and gave a little wave as I walked down the path.

23

"I am thinking that we should put the paintings back on the wall. Maybe then we will understand the reason why the killer knocked down some and not others." While Tyo was talking about the room, he was looking at me in disbelief.

"What's wrong? Sorry I'm a little late, I was talking with—"

"Why do you dress like that?"

"It's hot in that room," I protested lamely, looking down at my tight T-shirt and short skirt. "And these are all the clothes I have right now. All my others are at the laundry, and one pair of pants was ruined in the bike accident."

He shook his head. "You look like a prostitute. And that crimson hair dye only makes it worse. How do you think it reflects on my family to have you seen in our city like this? People know that you are my sister, my mother's only daughter."

That stunned me, even more than being compared to a prostitute. Sure, he called me sister, and yes, I felt an affinity to Ani. But I hadn't seen them in over twenty years. Why did they consider me a sister or daughter? Why would people know what my relationship to his family was? But it didn't seem the right time to pursue those questions. "Every European woman in this town has dyed hair."

"Henna. Not pink, or whatever you want to call it." He turned away with a dismissive wave of his hand.

"I apologize, but I didn't have a choice. I'll borrow a sarong from one of the girls when I go home today. I'll be more thoughtful in the future." Who the hell had put those words into my mouth?

The room was in the same state of disarray as on the day Flip was murdered. The only difference was the scrubbed bloodstain that spread in a Rorschach blob on the floor. I preferred the elegant arc of his supine body. As a visual, not as the reality. Tyo and I had eaten at the dining table on previous days, set apart from the living room area by a long, low cabinet. Seated with my back to the dying area, I'd avoided looking toward the body—toward where the body had been found—but was made aware of it by Wayan Tyo's distracted gaze.

"Jenna, are you listening to me?"

"No, sorry. I was . . . What did you say?"

"Help me put the paintings back on the wall. I think we should put the room back in order. It might help us make more sense of the crime, instead of looking at this mess."

"The crime scene . . . "

"The tape is down. We've photographed, dusted for prints, done everything we are going to do." He pulled off the tape that separated the area.

"Okay, but I don't really see the logic in putting the paintings back. After all, the mess originated from the time of his killing." On the other hand, doing anything was better than looking at that stain on the floor or having this pseudo–big brother chastise me like I was a child. Staring at the floor, I contemplated the bizarreness of Flip having been replaced by a stain.

"Jenna, help me."

He stepped over the dangling tape and got right to work. We put the cushions back on the couches and chairs and hung the paintings on the walls, placing them on the hooks closest to where they had fallen. I wondered if they had checked them for fingerprints. I avoided stepping on the bloodstain, as if it was a crack in the sidewalk.

Flip had to have been a complete narcissist, as he'd hung the walls gallery style with rows of his paintings one above the other. Only a few were by other artists.

I wouldn't have liked the man. I felt guilty for that, but all I'd learned about him made my skin crawl. The forgeries, the narcissism, fathering a child he hadn't acknowledged. I wondered if I would have learned anything from him. His death had been a reprieve for me, really, as it had allowed me to meet Made. His death had kept me from making serious mistakes in cataloguing the Searles collection.

Tyo stood holding a painting, looking from one nail to the next.

"It must go up there." I pointed.

"Are you being a curator? This is not your museum to decide where the paintings should go."

I ignored the jibe. "Look at the size of the spot on the wall that hasn't faded. And that's just where that composition should go to lead your eye back to the other paintings."

He stood back and looked. "You are right, curator."

I'd replaced all the works on my side of the room and now gazed at the single empty hook and small dark area before us. "I'm missing one here."

"Smaller work than most of his oils," he said.

"Likely a Balinese-style painting on paper rather than an oil?"

"Could be. And if it is, what does it mean that it's gone?"

"You're the detective."

"You've taken an interest, so it seems. What do you think?" He lightly touched my elbow with his finger. An apology of sorts?

"I think that the killer may not have wanted us to see that painting."

He scowled at me. "What else?"

"Key to the killing? Or the killer may have wanted us to think the painting was the key. It's hard to say."

"Yes."

"Maybe one of the servants could tell us what is missing. If not one of them, maybe Ulih. That's what I started to tell you. I was late because I stopped in her shop and looked at some textiles. I don't think she did it."

"I never thought she did. Why would you think that? I'll get the housekeeper." He went over to the coffee table and picked up the small bell that sat on a pile of picture books about Bali. Books on architecture, art, Bali's natural beauty.

Before the housekeeper arrived, Tyo scanned the room. "I feel that we are missing something. Some small piece of the puzzle that you have seen or I have seen and we don't know what it means.

Now he becomes a fortune teller.

"Jenna, think." I was thinking, and I was mentally clinging to the amulet as if it was a lifeline, but like Gollum, I couldn't let it go. Tyo was already angry at me, and I didn't want to compound his anger with my recklessness. With my folly. He would see it as something worse.

The head housekeeper didn't remember what painting was missing, nor did the head cleaning girl. A new girl who had only worked for Flip for a few months, and who spoke no English, seemed the most observant. Yet, she had no sense of the style or whether Flip had painted it. She repeated that it was a Balinese painting, and tried to describe it to Wayan Tyo. But his translation of what she said was so abbreviated—unless ten Balinese words were the equivalent of one English word, which I knew wasn't true—that my irritation drove me out of the living room to wander down the path to the pool.

An exquisitely pruned flame tree shaded one side of the flagstone terrace, the overlapping weave of its branches well worth the attention of an artist, the brilliant orange of its flowers echoed in the variegated leaves of the crotons that edged the patio. Beyond, staghorn ferns, drooping dramatically, grew on the tall trees that bordered the property, while yellow bamboo and the wild red ginger that grew at their base provided a further screen. There was no fence.

Clearly Flip had felt the landscaping sheltered his world. Was theft so rare that one didn't need to protect a multimillion-dollar collection? A multimillion-dollar collection of originals. If he knew that he could replace most of the paintings, maybe he just didn't bother worrying about security.

Wayan Tyo joined me.

"Do people ever put up fences, or isn't there a need?"

"Most people here worry more about their servants stealing from them than a burglar breaking in. The servants are also a deterrent. A person who owns a large property like this one always has so much help around that more defense against an interloper doesn't seem necessary."

"Yes, I can see that." I looked back at the girl, who stood submissively waiting for Wayan Tyo to let her go. "But here there were not enough people to keep Flip's killer from coming in."

"No."

"You would think concern for his collection might have made Flip put up a fence. Unless he thought the collection could be easily replaced."

"Possibly. After lunch Made is arriving. We will see what he says about the paintings."

Thinking of the amulet, I said, "Tyo, I . . ."

Thinking he knew what I was about to say, he cut me off. "I've given the housekeeper money to buy you pants."

"You're joking." My resolve turned to irritation.

"Hardly." He gazed at the pool, the tree, the idyllic haven. Yet, the busy sounds of Ubud still filtered through the staghorn ferns, the ginger, and abundant bamboo.

I couldn't tell if the moue of distaste that pursed his lips stemmed from my wardrobe or from the excess of Flip's home.

Picture-book perfect and expensive. The cost of the lawn furniture alone probably surpassed Wayan Tyo's yearly salary.

"The servants spend their time on the other side of the house, the kitchen, their living quarters. According to this new girl, this room and the pool terrace were off-limits except for serving and upkeep. They finish cleaning in there"—he waved his arm toward the living room—"by six in the morning, and the gardener had already cleaned the pool before that time. When Flip needed something, he rang, or more often yelled out to them."

"So, anyone who knew him might have deduced that no servants would be in this area. The killer would have felt that he had easy access to him in the living room. You can see that it's visible from that screen of trees. Which suggests it was someone who knew him." I paused to consider other possibilities. "Maybe he set himself up for this. Maybe he announced the extent of his privacy on this side of the house to anyone who would listen. Still, if the servants were alert, listening for him to call, it's amazing that they didn't hear anything."

"I want to show you something after we eat."

Why do men think constantly about food?

24

As we were leaving the living room after lunch, the housekeeper arrived with a small plastic bag, which she started to hand to Wayan Tyo. He waved her off and instead she handed it to me. I looked in at the pink elasticized-waist pants she'd bought from one of the tourist shops. They would better suit an aging housewife from a small town in the Midwest than an almost thirty-year-old Californian with a shock of pink hair. They were nothing like the clothes she'd seen me wearing the past few days or the day that I'd found Flip. I couldn't imagine what she was thinking. Then I realized that the color perfectly matched my hair. Surely, I thought, even Wayan Tyo would see how unattractive the pants were and wish me back into my short skirt.

I thanked her profusely and went into the bathroom off the front hall to change. Then I followed Tyo out the other side of the house, past the painting storage to another of the buildings dispersed along the path.

"The housekeeper couldn't find the key to this building when we were doing the search. She unlocked it for me later." He opened the door and switched on the light. "I didn't think anything of it when she couldn't find the key, as most of these buildings are housing for the staff and it was unlikely the search would turn up anything on this side of the house. Now I wonder why she kept this, of all the buildings in the complex, from us. ”

I was amazed that he wasn't angrier, that he didn't suspect her. I suspected everyone, but I said, "Maybe she just couldn't find the key."

The room was filled with Balinese art and crafts. Carvings, baskets, sculptures, stacks of textiles, and, along the long wall opposite the entrance, an array of weapons. Shelves at one end of the wall packed full of krises, swords, machetes, rice cutters, and next to them the longer weapons, the lances or spears stored upright. "Oh," I said.

"Exactly." He looked down at my pants and, to my horror, nodded approval. Apparently in Ubud modesty prevailed over fashion.

"Why didn't you tell me?"

Puzzled, he asked, "Tell you what?"

"About this room?"

He frowned, but didn't deem my question worthy of an answer.

I flushed and changed direction. "Do you think the servants had something to do with his death? I thought we'd decided a woman wouldn't have been strong enough. And the only man I've seen is that ancient gardener."

"There is a handyman, and the husbands of two of the women also live here."

"Jealousy? Do you think he might have been getting it on with one of them? Then to protect her, they all stick together. Maybe he was molesting all of them. Though one of them already told me he hadn't raped any of them."

"You shouldn't be questioning them," he said frowning. "You're getting ahead of yourself. There is no evidence. I'll ask Esa to come over and look at the weapons with me. I'm curious if these weapons are all old. If they are new, he should be able to tell me." He pulled out his mobile.

"He should be able to tell you if Flip had a reputation among dealers as a collector of weapons. If he did, they will all know who sold to him, or who made fakes for him. Did Flip have an export business or own a shop in town?"

"No, he didn't."

"The quantity of material suggests that he did." I had wandered over to the sculpture section of the room and was perusing the shelves for any piece that looked like the amulet. Damn, I'd forgotten to put it back in the drawer. It was under my pillow. "Or he could have just been an avid collector. Some collectors just pile up the goods."

There was a box pushed to the back of the bottom shelf, and, moving aside a few objects, I reached back and pulled it out. "This answers one question."

Tyo came over and took the box and opened it. A ream of old paper and lying on top of it, sheets of Pitamaha stickers. "Yes, it does," he said. He put the box back on the shelf and walked over to the lances.

Tyo pulled out one lance after another. "They look old to me."

"Yes," I said, though I wasn't thinking about their age. "I wonder if Eric came in here."

"I'll ask, but I think they would have told me."

"I doubt it. The way you were carrying on."

He glared.

MADE and I leaned over the painting, a slight breeze at our backs from the open door. "The strong diagonals give life to the composition, don't you think?"

"Yes," he said.

"All is ferment, not just the aristocrats committing *puputan*—with all the blood, the women and children piled in that corner, the frenzy of suicide—but the foliage, too. The juxtaposition of the mango trees with the palms, the plumeria entwined by bougainvillea, these provide real tension in the composition."

"Definitely," Made said. "This is a rare topic. It is the dark side of Bali."

"Yes, interesting, isn't it. Most of the paintings of this period are dark in their color, though the subject matter is often light—market scenes, village scenes." I stopped, then added, "I hadn't thought about the fact that even in those lighter scenes the dark forces are embraced in the colors."

"Foreigners don't think about the darkness that is here. They only want the light. They do not understand that the light must be balanced by the dark. Or that we have had our dark periods of history."

I thought about the 1960s and the thousands who were killed. "It's true." We turned back to the details of the painting.

"It sates me, like a hot fudge sundae." Then I realized he'd probably never tasted a hot fudge sundae, but I couldn't think of a comparable Balinese treat.

"Yes, it is very good, the way that he has used the landscape to support the feelings that come from looking at the mass suicide. It is all dark. The question is whether Flip painted it. As I said, it is a rare topic. I don't know that I have ever seen a painting of the *puputan* before. What do you think?"

"Yes. All dark." I leaned closer to the painting, studying the leaves of the trees.

"Fabulous," Made said.

"Very. The trees all identifiable."

"Except that one." He pointed at the edge of a tree in the upper right hand corner. "Not that one. While I was at university I worked with a gardener at one of the hotels on Kuta Beach. These hotels construct very beautiful gardens. Tourists think of Bali as one big garden, I think because the hotels give this impression." He pointed again. "Because I worked as a gardener, I know trees, and I don't know that tree."

I studied it. "Looks familiar." My eyes slid down the page to a beautifully pruned flame tree. "Let's go out into the yard. Bring the painting. I have an idea."

25

"We're just finishing up here. Made has found something very interesting. *Selamat siang*, Esa." I was thankful to Wayan Tyo now for playing big brother and forcing me into pants. Esa's disapproval last night when he'd seen Seth and me together would have doubled at the sight of my short skirt.

"*Siang*," said Made absently to the two. "Yes, I think that we can systematically identify the paintings Flip made himself."

I said, "Those three we looked at in the third drawer might tell the story best."

"Yes."

We laid the paintings on the acid-free paper we'd placed on the table. I readjusted the desk lamp.

"You see here that each of the paintings includes this tree. I cannot identify this tree, though I am able to identify all the other plants. Jenna and I just walked around the garden and we saw each of these plants growing there, just as they are sprouting in this painting."

"A plein air painter," I said. "In some of the detail at least."

"Jenna was even able to identify one plant in particular in the garden in this painting." He pointed at the flame tree. "You see this twist in the trunk? The same twist as the tree in Flip's

garden. We have not made this comparison with the other paintings, of the plants growing and the plants painted, but we think
that we could confirm our belief that he painted what is in the
garden. What is in Bali."

"Yes, Flip consistently painted the same plants. But there is
more."

Wayan Tyo and Esa moved closer to look as Made and I
stepped to either side of the table. Esa visibly tensed. Maybe he
was outraged at the fakery. Flip, a foreigner, painting in Balinese
style and doing it well. I said, "You can see in these three works
that he repeats those trees and shrubs."

"In each of the paintings that we have looked at closely, we
have also found this plant, which is not on the property."

"As far as we could tell, anyway. We only spent a short time
in the garden and didn't search as carefully on this side of the
property."

"That's correct. But it is not a plant that we can identify here
or that the gardener can identify." Made looked at me for confir-
mation. "We asked him."

"I think it's likely that it's native to the Netherlands. The
coloration he's given it makes it rather tropical looking, but the
leaves look to me like oak leaves." I pointed at one, then at the
photo of an oak tree I'd pulled up on my computer.

"Is this tree common in the Netherlands?"

"I believe it is. Oaks with leaves like that grow all across
Europe and North America. It's so common and so much a part
of my visual vocabulary that I didn't give it any notice. Made
didn't recognize it, so it stood out for him."

"It is his signature," Made said. "Every artist has one, know-
ingly or not. I am sure he knew. He painted it in intentionally.
He was taunting us. And, as Jenna says, we just accept that it is a
tropical plant. You have to be looking closely, searching."

"Thumbing his nose at us." They all looked at me blankly. I
guessed it was a rather odd phrase to them.

"What does this mean?" Esa asked. "Other than being further proof he was an evil man."

We were all silent, considering the various implications.

"That he was fooling a lot of people and someone might have gotten angry," Wayan Tyo said. He turned to Made. "Are any of the paintings in these drawers done by the artists whose signatures are on them?"

"Yes, definitely. He had a very fine collection."

"It's brilliant, really." I bent closer to peer at another of Flip's paintings, pointing at the oak tree as I did. "He was a true manipulator. He was mixing it up. Not just the foliage, he was mixing his own works in with originals. If he was selling to people like Eric Shelley, he would occasionally add one of his own works to a group of authentic works, or vise versa. He'd build confidence in the buyer, and even if that person was knowledgeable, they would be less questioning of a fake."

"You might think just the opposite. The fake might be more noticeable since it is in with real works," Wayan Tyo said.

"That would certainly be true of an inferior work. But Flip's paintings are of the highest quality. His ability to copy a number of different masters is uncanny. Look at these three here. We have a Lempad, an Ida Bagus Made, and an I Made Soekarja. Those three painters had radically different styles, but he captured each of them. Or so it seems to me."

"Jenna is right," Made said. "And look. He even captured their manner of underdrawing." Made turned over the one painting and held it up to the light to show us how we could see the drawing through the back of the paper. "And, of course, he had the Pitamaha sticker correct."

Esa walked over to the canvases and pulled one out. He propped it against the shelving and stepped back to look at it. It wasn't painted in the style of some well-known Western artist, but closely resembled the paintings that hung in the living room. Did Esa know about painting? I only knew he was a blacksmith.

Made said, "We haven't even looked at the canvases. Possibly he faked Bonnet or Spies or the other Western artists working here. Sorting this all out will be a full-time job for someone."

"For Ulih, no doubt."

Both Esa and Made looked at me. Damn my big mouth.

"I don't know about her, but for someone," Wayan Tyo said, trying to divert any questions. Being polite and reserved Balinese, Esa and Made didn't pursue my blunder, though I could tell they were giving it some thought. "So, what do we have?"

"A forger of paintings." I peered down at the painting closest to me, then reached for the magnifying glass as I moved to the next.

"Eric Shelley, who has vanished," Tyo said. "A room full of weapons, most of which Esa says are old."

I looked at Esa. "Do you know who sold them to him?"

He shrugged. "Probably everyone. Flip roamed Ubud; he roamed Bali. He knew every shopkeeper, every dealer, every beautiful woman."

I wondered if Esa had experienced Flip's womanizing firsthand. His tone was so bitter. A girlfriend stolen? A wife? Was he married? Perhaps our investigation of Flip and his paintings, his dealings, his fakery was unnecessary and his murder was a question of simple jealousy. "Jealousy," I threw in, though they all ignored me.

"Did he ever buy from you?" Wayan Tyo asked Esa.

"He had me make a metal railing for his patio, then decided it didn't fit with his decoration." As an afterthought, he said, "He paid me. Even though he did not take it."

"No weapons?"

Esa didn't answer. He knelt down to look at the Western-style painting. "He has signed this one."

Wayan Tyo leaned over to look at it. "Yes. Awfully close to Spies, isn't it?"

Esa agreed, put that one back, and pulled out another. "A portrait in the style of Bonnet." He peered more closely at the painting. "Looks like a Bonnet signature."

"Not quite right," said Wayan Tyo.

"No, it isn't," Esa agreed.

Made joined them. They dismissed the poor brushwork on that painting, then pulled out a few more, the three of them critiquing each one as they did. Style, signature, subject matter. They say that the Balinese are all artists, but until that moment I hadn't known that they were all art historians.

After fifteen minutes of their looking and my straightening up and putting away the works on paper and becoming increasingly disconcerted by the depth of their analysis, Wayan Tyo said, "Let's stop for the day."

"We can look more tomorrow," I said to Made.

Made turned to me. "I cannot come here tomorrow. As I told you, I have to install my exhibition at the museum. This afternoon has already put me behind. I will not be able to work with you on your project until next week, if that is good for you."

"Oops, sorry. I'm so absorbed in Flip's death and collection I forgot. Thank you for giving us any time. Whatever is convenient." I turned to Wayan Tyo and felt my jaw tighten as I looked at him. "I can come tomorrow."

"No. I think we have our answers about his collection. It is no longer our place to be here. We will—"

"But—"

"I will follow the leads that I have. I thank all of you for your assistance. I will get the housekeeper to lock up this and the other storage area. Jenna, would you like a ride to your hotel?"

"No, thanks. I'd rather walk." I knew I should contain my anger in front of the other two, but I couldn't. As I picked up my bag, I said, "So yesterday, when we were going through all those paintings, you knew who had painted, or who had purportedly painted, each and every one. Yet you let me struggle—"

He nodded. "I know that you have come here to learn about our painting. Esa, Made, and I trained as artists when we were young, and our earliest task was to copy the great artists. This is the way we learn as children, then we paint in our own style."

He could have gone through those drawers in half a day, and I could have been sitting by the pool or riding my bike around the island on a sightseeing tour. I charged out the door without a backward glance.

26

As I walked down Monkey Forest Road, I couldn't decide whether I was angrier at Wayan Tyo's dismissal of me from the investigation or at being tricked into spending two days going through Flip's paintings when Tyo could have done it much faster. Granted, I'd learned a lot, and that was what I was here for. At the same time, I wondered if going through Flip's paintings was the best introduction to this body of material. Maybe the experience had entirely warped my view of Balinese painting. Maybe the fake would seem the real to me. Of course, Made could—and would—set me right and all would be fine in the end. But damn Wayan Tyo.

I had the feeling one gets when a project ends—or worse, when it is cut off in the middle. I had been left hanging without the satisfaction of completion. Now I was uncertain what to do next. Made couldn't work with me until next week. I couldn't investigate a murder—not that I'd come to investigate a murder. I could sightsee, I supposed. Damn Wayan Tyo. I wanted to be somewhere else, so that I didn't have to deal with him.

I tried to ignore the drivers calling "Taxi," the touts from souvenir shops yelling, "Sarong, sarong, one sarong," but in my present state their advances were too much. When the third or fourth one touched my arm and began pulling me into her shop, I said forcefully, "Don't touch me."

Seeing her look of shock, I turned down a quieter side street. I needed to get away. Maybe I would go to Yogyakarta. I needed the familiar, and I'd been to Yogya to study the Hindu and Buddhist temples and knew them well. I'd visit Borobudur. I'd leave in the morning if I could get a flight. Just stay a few days and be back in time for the cremation and my meeting with Made at the museum.

Once I made my decision, I felt relieved and wandered absentmindedly, gazing blankly in shop windows or at the goods hanging outside. I didn't want to buy, but I touched the clothes that hung on racks at the storefronts, glanced at the masks arrayed by the dozens on metal stands, checked jewelry in dusty cases, showed an interest I didn't really feel. None of which helped with the hawkers, who continued to call out to me and offer me pink trousers.

The shopkeepers on the side street were no less aggressive than those on the main street, sidling up to me if I stopped, coming out to the road if I didn't. In my hurry to escape a particularly aggressive individual, I almost missed the weapons shop on the opposite side of the lane.

It was more discreet than your typical *oleh-oleh*, souvenir shop. Only the metal sign displaying a kris handle identified the merchandise inside. I crossed and entered. Three men sat together on stools on one side of the shop, and if they were surprised to see a woman in this man's world they didn't show it. "*Selamat sore*," I greeted them. They answered, then went back to their discussion, leaving me to peruse.

A long glass case held krises from many regions of Indonesia and Malaysia. There was also a single Indian blade and what looked like a machete from the Philippines, if I could trust my understanding of the Filipino technique of plaiting grasses to hold the hilt in place.

The krises were displayed to appeal to the Western eye, with the sheaths covering the blades. Indonesians would want to see not the hilt, but the blade with its many possible variations and the *pamor* or design of the damascening, the layering of metal that creates a rippling pattern on the surface. Knowing that the style of the hilts provides regional identification, I looked for a Sumatran kris like the ivory one that had just recently been given to the Searles Museum. No examples in the case matched exactly, but some were close, particularly one of wood.

Out of the corner of my eye, I looked at the practical bamboo racks that stuck out from the back wall and accommodated about ten spears each. Flip could have used this same method of storage. His spears had been piled in a surprisingly haphazard manner, considering the care with which he stored his paintings. The blades were uniformly displayed upward, unlike Flip's weapons. Not wanting to give away my true interest, the spears, I spent time looking at the krises, many of them old and the new ones of the highest quality.

Since the men were speaking Balinese and I could only understand an occasional word, I didn't pay too much attention. But my ears pricked up when I heard one say *kremasi*. That was the word Ulih had used when she was talking about the cremation. Then I heard one of them say *Belanda*, the Indonesian word for "Dutch." I was certain they were discussing Flip's funeral. They undoubtedly knew him and had probably sold him weapons.

"Would you like to look at anything, Bu?"

Because I'd stood so long in one spot, the shop owner thought I was interested in the weapons in the case before me. "Yes. May I see that one?" I pointed at a Sumatran kris with a wooden handle, similar to the hilt on the Searles Museum kris.

He pulled a little velvet pad out from below the case and lay it on the countertop, then unlocked the cabinet and placed the kris on the pad.

I leaned down to look at it.

"You may pick it up if you like."

I set my bag on the floor at my feet, then with two hands picked up the kris. Carefully I held the sheath, then grasped the part of the hilt closest to the sheath and gently pulled up the blade.

He nodded his approval, seeing that I had pulled the hilt out carefully.

The new blade of this kris was a disappointment, but not unusual, as many of the krises that one saw on the market wedded components from different periods and areas of production: a new blade, an old hilt, a questionable sheath. As I held the hilt up to my eye, I realized that it too was probably new. Sliding the blade back into the sheath, I asked, "Do you have any older Sumatran krises?"

"You know about krises?"

"Very little. I would like to learn, but I will tell you right away that it's curiosity rather than a desire to purchase that brings me in today."

"That's fine. Here is another kris from Sumatra, older, maybe one hundred years old, and the owner used it." He took the kris I held and placed the older one on the velvet pad, pulling the blade out as he did. The *pamor* was delicate and many-layered. It was also worn from frequent cleaning and use.

"Not terribly old, but very finely made," he said.

"Lovely. Are there *pande* still who are as skilled as this artist? Or has the blacksmith's art completely died out?"

"Not completely. There are a few who are very skilled, but unless they teach their sons, the art may well die. Our culture no longer values the magical power of the kris. First guns, now bombs. These are the new weapons with power."

One of his friends called across the shop, "You have seen the children play the games on the screens? No one ever kills another with a kris. They all use explosives."

He was right. It was the burst of the explosion on the screen that kept the player engaged. A kris doesn't explode. "I doubt that I can afford a kris such as this one, but I am curious what it costs?"

"Two thousand, U.S."

"Ah, well. This may be a stupid question, but traditionally did the same person make both the kris and the spears like those?"

"Yes." He put the kris back in the cabinet and walked over toward the spears. "You can see this *tombak*. It has a circular base to the blade, and you see the *pamor* on this old blade."

"This *tombak*, too." I said.

"That is not a *tombak*. That is a *lembing*."

"I don't see the difference."

"The *tombak* is not thrown and the blade has a circular base, while the *lembing* can be thrown. You see here how it attaches to the bamboo pole, narrow then getting wider."

I nodded. I couldn't remember what the base of the spear or lance that had killed Flip looked like. I thought it had a circular base, which would mean that the killer had planned to run him through, not to throw the spear at him. Assuming he had such refined knowledge about spears. "So the one is only thrown and the other only driven through someone?"

"No, the *lembing* can either be thrown or the warrior can pierce his opponent with it."

"I remember that the spear, or lance, was the weapon that many of the people carried in the early twentieth century at the *puputan*."

"Yes." He didn't elaborate, but searched through the stacked weapons for something. "They carried both *lembing* and *tombak*. Here it is."

"What is that? No, wait, that's a *tombak*."

"Correct. It is a *tombak benderang*. You see the red hair that hangs from it? This is horsehair that has been dyed red and tied near the blade to catch blood as it drips down from the blade."

I thought of the blood pooled around Flip. "How does one learn how to use these? I mean, they wouldn't seem to be a weapon that a person would buy today. You have a lot of them."

"Tourists want them."

I tried to imagine carrying home a spear. A broom maybe, a large puppet or pinwheel or an umbrella, but a spear? No. "A little hard to transport, I would think."

"*Bule* will carry home anything," said one of the men, using the derogatory term for foreigner.

I laughed.

"Some have even purchased houses here and taken them home. As if they do not have the wood at home to make themselves a new house," the other man said.

"I suppose they want the Balinese workmanship." I paused. "Do local people collect these weapons, too?"

"Of course."

"Is there a blacksmith here in Ubud who makes *tombak* and *lembing* of this quality?"

I waited for him to answer.

One of the men rose, picking up a teapot. "Join us for tea, Anak Ani."

I looked at him astonished. I'd been in town for less than a week, yet this stranger knew me as Anak Ani, Ani's child. How could they single me out from the millions of tourists each year? And why? Did they think me some changeling, raised by foreigners but truly belonging to them? If I am one of them, does it mean that they accept me? That I can ask anything? About Flip's murder? Or about who they think I am?

"Esa," one said. "He can make a new one that looks old."

"Yes," another said.

The bearer of the teapot walked into the back room, the shopkeeper was settling back in his seat, the third man had turned his attention to a newspaper in his hand, and I had finally managed to drag my lower jaw closed. "*Terimah kasih. Dengan senang hati.*" I threw in a little Indonesian, hoping they wouldn't take it to mean that I would prefer to speak in that language.

I had thanked him with the greatest pleasure, a pleasure that was real, as my conversation with the shopkeeper had not only been agreeable, but I'd learned something about spears. I made my way to the fourth stool by the tiny table, wondering if Flip had sat there.

"You are interested in Flip's weapons," the shopkeeper said, as if he were reading my thoughts.

"Yes," I answered.

"He bought weapons from me, but I never saw his collection." He poured the tea. "I saw the weapon that killed him."

I realized Tyo had been here. "Was it old?"

"Yes."

"Not new," I muttered to myself, though the significance of whether it was old or new seemed irrelevant.

"Any good blacksmith can make a new weapon look old. Any dealer of weapons can, too," said the owner.

The man who had been ignoring us chuckled.

"Including you."

"Yes," he smiled. "Including me."

SETH and Randall were at the pool when I arrived home. "Join us," Randall called out cheerfully.

I walked over. "Will you be here a while? I've decided to go to Yogyakarta tomorrow, to visit Borobudur, and I want to get a ticket now."

"How long will you be in Java?" Seth asked, frowning.

"Just two nights. I have to get my passport so reception can book me a ticket. I'll be right back." It wasn't until I was at my door that I realized Seth had followed me.

"Would you mind if I joined you? We didn't go to Java because Randall didn't want to, but I'm very curious. And we don't leave for a few days."

I hesitated. I was going in part to avoid embarrassing Wayan Tyo and Ani with my Seth fling. And to get away from him. It wasn't rational, but I didn't trust him. Finally, there was my need to get away from Tyo.

Seth watched me.

I wavered, thinking of the amulet and the fact Seth had seen it. Of the connection I'd imagined between him and Eric Shelley, though that seemed farfetched and paranoid.

He turned to walk away, his shoulders tense, his hand raised in what I could only interpret as a wave.

And I thought of the saying "Keep your enemies close." "Sure, why don't you come? But we have to be discreet."

"Great. Of course, we can be discreet." He walked back and gave me a kiss. "I'll go down the street to that travel agent to get my ticket."

In the bungalow, I was relieved to see the silk bag lying on the bedside table where the housekeeper had put it. I tugged at the strings to open it, but stopped myself and squeezed it instead, hesitant to look the little guy in the eye, yet reassured by the outline of the small figure inside. I hadn't thought to ask the men at the weapons shop who might have made this sculpture, but I had learned a good deal about weapons and discovered I could learn even more from Esa.

When I returned from Java, maybe I would go by and see what they had to say about the amulet. Or I would visit Esa's smithy and ask him. Wayan Tyo had been correct. Esa did know weapons. What he hadn't told me, what I had learned at the weapons shop, was that Esa was the most adept smith in Bali when it came to making them.

27

In the car taking us from the airport in Yogyakarta toward the great Buddhist stupa of Borobudur, I leaned against my door. Seth complacently looked out his window. "I don't know what you're so riled up about," he said.

"You said you were going to the travel agent."

"They were closed." He shrugged, his expression unchanged. "Who's to know? It's one of the great things about travel. You go to a distant place. You're anonymous. You can be anyone you want. Do anything you like. No one cares." He reached and took my hand.

Still looking out my window, I said, "My Balinese family would care, and I don't want to do anything to harm my relationship with them."

"Ah, the detective. You have a thing for the detective." He looked pleased that he'd had this thought, then amused.

"It's not funny. I've known them all my life." A stretch, but it made my point. "I feel a connection with them."

"Ah, very California, very touchy-feely." The words teased, but the edge in his voice mocked.

"It has nothing to do with touchy-feely. I want to be discreet." I thought as I said it that "discreet" was not my middle name. I gazed at the blurring cassava trees that lined the road, a road wider than I remembered. "I planned to get away for a few days."

"From me? Knowing I was leaving soon?" His voice was flat. I'd hurt him, and he didn't like it.

I felt stupid for having gotten involved with him. Especially since there was a very nice man at home. "That was my plan." Of course, it wasn't a plan, and that was the crux of all matters of the heart for me. Which was how I'd ended up in his bed, or rather, he in mine. Anything to create a new kink in my life, a swerve away from ease, an adrenaline rush.

"Plan? I don't get the sense that you plan, Jenna."

His insight startled me, and I laughed. "Too, too true. Just ignore me and I'll get over it. I'm on edge."

"The murder?"

"Yes." I didn't add, and the attempted murder.

As we approached a turnoff, I read a roadside sign and said to the driver, "We want to stop at Candi Pawon and Candi Mendut, please." I told Seth, "They were way stations for pilgrims visiting Borobudur."

At Candi Mendut, I walked ahead of him and began to circumambulate the small temple, looking up at the carvings on its exterior. He followed behind me until we got to the rear of the temple, then stood next to me. "Who are these figures?"

"The relief carvings of standing figures are the eight great bodhisattvas. Lovely, aren't they? The simplicity of Central Javanese sculpture, the wonderful play of jewelry against smooth flesh is so appealing, don't you think?"

"Bodhisattvas are saints, right?"

"Not exactly. They're beings who could be enlightened at this very moment, but forgo enlightenment to aid other living beings."

He moved closer to me. "And the seated figure?"

"That's Chunda. She's a manifestation of a *dharani*, a sacred incantation. This particular incantation was very popular during the period this temple was built. It spread throughout the Buddhist world."

"Ah. Magic." He gazed up at the temple wall and the voluptuous Chunda.

"To us, maybe, but to the Indonesian the spirit world is close and a belief in incantations, amulets—all the paraphernalia that we disregard—is potent." I thought of the amulet and wondered what it had meant to Flip. It certainly hadn't saved him. We continued walking.

"You know, I think the most magical thing I've seen here in Southeast Asia is that amulet you carry in your pocket. It's tiny, but it seemed large." He thought for a moment. "And oddly powerful. It's your good luck, isn't it?

I gripped the amulet as I nodded, aware that it might well be the worst luck.

"Funny that an educated person like you is superstitious." He glanced at the reliefs carved on either side of the front steps to the temple. "I've never understood superstition or people's belief in magic."

"Really?" I shrugged, trying to diminish the importance of the little sculpture as I started up the stairs to the temple chamber, while at the same time feeling wary that it interested him so much.

A bodhisattva sat to either side of the enormous stone Buddha Vairocana. The sheer scale of the figures inspired awe. "Many believe this small temple represents a mandala that complements the stupa of Borobudur, which they also believe is a mandala."

"What would that mean?"

"Mendut would have been essential in the worship of Borobudur." I looked up at the Buddha, the simplicity of the carving, the serenity of the face, and my heart stopped, suspended in his presence. "I disagree with you. There's magic everywhere."

THOUGH it's a mountain of a temple, from a distance you can't make out Borobudur's mass amid the volcanoes that surround the Kedu Plain. Stalls overrun the approach, selling food, clothing, toys, crafts, and more. Hawkers tried to lure visitors to buy, to eat. The place bustled. I was astonished to see hundreds of schoolchildren converging on this Buddhist holy place.

The driver slowed as he maneuvered his way past open car doors, around dazed tourists, and through the buses disgorging crowds of uniformed students.

"Wow," said Seth. "Quite a crush of humanity. And it looks as if most of them are Muslim."

Seth was right. Most of the schoolgirls wore head coverings. "All those kids are going to want to practice their English."

"Right. What do you suggest?"

"We'll play it by ear with the kids, but no eye contact with peddlers."

"Sounds like a plan. How do we get in?"

The driver stopped the car and said, "I will be here. This tree." He pointed at the license plate number on the tag that hung from the rearview mirror, wrote it on a scrap of paper, and handed it to Seth.

"He must have lost a tourist or two," I said as I climbed out.

Looking around us, Seth said, "Or maybe the fact that almost every vehicle is a white minivan creates tourist befuddlement. So tell me more about Borobudur. I read that there are thousands of reliefs."

We wound our way through the stalls. "That's right, and hundreds of Buddhas on the five square platforms and the circular levels at the top. There isn't any interior space. The tales depicted in the reliefs begin with the mundane and become more spiritual as you climb."

"But if there's no interior, where are the reliefs carved?"

"On the exterior corridors that skirt each of the lower square levels. You'll see. It's quite amazing."

"What do the reliefs depict?"

"The base has hell scenes. Then the first gallery includes the life of the Buddha and his previous lives, the *jataka* tales, along with some noncanonical stories. They're the ones that I like the best, because of the narratives."

"And are you at the top then? Once you've passed the reliefs you've described."

"No. The next three galleries tell the story narrated in the *Gandavyuha*, the pilgrim Sudhana's search for Wisdom—Wisdom with a capital W. We begin on the east side, climb to the first level, and circumambulate until we're back where we started, then climb to the next and so on. At the top there are Buddhas seated in perforated domes, though by then we've passed many Buddhas on the lower levels. But you'll see soon enough."

The government had expanded the grounds around Borobudur, so now the massive monument sat in an extensive park laid out with stamped earth footpaths and paved roads, all beautifully landscaped.

We set out on the long approach from the entrance. Hawkers hunkered down along the path pressed sarongs, small sculptures of Borobudur, miniature buddhas, and brass stupas upon us. We soon discovered that a polite "*Tidak, saya tidak mau,*" no, I don't want it, worked well. These were the most polite hawkers in the world.

People swarmed up the path, but the throng didn't matter. Once Borobudur was fully within sight, I was oblivious to all around me, and the worries of the previous week faded away. I picked up the pace as we approached.

"Whoa, slow down. I want to get a look at it."

"Sorry, I got excited."

Seth stopped to gaze at the monument and to take a swig of his water. Sweat was already forming on his brow. "How long did it take to build this? And who built it? It's formidable."

"Yes, it is. No one knows how long it took, but it seems the rulers of the Shailendra dynasty completed it in the early ninth century. This afternoon we'll see more Buddhist temples and the Hindu answer to Borobudur, Loro Jonggrang, on the

Prambanan plain near Yogyakarta. Then tomorrow we'll go to visit Candi Sukuh outside Solo, and you can see what happened in later centuries once the Javanese asserted their local vision of what a temple should be. Local versus Indian."

I paused. "Not that there is much Indian about this structure other than its general form—the stupa, a reliquary, is an ancient architectural form in India. Of course, Indian style influenced the reliefs. Well, also the texts that formed the basis of the reliefs come from India. Let's go."

WE stood in front of a scene filled with figures. He laughed. "I think I like it better than the sculpture that Randall and I saw in Thailand."

"Me too."

"Randall was crazy about Sukhothai. I think he took a thousand photos of the Buddhas there."

"They're beautiful, but more idealized, less human."

"Yes."

"I feel as if we're inside a building," said Seth, shifting closer to me.

"Yes, amazing, isn't it, the way the architect moves us through the monument without our ever going into it. Not that anyone could enter, as there's no interior. Instead the architect gives the impression through these corridors, which don't exist on other stupas."

I could tell he was gauging the effect of the architecture and the reliefs on me as we walked along a corridor, then climbed to the next level. He sensed I was beginning to relax with him. "That says it all, *through* the monument," he said. "We're outside, but we feel in."

"When we get—" I stopped, leaning my shoulder into his arm. "Never mind, you'll see."

As we mounted the steps above the top square level, through the jaws of the carved head of Kala who swallows time, I heard his sharp intake of breath. "My god," he said. "Brilliant. It's just like you said. You move from the everyday to the sacred."

"Exactly. In the lower terraces you don't have any sense of the surrounding plain or the volcanoes in the distance, but here on the top it all opens up."

"Right. It opens up at the same time it becomes a mountain like all of those." He swept his arm to embrace the vista.

"It takes your breath away." I pointed at the closest perforated dome with its Buddha inside. "And I think the Buddhas, the Buddhas are the culmination of having read all the reliefs below. The reward for the achievement of it."

"How many times have you been here?"

"Just twice, once when I was a kid and a few years back, but it feels like more. I've studied it and taught it, so I've put a good deal of thought into understanding the place."

WE had walked around the circular terraces and now stood looking off into the distance at a volcano that steamed away. I didn't know its name; maybe it was Merapi, the volcano on an axis with the Yogyakarta *kraton*, the palace the Javanese believe is the center of the world, the *axis mundi*.

"What do you remember of this place from when you came as a child?"

"I remember being tired. Or rather, I should say that when I visited here last time, I remembered being tired as a child. Now that early memory has been supplanted by the memory of my last visit."

He touched my arm. We both tried to ignore the group of children who stretched their arms, trying to reach the Buddha inside one of the perforated domes. Even an adult's arm was not long enough. I took a deep breath, relieved to be away from Flip and Tyo and death. Happy with the familiar.

A voice behind me said, "What's the time, mate?"

I was sandwiched between that Australian accent and Seth. The comfort I felt fell away as I pictured the Australian Eric

Shelley, the Wild Man, standing behind me. This is it, I thought, Seth told him we were coming here.

I imagined a knife, a kris, the short blade driving into me up to an elegant hilt. I pictured them leaning me against the perforated dome that enclosed a Buddha. Me unable to reach the Buddha, not because my arm was too short, but because a knife had pierced my heart. I imagined the blood expanding over my chest until my white shirt was so red someone noticed. And then a scream of horror from a schoolkid who wanted to speak English with me. Men carrying my limp body down the steps, through Kala's mouth that swallowed time. All my time gone.

I tried to move, but Seth had inched closer, and if I stepped back I'd tumble down the step into that Australian. I pushed at Seth and saw his startled look. I flashed anger. I'd been right in distrusting him. And now, now who knew what would happen?

Wedged and in a panic, I tried to turn to get a look at the Australian, to see my killer. At the same moment, a group of wild teenage boys racing after one of their group crushed Seth against me. I opened my mouth to scream.

Seth raised his arm and I cringed at the anticipated blow.

"One-fifteen," he said.

"Thanks, mate."

He looked up from his wrist, his hand on my waist to steady himself, or to steady me, and said, "What's wrong? All the color's gone from your face."

Twisting, I watched the short, dark-haired man walk away, his arm around his girlfriend. "Fine. I'm fine. I seem to have an overactive imagination." I looked around, trying to ground myself in the moment.

He frowned. "Are you sure you're okay?"

"Sure. I'm sure." I hesitated. "I have to ask you something."

"What's that?"

"The other night, at the bar. When Randall and I were walking back to the table, I saw you nod at someone."

"I was afraid you saw that." He watched the kids climbing the perforated stupas, while a teacher yelled at them to get down. Finally he said, "A woman I'd been talking with the night before."

Now I frowned.

"I thought she might come over. But I'd met someone much more interesting than her." He slid his hand down to my hip.

"You weren't nodding at the man in the red shirt? The Wild Man at the bar, the one staring at me."

"The one looking at you? Never seen him before."

"Is that really what he said? That I looked like an old girlfriend?"

He flushed. "No. When I walked up, he said right away that I'd found myself a good-looking woman. Better than the one I'd been talking with the night before. I couldn't tell you that, so I just chatted with the guy for a while."

Under other circumstances I would have been furious that Seth had ignored my concerns, but now I was relieved.

"Excuse me. I would like to talk with you now," said a young boy.

"*Mujhe samajha nahīṁ ātā,*" I said in Hindi.

The boy frowned and walked away. "What did you say?" muttered Seth.

"I don't understand." But I did understand something. There was no getting away from Flip until the murder was solved.

28

We were exhausted and the driver was impatient. We'd agreed on a twelve-hour day with him when we figured out payment, but I don't think he'd anticipated we would use all twelve hours. We were now driving through Muntilan, the road lined with stonecarvers' shops, Buddhas and goddesses, demonic guardians, Western-style figures, all in black stone and lined up in front of the shops.

"Stop here, please," I said, spotting a particularly fine sculpture and beyond it a few large bronzes. "This one, please."

"*Lebih bagus.*" He pointed down the road at a shop where he would probably get a better commission.

"No, please stop here."

He glared at me in the rearview mirror, but pulled over.

"Aren't you exhausted? Don't you want to get back to that lovely hotel, the swimming pool, a soft bed? I'm worn out." Seth looked hot and tired.

"'Exhausted' isn't in my vocabulary." I climbed out of the car then stuck my head back in. "The word is in the same category as 'bored' for me. I won't be long. If you want to stay here, the driver can keep the air conditioning going."

"No, it's all right. Keeping up with you on a full-time basis would be hell." He dragged himself out of the car.

"Right." We slammed our doors in unison. "These sculptures look like stone, but they must be concrete or some other composite. There are too many that are alike. Has to be a mold."

To my surprise, no salesperson rushed out to sell us a three-hundred-pound sculpture that would cost a fortune to ship home. We wandered unhurried through the forest of figures, Seth in one direction and me in the general direction of the bronzes. I had stopped in front of one of them when a small man, my height, emaciated, very brown and wrinkled, arrived at my elbow. "Can I help you?"

"*Terimah kasih.* Are these bronzes made here?"

"No, from Solo."

I glanced over at Seth, who was in conversation with an attractive young Indonesian woman. This place had its marketing strategy down. "No bronzes made locally?" I pointed down the road.

He shook his head. "Solo, Bali. Not here."

I pulled the silk bag out of my pocket and extracted the tiny sculpture. "Can you tell where this was made?" I asked, though I had a pretty good idea.

"Bali," he said immediately. "Bali style. Bali craft. Batuan, maybe Ubud."

"Old or new?"

He shook his head as he took it from my hand, then he nodded. "New." He looked closely at the piece, turning it round in his hand, admiring the tiny kris at the back. "Yes. *Baik. Bagus.* How much?"

I laughed. "I'm not selling it. I just want to find who made it."

"Bali. Very good. Very powerful," he said as he handed it back to me.

"What do you mean?"

He just looked at me and didn't say any more. His black eyes observed me thoughtfully.

I knew what he meant about it being powerful. I'd felt it, Seth recognized it. It was an amulet, after all, and Flip had seen enough power in it to wear it around his waist.

To change the subject, I asked, "Which of these sculptures did you carve?" Then I wondered if the murderer had sought this amulet for its power and if I was in danger because I had it. Of course, the murderer couldn't know that I had it. Even Tyo didn't know. I wondered, not for the first time, how I got myself into the messes I seemed so easily to find.

He waved his arm, taking in all the sculptures.

"All of them?" I said incredulously. "You mean you made the mold. So they're concrete?"

He shook his head vehemently. "Stone, crushed stone mixed with resin. Yes, molds."

"Do you carve any small ones?"

He led me into the rickety building and offered me a seat, I started to say no thanks before I realized he was headed to a cabinet against the far wall. I sat.

When he opened the door, I got a glimpse of shelves filled with small, white stone sculptures. He chose one and brought it to me. The soft, smooth stone was tuff, a stone compressed from volcanic ash. I was familiar with this type of sculpture carved in Eastern Javanese style. A group of them had suddenly appeared in the 1980s. I was just a tot back then, but in graduate school my professor had discussed them, and I'd seen a catalogue of them. There had been extensive debate about whether they were new or old. Since there were comparable examples that had been in museums for decades, it seemed certain that some were old, but many were probably new. Maybe this was the sculptor who could answer the question of that group's authenticity.

The figure he put in my hands had a magnificent asymmetrical chignon that curved off the left side of her head. She knelt, her hands on her knees, one palm up and one down. Her expression was straightforward and serene, perfectly matching her relaxed, though alert posture. "*Cantik sekali*," I said. Very beautiful. "You carved this?"

He nodded, watching me.

"How much is this?"

"Trade," he said, pointing to my pocket that held the silk bag.

"No. I can't trade. If the price is not too high, I would be interested in looking at more of the tuff pieces."

He shook his head. "This one. Five hundred dollars, U.S."

The price was surprisingly steep, considering how he must have assessed my financial capabilities. My T-shirt and baggy pants sweaty from a morning climbing Borobudur, and my age—people tend to guess early twenties—wouldn't have suggested someone who could pay that much. But then, he'd seen us arrive in a private car.

"Two hundred," I said. "It would have pride of place in my home."

He gave no response.

I continued to look at the sculpture, examining it every which way, hoping in time he would make me a counteroffer.

He lit a *kretek*, the fragrant clove and tobacco filling the air, crossed a leg, and gazed off into the distance.

When I finally put the piece on the table, he said, "Last price four hundred."

"Two fifty."

"Three fifty."

"I can't go that high." I pulled three hundred-dollar bills from my wallet, set them on the table, and waited to see if he would pack the piece for travel. If he did, I would need another suitcase.

He'd fed me a crumb, telling me that the guardian was made in Bali, but that was something I already knew. I would have to grill Esa about bronze casters without letting on that I had the amulet. I would also need to ask him about weapons.

So many things to do before I went home. Wayan Tyo might try to derail me from the investigation, but he certainly couldn't stop me.

Seth came over. "How's it going?"

"It's going well," I said, watching the stonecarver pick up the money and put it in his pocket. He'd scooped it up as soon as he saw Seth coming, not wanting to reveal to another potential buyer how much I'd given him for the sculpture. "I just bought something."

"I see."

"I'll be ready to go to Prambanan in just a minute."

He groaned and said again, "Exhausted."

29

Morning and we were off again. Looking out the car window, I thought of the hotel and our exhaustion the day before. Seth had been right about the soft bed, the piles of pillows, the sensuous luxury of it. We hadn't slept as much as we should have.

The hotel room could have been in any town, except for the table lamp with the base in the shape of one of the perforated stupas at the top of Borobudur. What had tourism done to this place? The visiting hordes were better for some, bringing in jobs, but . . .

Seth stirred. "Strenuous night?" I asked. He twisted his body and curled into the corner of the backseat.

"Yes, and the only thing saving me right now is the fact that I'm sitting in a car and not on a motorcycle like you wanted."

I laughed. "Well, you wouldn't have done very well this past eighty kilometers if you'd been sleeping on a motorcycle, so I would have to agree."

"Are we there?"

"Just about. Candi Sukuh is up this mountain."

"I guess that means I have to wake up."

I didn't answer, finding it hard to believe that anyone could have slept through the drive we'd just taken. We wound up the hill, curving in and out of picture-postcard views of patchwork fields in their varied greens. The air was clear, and rice paddies stretched for miles below us.

"Tell me about this place."

"Okay. Inscriptions date it to the mid-fifteenth century. We don't know who built it, nor why, though we can guess. Some scholars think that it served as a place to revere ancestors or to call the ancestors back to earth. Others focus on fertility."

"Fertility?"

"A two-meter-tall carved lingam, a phallus, was found here. It's an impressive thing, but it's now in the museum in Jakarta, so you won't get to see it this trip. It has four balls."

"Big and bold. Do these ideas have relevance today? I mean, do the Indonesians worship ancestors still and worry about fertility?"

"They definitely revere their ancestors. In Bali right now, the Galungan festival is a time ancestors come back to earth. And fecundity is always an issue, isn't it? Here in Java, in Bali. Everywhere in the world."

"True. And as far as ancestors, didn't you say Borobodur was a giant reliquary?"

I nodded. Somehow the thought brought Flip's cremation to mind. We pulled into the parking lot, paid our fee, and entered the compound.

Seth stopped in front of a tall horseshoe-shaped relief. "What's this?"

"A Dutch scholar suggested that these are all stories of deliverance." I waved my arm to encompass the site. "That idea would fit with this being an ancestral site. Remember when we went to Klungkung that first day of sightseeing in Bali, the paintings on the ceiling of Kertha Gosa that had the scenes of Bima trying to get his father released from hell?"

"Sure. Is this the same story?"

"Most likely."

We climbed up the pyramid, then back down a series of steps to the gateway. I was looking for a particular relief, and feeling puzzled because we ought to have seen it already. But as we came back up the path, there it was, off to my right. We'd walked behind it when we'd come from the ticket kiosk.

On the tall stone relief a blacksmith squatted in front of a workbench laden with tools and weapon blades. My life seemed filled with weapons these days.

"Is that Ganesha?" asked Seth.

An anthropomorphized elephant, carrying a small dog, lifted one leg in dance. "Yes. Though he isn't usually shown with a dog. A dog generally accompanies a horrific form of Shiva found in cremation grounds. Shiva is Ganesha's father, so maybe he's a stand-in for Dad. At the very least the dog connects the site to death and cremation."

"Ah."

The powerful scene of blacksmith, helper, and Ganesha quieted us. "The blacksmith was an influential figure in ancient times. His ability to work metal was akin to magic."

"Why would that be?"

"Meteors fell from the heavens, and the blacksmith had the skill—the power—to transform meteoric ore into something functional, something earthly. In Bali, that power and magical ability are still ascribed to the blacksmith. Pande is the hereditary name and clan."

"Is that little sculpture you have made from meteoric ore? It's certainly powerful."

I didn't want to have a conversation about that little sculpture and pointed at the weapons on the blacksmith's workbench. "Look here at that wavy blade. He's fabricating a kris, the weapon that the Indonesians consider a source of power and magic for the owner."

After a while, Seth wandered off toward a large, winged figure that stood behind us. I continued looking at the blacksmith, hunkered down in front of his bench. No tools in his hand, instead a blade, which he aimed in the direction of Ganesha, though it was more likely intended for a figure that would have been carved between the two of them on a stone panel now missing from the relief. One of the blades lying before him looked like the blade of the spear that had killed Flip.

Had blacksmiths funded this temple, as they had the one we had seen at Besakih? Was that the reason for this large-scale relief?

"He was a complicated figure, the blacksmith," I mused to Seth when he wandered back. "Commoner class, worked with his hands—dirty work—yet he was a priest because of his ability to transform."

"What are you thinking?"

"Nothing really. Just about the blacksmith's work. They create weapons as well as agricultural tools. I want to talk with that blacksmith, the one we ran into the other night, Esa, when we get back. But he's not very chatty."

"I ran across his smithy in my wanderings day before yesterday," Seth said.

"You did?"

"Yeah. He showed me around. He was pretty chatty with me."

"You're kidding."

"No. Told me about the kris he was making, the thicknesses of different metals on the blade. Its meaning. Really interesting. I asked him how much one would cost, but it was way beyond my budget."

"Did he ask about me?" I said.

"No, why?" He looked at his watch. "Shall we head back?"

"Okay."

"What do you need to know from the blacksmith?"

"Nothing specific. I'm just curious." I doubted I would be able to get Esa into a conversation about the role of the blacksmith in society. Or in the meaning of Candi Sukuh.

"He doesn't know any artists who make really good small sculptures," said Seth as we walked toward the car. "I asked."

"You told him about my sculpture?"

He thought for a moment. "I don't think I said it was your sculpture, but I did describe it."

"Ah." My heart sank. If Esa told Tyo before I did . . . I shook my head at myself, and Seth looked at me quizzically.

30

Back in Bali, I made Seth take a separate taxi from the airport back to our Ubud hotel so that we wouldn't arrive at the same time. He wasn't happy. We'd had a nice interlude, but I was looking forward to his departure. I might be angry with Wayan Tyo, but I didn't want to embarrass or bring shame on him or Ani. That the men in the weapons shop recognized me as part of Ani's family had made me realize I had no anonymity in Ubud. When I'd asked them how they knew who I was, one had tugged at his hair.

I greeted the receptionist as I passed through the lobby and back out onto the garden path, the click, click, click of my suitcase clattering along behind me. The light dappled the trees, and I slowed to take it in.

When I climbed the steps and opened the door to my room, the mattress was halfway off the bed, the drawers were open, the cosmetics I'd left on the dressing table were no longer there. Clothes I'd hung on the hooks along the wall were strewn across the room like a trail of crumbs.

No, I probably didn't put my hand to my mouth, as the heroine always does in films and books. I was too pissed. Who had done this, and what were they looking for? I felt the sculpture in my pocket. My first thought was Eric Shelley. Then Seth. Had he lied to me about knowing Shelley? And then Randall. Had I misjudged Randall—was he in league with Seth and the Australian? For what possible purpose?

Someone was creeping up behind me. I whirled.

"Whoa. What's the matter?" Randall asked.

No, it couldn't be him. He wouldn't be standing here now if he had searched my room.

"What happened?" Randall asked, looking over my shoulder at the chaos.

"Good question. Did you see anyone lurking around here?" I asked.

"No. What a mess."

I stepped into the room to survey the damage.

"Are you missing anything?" Randall asked.

"Don't know. There's not much of anything to go missing. I had my valuables with me and my favorite clothes, my computer."

"Wonder why they tore the bed apart. Almost looks as if they were looking for something."

"Yes, it does."

"We better call the police."

"No. I don't want to do that." I thought of Wayan Tyo and how he might read this. The questions about where I'd been, the realization I'd been with Seth. "No. Help me get the mattress back on the bed. There was nothing here that they might have taken."

"Is anything wrong, Miss?" One of the men from reception had stopped at the bottom of the steps.

"Yes. Someone has been in my room."

"The maid, Miss," he said as he moved up behind us.

"I don't think so."

"Oh. This is not good. I am so sorry."

"It's okay. There wasn't anything valuable in the room. Just help me get it back in some livable state."

"Of course. I will get the maid."

"No, come in and help us get the mattress back on the bed. I'll do the rest. Not that much amiss." As I said it, I realized that though nothing was gone, I felt a tightness in my chest. My space, no matter how temporary, had been invaded.

"What on earth could they have been looking for," Randall muttered to himself. "If they knew you were gone, they would have assumed you had your money and passport. And it's only logical that you would have taken any jewelry or valuables."

"Maybe the computer," said the receptionist. "Every tourist has the computer or the tablet, and most Balinese cannot afford these."

I fingered the silk sack in my pocket, wondering if he was right. But what would Eric Shelley know about the tiny sculpture? And why would he want it?

The mattress back on the bed, the pillows on the mattress, I said, "That's fine. That's all you need to do."

"Your clothing. We will be happy to wash your clothing."

"No, really. I'll deal with it. It will only take me a few minutes. I'd like to be alone now."

The fellow walked out, looking over his shoulder.

"Don't call the police," I said.

"I can stay," said Randall, a sensitive offer that acknowledged I'd been violated.

"Thanks, but no." I gave his arm a squeeze as I ushered him out the door. Then I knelt on the floor to see if my cosmetics had rolled under the bed. No, but as I rose I saw them in the wastebasket. Weird.

Finished straightening, I lay on the bed, then jumped up and bolted the door and lay back down again. I thought about what I was going to do next, trying not to think about the mess that we'd just put in order and what it meant, but I couldn't avoid it. I listed the possibilities, but nothing made sense. Sighing, I tried to calm myself, and my best chance of ordering my thoughts was to create a list of what I needed to do in Ubud. A list helps tame one's mind.

Visiting Esa was near the top of the list. I sat up. Seth had told Esa I had a small sculpture. But why would Tyo's good friend try to rob me? It didn't make any sense. I hoped Esa wouldn't say anything to Tyo, though I couldn't imagine why he would. So I had a nice little sculpture; I could have gotten it anywhere. There was no reason for Esa to connect it to the murder.

But if for some reason he did connect it to the murder, by telling Tyo about it, he could discredit me. A foreigner, his source of evil. I lay back down, my thoughts racing.

Esa didn't like foreigners, and in particular he didn't like me. Jealousy, I thought. But this entire line of thought was preposterous, for he didn't know where I'd gotten the sculpture. In fact, if Seth was telling the truth, Esa didn't know I owned the sculpture Seth had described. I debated whether I should show it to him. After all, he knew about it already.

I lay on my side and rested my head on my elbow. Surely it had been the Wild Man who had broken into my room. As a foreigner, he could have walked right into this hotel. If anyone questioned him, he could have said he was visiting a friend. I rolled onto my back and put my hands under my head, listening to my stomach growl.

I needed to find that Wild Man, that Eric Shelley. I could confront him about my ransacked room. If he'd been the one looking for the sculpture, how had he known about it and why would he want it? I took it out of my pocket and looked at the face, then the kris at the back. The old man in Java had said "powerful," and I knew exactly what he meant. Size meant nothing. This little bit of bronze radiated strength. Looking at it almost made me dizzy.

I laid it on the bedside table, then thought better of leaving it there. I either needed to keep it on me at all times or find a good hiding place for it. Of course, there was another possibility. I could give it to Tyo. The fact that someone was looking for it, which my chaotic room suggested, meant it might be a motive for the killing. Maybe *the* motive.

I kicked myself for having taken it. Sheer madness. But it had drawn me like a magnet. Radiating power. No, now I was going off into gaga land, imagining the thing had some magical power. Like a kris, like meteoric ore.

Of course, my knowing about it, when Wayan Tyo didn't, gave me a lead in finding the killer. That thought sat me up. I didn't have access to any of the information that Tyo had, but I had the amulet. I looked at the squatting body firmly planted on my bedside table. Of course, this assumed it was related to the murder. I groaned and slid back down my pillow.

I both wanted it to have import and didn't. If it wasn't relevant, my taking it wasn't important; if it was, I might have hindered the investigation. "It can't," I said to myself. "It just can't."

I reached over to pick it up again, but resisted and went back to my mental list.

Go back to see Ulih. She might know something she didn't know that she knew.

Convince Wayan Tyo to allow me to finish cataloguing Flip's collection.

Flip's oil paintings would be interesting. If he'd copied Western artists—Spies, Bonnet, any of that crowd—I would need to consider how that fit in with the murder. And I wanted to look at the Western works for other reasons. I was concerned about the two oils that were in the Searles collection. They might be Flip originals for all I knew.

Then, of course, there was the reason I was in Bali. To better understand the collection sitting in my museum. I needed to go through my photos of those paintings to figure out what questions to ask Made when we met again.

My finger shifted and I realized I'd picked up and been rubbing the amulet as I thought, the curve of the tiny body, the minuscule bump of the kris at his waist, the detail so fine. I slid it back into the silk, relaxing as I pictured it in my mind's eye. I couldn't keep my focus on my list.

The amulet might not be the key to the murder. For that matter, the pre-war Balinese style paintings might not be either. Instead, Flip's collection of Westerners who worked in Bali might be. I considered ways I could explore that question. There were more museums to see here in Ubud, and my credentials could help me meet fellow curators. For that matter, Made would surely be willing to give me introductions. I had a perfect excuse to ask questions at these private museums, most of which featured twentieth-century Balinese painting of one sort or another. And I could combine my questioning with work.

I had to work. I'd learned an enormous amount in the week that I'd been here. I could now identify many of the better-known painters because of Flip's inclination to paint those artists. And I could identify a good fake of those artists. Made had been extremely helpful in the few hours I'd spent with him at his museum.

Basically, I needed to look at as many paintings as possible during the remainder of my time in Bali. Also, Made's museum might have a library I could use. And I needed to buy some books. Very few on such paintings were available in the West, and our librarian had given me a budget. That was another task, another suitcase. I looked at the white stone carving that now sat on the dresser across the room from me. I had paid too much, and it had cut into my budget for Balinese paintings, but I liked it, and the old man had intrigued me.

I thought of the painting school I'd discovered the other morning. I had to get back there. I also had to contact the shop at the Searles and see if they would be interested in getting work by youthful painters to sell at the time of the exhibition.

Also on my list, art galleries. Made had told me that there were some that I should see. And I could go to Kamasan to watch artists working on traditional painting in that town. Short of that, surely there were painters here in Ubud. Some entrepreneur was probably even giving painting classes. Given my lack of talent, that was probably going a bit too far.

There was a knock on my door, and I lay very still. Of course Seth knew that I was here, but I really didn't want to see him now. I felt raw from my room being trashed. I felt crowded. I didn't want to talk about the break-in. I didn't want to talk about us. I didn't want to talk. We'd been together nonstop for two days, a pleasant enough two days, but that was enough.

Another knock. It wouldn't be too difficult to get up and tell him that I didn't want to see him. I knew it was childish to pretend I wasn't in my room. If he knocked again I'd get up. But instead I heard the sound of his footsteps lightly moving down the steps. I thought of his body, his arms around me, his breath on my neck. I thought of Alam.

Then I shook myself. I'd see Seth tomorrow and the next day he would be gone.

In the meantime, I needed to eat something. We'd left Yogya without dinner, our visit to the palace, the *kraton*, having taken longer than we'd anticipated. Now I needed to get out of the hotel to get some food without Seth seeing me.

I grabbed the purse I'd been carrying in Java, decided it was too heavy, and got the small purse I'd left here in Bali from the dresser. As I transferred wallet and flashlight, tissues, and mints to the smaller bag, I felt my Balinese mobile in its outer pocket. My heart skipped a beat: this proved that the burglar had not been your garden-variety thief, looking for electronics, money, and jewelry.

When I was in Java, I'd been too preoccupied to realize I didn't have that mobile with me. I flipped it open to see if it was charged, and the face showed that I had five messages. All of them were from Wayan Tyo, who sounded increasingly distressed that I wasn't responding. I needed to call him immediately.

"Wayan Tyo, I . . ."

"Where have you been? We've been very worried."

"Sorry. I left a message for you here at the hotel." Not exactly for him, but I had told the desk to tell anyone who called that

I'd gone to Java. "I forgot my phone. I didn't even notice I didn't have it with me until I returned this evening. If I had noticed, I would have called you." Was this true?

"My mother has been very concerned. We spoke with the hotel. They said a man who was staying there left at about the same time as you, and we were afraid that you had been harmed. Also, you kept your room. That didn't make sense."

"No, I'm fine. I went to Yogya, that's all. I really am sorry. Tell Ani that I will come to see her tomorrow. I'm tired tonight and need to get a bite to eat. When I got back—"

"I'll tell her." He hung up abruptly.

I looked at my phone and cursed. He'd cut me off before I could tell him someone had broken into my room. I cursed him again. He hadn't said anything about the case. Well, of course he hadn't. I thought of the mental list I had just created, with the murder case at the top, my work second. If I did what I should, I would invert that list, and I would give Wayan Tyo the amulet. If I did what I should.

I fingered the phone, pulled up contacts and his name. My stomach rumbled. The heck with him. I closed the phone, thought of calling my mother on Skype, and decided to call her after dinner.

As I walked down the path, past Seth and Randall's bungalow, I thought I saw the curtains move. I held my breath, afraid Seth would come out the door.

31

"Ulih?" I called, relieved to be moving from the hot sun into the cool shop. I could hear sounds from the backroom. A bamboo shade kept the harsh equatorial sun from fading the textiles. A display of gaudy sequined scarves, a type worn by half the tourists in Ubud, sparkled in the rays that squeaked through the slats. It surprised me that she had cheap scarves in her shop, though I supposed she probably sold more of them than of her more expensive textiles.

A muffled few words floated back to me, so I waited, looking at a pile of new textiles on the table in the middle of the room. Funny how collectors want old textiles, when modern weavers create fabric as beautiful and as skillfully woven as the old. I held up a *tampan*, a traditional Sumatran wrapping cloth, appreciating the finely balanced composition of bold ship and three small figures in the foreground, the subtle colors of the supplementary weft pattern. The price was probably right. I could buy this and hang it on a wall to enjoy daily. Why did I feel I needed to spend all my savings on an old *tapis* that I would store in a box and pull out to look at only a few times a year?

She came out carrying a large box. "Oh, hello. I was packing this shipment and wanted to finish taping it. Did you have a good journey?"

"How did you know I was gone?"

"This is Ubud," she answered simply. As if that explained it all and there weren't thousands of tourists roaming around town on any given day of the year.

"Yes, I did have a good journey." I walked up to the counter, where she stood writing an address on the box. "I was passing and thought I'd stop in and say hi. Also see how your preparations are going for the funeral, the *kremasi.*"

"The preparations go well. The priests have agreed with me that Flip should have a Balinese cremation." The tall counter dwarfed her and I suddenly felt clumsy and large, an unusual sensation for me. In the States I feel small.

"That's very good. You must be happy." What a stupid thing to say. No one would be happy about a cremation.

"They agreed since Flip had become Balinese."

"Become Balinese? How does one do that?"

"In the temple. It is a ceremony."

I hadn't known there was such a ceremony.

"There is still resistance, but it will happen on Thursday."

"Thursday? I thought that you told me it would take place next Monday."

"Yes, but the priests decided that day was not auspicious. They said the reason why we were meeting resistance about the cremation was because it was a badly chosen day. So they changed the date."

"Oh, well, I'm glad I didn't stay in Java any longer. Since I . . ." I stopped and said simply, "I would like to be there."

"Yes. The ceremony will be larger than I had planned, as two of his servants have had family die in the past year, and they will also cremate their dead. At least one or two other families who knew him will also join. Maybe more. One family will burn an *adagan*, as the man died many years ago and the family could not afford to have a cremation these many years."

"I don't understand. I didn't think he was well-liked."

"When a wealthy person is cremated, often people with less money will cremate their dead at the same time. It is a financial decision. Also, he was their patron, their boss. So he helps them even in death."

"That seems sensible. And what is an *adagan*?" As we spoke, I went back to the table in the middle of the room and sorted through a pile of textiles, thinking I would buy one for my mother and maybe one for Breeze, the museum registrar. Or maybe I'd get her a sparkly scarf.

"If the family cannot afford a cremation, they bury the dead and wait until they can afford to cremate. Sometimes years will pass before they are able to raise the money, so many years that there is no body. When this happens, they burn a wooden statue in its place. This is an *adagan*."

"A cremation in the U.S. is cheaper than a burial."

"Here many people spend all their money or go in debt for the cremation. Now some people in villages put their money together and have the ceremony once every five years. I am happy that some will benefit from Flip's cremation."

Looking at her, I noticed that the painting hanging on the wall by the register was not the same one I'd seen on my first visit. It gave me a little shock of recognition. "Is there anything that I can do to help you?"

"No, I don't think so. Oh, I brought in a couple of textiles in case you stopped by again. They are not *tapis*, but I thought that they might interest you, as they are unusual. You shall still come to my home to see the *tapis* I have there. Now that the *kremasi* is earlier we will have plenty of time before you leave." She went again to the back of the shop, her long, loose ponytail swinging as she walked.

I stepped over to the painting. I knew this painting. I'd catalogued this painting and noted it as one that Eric had taken from Flip's storage. When she returned, the textiles in hand, I asked, "Is this painting new? Where does one get a painting like this?"

"Another dealer owed me money and I agreed to take it as payment. I do not think he knew what he had. I think it is worth much more than he owed me." She gazed at it with me. "It's fantastic, isn't it?"

I looked at the Lempad. A single, wild demonic figure twirling in the center of an empty ground, his characteristic style. When I saw it in Flip's top drawer I had expected the demon to leap off the page. Without foliage around the figure, Flip's signature plant was nowhere in sight. Then I noticed a single leaf, hidden in the extravagant hair, an oak leaf, drawn to look like a matted knot of hair. "He stole it," I said, closely watching her expression.

"What?" She seemed honestly shocked.

"From Flip."

"I do not understand." She peered at the painting. "Flip never showed me this painting."

"Flip had hundreds of paintings. He couldn't have shown you all of them. Unless you've been in his storeroom?"

"No. He never took me to the storeroom. I followed him once—we were having a conversation. He became angry and told me to wait."

This didn't surprise me. "I catalogued the works on paper for Wayan Tyo." I tried to suppress the edge of annoyance in my voice when I mentioned him. I didn't want her to think it was directed at her. I hadn't sorted out if I was angry with him for giving me that job or for excluding me from his investigation. "Even though he could have easily done it himself."

"And this was one of the paintings? Are you sure?"

"I remember it. It's a memorable painting, a Lempad. And I photographed all the paintings in the drawers, so we can verify it." I saw that she had paled. "Don't worry. I know that you didn't take it. We know that Eric took it."

She looked surprised. "You know him?"

Her response told me that it was Eric who gave her the painting. "I met him the other day. He was in the storage when I arrived. He managed to convince Flip's servants that he should be allowed in. After he left, we went through the drawers that I had already catalogued and discovered that at least seven paintings were missing. This is definitely one of them."

"I am very angry at him." Her voice was calm, the slight narrowing of her eyes the only evidence of her anger. She probably didn't usually show her emotions, which made her hysteria the day of Flip's death all the more heartbreaking. Not to mention all the more convincing she was innocent. His death had deeply wounded her. "What shall I do?"

"You should call Wayan Tyo and tell him."

"He will arrest me?"

"No, but he will probably take the painting. The police are trying to find Eric Shelley, so all you can tell them will be helpful. When did you get the painting from him?"

"Yesterday."

"Good. That means that he may still be on the island. Do you know where he's staying?"

"No. He often stayed with Flip, until this past year. Now I do not know where he stays. I think he has a Balinese girlfriend, but I do not know who that girl might be." She was thoughtful. "When he left, he went in the direction of Campuhan."

"That's helpful. Yes, call Wayan Tyo the second I leave."

"I can call him now." She raised her mobile.

"No, it's better to wait. I'll leave shortly. Let's see those textiles you were going to show me."

She pulled a textile out of the pile in her arms and laid it on the table in the middle of the room. "I brought this beautiful old *geringsing*. Here, let us compare it to a new *geringsing*." She took down the example hanging near the door and spread it out over the textiles on the table alongside the old one. They were of a similar size, narrow, indicating they were woven on a backstrap loom, and about six feet long. "You know this cloth?"

"Yes, double *ikat*. I was admiring the new one when I was here the other day. It's lovely, but this is so much more refined. It makes the new one look downright primitive."

"Yes. You know this is a ritual cloth, used in a person's life from birth until death in Tenganan Pegeringsingan, the village where they are made. This traditional use of the cloth explains why there are so few of the old ones that have survived. Of course, now the villagers make them for tourists, so it is possible to buy a new one. The colors are always the same, brown, reddish brown, a black, almost blue color. All natural dyes in the old ones."

"Not in the new?"

"Some. This one, I think." She lifted the new *geringsing* up to her face. "Yes, this one has natural dyes."

"Still, old or new, it's incredible to think that the weaver dyes the design into the threads before weaving. And the double *ikat*. That technique is beyond belief."

She laughed, "Yes. Dyeing the design in both the warp and the weft before weaving. This takes a very patient person."

"That would not be me."

She opened up a natural-colored handspun cloth that she'd pulled out of the bag with the *geringsing* and spread it over that textile. "This is another ritual textile, a *kajang*."

"I love the way you textile dealers handle your cloth. It's so casual, so comfortable, like an extension of your body, a sort of dance with your wares."

She smiled as she smoothed one edge, touching it with only the tips of her fingers. "Yes, they are like children. This is a *kajang*, a very rare and old *kajang*. I have never seen any other like it. This is not surprising, since it is a cremation shroud and they are burned with the dead. I do not know how this one survived."

Faded drawing and writing covered the surface of the six-foot-long cloth. The outline of a single nude figure filled the center of the fabric. Medallion-shaped emblems were painted on the *chakras*, the power points of the body. The male figure floated in a field broken only by words. Down in one of the lower corners a finely detailed figure stood astride a twisted demonic form.

"What does all this say?" I touched one of the inscriptions.

"I do not know. I showed it to one priest, but he became so angry at my plan to use this as Flip's shroud that he would not tell me the meaning."

Incredulously, I said, "You're going to burn this?"

She didn't need to respond. Her slumped posture told it all. "It belonged to Flip. He gave it to me and said to burn it with him if he died before me."

"Did he have a premonition?"

"No, not at all. He was not that kind of a person, in touch with spirits." She paused. "He was not a nice man." She began to fold up the textile.

"Wait, I would like to photograph it if I may. It would be nice to have a record of it."

"Ya, okay."

I pulled my camera out of my bag. "Can you hold it up over there where the light is better?"

"I never should have shown this to that priest. Now he is against the *kremasi*, I think both because of my burning the *kajang* and because it is Flip." She spoke from behind the *kajang*, which she held up over her head. "He must know how difficult it is for me, a textile dealer, to burn this cloth. I could sell this for a great deal of money."

"Why did you love Flip? You say he wasn't a nice man, yet you obviously loved him. You had a child with him." I thought of the man I had loved, his betrayal and how I had continued to love him in spite of it.

She put the cloth down. "We do not always choose who we love."

"True." I didn't move, waiting to see if she would say more.

"He was very alive. I was young. This is not a good excuse, I know. I think, too, that over the years he became less nice. He was kind at first. You're done?"

I scrolled through the photos on my camera. "Yes, I think so. Do you think that the writing on the cloth pertains to a specific person?"

"Each shroud is made for a specific person. At least that is how it is done today. The symbols relate to the person's caste. Maybe that is a reason not to burn the textile with Flip. It is very difficult for me to know what to do. I need to honor his wishes, but as I say, burning it does not make me happy."

"Well, if you honestly don't want to burn it, maybe you need to show it to someone who can read what it says. A different priest."

"Yes, maybe I should do that." She folded the textile.

"I really appreciate your showing it to me. I saw something like it in one of the tourist shops and didn't know what it was."

"Yes, maybe they make these for the tourists who don't know their meaning and merely like the symbols they see."

"That's possible." I thought of the way tourists' commercial interests alter Balinese rituals and wondered if this would be the case with the *kajang*. "Tourist interest can change ritual, I suppose. Can change your beliefs."

"Yes." She was thoughtful. "But we will always have Barong and Rangda."

"What do you mean?"

"The good and the bad. The dark and the light and the constant struggle between the two. The bad, the evil rises up sometimes. As it did in 1965. All the killings."

I thought of the anti-communist purge and how Suharto had displaced Sukarno. "That was a terrible time."

"Family against family within small villages as well as in the larger cities. These were not minor slights, these were fathers dragged from their homes, leaving their children orphans. Children killed along with the parents. This is not easily forgotten."

"Genocide," I said.

She didn't answer, instead folding the textiles and picking up the pile.

"I'm going now. Be sure to call Wayan Tyo."

"Yes. I will. Thank you for talking about the shroud. I will try to find another priest who will not condemn me for thinking of burning the *kajang* and who may give me a more thoughtful opinion."

"Sounds perfect. I'll see you soon."

As I turned to go, she asked, "Did he suffer?"

I looked at the floor, bamboo like Flip's. It dawned on me that other details of the shop were similar to his house: the same windows, the carved door. He must have helped her in her business. I pulled myself back to her question. "No, he didn't. It was quick."

"Yes? Good." But knowing this didn't erase the sadness in her eyes.

I felt for her and understood how much she had wanted to see him again. "I'm very glad that Tyo wouldn't let you in to see him."

She thought about this for a moment. "I would have liked to see him one more time."

"Not like that. You must believe me. Not like that."

32

Esa stood at the side door of his smithy, sweat glistening on his chest and arms. He wore his sarong like a farmer in the fields, the back pulled through his legs and tucked in at the front to create the Southeast Asian version of shorts. A man of no words as far as I could tell, he nodded at me and turned to go back into the workshop that stretched behind a small storefront.

I followed, not knowing if he intended me to enter or not. The young boy sitting by the entrance to the shop, his eyes glued to a handheld screen, didn't look up. A few knives rested in a glass case. Sturdy handmade gardening tools, scythes, and hammers hung along one wall, and as I passed I reached out and touched a small pair of clippers. My mother loved gardening, and this would be the perfect gift. A small hammer would be a great choice for my brother Sean.

A fire blazed in an open furnace at the far end of the room. Beside the furnace stood the same cylindrical upright bellows I'd seen carved on the Candi Sukuh relief of a blacksmith. It said a lot about Esa, this bellows. He could have found a more up-to-date alternative, but chose to maintain a traditional shop. This type of bellows is found throughout Southeast Asia and is considered one of the characteristics linking the culturally diverse region.

Dust from the burning fire covered every surface, lending a grim gray ambiance to the orderly room. There wasn't much to see in the way of equipment or other metalworking paraphernalia, so it was difficult for me to tally the complex, completed work of a kris or a spear with my surroundings. The tools I had just passed looked simpler, and easier to fabricate.

Ignoring me, which I took as acceptance of my presence, he squatted in front of a low bench, much as the blacksmith in the Candi Sukuh relief had. As I neared the fire, I could see that he was working on a rather deadly looking wide, curved blade.

"How does one use a blade like that?" I asked.

"Weapon," he said, grasping the long tongs and picking up a metal bar. Tightening his grip, he began the annealing process that increases the ductility of the metal, as he thrust the blade into the scorching fire, then pulled it to the anvil and pounded it with his mallet. As it began to cool he put it back into the fire. The surface heated unevenly, ripples of different colored ores shining brightly, the coal flashing.

"Do you only make tools and weapons?"

"No." He moved again toward the burning coals, inserting the blade into the reddest, hottest part of the fire, twisting it right and left as he again picked up the mallet from the shelf beside him. He repeated this four or five times while I watched, fascinated. Each submersion in heat, each strike of the mallet lengthened and widened and thinned the blade. Finally he went back and squatted in front of his low bench.

I would never get information from this man. Not only was he barely speaking, but he clearly didn't want me here, whether because he was in the midst of his work or just because, I couldn't tell. I wandered around the workshop, eventually stopping in front of a shelf that held tools, wax, and blades in various stages of production. They were of assorted shapes, finely made, the acid-etched layering of iron and nickel-bearing iron creating the marvelous rippling pattern, the *pamor*, favored by collectors.

I picked up a book on Indonesian weaponry that lay on a lower shelf and flipped through it in search of examples of the blades before me, trying to figure out how they were used. A few of them were so oddly shaped that I could not imagine their attachment to the haft.

Behind me Esa moved again toward the furnace, where he perched on a chair that he had elevated by placing a section of a tree trunk on top of the seat. He picked the blade up with his long metal tongs and began pounding again, still annealing it. He held the blade over the fire then drew it out as he concentrated on the edges, thinning and refining the metal with strong confident strokes. He never looked at me.

"Did you learn this skill from your father?"

"My uncle more than my father. He learned from my grandfather. My father was not a smith when he was young. He only learned after my grandfather was killed."

"In the purge? In 1965?"

"Yes. Then my father regretted not learning this skill from him. He left his job as clerk and became a smith. But my uncle was the true teacher."

I hesitated, but since he'd finally begun to talk, I didn't want to end the conversation. "Was he a communist, your grandfather?"

He didn't answer, and I realized the question would have been irrelevant to a child. His grandfather had been killed, and so he had never met him. That was all that mattered.

We sat quietly as he waited for the blade to cool. Eventually I asked, "Did we meet as children?"

He looked surprised at the question. "Of course."

His response was as brief as usual. And then I wondered, is there an "of course" to memory? I think only if a momentous occasion took place could you say, "Of course I remember." Otherwise I would say there was no "of course." I wanted to pursue my question and his response, but he had walked to the storefront and was speaking with a customer.

Probably his life experience had been more predictable, more routine than mine, so that meeting and playing with an eight-year-old girl from a foreign country when he was twelve years old was notable. Certainly my life had been less so, though it didn't seem particularly exciting to me. What did I remember from the summer when I was twelve? Camp, music lessons, my friends.

I thought about my three closest friends from that time. A Japanese girl whose mother cooked food that filled their home with unrecognizable smells that I learned to love. A girl whose parents were divorced and whose mother dated a new man every week, much to our horror and amusement. And a girl who was diagnosed with cancer and survived, but with consequences for all of us that I still hadn't sorted out.

What else had I done the year I was twelve? Maybe that was the year that we went to the Grand Canyon for vacation. Or was it Vancouver? Summer camp for sure, circus summer camp in Mendocino. It wasn't until I was fourteen that I flew alone to my grandmother's for the first time, so surely we had taken some camping vacation that year, as we usually did. Nothing epic, but with the constant new input that my parents had wanted for us, that they scraped and saved for through the rest of the year.

What had Esa done? Worked in his uncle's blacksmith shop. Gone to school. Followed the set of routines and rituals that structure the average Balinese person's life. Traveled? I doubted it, but maybe I was wrong. Met a family from California with three kids younger than him, whom he and Wayan Tyo befriended.

He came back into the workshop.

"Thank you for letting me watch you make that blade." He was silent. I fingered the amulet in my pocket. "Do you ever make sculptures? Of bronze?"

He gave me a long look, bent to his blade, and finally said, "No."

"Can you tell me a workshop where I could go to watch bronze-casting? I see small bodhisattvas and buddhas in some of the shops, and I would like to see them being made." His cold reserve was like a shove, and though I held the little sculpture in the palm of my hand, I didn't show it to him.

"Any special type of figure?" A long sentence for Esa.

"No, not really." I tried to sound casual. I let the amulet drop to the bottom of my pocket. "Just an artist who produces high-quality pieces. I have a friend in California who asked me to look. There's a piece he's thinking of buying. Supposedly it's old, and I want to see what the best artists are capable of producing here. To see the fakes."

He gave me a name and address that I wrote down, and as I put my notebook back in my purse, he said, "*Selamat jalan.*" Safe journey.

My time to leave. I'd go home, change my clothes, and ride—away from busy Ubud. Maybe to Tampaksiring to visit Gunung Kawi, maybe just down a road, past rice paddies and through villages. Maybe I would stop somewhere and drink a Bali coffee. Maybe I would just feel the wind on my face. Then I would go say hello to Ani. Maybe I would do that first, before Wayan Tyo arrived home.

33

The French couple and I seemed to be on the same clock, as once again they were eating breakfast when I arrived. We greeted each other, and I sat in the seat I had decided was my own. Before I could ask, one of the waitresses brought me tea with honey, and I opened my computer to check my e-mail before going up to the buffet. The Internet access was much quicker in the dining pavilion than in my room.

P.P. had written, and I had to laugh at his need to chat about his collecting, though I shouldn't have been surprised. This collector spent more time in the museum—in my office—than any of the museum staff. His wife preferred being in Kolkata and so lived there most of the year, leaving P.P. to fend for himself. He loved to talk and to socialize, and I suspected that I was one of many people whom he sought out to fill the loneliness. We also had a regular schedule of lunches since he hated to cook and ate almost every meal in restaurants. I had become quite fond of P.P.

He'd come to the States for graduate school and upon graduation had started up a tech company with two of his classmates. It wasn't a rags-to-riches tale, as his family was wealthy, but the company had catapulted him onto the Forbes 500 list. Though he still spent a few hours each day in the office, the remainder of his time was dedicated to buying art.

I would call him once the French couple left.

I ate *nasi goreng* with a fried egg, fresh fruit, and yogurt with a few peanuts thrown in.

"Do you go sightseeing today, Bu?" asked the waitress as she took my empty plate.

"I thought I would visit a few art galleries." I poured myself some more tea and took another spoonful of yogurt.

By noon it would be hot. Unless it rained, and then it would be even hotter. Rain increased the humidity to an unbearable hundred percent.

She lingered. "There are many artists in Ubud."

"Yes, there certainly are." Before I could ask her about artists she knew, she was gone.

Seth entered the breakfast area alone, earlier than usual. He joined me without asking and without preamble said, "I thought that we got along quite well. I was thinking that if I took the San Francisco job, maybe we could continue seeing each other."

The waitress came to ask what he wanted to drink, but he didn't look at her. After hesitating, she walked away.

It was a question, two questions, and with the spoon raised halfway to my mouth, my computer open beside my bowl, I couldn't see any possible escape. I put down my spoon. "We do seem to get along fine. But I don't want to see anyone on a regular basis. I also don't want to threaten my relationship with this family I've known most of my life." I'd already threatened my relationship with Ani's family by going to Java with him, but I didn't need to reveal that.

"You should have considered that before you let me in your bed." He stood. "And it would have been kinder to just say that you were having second thoughts than to vanish."

"True. I'm sorry." He was already walking away when I said it, and I wasn't sure whether he heard me or not. I hadn't meant to be unkind. I was a chicken when it came to matters of the heart.

He was right; I had behaved badly. There wasn't much I could do about that now. I closed my computer, looked at my unfinished breakfast, and headed back to my room, so that Seth and Randall could have the dining pavilion to themselves when they returned. Or, to put it more honestly, so that I wouldn't have to encounter him again. I would try to contact P.P. from my room and hope for a good connection.

34

Six Balinese pre-war modernist works on paper hung in the entryway of the gallery Made had recommended. Bigger oils and gouache works, many painted by Western artists, hung in open-air pavilions that climbed up the hill. As I wandered, I saw that some of the works were old and some contemporary. None related to my interests of the moment.

I was about to leave when the rain began to fall, drops plummeting straight down unhindered by wind. When I stuck my hand out the door, rain hit me like a bombardment of Ping-Pong balls. I watched a vast puddle form at the bottom of the steps and turned back into the gallery, preferring a longer look to getting drenched. I'd only glanced at the modernist works in the entryway, but now I took the time to scan them for oak leaves. The first painting was signed "Sobrat," a second-generation painter who had completed this work, according to the label, in 1950.

Thunder rumbled the building and the town. Lightning flashed nearby, brightening the dark hallway. Suddenly the overhead lights came on.

The man who had kept his distance on my first foray through the gallery now stood at the light switch across the room. He nodded at me, and I smiled back. "*Terima kasih,*" I said, thanking him, and went back to looking at a painting of demonic Rangda. The sinuous figure swung a garland around her shoulders, flashed long, curving fingers and toenails, and stuck out her snakelike tongue. Flames floating in the sky haloed her. One of them was an elongated oak leaf.

"Can you tell me about this painting?" I called to him.

He walked toward me. "It is by Anak Agung Gde Sobrat. It is Rangda."

"Yes, I see that. How did it come to be in your possession?"

"I bought it."

This was a bit like talking to Esa. "From the artist's family?"

He hesitated long enough with his answer that I knew that he was lying. "Yes."

Well, I'd fed him that line, certainly. Foolish of me. "Recently?"

"Yes. Recently."

The rain was letting up, but I needed to look to see if any more of his paintings had oak leaves. "Can you tell me the price of the Sobrat?"

"It is $3,000."

"Thank you." I looked more closely at the other paintings in the entryway, aware of the man hovering nearby. If he knew I was Anak Ani, he didn't let on.

The rain seemed to have stopped. "Come back anytime," he said as I ventured forth.

"Thanks. I will." So Flip had spread his paintings around. If this dealer knew that he had a fake, it hadn't kept him from hanging it on the wall. Nor had it lowered his price. Of course, since the painting was an excellent forgery, he may have had no idea.

Hungry now, I decided to go to a little Balinese tapas *warung* that I had read about in the guidebook, nearby on Goutama Street. I made my way past shops and cafés, a market, avoiding puddles as I stepped on and off the sidewalk.

SEATED at the counter that ran along the front of the *warung*, I watched the passersby. Across the street, four men constructed an extension to a small homestay. Huge bamboo poles supported the concrete forms of the main frame of the building. Though it had begun to rain again, they continued working.

"What is *nasi campur*?" I asked the waitress.

"It is a plate of rice with small amounts of different dishes."

"Sounds good. I'll have that and the *gerong goreng*." The guidebook had recommended those tiny, deep-fried fish, which sounded, in theory at least, like the deep-fried fish skin that I had so liked in the Philippines.

"Fearless," the man at the next table said.

For a moment I thought he was talking about my order, but when I followed his gaze, I saw he was looking at the construction across the street. "Yes, completely fearless."

A man stood casually on a narrow beam fifteen feet above the ground. Lightning lit the sky as he laid a twenty-foot piece of wood he'd taken from another worker across the width of the roof. The lightning strike proved the only transition from light rain to a torrential downpour. The worker looked up, straightened the wood he'd just laid down, hunkered, then dropped to the ground.

He and the other workers scurried to shelter. A woman on her motorbike struggled to put on her poncho. Three schoolgirls squealed and held their backpacks over their heads for imagined protection. My *nasi campur* arrived.

"Good, I'm glad he got down. I wouldn't have been able to eat." My neighbor turned back to his book.

I ate, watching the growing rivulets flow down the gutters until they almost met in the middle. A very grumpy-looking woman ducked into the shop next door. A young woman hurried to the homestay across the street, and as she jumped the flowing water she lost a shoe. She glanced at it as it was swept away, then continued inside without trying to retrieve it.

The waitress delivered my *gerong goreng*. I dipped one of the tiny fried fish into the spicy *sambal*. Salt, crunch, and spice combined in my mouth in a pleasant burst. Rain blew into the open front of the *warung*, and the waitress helped me move farther inside where it was dry. I chatted with the man, who had also moved out of the rain, and with the other diners, who ate slowly and sipped, waited for the rain to subside.

I thought about all I had to do as I watched those around me. I ordered a soda, stretched out my legs, listened to the rain beating on the tin roof. I thought of my mother, whom I'd spoken to on Skype when I was unable to contact P.P. She was worried about my brother Eric, but she was always worried about him, so her concerns were like white noise. His escapades loomed over the entire family: the drugs, the DUIs, the drama. I sighed, then pulled out my mystery novel and began to read.

"DID you have a good day, Bu?" asked the receptionist.

"Yes, thanks. Any messages for me?"

He handed me my room key. "No."

Walking toward my bungalow, I saw Randall by the pool. I waved and he waved back, then said something to someone I couldn't see. Seth, I assumed. I hurried on, thinking of the galleries I'd visited.

I'd found two more Flip paintings and some other, less skilled forgeries. Of course there were more original paintings than fakes, but they tended to be by artists less important than Ida Bagus Made and Lempad. Flip must have made a considerable amount of money from his work. I guessed that he had gotten away with selling fakes to different dealers in town because they were all secretive with each other. Without knowing where the others had purchased their stock, they wouldn't have been suspicious when he offered them a "good" painting.

I had to wonder how long he'd been painting forgeries to sell to the local dealers. Eventually he would have been caught out, for even though they kept secrets from each other, if too many Lempads turned up on the market, or a surplus of Ida Bagus Mades appeared in gallery after gallery, the dealers would eventually have talked with each other. Flip would not have been a popular fellow when that moment arrived.

Maybe it had arrived, and that was why I'd met him with a spear through his chest.

35

Drivers in Bali are not as fast or as reckless as drivers in mainland Southeast Asia, and there aren't as many motorbikes on the road, but the negotiation of space is similar. A lot of horn honking. Size dictates right of way. Intersections require merging that only the gods could choreograph.

As a bicyclist, I had the fewest rights, fewer than a pedestrian, but I was learning to negotiate the merge. My scare the previous week had made me cautious. Flocks of ducks and the occasional racing motorbike presented the only challenges on the back roads outside of Ubud. As I neared town, spatial negotiations increased, and I found that I had to stop frequently in order to avoid being squished or driven off the road. Fortunately, the one time that it happened, I ended up on solid ground rather than in an irrigation ditch.

Avoiding the heavily trafficked streets of Ubud, I could survey the scenery and could ride with less fear of being hit by a truck or of hitting a pedestrian. From what I could see, biking was better than driving, but not as good as walking.

The West had spread its tentacles into all aspects of life: the dress, the commodities for sale in the shops, the menus chalked on roadside signs. Hamburgers, facials, dance classes, manicures.

I supposed some people had come for the inexpensive spas, the cheap clothing, the culture secondary.

I thought of the man ahead of me in the immigration line when I arrived. He said to the woman ahead of him, "It's just such a cute little cultural place. I come back every year." They then tried to best each other with their knowledge of the most obscure pristine beach. When she said to him, "Pasar Putih has been discovered," as if that ruined it, I wondered if she saw her part in that ruination.

Paradise was created, as one author had written, by Westerners and by the Indonesian elite. The problem was that paradise was having trouble keeping up with itself. Sure, it was possible to accommodate five hundred thousand tourists a year, but multiply that times five as it was now, and suddenly there wasn't enough water. Rice paddies that had fed families were paved over or turned into hotels. Plastic bags and water bottles, tourist detritus, piled up everywhere.

I pulled to the side of the narrow road to let a truck pass and looked through the trees at a family working their land. One sometimes felt as if the shops, *warungs*, and hotels were all a veneer, while the real Bali simmered beneath the surface. Buildings dedicated to the gods protected courtyards around the island and embraced tradition. The rituals, with their offerings, the dance and art and performance that underpinned Balinese society, seemed to strengthen with the influx of tourists.

I climbed back on my bike, and before I'd pedaled ten feet I had to swerve to miss two small children playing at the edge of the road. The scabs on my legs tightened with each stroke, and I tried to ignore my aching side.

I glanced down at my watch. Five. Ani had insisted on my coming to dinner, so I wasn't going to be able to avoid Tyo. He had texted me, in fact, to say that I should come to their house around six, or earlier if I felt like it. If I went back to the hotel to change, I would be late. Since I was hungry, I decided to continue directly there, hoping that Ani would excuse my sweaty attire. A bit lost in the maze of neighborhoods, paved streets, and dirt lanes, I stopped to get my bearings.

"Anak Ani, you look here," called a shopkeeper from across the lane.

Geez, Louise, I needed to change the color of my hair. Word had spread like wildfire that Anak Ani was in town and she had a pink forelock. I didn't think I'd even walked down this street before.

Hopping back on the bike, I headed in the general direction of Ani's house, continuing to avoid the busiest streets, riding slowly so that I could take in the scene. I stopped when I saw a workshop that looked like a promising venue for bronze sculptures, but the brassy tourist souvenirs didn't come close to P.P.'s bronze. Eventually I found a familiar road near Ani's and headed out of the hustle and bustle toward the peace that her home offered.

I was sauntering—if one can saunter on a bike—swerving lazily around potholes, people, and transport, when I felt something fly by my head. Or maybe I heard it. It was a sensation I'd only experienced from the safety of a movie theater or sitting on my parents' couch watching TV—the whizzy sound-feel of a bullet, or an arrow, or a poison dart. Not a spear or arrow, because I definitely would have seen that. I crouched down over the handlebars, drove my feet down on the pedals, careened this way and that to make myself a difficult target.

A truck came out of nowhere. It provided cover for the few moments that I needed. I had to get out of the vicinity. I veered around a few kids playing out in the street and rode directly into the courtyard, swerving around the wall just inside the entrance, the wall that kept out evil forces, who can only move in straight lines. Judging by the look on Ani's face, riding in the courtyard was not allowed. "Someone just shot at me," I said in explanation.

"I'll call Wayan Tyo. Here? In front of the house?"

"No, back there." I waved my arm behind me.

"Where? What street?"

"I have no idea. I didn't stop to read the street sign. Near. I could take Wayan Tyo there."

Ani called Tyo and went into the kitchen. She came back with a thermos and poured me a glass of tea.

Had I fantasized the episode? No, that sound was real. I sat beneath the old tree.

"I think that you have something to tell Tyo," she said as she sat beside me.

I glanced at her, then concentrated on my tea. "No, I don't think so."

She crossed her arms over her chest. "Then tell me."

I tilted my glass, the amber liquid sloshing to one side.

"I will not tell him if you do not want."

I took a sip.

"There is a reason someone shot at you."

I looked up. "Yes. I caught him stealing from Flip's house. Eric Shelley, the Australian dealer who was in Flip's storage. It must have been him."

She refilled my glass. "Is there another reason?"

I blurted, "I took something."

Her expression didn't change.

"At the murder scene."

When I didn't continue, she asked, "What?"

I didn't answer her, mentally kicking myself for saying anything, while at the same time relieved to get even this much off my chest.

"Something to kill for?" she persisted.

"I don't know. I really don't. I took it because I thought it might be a clue."

We sat in silence, me wrapped in my guilt, guilt that her silence amplified. If it was something worth killing for, I didn't need to involve Ani. My relief from having told her now intensified my guilt. I changed the subject.

"Bu, why is it that everyone in this town knows me? They call me Anak Ani."

"Strangers?"

"Yes, a shopkeeper yelled from the side of the road, and men in a weapons shop invited me for tea."

"You have made an impression." She smiled. "When you were young and more recently when you were the person who discovered Flip's body."

"When I was young?"

She didn't answer me.

"Finding Flip's body wasn't exactly an act of any consequence. I mean, I didn't do anything."

"Yes, anyone could have found Flip's body. But you found it and you once again met Wayan Tyo, who was your close friend when you were small. Twenty years separate these two events, but it is clear to everyone that fate played some part."

"Fate—you mean I was fated not to meet Flip alive?"

"No. You were fated to meet Wayan Tyo and me again. This is a coincidence that must have greater meaning. We do not know what that meaning is, but it must be. Do you see this?"

I thought for a moment. "I see that it's an unusual coincidence, unusual and unlikely and a bit weird. Whether it has greater significance, I couldn't say. Maybe the way we each think about it is cultural."

I heard a motorbike roaring down the road. Wayan Tyo did not ride into the courtyard; he knew better.

As he hurried toward us, she said, "You must do the right thing."

I thought, true, but not tonight.

36

"You taught me how to fold those," I said from the doorway. Morning moisture permeated the air.

Ani was squatting on the floor of the kitchen folding offerings from young coconut leaves. "Yes, I did. And do you remember how to make them still?"

"I'm not sure. I'd like to try." I entered and joined her. The room was dark and cool.

Ani had insisted that I stay the night to be safe. I slept in the girls' room while they slept with their dad.

When he'd arrived the previous evening, Wayan Tyo said he was skeptical about my misadventure. Yet I noticed he got to us in record time.

We'd returned to the street where I heard-felt the whizzing.

"Did you see anything strange?" Wayan Tyo had asked one shopkeeper after another.

"No," came the response.

"Were there any foreigners?" This had brought a laugh.

"Always," one said.

"Yes, but they all look alike," said another, and they all laughed harder.

"Her, I see her," chimed in a child who pointed at me. "She ride the bike like crazy." And he proceeded to dash down the street, hunched down, hell-bent, mimicking my escape.

"When you saw me, was there anyone suspicious?"

"Not more."

I had taken that to mean not more suspicious than me.

"A tall, skinny man? Wild hair?"

The shopkeeper shook his head.

The child said, "Yes, yes. He cowboy." Then he mimicked shooting a gun.

Tyo and I looked at each other.

Tyo asked, "He shot at her?"

"No, me," said the boy. "Like this." He aimed his finger at Tyo and pulled the trigger. Then he blew into his fingertip and holstered his hand.

"Kids everywhere," I mumbled. But I thought we knew our culprit.

Tyo had questioned the child further in Balinese, but hadn't gotten more out of him. The shopkeeper glared at the boy, who became evasive.

We hadn't found any evidence of bullet or poison dart, or any other projectile. Of course, why would we?

Since my description of where I had heard the sound was so vague, we would have had to comb an area far beyond Wayan Tyo's and my available time or the capabilities and the resources of the Ubud police department. We just had to take the event for what it was and add the fact that Eric might have again tried to harm me into the mix of information available about Flip's murder. The fact certainly cemented his position in first place on my suspect list.

ANI smiled as she looked at my Hello Kitty T-shirt. Big on Wayan Tyo's older girl, but I could have won a wet T-shirt contest without getting it wet.

"This one, the *porosan*, was your specialty." She held up the small, folded offering.

"My specialty?" I said as I sat down.

"Your small hands were good at making the *porosan*. It is placed in many larger offerings. The ingredients of each of the offerings are fixed," she explained. "One of the most common elements for an offering is the quid."

"The betel quid?"

"Yes. Traditionally one always offers the quid to one's guests to chew. The betel quid is also offered to the gods and spirits. The quid has many parts—the areca nut, the limestone paste, the leaf—and the *porosan* has tiny bits of all of these wrapped in a piece of coconut palm leaf. Like so." Ani demonstrated.

"Could you do another?"

She made a second slowly as I watched. "One large festival took place when you lived here as a child. We needed to make many offerings, and you and your mother helped me."

"Ah," I said. But it wasn't her describing my making offerings that caught my attention. It was the phrase "when you lived here." As if my childhood had been spent under her gaze.

Ani handed me the components of the offering, and I set about making a *porosan*. As I finished the third tiny folded lozenge, I said, "My hands seem to remember making these."

"Not surprising," she said as she adeptly folded a more complicated piece. "You made hundreds of them and became famous in the village for your persistence and determination. During the week before the festival all the women in the neighborhood gather in this courtyard to make offerings together. They bring their daughters and granddaughters—these days it is more often grandmothers like me and our granddaughters, as the daughters of your age are out of the house working. You could make them faster than anyone. You were very happy for the many compliments that were given you for your skill."

I laughed. "I'm sure I was. Today I'll make these, and maybe tomorrow you'll teach me to make something a little more complicated."

230

Ani stopped her work and looked thoughtful. "It is not how complicated the offering is, it is the state of mind of the maker. If you make it truthfully for the gods, and in your belief in the spirits, that is what matters. Some women are more skilled than others, but those with skill are not always those whose hearts and minds are correct."

That quieted me.

"Offerings must please the gods and should be made properly and well. Our making the offering in the proper manner as best we are able is an expression of our belief and faith." She turned back to the small dish, with its careful arrangement of flowers and other bits, and finished folding in silence, effortlessly and carefully.

Thinking back on the group of women making offerings at Besakih, I remembered one woman who wasn't distracted by chatting. Her focus had been entirely on her hands and the materials before her, and I'd been struck by the serenity of her expression. Then I had noticed that her offerings were clumsier than some of the others, and I'd turned to watch those women who were quicker, laughing and chatting as they churned out one offering after another. The clumsy woman's calm, her serenity, suggested she may have been the one with the faith and, though without creative skill, the one whose offerings did her and all of us the most good.

"What are you going to do with these offerings?"

"Take them to the temple," said Ani as she rose.

"Now? May I come?"

"Of course. But . . ." She looked pointedly at my T-shirt.

"I'll change and be right back."

"Wait," she said, and went into a room in the largest of the buildings. She came out carrying a *kebaya* and a sash, which she handed me.

"I'll only be a minute."

37

As we walked toward the temple, a steady stream of women exited their houses and headed in various directions, all of them with shallow offering baskets in their hands or on their heads. Some were going to the same temple that we were approaching, others to one of the many other temples that dotted the landscape. A heady smell recalled my childhood. "I recognize the smell."

"Clove tree." She pointed at a tree with big, glossy leaves and tiny flowers.

"I don't just remember that smell, I associate it with walking with you."

"We are going to the ancestor temple where you've been. There are three different kinds of temples, for the ancestor, for the village, and the third, the temple of origins. This has been my ancestors' temple for many generations. It is a link to my past and to my children's past. Many of my neighbors feel deeply about this temple, as it is their ancestors' temple as well."

We mounted some steps, passed through the split gateway, and entered a large courtyard with few buildings. Forty feet in front of us a wall with doorways led to two other courtyards, each with numerous small shrines. Ani walked toward the courtyard on our left, and I followed hesitantly. A sign at the main entrance stated no one was allowed who was not worshipping, and though I did intend to place my offerings I hesitated.

Each of the small buildings was raised on stilts. Porches fronted them, and though each had a door to an interior space, those spaces were not large enough for one to enter. Thatched roofs formed a lovely, irregular skirt above each building. All three of the courtyards bustled with people, mostly women, attending to their spiritual duties in the early morning.

I wondered why some of them let Ani pass ahead of them, or deferred to her in other small but subtle ways, as we walked around the temple grounds. From the right a nod of the head, from the left a shrug of the shoulders. It couldn't be only her age, as one ancient who could have been her grandmother stepped back for her to pass.

I hesitated as she moved toward one of the structures, uncertain if it was okay for me, a foreigner, to approach. She waved me forward. I followed her lead in placing the offerings, which she did with an economy of movement. In her left hand she held a basket containing at least a dozen small baskets holding leaves, flowers, rice. She'd produced many offerings before I'd awakened.

A flower flashed between her fingers as she dipped it in a small water pot on her tray, then, flicking her finger, sprayed water over the offering she had placed on the shrine's porch. She approached another shrine, where she did the same. Unable to mimic the quick casualness of her floral blessing, I set down my offering without the requisite ceremony.

While she moved from small shrine to small shrine, I looked at the offerings that were piled before me and fingered the amulet in my pocket. On impulse, I pulled it out and set the small bag with the kris-carrying figure in the back corner of the altar in this, the largest of the shrines in the left-hand courtyard. The figure belonged here, not in my pocket, not on the body of a dead man.

The Balinese believe that some places are *tenget*, sacred or metaphysically charged. You could feel the charge in this temple. This was where man communicated with his ancestors through the gods. This was where this small but powerful figure would be at home.

I looked around to see if anyone had watched me. The busy priest dressed in white who was now occupied clearing offerings from another altar would clear this one away shortly. And what would he think of this small figure? Would he place it in the temple's storehouse? Or was that only for the ancient relics belonging to the temple? Maybe it would burden him as it had weighed on me these last few days. Weighed on me to the point I could not bring myself to look at it. I would have liked to stay to watch how he dealt with the tiny sculpture, but he would have known that I put it there. I was the only other oddity in the place.

I followed Ani from the inner courtyard to the outer. As we neared the main entrance, Esa entered. Though he was clearly surprised to see me, he nodded politely to both of us and continued walking.

Once out the gate, I said, "This is his temple too? He lives on the other side of town. I thought people tended to go to their neighborhood temples."

"Yes, but his family lives near here, and this was his temple when he was a child. He is a priest, as he is a *pande*."

"A priest? Really?"

"Why does that surprise you? He is a very serious young man. And he is a blacksmith."

"I do know their caste are priests. But, somehow . . . He's so quiet and reticent. I just don't quite imagine him as a priest. I think of a priest as someone who can communicate with people."

"Reticent? Esa? I do not think that is so. Even if it were, he doesn't need to communicate, really. A priest needs to be able to perform rituals. It is not like your Western church, I think." She greeted an approaching woman before continuing. "One day he will be a very important elder in our community. He is well respected because of his seriousness. Now he is young and is very strong in his opinions. Once his opinions calm down, he will rise to his duties for our community."

I found this difficult to square with my impression of the man, who seemed withdrawn to a point that in the West would probably be diagnosed as Asperger's, if not autism. Clearly the Balinese valued quiet in a way that we in the West do not.

"Last year when thieves broke into this temple, Esa called Wayan Tyo right away. This angered the other priests, who are Brahmans. They felt that they should deal with the problem themselves. This meant keeping it secret. It meant continuing a secret."

"Why would someone break in?"

"Many temples have sculptures that remain hidden in *gedung penyimpanan*, storehouses. For centuries the priests have kept it secret that these important religious objects were in their temples. Our temple held one small icon that we thought very powerful, and so we kept it safe in the storehouse."

"I have read that many temples have icons that they take out once a year and process around the village. Was this one of those objects?"

"No, it wasn't. It was hidden and not seen, and only the priests knew about it. But a thief broke in and stole it." Ani turned from the path to cut across the rice paddy.

I thought of the small sculpture that I had just left at the temple and felt a chill. "Do you know what it looked like?" We were walking along a narrow berm, and I needed to concentrate on where I put my feet. Ani never looked down. She couldn't, for she carried her basket on her head.

"Yes," she said, but didn't expand.

"How do you know what it looked like? Isn't it only a priest who would know?"

"Yes. I am a priest."

"At this same temple?"

"Yes."

So that was why everyone deferred to her. "But you didn't tell Wayan Tyo? Esa did?"

She didn't answer right away. Finally she said, "I was the one who discovered it was stolen, and I immediately called Esa."

"The others must have been angry at you, too."

She didn't say anything, so I veered away from the blame that must have been flying. "Was the icon found after it was stolen?"

"No. Wayan Tyo had some ideas who might have stolen it, but was unable to prove them. They felt that they had lost face by people knowing that they had not taken care of the temple properly. She shook her head at the memory. "They were embarrassed. The priests were very angry."

"But it had been stolen."

"Yes. It was not very sensible, and most of the people in my village felt that it was not sensible, and so they admired Esa for calling the authorities. It cost Esa in his relationship with the priests but gained him standing with the village."

"Which probably lost him more with the priests."

"Yes, jealousy combined with anger. The situation turned out to be good for Esa in the end, as he gained stature. At the same time, I think that he also learned that he must not make a decision alone, which was a lesson that he needed to learn. Since that time he has become much more . . ." she searched for the word.

"Compliant?"

"Yes, I think that is right." We passed onto the road, and as we made our way toward home the traffic increased. I felt lighter. Visiting the ancestor temple? Making offerings? Getting rid of the amulet? I didn't know for certain, though I imagined it was the amulet. At the same time, I felt sad that I no longer had it in hand. It was a beautiful thing. Add to that the fact that it had come from a murder scene and that if I wanted to tell Wayan Tyo about it, it was now that much more complicated.

I stumbled at the thought. I'd done it. Jumped when I should have taken my time.

She turned her head toward me, and the basket didn't even jiggle. "Do you have a boyfriend at home?"

The question surprised me, since I felt very much in Bali at the moment, not at home. It wasn't a topic that I wanted to explore. "No. Well, sort of."

"Sort of?"

"There's a man who is interested. I like him, but it's complicated. It won't work out."

"Why?"

"Just won't. Really, there isn't anyone that I want to see right now."

"See?"

"I don't know any men right now that I want to date."

"But you have had a boyfriend? Other than this one you don't want."

"It's not that I don't want him. It's that our situations make it complicated."

She waited.

"We are too different."

This seemed to satisfy her. She said, "But in the past you had one. And did not keep him?"

Them, I thought. "No, I didn't keep him."

"You do not like men? You like women?"

I laughed. "I do like men. I like men quite a lot. I just haven't settled on one yet."

"You do not want children?"

"I don't think I do. At least right now I don't. I know some women want children even if they haven't found the right man, but I don't. I see it as a package deal, and the first component of the package—the man—is nowhere in sight." But, I thought, maybe he is, and that's what frightens me about getting involved with Alam.

"What do you want from a man?"

That was a question to ponder. "I don't really know. I suppose I should be able to answer that, shouldn't I?"

"Yes. I recall before I was married, how surprised I was by what my friends wanted from men. One wanted a man with money. One wanted a man who was handsome. Some wanted beauty in the body, while others cared more for the mind. We talked about it a great deal."

"What did you want?"

"Steadiness."

"Steadiness?"

"Yes. I wanted a husband whose hand held me to the earth."

"You? You seem very much bound to the earth, caring for Wayan Tyo's children and the rest of your family. You seem to be the core, the stability, of your courtyard."

"He gave me that. I was not always like this. When I was young, I was like a butterfly, flitting from one flower to the next. No, worse, like a bee, drawing in the pollen in deep drafts."

That was a rather naughty metaphor. I didn't dare ask if she meant it to sound so profoundly sexual. We were both quiet as I pictured those bees and butterflies flitting around, wondering if in Indonesia they referred to the "birds and the bees." "And?"

"I met my husband, who had a very steady hand. Not a hand that pressed me down, trying to stop me, but a hand that gave me room and a safe home. He was very patient with me. I miss him now, even after ten years."

"Ah." I thought of Alam, a steady man.

"I believe I was like you."

This might have been an astute observation, or it might have been a complete misunderstanding of who I was. "Quite possibly."

"I recall telling your mother that I was much like you as a child. She understood this and said maybe you were my daughter and Wayan Tyo was her son, as she thought he was very much like her."

I stopped short. "Is that where it comes from? 'Anak Ani'?"

"Maybe, yes, I suppose."

Nothing more than a couple of women talking about their children. I had begun to think that they had performed some Balinese ritual where my parents had relinquished me to Ani. I was relieved to find that wasn't so. One does want to feel certain one knows one's parents, no matter how good or bad the relationship.

Back at the house, we found Wayan Tyo feeding his daughters breakfast. "You have been to the temple," he said.

"Yes. First we made offerings, which Jenna remembered how to make, then we went to the temple."

"*Porosan?*"

"Yes, they're my specialty."

He laughed. "I recall that. My girls are quite good at making those, too. Did you sleep well?"

"I did, though when I woke I was very aware of my dream, or rather I should say the soundtrack for my dream. My dreams don't usually have soundtracks, so that was odd. I don't recall exactly what happened, but the gamelan playing in the background stayed with me. Then during a tense scene—"

"A tense scene?" Ani asked.

"I think someone was chasing me. At any rate, during that scene the voices of men performing the *kecak* provided the background. That rat-a-tat-tat chatter of monkeys that they imitate. There was a brief *kecak* performance at the palace the other night, and walking down the street I've heard the chanting at other performances. We saw a show when I was a child, and I found it scary." Tyo's younger daughter climbed onto my lap, and I began to braid her hair.

"Yes, many children find it frightening," said Wayan Tyo, watching us.

"And adults," said Ani.

"Even hearing the sound, I can suddenly visualize those men, their arms extended, fingers fluttering, shoulders swaying. I had a strong impression, or memory, when I saw it the other night. I think that for me it wasn't really dance, but body language. The extreme postures brought up all sorts of feelings, mostly dark feelings. So, in my dream, the sound of their chanting caused me to run."

"Are you still frightened?"

"Frightened? You mean from last night, from the whizzing?" I looked at the girls as I spoke, then thought for a moment. "I suppose I am. I suppose I wonder if the person will try it again. I've been wondering why Eric would have a gun."

Wayan Tyo looked pointedly at his children, who were now looking at me.

"Mmm. We can talk about this later, I guess."

38

I'd whiled away my morning with temple and breakfast, and now it was too hot for a bike ride, so I decided to visit the Puri Lukisan Museum. Then I would spoil myself and take advantage of one of the many spas that line the streets of Ubud.

I looked back at the parking lot as I paid. "No tour buses?" I said.

"No, Bu. Here is a brochure."

Steps rose from the ticket kiosk up to a peaceful and pleasant garden, an oasis on Jalan Raya, Ubud's main street. A series of buildings held the permanent collection and a special exhibition of traditional *kamasan* paintings, where I went first. I particularly liked a scene from the *Mahabharata*, the great Indian epic, with its one figure so much larger than the others. Bima, the son who travels to hell for his father.

I thought of the theme of deliverance, which I kept bumping up against: the relief carvings at Candi Sukuh, the paintings on the Pande temple at Besakih. Clearly the theme still engaged the Balinese. But it was the style that caught my attention even more than the theme. I tried to formulate the steps that would have led an artist from the flat, silhouetted figures before me to the dense, overactive, and charming paintings of the 1920s and '30s.

Could we really credit Westerners with responsibility for this radical shift in artistic production? I worried the puzzle as I walked through the exhibition. Surely I had chosen the best profession anyone could have, thinking about and looking at art. Little by little, I was able to leave behind my thoughts of Flip, provocative even in death.

DEPARTING the museum, I decided to make a quick stop at the hotel for some clean clothes before heading to a spa. If I was lucky, I wouldn't run into Seth and Randall on their way out.

"Can you recommend a spa?" I asked the receptionist when he finished up with another guest. "For a massage."

"Here, Bu." He led me out to the garden and pointed at pavilions that were partially hidden by the landscaping. Behind a screen of plants, each pavilion had a mattress and triangular cushions where one could sit when the pavilions were not being used for massage. They also had thick mosquito nets, which the masseuse had pulled down. "Very good massage. Best Ubud massage."

"You're not biased, are you?" I joked.

"Yes, Bu," he answered seriously.

I laughed. "Fine, in half an hour. Is that okay?"

"Yes, I will tell her."

WITHIN half an hour I was entering a pavilion where the masseuse said, "Take off. Keep underwear."

"I feel exposed," I said. Even though plants and netting blocked the view, I was in the middle of the hotel garden.

She held up a sarong while I stripped, then covered me with it when I lay face down.

I could smell the plumeria, the fragrance like a bowl of just-cut peaches. A bird chirped, then skittered across the pavilion roof. A gentle breeze rustled the netting. She had strong hands, and I had to tell her to rub more gently as she worked first on my feet and legs, then my shoulders and upper back. She told me to turn over, holding the sarong modestly over me as I did. Before she covered my eyes with an eye cover, I glimpsed a bird jump from the roof to a nearby tree. If she hadn't been massaging quite so powerfully, I might well have gone to sleep.

There was a pause as she moved to the head of the table, then she began to massage my shoulders. She continued to work the pressure points, but no longer used the long smooth strokes she had used on my back, and her hands felt harder and larger.

"You haven't changed, have you? Your impulses always get the better of you, don't they?"

I pulled the cover from my eyes. He was bending my left arm back and massaging my forearm in short bursts. Above him the ceiling fan seemed to have picked up speed. The masseuse stood wide-eyed at the edge of the platform.

"I was rereading the report and noticed a mention of a broken thread around Flip's waist. So I went to the house to ask his servants about it." Tyo massaged harder. "They told me that he always wore an amulet in a little silk bag. They said that it was a small sculpture. A god, they thought. Once, when drunk, he showed it to one of them.

"When I asked them why he hadn't had it on him the day he died or if they had taken it, they said no. He had been wearing it. His servant who took you to him, who was with you when you found him, remembered seeing it. She said his sarong had fallen open and she had seen his penis and his amulet, lying next to it. She distinctly remembered."

"Naughty girl," I said.

His eyes flashed. Maybe he didn't have a sense of humor.

"This is not amusing. This is a murder investigation."

"A double murder if you keep rubbing that hard. Gives new meaning to the phrase 'rubbing someone out.'"

He rubbed harder. "Where is it?"

I didn't answer. It was a rope burn, and I recalled he had done that to me as a child. And another memory came to me: his hand yanking me back from the riverbank as it began crumbling beneath me; his shout, "You're crazy"; the beating of our hearts as his twelve-year-old arms hugged me to him, the water rushing below us.

"I'm not going to ask a second time, Jenna. This is a murder investigation."

"Did you, when we were kids, save me from . . ."

"Don't try to distract me. Where is it?"

"I left it at the temple."

"You what?"

"I left it at the temple when I went there with Ani. I don't know why. Suddenly I didn't want to have it on me anymore, and I put it next to the offerings that we had just placed on the altar."

He leaned away from me, though he didn't let go. "You are not serious."

"I'm afraid that I am serious."

"Jenna, that amulet may well have been relevant to the crime."

I nodded. "Yes, maybe. I don't know."

"You know this makes you a suspect. Taking evidence from the scene."

"Do you always interrogate your suspects when they're naked?" I shot back. Of course I was covered by a sarong.

He glared at me. "Should you have been a suspect from the beginning?"

"Of course not."

Absentmindedly massaging my arm, he waited for me to say more. He began to do something nice with my hand, then my fingers, grasping them in both of his hands and rubbing away from the palm. I closed my eyes for a second. He had us both in a trance, a trance that I broke when I pulled at the sarong to better cover myself. He seemed to realize the inappropriateness of what he was doing, and our eyes locked. He hesitated, then picked up my other arm, rubbing it, deep in thought. I felt our breath suspended between us.

Finally he let go. "Stay out of this, Jenna. That sculpture had better be at the temple when I get there. If it isn't, there will be hell to pay."

Where had he heard an expression like that? Did he watch old movies? "I photographed it," I said as quietly as I could.

"Well, that's something. If I don't find it, I will be back here." He stepped down and pulled at the netting. "I'll be back here anyway." Then he walked purposefully across the garden.

I watched him as he reached the path to the lobby. Then I followed the progress of two men rolling their suitcases along behind him. Seth and Randall, headed home. Tyo looked back at the two of them for just a moment, studying Seth. Long enough to suggest he knew I'd been with Seth. My face went hot.

"May I, Bu?" asked the masseuse. Did she know him? Surely she did. Everyone seemed to know him.

I was tempted to say no, but it had felt good. Even when Wayan Tyo had been massaging me. Especially when he had been massaging me. "Please. Can we make it an hour and a half instead of an hour, since we were interrupted?"

What did he mean, he'd be back, anyway?

39

I waited for him at a restaurant across the street from the hotel. I had my dinner at a window table, never taking my eyes off the hotel entrance. I ate quickly, which was just as well, as the *nasi goreng* stuck together as if each individual grain of rice had been glued to the next. The shrimp chips, *krupuk*, were soggy from leaning against the rice, and I made the mistake of ordering a fresh lime soda. They brought me a soda and one small section of lime instead of what I expected, soda mixed with the juice from half a dozen limes.

I'd eaten half the rice and lost my appetite, and was about to pay and go back to my room, when I saw Ulih walking by. I ran to the door and called out to her. She walked distractedly toward me.

"Someone has broken into my shop."

"Oh, no. Did they take much?"

"No. Only a few textiles. But they did take the *kajang*."

"Flip's?"

"Yes. That textile has caused me so much trouble. I had finally decided not to use it in the *kremasi*. The priest I spoke with convinced me that I should not burn it. It was made for another person and would not have been right to put it on Flip's body." She sat opposite me.

"Ah."

"So I was feeling relieved. Then this afternoon I went to pick up my daughter from my sister's. My sister had to go out and could not watch her as she often does. I was gone only a brief time, but when we returned to the shop, the lock on the back door had been broken and someone had been in."

"You don't keep the valuable textiles in a safe?"

"Usually, but I'd been looking at them and was in a hurry to get my daughter, so I hid them behind many other newer textiles. I often do this. I don't worry much about theft."

"Is that what the thief took?"

"Yes. Only that box."

"Who knew about the box?"

"My employee, my sister, my daughter. I am careful when I take something from there. I don't usually pull out my valuable textiles when someone is in the shop. When you were there the other day, I had to get them out of the safe."

"Has anyone else been in the shop when you pulled out the *kajang*?"

She thought for a few moments, then looked at me as if a light had dawned. "Eric Shelley."

"Did he go in the back room with you?"

"No, he was waiting out in the shop."

"Where was he when you came out?"

"He was near the door to the backroom. We'd been talking while I was back there." She ran her finger down my sweaty water glass. "It was him, wasn't it?"

"I suspect it was. Unless there is someone else who might know where you put it."

She thought for a few moments. "The only other person who was in the shop and who I showed the *kajang* to was Esa, but he did not come to the door as Eric did. I had the *kajang* out when he came and he left before I put it away. I am going to the police station." She stood. "I am going to report Eric."

"Why did you show it to Esa?"

"He'd heard I was going to use it and was angry. He wanted to see it."

"That seems an odd reason to show it to him."

"He is an old friend. A childhood friend."

Having given up on Tyo, I walked back to the hotel, wondering if I had met Ulih as a child.

BACK in my room I tried to read, but even detective Dr. Siri in my Lao mystery couldn't hold my attention. Poor Ulih. She had had a terrible time. First Flip, now the textiles. Tyo had to find Eric.

Tyo. I thought of the feel of his hands. I thought of the sensuous strokes as he'd massaged my arms. I thought that he was my brother.

But he wasn't. Saying that you are someone's brother doesn't make you siblings. We did not have the same parents. We had no familial relationship. What was I thinking? My brain felt like a racquetball court, the ball my thoughts. I put down my book and tried to focus on my breathing. Was I really panting? Panting at the thought of him? Panting from apprehension?

I opened my computer to check my emails and before I'd gotten through half of them, my Skype account began to chime. It was Brian.

"You're up early," I said, pleased to hear my friend's voice. I turned on the video.

"Didn't sleep well." He looked a bit rough.

"Lane?" I asked. Brian's partner Lane was very ill and the strain of caring for him was beginning to show on Brian.

"He didn't sleep well either."

"I hope if I'm ever sick, you'll take care of me."

"I'm sure Alam would take good care of you," he countered, but didn't continue along that line. "How are things with this other man?"

I could hear the annoyance in his voice. I knew he liked Alam and thought I should . . . Should what? Give in? Succumb? That's what it felt like to me, that I would be losing a battle. It was not a good way to think of a relationship.

Then I thought of Tyo, but rather than dig myself deeper, I said, "He's gone. Left today."

"I'm glad to hear it."

I ignored that and said, "What's up?"

"Nothing in particular. I was up and thought I'd try you—haven't had much luck getting through."

"No, I've been busy."

"Detecting or studying paintings or biking?"

"A little bit of everything. I went to Java, to Borobudur."

I could see that he was wondering if I had gone alone, but he showed restraint and asked, "Have they caught the killer?"

"No."

"Have you gotten into trouble yet?"

"No." But he must have heard hesitation in my voice.

"No, but?"

"Someone shot at me."

""Why did I ask," he groaned. "I'm taking it that the bullet didn't find its mark?"

"No. Not even close." I'd tell him about the whizzing when I got home. No point worrying him. "I had a great massage today."

He smiled. "That's more like it." He turned from the video cam and said, "I'll be right there."

I wanted to talk more. I wanted a conversation that allowed me to tell all, a talk that would tire me out. He'd been my confidant and I wanted to tell him how I was feeling. He was also a smart man who might well help me think through the clues of the murder. I could tell him about the amulet and he wouldn't judge me. I could, but I stopped myself, and said, "Say hi to Lane for me."

"I will. And keep out of trouble. We'll continue this conversation later."

He was gone.

I got up and paced, reaching for the amulet, remembering as my hand slid into my pants pocket that I'd gotten rid of it. I'd created a problem there. I'd walked into a temple and put a piece of evidence for a murder investigation on an altar. Tyo hadn't come back, so maybe he'd found it.

I picked up my phone, then looked at the clock. Ten-thirty. I'd spent hours not reading, obsessing. He wasn't going to come, and I wasn't going to sleep.

He'd probably meant that he would be back to arrest me if the sculpture wasn't at the temple. Or maybe he was just quoting Arnold.

My conversation with Brian had slowed down that racquetball, but it hadn't stilled it. If I could do that, maybe I could figure out what I was thinking. Maybe I could figure out my relationship with Tyo. When he'd said that he would be back, I had jumped to a conclusion based on my usual relationship with a man. Lover. But he was not a lover. He was a man I'd known as a child, an old friend. He was a cop investigating a murder that I had discovered.

I stopped at the window and pulled aside the curtain to look out. Maybe he really did suspect me, and that's why he was sticking close. And that's why he had said he would be back.

I sat on the bed and crossed my legs.

But there was our breathing. There was the electric connection that passed between us when we touched. There was comfort and an understanding when we were together. We kept drawing close, then pulling back, or at least he pulled back. At least he pulled back about discussing the murder. But he hadn't pulled back when he was massaging me. Even when I'd joked that it was inappropriate, he'd continued. He might be as confused as I. Maybe he was lying in bed wondering what he'd meant.

I'd see him tomorrow at the cremation. Or maybe he would come by my hotel to tell me that he had or hadn't found the sculpture. He might avoid me. I fell back and closed my eyes.

40

Because I was with Ani, the people controlling the crowds allowed me to walk in the funeral procession rather than pushing me to the sidewalk with the tourists. We followed the cremation tower, carried aloft by a dozen men arrayed amid a bamboo latticework tied together with rope. The men wore black polo shirts, a uniform of sorts. The tower was tall and multi-leveled. Ulih had told me the number of its levels for Flip's funeral had been a source of dissension. They had decided on seven. On one side of the tower, a painted styrofoam Boma face, a protective deity, watched over the proceedings. Animal heads adorned the other sides, all brightly colored and slightly whimsical. A priest dressed in white led the procession, and musicians striking gongs and beating slit drums followed us. Women carried offerings on their heads, and some of the men not supporting the bamboo platform were clustered around its edges, giving moral support by shouting to their friends. Others marched ahead of the tower.

"Where is the casket?" I shouted to Ani in the din. We'd briefly stepped out of the procession and were now watching the tower pass along with the tourists cramming the sidewalks.

"It is above Boma's head. There. You see the white cloth draped over it and umbrellas shading it? The umbrellas above it indicate its importance. You see the sarcophagus behind." She pointed to a second group of men who carried the bull-shaped sarcophagus on another latticework platform. They wore yellow shirts, and I wondered if there was a reason for the distinction in what people wore, but the crowd was too noisy for me to ask too many questions of Ani. "The casket will be transferred into there at the cremation grounds."

Westerners surrounded us, cameras raised, cheerfully talking about what they were seeing. The Balinese were just as loud, just as cheerful. "It's not like a Western funeral," I said. "Not the usual solemn and sad faces." People joked amongst themselves or called out to friends in the crowd. Young children rode shoulders, while the older children darted in and out, chasing each other, teasing and taunting.

"No," was all she said as she took my hand and we stepped back into the procession.

Though it felt as if we were moving at the same speed as the other participants, I noticed that people seemed to make way for us as we walked along, and I was uncertain if it was because of Ani or if they moved away from us because they thought that I was polluting.

Ani spoke in my ear as we continued to move toward the cremation grounds. "For the cremation, we make many offerings. First the bier and the sarcophagus are purified and blessed by offerings and the priest's words. You already know that we use a shroud to be burned with the body. Like the one that was stolen from Ulih, but you see that a plain white cloth is stretched over the body now."

Her mention of Ulih made me look around for her, though it would be difficult to find anyone in the throng of locals and Westerners. I scanned those around me, trying to focus on individuals. I saw a young woman crying, huge fat tears rolling down her face.

All that I had learned about Flip over the past week had not prepared me for the fact that people had cared for him. Ulih's mourning made sense to me, as he was the father of her child. They had more than a passing relationship. But I saw now that he'd touched many lives, women's lives by the look of it. The lump in my throat reminded me that our hearts are not rational organs.

"I'm surprised so many mourn him."

Ani said, "Loss is a powerful emotion. You know this, I think."

"Yes," I said.

The procession wound onto the cremation grounds and stopped. Ani nodded toward the sarcophagus, which had preceded the tower.

While the tower's multiple levels were adorned with various brightly colored animal heads, the bull's grandeur lay in its simplicity. A deep maroon fabric had been stretched over a wooden frame and batting. Gold jewels hung around his neck, and gold paint covered his testicles. He stood head and shoulders over the crowd, a smiling creature.

Moving the body from the height of the tower took a large number of men and a great deal of time. The transfer of the other bodies being cremated happened more quickly, and I turned my attention from one to another. I didn't think Ulih had said that she was related to any of the others, but maybe I was mistaken. Maybe she was with one of them. The crowd milled around; hawkers sold food; a few others attempted to sell souvenirs to the tourists who watched. While the crowd had been segregated on the walk to the cremation grounds, now locals mingled with foreigners.

"You see that large tray over there." Ani pointed to the other side of the bull, beyond the commotion of the transfer.

"Yes."

"There are many objects on the tray, and they represent different parts of the body. Flip's body. There are eggs for eyeballs and corn for teeth. The heart is a banana bud. You can make that out from here. See those cucumbers? They represent the legs. It is prescribed that we use the many parts of the body, dozens of parts, for the cremation. Sometimes it is difficult to find all the plant parts of the body for the cremation, which is a problem. They are all a necessary part of the offering that will be burned with the body."

"Can't you substitute?"

"No. They are the body. You can no more substitute a gourd for a cucumber or beans for corn than I could cut off your leg and attach a cucumber in its place." She took my elbow. "Let us walk over there. We are in the way of the wind here, and when the fire begins we do not want to breathe in the smoke. It will be some time, as the priests must perform the burial rites."

I wondered if the smoke coming from the burning body emitted some sort of negative force or influence, or if Ani just didn't like smoke. Surely we could see more clearly from here. Then I noticed that few of the locals stood to this side, which was where most of the foreigners stood. "Do you see Ulih?" I was getting anxious.

Ani stopped and looked off toward the priest and the group of men who stood to one side of him. She frowned. "I do not. That is very odd. Unless . . ."

"Unless?"

She shook an idea from her mind. "She would not have arranged the cremation for her time of the month. No woman would be foolish enough to do that. She should be over in that area, near the priests and Flip's servants. Her daughter is there with Ulih's sister, but I do not see her."

"Is there any reason she would be watching any of the other cremations?"

"No, I don't think so. Let's just have a quick walk to see."

We didn't find her in any of the other groups clustered around bodies and sarcophagi, so we returned to the ceremony at Flip's body.

We watched Ulih's sister, her hands on her niece's shoulders. They also seemed to be looking for Ulih, worried expressions furrowing their brows.

"Let us go to find her." Ani held my elbow more tightly. Again the crowd parted as we turned away from the sarcophagus and hurried from the ceremony. Ani steered me to the left, toward the center of town and Ulih's shop.

"You could wait here and I could go alone," I offered, not really wanting to leave but thinking it was silly for both of us to go. I did want to watch the cremation.

"It is close. We shouldn't take long. The transfer of the casket and the rites will take a long time."

"Where are you going?" Wayan Tyo called from behind us. We stopped. I hadn't seen him in the midst of the men surrounding the two platforms. He walked toward us, away from Esa, who scowled at us.

Both men wore traditional sarongs, the shorter top cloth revealing the folds of a longer sarong beneath. Wayan Tyo's upper sarong had a band of gold threads at the bottom, while the under sarong was a Yogyakarta brown-and-blue batik. Ani had encouraged me to wear a sarong, and I had bought an orange *kebaya*, a blouse I thought would look good at home with a pair of leggings that I favored as much as the multicolored sarong I had also purchased. I wondered if it was my attempt to look native that caused Esa to scowl, though it was just as likely that it was my very presence.

"Ulih isn't at the ceremony," Ani said. "We are worried and are going to find her. We will not be long."

"I will join you," Wayan Tyo said.

He walked ahead, and I noticed a kris stuck in the back of his sash in the traditional manner. I supposed he wore it for the ceremony. "I find that reassuring," I said, pointing to it. One murder and now the missing Ulih put me on edge.

He didn't answer, clearly still angry with me.

She wasn't at the shop, so Wayan Tyo decided we should check her home, which was not far from the center of town. I was surprised to see the town as crowded as it was, since it had seemed that everyone was attending the cremation, tourists and locals alike.

Her house lay down a short lane amid a profusion of fruit-bearing trees: banana, mango, and rambutan. Chimes hung from low and high branches and tinkled in the slight breeze, the thin metal rods sounding light and delicate, while pieces of bamboo clonked together in deeply resonant tones. The circular stepping-stones leading to her front door consisted of small, smooth river rocks and sparkling rounded glass, and I realized that each individual stepping-stone was not a composite whole but small stones clustered together and set into the ground. I could imagine Ulih and her daughter creating the abstract form made up of one stone, one piece of glass after another, little magical steps to their front door.

As in all Balinese homes, the door was not locked, and we entered as we called out. Flowered plants filled the hallway, while orchids of various types drooped from the containers on the walls and from planters, their heavy buds arching over the long narrow table along the wall on the left. A small fountain muttered at the foot of the stairs. Above it hung the most beautiful Sumatran textile I had ever seen. Gold threads whose patterns approximated sea creatures crowded over the muted, natural dyes of the *ikat* sarong, drowned in their writhing and twisting on the abstract ground, where they lay on the seabed for eternity. I shivered.

"Ulih," Wayan Tyo called.

The silence felt heavy, as everyone was probably at the funeral. We walked into the living room. More textiles hung on the walls, each as exquisite as the next, their colors dark and saturated. Ulih had told me that she had her best pieces at home. That was an understatement.

"Not in the other rooms downstairs," said Ani as she moved past us to look out at the back garden. "Let's look upstairs."

I led the way, slowing as I passed a superb woven mat that graced the wall on the stairs. The woven reeds appeared like tiny spears, small darts held together by darker threads. Wayan Tyo took a step that brought him close enough that I felt his breath on my neck. "Sorry," I said.

The first room was her daughter's, simple with a narrow bed covered by a pink coverlet and a shelf with her toys neatly arranged. A lovely batik took the place of a closet door.

Walking down the short hall, I saw the curtains in Ulih's bedroom billowing in a sudden gust of wind and heard the chimes in the front and backyards throw up a cacophony of sound. The bamboo chimes rose above the more delicate ceramic and clinking, the drumbeat of the gamelan, endless, haunting. I stepped into the room. "Oh, no," I said. My stomach lurched. I felt lightheaded.

She lay before us, dressed for the funeral. Her right arm, bent behind her, grasped the kitchen knife stuck in her back, as if she was trying to pull it out. Her left hand held a white scarf in preparation for the cremation.

I wobbled. Ani moved next to me and grasped my arm tightly.

Because Flip had been a stranger, seeing him had been unreal, looking down on him like viewing a movie. This was different. Ulih and I had begun a friendship, woven together by her textiles, by Flip in her life, his death in mine. I covered my mouth with my hand.

Seeing my distress, Wayan Tyo said to Ani, "Take her out."

Ani pulled at my arm.

"No," I said, kneeling down. "I think she just moved."

WE agreed that Wayan Tyo would accompany her to the hospital. I wanted to go with them, but he prevailed, and Ani and I went back to the ceremony to inform her sister and daughter. The poor little girl had already suffered enough grief. First the loss of the father she barely knew. Now her mother on her way to the hospital.

We arrived just as the flames of the pyre rose to engulf the sarcophagus. The fires on the smaller cremations were dying out.

"Let's wait a few moments," Ani said as we approached Ulih's sister and daughter. But her sister started at the sight of us. Dragging the girl behind her, she rushed over.

"What is it?"

"She's injured. We have a car waiting to take you to the hospital."

"Injured? How? What happened? Did she fall?"

Ani and I looked at each other. Ani said, "She was stabbed."

The child burst into tears.

"Let me take you to the car. Wait here," Ani said to me. "I'll be right back."

As they rushed away, long snaky flames wrapped around the bull's head, and he breathed a billow of smoke from his mouth. The crowd let out a united "Ah." I was too emotionally drained to think about what it all meant.

41

"There is a good chance that she will live," Tyo said as we greeted him by the entrance to Ani's house.

"Did she tell you who did this to her?"

"No, she is unconscious, and they think she may well be for quite some time. Hopefully she will live long enough to tell us." He looked grim as we followed him to the main courtyard.

"Hopefully she'll live long enough to raise her daughter."

He looked at his mother. "I need to eat something."

Ani headed toward the kitchen.

"I have never had anything like this," said Tyo as he sat on the bench at the base of the tree. "My cases are usually straightforward. A man kills his wife for adultery. Or gets drunk and in a fight that accidentally ends in a death. Once I had a suspicious drowning."

"A drowning?"

"In a swimming pool in one of the hotels. It turned out to be an accident. Rarely have I had to figure out who did it. It has generally been clear, as the murder was committed out of anger or jealousy. Because of a simple, straightforward emotion that a person can understand. I do not understand this."

"You're right. This attack on Ulih doesn't make sense. It doesn't fit in with anything else." I tilted my head back and looked up, the blue of the sky becoming the positive, the leaves of the gigantic tree the negative. I needed that light.

Wayan Tyo took the plate from Ani, then remembered himself and offered it to me.

"I am getting her one now," Ani said.

"I'm fine. I don't need anything." I sat next to him, the hairs on my arm standing up as my elbow hit his.

Ani ignored me and headed back toward the kitchen.

"Except Eric Shelley," said Tyo as he spooned up some rice. "It fits with Eric Shelley."

"The painting he traded her, you mean?"

"Yes."

I tried to think why Eric would kill her because of the painting. Had she told him that the police knew he'd taken it? But then wouldn't she have said that the police had the painting now? Maybe he hadn't even given her a chance to say that. Maybe since he'd already killed Flip, it wasn't anything to kill her. "Seeing her lying there like that was awful."

"Yes." He held his spoon, but made no move to eat.

"Because I had met her? Or do you think it's because she's a woman?"

He shook his head.

"I thought we were becoming friends," I said, then caught myself. "*Are* becoming friends. Seeing her like that hit me so hard. I thought I was going to pass out."

"Yes." He ate the mouthful of rice.

"Maybe it's the feeling that life is so uncertain. That bad things can just keep happening again and again, and we have no control over them."

Ani set a plate before me, briefly put her hand on my shoulder, then walked away.

"Nothing is certain."

"I came back. You said you were certain that I would return. Ani said the same."

"Yes, you came back. But you will not stay." An edge of sadness crept into his voice.

"I'll keep coming back. I'm drawn to this place. I have to make my pilgrimages to Borobudur, to Angkor." I spoke without thinking, until I saw the pain crease his brow.

"You've been back before. You came back, but we did not see you."

"No, I haven't been back here, not to Bali. I went to Java about eight years ago. Between undergraduate and graduate school. I had three months to travel and little money. I spent two months in Southeast Asia and a month in India and Nepal. I had to make choices, and one choice that I made was to visit the temples of central Java rather than come back to Bali. I saw what I was doing as work, seeking the direction of my future studies, and Bali sounded like pleasure. It had nothing to do with you, your family, us."

He looked past me beyond the large tree that dominated the courtyard. He moved his fingers as if counting.

I fiddled with my spoon and suddenly saw the expanse of my life, my travels through Asia, through Europe. My years in school and the possibilities of my career. I saw the circumscribed space of Wayan Tyo's existence here in Ubud. Saw it as I had imagined Esa's. "My time here is only bits of memories, nothing coherent. A smell, a moment, a passing feeling. I was too young. I can't put the experience in any order, and now any order that I would have created is altered by being here. Now that I'm here, gaps are filled in, bits of memory have become complete memories.

"That first night that I saw Ani, I told her a complete story of a young artist selling paintings all those years ago. It was complete because over the years that memory was embroidered by my parents. Of course I remember you, but I remember you as a boy who was older than me and who I chased when we played tag. I recall holding your hand. There was a time that we sat on a log and the light around us was filtered. A forest? Recently I remembered the river. Your hand grabbing my collar."

I waited, but he didn't volunteer any details.

"I think when I was younger I remembered more. Ani was more present to me, though if you had asked me about her before I arrived here last week, I wouldn't have been able to tell you more than that she was lovely. Even those later memories are merely . . ." I moved my hand in an arc. "They passed, they faded. So when you say to me, don't you remember? I have to say no, my summer here when I was eight had probably lost its weight by the time I reached twenty."

I took a bite of rice, with some *sambal* on it to add a little spice. He continued looking into the distance, at the wall of the compound. Finally he spoke. "Your time here shaped my life. For the first ten years after you stayed with us, we heard from your family. Then we did not hear anymore. It was difficult to know what that meant. Still I waited. Meanwhile I chose a moral life, working as a policeman helping people.

"It was the summer that you were in Java, maybe after you left Java, maybe the moment you decided not to return to Bali, that I proposed to my wife. She was not a good choice for me, my mother told me. I did not listen. Most mothers tell their children, marry, marry, have children. My mother tried to keep me from marrying Manis. She told me to wait for the right one. I couldn't. Since I was a boy, I thought the right one was you and that you were never coming back."

I was shaken. Our connection felt deep, but was that what it was? And how would our lives ever come together, him here, me there?

He echoed my thoughts. "Not that I believed that you would come back and we would marry. We live too far apart. Our worlds will only occasionally converge. Our lives are threads the shuttle joined when we were young. Like brother and sister, we did not choose each other, yet our fate is intertwined. We complete each other."

He shook off his reverie. "I find it very difficult."

Had he woven us with his words? Or was he correct in saying that we had been woven together as children and would find ourselves always intertwined? I didn't know and wondered at my own lack of self-awareness. But, then, I realized it wasn't that. Our histories, our cultures, had led us to view our relationship in radically different ways. His traditional point of view had seen our only possible link as marriage, while I had seen him as one of the many people I had met in my travels, in my much more unstructured life.

If I looked at it from his perspective, would I wonder if I had stumbled all my life in search of this man? I hoped that wasn't the case. He was right that our paths could never easily become one.

42

I was lying in the cocoon of mosquito netting, the curtains still drawn, the cacophony of competing roosters dying down. Morning was happening out there, and I was immobilized. I would have been far better off if I'd gotten up early, mounted my bike, and ridden all the way to the east coast of the island for a swim. I wouldn't have been able to think beyond the worries of what trucker, what motorcyclist might run me over.

I'd botched many things in my life, and now I had to figure out a way not to botch what I had here in Bali. First I had to figure out what I had. Or I needed to not figure it out and just go along and see what happened. But wasn't that what Wayan Tyo had said to me as he rubbed my arm in that seductive and voluptuous way? That I brashly ran into everything.

I'd come to Bali to do research. That was what I should do. Maybe if I narrowed my focus and took it one painting at a time, the path would lead me out of any potential muddle in my personal life. I imagined an Ida Bagus Made before me, the concentration I would need to consider all aspects of the work—the brushwork, the composition, the influences on his style. Who he influenced. The subject matter of the painting, the details. But even in my imaginings, I found myself getting into trouble with this basic art-historical task. I searched in my fantasy painting for an oak leaf.

Here lay the root of my muddle, one of my muddles, this intersection of my research with the role of Flip and pre-war modernist painting in the murder. I found a motive for murder in every painting that I looked at. If I convinced myself that the motive for the murder lay elsewhere—an angry husband, a fired employee, some other dealing of Flip's—then I might be able to do my own work without straying back to his murder. Of course, the attempt on Ulih's life gave us a suspect—Eric Shelley—and the motive—paintings. He'd given her that painting to repay a debt and then realized he'd made a mistake. Maybe she had confronted him. But was that right?

I needed to separate the forgeries from the murder, since the murder didn't have anything to do with me other than the fact that I happened to find the body. But that wasn't true. Someone had tried to run me over. Someone had shot at me. Eric Shelley, no doubt. I thought of Tyo. Oh, god. I rolled on my side, reached under my pillow. My hand came out empty.

The other muddle. Tyo. A larger, more personal muddle, not easily considered. My mind ran from its confusion, a confusion compounded by thoughts of Alam.

I would spend this morning on my computer, going through the Searles collection of paintings to compile a list of questions for Made. I'd come to Ubud with questions for Flip, but that list of questions had grown since I'd arrived. With my new understanding of the fakery involved in Balinese painting, the questions I needed to ask were different. I needed a foundation for understanding each individual painter and his style before I could come to terms with the forgeries. Made's teaching had furthered my research and knowledge. He had also shifted my thinking on the subject from a purely stylistic analysis to a deeper comprehension of genealogies of teachers and the influences among artists.

On my back again, I pulled my knees up to make a tent. The simple, repetitive exercise of examining one painting after another should focus my mind. No thoughts of murder. No deeper reflection on Wayan Tyo.

Ulih was unconscious in the hospital. I twisted, leaning up on one elbow. I had to go see her. I couldn't even consider that she might die. She had to be doing well. I'd work in my room today and keep out of trouble, only venturing out to the hospital this afternoon. I would also avoid Tyo. Of course, tonight I needed to go to Made's opening, and I suspected Tyo would be there, but in the midst of a crowd our conversation shouldn't be too fraught.

If I worked for an hour or so before breakfast, it would be easier for me to continue working after. Enjoying a last few minutes in my mosquito net tent, I sank back into that liminal state between sleeping and wakefulness and thought of Seth, whose hands became Wayan Tyo's. All the while, Alam was watching me, a disappointed expression on his face. Aargh. Pushing them all out of my mind, I stepped out of the bed into my room.

THE French couple had either finished eating or left Ubud. A family of four, the parents intent on making their children eat things the children didn't want to eat, had just begun their meal. As I took my usual seat, two boisterous Australian couples, clearly traveling together and making up for the eight hours apart since the previous night, entered, reciting to each other their recent bar-hopping escapades. One woman kept saying, "I don't remember that," while the other three gleefully detailed her inebriated adventures. I watched them as they moved my way. Just my luck that their table of choice was the one next to me. I considered flight, but I was hungry.

Ketut set down the pot of tea in front of me and gave me a rueful grimace. "What can you do?" I said. We shrugged in unison.

One thing I could do would be to eat a light meal and eat it quickly. I went to the buffet and withstood the temptations, settling on yogurt and papaya.

Cutting up my papaya, I didn't see Wayan Tyo until he pulled out the chair to sit opposite me.

He didn't speak.

"*Selamat pagi,*" I greeted him, then asked if he was well. "*Apa kabar?*"

"*Baik. Anda juga?*" he asked in return.

"I'm well."

"No nightmares with soundtracks?"

I shook my head, thinking about the intimacy of having breakfast with someone. So close to sleep, so close to the bed, not yet completely in the world. I'd been up for hours and was entirely present, so I tried to shake intimacy from my thoughts. But when he'd pulled in his chair, his knee touched mine, and he'd made no attempt to move it. I took a breath, "No nightmares, with or without soundtracks. Did you sleep well?"

"My daughter had a bad dream. And I didn't sleep at all."

I spooned a bite of yogurt and papaya into my mouth and didn't take the bait. "Would you like something to eat? Tea? Coffee?"

"Bali coffee," he said to Ketut.

"*Susu?*" Did he want milk?

He declined. "*Tidak.*"

Neither of us spoke for a moment. There was no need for words. Or there was a terrible need, but I had no idea what words to use.

"Where is the man?" he said.

"What man?"

"Who went with you to Java."

I hesitated, remembering him watch Seth and Randall trundle down the path with their suitcases. He hadn't known it was Seth, had just been speculating. "He went home."

He looked at me thoughtfully. "Is that why you were with him? Because you knew that he would go home soon?"

"In part." I didn't want to ask, but couldn't stop myself. "Does Ani know?"

"No. I wouldn't want to disappoint her."

"Neither would I," I countered, though I wondered if she would be more disappointed than Wayan Tyo. I had finished my yogurt and papaya but still had tea to keep me occupied. I spooned honey into the cup and looked out at the garden, hoping to catch sight of the nectar-eating bird. "How is Ulih?"

"They say she will live. I just came from the hospital. She's not awake yet." He fiddled with my water glass.

"Thank goodness."

"Jenna," he began, then seemed to change his mind about what to say. "I have given more thought to your cataloguing of Flip's collection."

"And that bloke from Perth, the one who sells art," said the loudest of the four Australians. "He was something, he was. Drank more and faster than any of us. Even you, Stacey."

They all laughed. Wayan Tyo and I looked at each other, both of us listening attentively.

"What was his name?" Stacey asked.

"Who knows? Bloke didn't tell us, did he? He just drank and drank, trying to put us all under the table. Grim, he got, didn't he?"

"Maudlin, you'd say. Downright maudlin, hanging on you, Stacey. You'd a thought he was your long-lost lover."

"She acted it," said the other woman.

Stacey glared at her. "I'm getting one of those pancakes. You want one, honey?" she asked her boyfriend.

He wasn't having any of it, including the pancake, clearly not liking Stacey's interaction with the bloke from Perth.

Wayan Tyo turned toward them. "Excuse me, *maaf,*" he said.

The woman facing us looked startled.

"Could you tell me what your Australian bloke from Perth looked like?"

"You listening in on our conversation?" said the boyfriend, shifting his bulk in Tyo's direction.

"I couldn't help but overhear. I have been looking for an art dealer from Perth, and it sounds as if you may have found him for me."

"What for?" asked the other man, as aggressively as his buddy. The two undoubtedly had participated in bar brawls together.

"He has a painting that we want," I said in my most concilia-tory voice.

Tyo looked at me. "Yes, that's right. But he seems to have moved hotels."

"Wasn't staying in a hotel, was he?" said Stacey as she re-turned to the table with a plate piled high with crepes. How on earth could she eat, as green as she was?

The other three looked at her.

"Thought you didn't remember him," accused her boyfriend.

"I remember when he introduced himself and you were talk-ing about our hotel and asked him where he was staying, and he said with a friend. Didn't he?"

The other woman said, "Yeah, that's right. He was staying with a friend."

"Did he tell you where his friend lived?" asked Tyo.

"Nah," said the boyfriend.

The other was more thoughtful. "Wait a minute. He said he was staying near our home-stay, in the neighborhood, didn't he?"

I asked, "Was he tall and thin? Kind of wild blond hair, dried out, like he did a lot of swimming in a chlorinated pool or had never heard of conditioner?"

The two women laughed, and the one said, "Sounds about right. Bad teeth."

"Blue eyes," said Stacey, digging an ever-deeper hole for herself.

Her boyfriend gave her a look. "But you thought he was kind of cute, didn't you?"

"Not really," she said mindlessly, slathering butter on her crepe, which was already cold, so by the time she finished it looked like a sheet of paper covered with a thick coating of gesso.

Wayan Tyo looked at me questioningly and I nodded. "Sounds like him."

"This is your hotel?" he asked as he stood up.

"Nah, ours doesn't have breakfast," said one of the men. "Came here to eat. We're trying out as many hotels as possible. For next time."

The other woman delved in her bag and pulled out a card. "I have a couple of them. You need them if you want the drivers to get you to the right place. They never understand what you're talking about. I wish their English was better."

They probably wished you could say two words in Indonesian or Balinese, I thought. "I'll go with you."

"No. I've arranged for you to go back to Flip's to look at more paintings."

"Really?"

"Yes, the girls are expecting you. I'll see you at lunch," he called over his shoulder.

"You'd think he was a copper the way he hurried out that door," said Stacey. "On the trail of a murderous suspect."

Yes, you would, I thought, relieved that he'd left without us having a serious conversation. And a bit peeved that he'd left without me. But then I didn't really want to go searching for Eric, especially if he was the one who had killed Flip, tried to kill Ulih, and shot at me. I'd much rather look at paintings.

I opened my computer to check my e-mail and discovered a lengthy message from P.P. Lengthy for him. Three lines telling me that he might not come and asking again what I thought of the sculpture that he was considering. Come? I thought I had dissuaded him of that idea. I needed to make certain he didn't.

That was something else I needed to do. Find someone who made bronze sculptures of buddhas and bodhisattvas. I'd have to search for that name Esa had given me. Which reminded me, Wayan Tyo hadn't told me if he had found the amulet at the temple. Withholding information once again. Well, I hadn't asked, both wanting to know everything and not wanting to know anything. I also didn't want him to think too much about my taking the amulet.

I quickly typed an e-mail to P.P. telling him that he should definitely not come and definitely not bring the sculpture to Bali, that I hadn't yet located a foundry where they made high-quality bronzes, nor had I seen anything like his piece in Bali, and reminding him that I would be back soon. Then I deleted what I'd written, deciding that going back to the room and Skyping him would be more persuasive, even though the online connection had proven frustrating before. I sensed he needed face time, and maybe I did, too.

The Australians stood to go. "Good hunting," said one of the men. "Is that guy a cop?"

"Yes," I said, seeing no harm.

"What did that bloke do?" asked the woman.

"He's a suspect in a murder case and in an attempted murder case."

Stacey's eyes widened. "Yikes," she said. "That's scary."

"Yes, it is."

"Better watch who you cozy up to," said the other girl to Stacey.

"I wasn't cozying up to him!"

"Yeah, right," said her boyfriend, grasping her arm roughly as he steered her toward the door.

43

"P.P., I told you it's pointless to come here."
I adjusted the screen on my computer to avoid the glare from the
window behind me.

"Yes. Bought the miniature. Lovely. Mewar."

Thrown off track, I said, "Sounds good."

"Portrait. Raja such and such."

"On a horse?"

"As usual." He was rummaging in a drawer as he spoke, so
that all I could see was the top of his head.

"That's great, P.P., but about Bali. I haven't located a foundry
where they make such things. I suspect they're producing them
in the area of Solo, but I haven't been able to go there to research
it." It had proven more difficult to find a foundry in Bali than I'd
anticipated. I thought of Mandalay in Myanmar or Chiang Mai
in Thailand, where one could easily see bronze sculptures being
made. I didn't need to tell P.P. that I had driven through Solo on
my way to Candi Sukuh. Or that I had the name of a foundry
from Esa, but it was on the other side of the island.

"Anyone else murdered?"

"As a matter of fact."

"Not you. That's good."

"Well . . ." I debated whether to tell him about my brush with a bullet, my close call with a car.

"The investigation?"

"It's not going so well. We think that it had something to do with Flip's forgeries."

This caught his attention. He raised his head—thankfully, as it's disconcerting speaking to a man's bald spot. "Forgeries? This is art related?"

I told him about cataloguing Flip's paintings, about Eric.

"But why?"

"Why what?"

"Why do forgeries have anything to do with it?"

"Well. I suppose we thought they did because it was illegal business that he was involved in. Seems likely, doesn't it?"

"No other possibilities?"

"He was a philanderer."

"Good possibility." He bent over again and straightened up quickly, so that I only had to view his thinning hair for a moment. "Here." He held up the painting he had just purchased.

"Move back a little."

The portrait filled the screen, the raja seated on his elegant piebald horse, two of his children walking to one side and a servant holding the horse's lead. "You didn't tell me it had children in it. They add charm to the work. Wonderful purchase."

He turned it around and looked at it. "What else?"

"What else?"

He looked around his office. "An echo?"

"Very funny. You mean what other possibilities are there? Well, a servant, an irate husband or boyfriend. Painting forgeries, though it could have been some other kind of forgery. He had an entire building of weapons, sculpture, and decorative art. He had some sculpture."

"Wealthy?"

"By Western standards? Probably not terribly. By Balinese standards, yes."

"Heirs?"

"His daughter, though no one knew she was his daughter."

"The daughter?"

"She's about ten."

"The mother?"

"No, I've met her and like her and she couldn't have driven a spear through him. I think, we think, it had to be a man." I hesitated. "Plus, someone tried to kill her and me."

"Nice spear?" The collector rose in him at the mention of an object. He either ignored or didn't want to hear that someone had tried to kill Ulih and me.

"Yes, nice spear."

"Old?"

"Probably."

"Why you?"

I told him about finding Eric Shelley with his hand in the till, so to speak. I didn't mention the amulet.

He squinted at me. "Nothing else?"

"No." I could tell he didn't quite believe me.

He was thoughtful, running his finger around the outline of the raja and his horse. Fortunately, the painting was mounted and behind glass. "Painting forgery and theft are possibilities. No more likely than a servant. You need to explore other avenues."

"You may be right. Now, about Bali."

He shook his head as if Bali were a ridiculous idea. "Going to Paris in two hours. Have to go. Bye." He closed our connection, leaving me with my mouth open.

I continued to sit in front of my computer. It was right what he said. There was no logical reason why the murder had to do with paintings rather than an angry husband. Well, Eric Shelley was in the art business, but his actions might be separate from Flip's forgeries. They might have to do with his theft of paintings after the death. Though that might mean that there were two murderers—the person who had killed Flip for some unknown reason, and Eric, who was the logical suspect in Ulih's attack and the attempts on my life.

My finding Flip, my being in Bali because of paintings, had steered both Tyo and me to exploring Flip's painting interests—and business—as the motive. Maybe I'd sent us off in the wrong direction. Because of my own focus, I'd steered Tyo toward forgeries when the real reason might be something completely different. Throughout the investigation, I had single-mindedly focused on Flip and his painting. Whenever Tyo and I spoke, I had asserted some new aspect of the forgery issue, pushing the investigation back toward that.

Of course, maybe Tyo was exploring other avenues, which would explain why he kept trying to block my participation in the investigation. I looked out the window.

What did we really know? There were no clues, other than the spear and the fact that the person who drove it through Flip was probably male. An angry act. A crime of passion. But wronged husbands don't carry around spears. Or maybe they do. I shook my head.

Then there was Eric. True, his theft of Flip's paintings had fueled the forgery fire. Surely it did more than fuel it. Maybe Flip's murder and the attempt on Ulih weren't connected, though that would be difficult to believe, given the low murder rate in Ubud. Eric was the only connection between the two. He had to be the murderer.

What did Flip and Eric have in common? Paintings. An interest in Balinese women. Maybe they had both had an affair with the same woman and her husband/boyfriend had done Flip in. Which would mean that Eric was in danger. Though that didn't explain the attempt on Ulih's life. Still, I'd have to ask Tyo to check that out. P.P. was right. There were other avenues to explore.

I thought of the amulet and groaned.

I powered down and closed my laptop but continued to sit there, my hand resting on the cover. The other thing that Flip and Eric had in common was that they were both foreigners: not just tourists but foreigners who either lived or spent a great deal of time in Bali. Maybe they'd been involved in some business deal together. Something other than painting. Property. Or . . . I couldn't think of anything else. Flip had been killed with a traditional weapon, which made his murder appear to be premeditated, since who carries around a kris or, more to the point—terrible pun—a spear?

I needed to talk with Tyo.

44

Studying small works on paper is a pleasant and easy task. You pull open a drawer, extract the drawing or painting, place it before you, and voilà. But this afternoon I was following Wayan Tyo's instructions and cataloguing the large paintings. I'd been working for three hours, and my shoulders and my bruised rib were feeling the strain. I needed to pull out the painting from the stack, lean it against the other canvases, then go back and forth between paintings and desk as I entered the information into my computer. The process took longer, the light was worse on that side of the room, and I was tiring quickly, for although most of the canvases were unframed, some had bulky, ornately carved frames.

I needed help. Maybe Wayan Tyo had a strong policeman he could spare. Or maybe Made knew a student who could help me. I would ask them tonight at the opening.

While Flip's servants had paid me some attention during my first stint of cataloguing, dropping by to give me something to drink or asking if I wanted anything, they were steering clear today. I think Tyo had put the fear of God in them with his admonitions about Eric. Now I needed a cup of tea. I also needed some lunch, which reminded me. Tyo had said that he would see me at lunch. Surprising that he was so late, as he seemed to have a stomach that worked like clockwork. If I went ahead and ate without him, I could avoid a conversation, deep or otherwise. I decided to lock up and go find food.

I pulled out my phone to check the time as I walked along the path toward the main house. One-thirty. No wonder I was hungry. I noticed that there was a text and checked it as I neared the kitchen. Another terse text from Tyo, "Cannot make it." Maybe he had found Eric. Or maybe he hadn't and was still looking? Either way, I was relieved.

Looking in the kitchen door, I was surprised to see a Western kitchen straight out of *Architectural Digest*. Granite countertops, stainless-steel appliances that included a six-burner gas stove, a convection oven in addition to a regular oven, the most enormous refrigerator that I'd ever seen, and a smaller, narrower one by the door where I stood. Three women puttered around the kitchen, talking and chopping. Both activities stopped as one by one they saw me standing at the door. A beautiful bouquet sat on a large table by the window. The chairs were pushed back. Probably where they had sat crying the day of the murder.

"Bu. Lunch?"

"Yes, please. Wayan Tyo is not coming."

They looked relieved. Pulling me into the kitchen, they waved me down a hall into the living-dining area. It was close enough that from the kitchen you should have been able to hear much of what went on there, and once again I wondered why they hadn't heard anything the day of the murder.

Being in Flip's house made it impossible for me to avoid thinking about him. Especially being in the living room.

The table had been set for two, and the servant who had led me down the hall cleared away the extra setting. Another woman came into the room carrying a tray. Remembering that I liked fresh lime soda, they had prepared a glass and a small pitcher filled with ice and floating with lime and a few sprigs of mint.

The meal consisted of rice and one of my favorite dishes, *ikan pedas*, fish and a few vegetables and spices cooked in banana leaf. "That looks delicious," I said. "*Enak.*"

"Anything else?"

"No, thank you. This looks perfect. Wayan Tyo is missing out on a lovely lunch." I wasn't sure if they understood what I'd said, but they both cringed at the mention of his name.

They left and I sat looking out at the yard, framed and picturesque. Maybe I sat where Flip had sat, enjoying the luxurious life of the expat. I wondered how far he would have gone to maintain this lifestyle. Given his penchant for upsetting the local norm, I expected he would have gone to any extreme, beyond any extreme.

The *ikan pedas* was the best I'd had since my arrival. Flip not only had created paradise, but he'd found a great cook. I concentrated on my food. The sound of the fountain outside the door and the birds singing in the trees soothed me, holding the jitters just below the surface, while his ghost poked and prodded, asking for revenge. Crazy, why ask me for revenge? We'd never met. I shook myself.

An empty birdcage hung desolately from the branch of a tree. I seemed to remember there being a bird the day that he had been killed, but now that day was with me as a dream, not as a real memory. Hazy and filled with silences and abrupt sounds, people appearing and disappearing. Imaginary birds. Even Flip, who had since invaded my dreams, had lost the immediacy of an actual body and become a silhouette on the floor. Which is how I wanted it to be.

I looked around the room at the paintings Wayan Tyo and I had hung: the Bonnet, the Spies, and Flip's many efforts. We needed to put those paintings in storage. As I finished eating, I texted Tyo to ask if I could do it, pointing out that the Spies and Bonnet alone were worth a considerable amount of money. Flip's daughter's life would change with all this wealth.

Hopefully her mother was as sensible as she seemed. Hopefully she was doing better.

I lingered over my fresh lime soda, knowing I had to get back to work but sluggish from the food. When the servant returned, I asked if they had Bali coffee.

She brought it in record time, and I drank the strong, rich coffee hurriedly, so that I could do a little more work before going to see Ulih. I also needed to go back to the hotel to change before the opening.

I stood and glanced again at the garden and the pretty scene Flip had created for himself. "Was there a bird?" I asked the girl who was wiping down the table.

"A bird?"

I pointed at the cage.

"Yes. Outside." She pointed toward the other end of the property, where the servants' quarters and the storage house lay. Then she said carefully, testing a phrase, "He is there."

I was relieved to hear that they hadn't just let it free. A domesticated bird might not survive in the wild. I looked for a cage on the path as I returned to the storage area, but it must have been at one of the houses beyond. Maybe it was the bird that I had seen sitting on the small boy's shoulder a few days before.

My phone vibrated, and I pulled it out of my pocket. Wayan Tyo's text read, "Yes, catalogue and move."

Right now I would continue in the storage area and do the living room when I had help.

45

"Yes, I went to see Ulih," I said. "She wasn't awake, but I was able to speak with her daughter and her sister and give them my good wishes."

"That is very good," said Made as he scanned the room, which was festively decorated for the opening of his exhibition. He marked who entered, who spoke with whom. Curatorial duties are the same everywhere. Mounting exhibitions and doing research are the fun part of the work. Coping with patrons and parties are not necessarily in the skill set of the more scholarly. Made didn't look comfortable, but he knew his role and played it well.

I didn't intend to stay long, just to make an appearance. I didn't know any of the people who milled around me. "Will Tyo be here, or Ani?" I asked Made.

"He texted me to say he couldn't come. Something came up. He sent one of his policemen to be here."

"That's odd."

"I thought so." He shrugged. Made excused himself and walked away, his eyes on a couple who had just walked in. They seemed to be attracting a great deal of attention. Potential donors? The museum founders? I'd seen photos, but couldn't match those pictures of a young couple with this middle-aged pair.

An elderly man approached me tentatively. "Anak Ani?" he asked.

I opened my mouth to disavow my Balinese affiliation, but his expression was so uncertain, the lines in his face coalescing into a map of wrinkles, that I couldn't be abrupt. Then I realized that we had met. "*Ya*," I answered.

"I am I Nyoman Anariksa."

I raised my hands together in a polite greeting. "We met when I came to your studio last week. I'm so sorry that I haven't been back. I promise you that I intend to buy your student's painting."

"Yes, yes. I know that you will return. I have the painting for you."

"It's so nice to see you here at the opening." I meant it. Now I would have an opportunity to talk with him about an idea that I had.

"I am also the painting teacher of Esa and Wayan Tyo. I also taught Made when he got older and his father wanted him to have another teacher."

"Really? That's wonderful." I liked that I could picture them in his courtyard. "Made has been so kind in helping me understand Balinese painting. Thank you for teaching him so well."

"And Wayan Tyo? Has he not been kind?"

Flustered, I said, "Yes, of course, though he has not been teaching me about Balinese painting."

"No. He is a detective." He spoke sadly. "It is a loss. I ask him to paint sometimes, as Made does. He agrees but does not. He thinks that he is being kind to me by telling me he will paint someday."

"Maybe he will. Some calm day."

"Yes, maybe. Made tells me that you have discovered the key to Flip's painting."

"Made discovered his 'signature,' an oak leaf."

"He discovered the odd leaf and you identified it. The foreign scholar working with the local scholar. Very nice, very clever. I am proud of him. There are elements of Flip's teacher's style in some of the forgeries, and I have been very worried that he might be the forger. This is a great relief to me. It is far better that it is a foreigner than a Balinese."

I agreed, though I wouldn't have been able to explain why. "I'm sure it must be. You knew that there were forgeries?"

"We knew, but we did not know, as we were not able to identify who was doing them or exactly what was incorrect about these paintings. His fakery has been very bad for our profession. We do not want people to think that we are all making such paintings."

"No. No, you wouldn't."

"All elements of our culture are being copied. Even within our culture."

"What do you mean?"

"Well, let me think of an example." He pondered a moment then pointed toward a sculpture at the foot of the stairs. "For instance, the *lamak*, the textile we hang beneath the shrine or over the base of a sculpture, is now made by factories and sold in shops. In the past they were made in the home out of leaves, but now they make them of machine-made textiles and sequins."

"Ah."

"Of course, always sculptures and paintings have been copied. They have been copied for teaching, the young students following the work of their teachers. Just as you saw my students doing." He raised his hand, as if pointing toward his studio. "Then when the Dutch arrived, we sold copies, and originals of course, to the Dutch and to the other Europeans who followed them. We have a long history of making copies. It may be difficult for you to understand that the original intent was not to deceive. It was to honor those works of art of the past."

"Yes, I understand that. Funny, isn't it, that paintings or sculptures that have age often have more value than works of higher quality made today?"

"It is sometimes confusing."

A waiter held out a tray of small *lumpia*, spring rolls, and we each took a napkin, then dipped the *lumpia* into a tomato *sambal.*

"Very good," I said, raising the last bit of *lumpia.*

"Yes. He has the ability to pay for the very best food and the very best painting." He nodded his head toward the couple that Made had joined. "He also has excellent taste and has had since he was a boy."

"That is the founder of this museum?"

"Yes. He is a hungry collector. Would you like to meet him? He, too, was one of my students, but only briefly. Like Wayan Tyo he did not continue painting."

"That would be very nice. Thank you."

"I can introduce you to other collectors as well. I think that they will be happy to invite you to see their collections while you are here. And of course you will return to my studio."

"That would be wonderful. I'd like to meet collectors. And I want to return and look more closely at your students' work. I have an idea that I might be able to get the shop in my museum to purchase some of their paintings to sell next year when we have an exhibition of Balinese paintings."

"That would be very good for my students. Two of them are ready to go off on their own. Their work is very accomplished, as you have already seen. Some of the younger ones are doing fine work as well, and their paintings could be purchased very inexpensively. The money will be a great help to them and their families." Many of the wrinkles had vanished from his small face as he relaxed, and I had a glimpse of the handsome young man he once was.

I handed him one of my business cards. "I've written my Indonesian phone number on the back."

I Nyoman Anariksa took me under his wing and introduced me to collectors, painters, and friends. He explained that most of the collectors had only a few paintings each, but some very fine, and if I had time I should take advantage of the opportunity to visit them. I saw the days filling before me with cataloguing and collectors and galleries, my personal life flowing into my work in a seamless blend. My concerns about my project gave way to excitement, and I stayed longer than I'd intended.

AS I bade good-bye to Made and Nyoman Anariksa, a young man approached. "This is the policeman who is here to guard you," said Made.

"Guard me? You didn't say he was here to guard me."

"No, he only told me later in the evening."

"Why do you need to guard me?" I asked.

"Wayan Tyo sent me."

"I understand that. But why did he send you?"

He looked uncertain.

"They have another murder," said Made. "An Australian and his girlfriend."

"Oh, no." I shuddered as I thought of that bullet that had whizzed by my head, and the attack on Ulih. "What is his name?"

The officer said, "Shelley."

"How was he killed?"

"A knife," he said. "Both were killed with a knife."

"A knife? Or a kris?" Only realizing as I asked the question what the answer meant.

"A kris. I will drive you back to your hotel and stay there overnight."

"Thank you. I don't think it is necessary," I said politely. But I didn't mean it.

46

I didn't sleep well, my dreams filled with violent attacks, blades dripping my blood as they were slowly and painfully pulled from my body. Men with blank faces lunging at me as I tried unsuccessfully to dive to right or left, always choosing the wrong direction, and the men then going through me in a puff of smoke or piercing me with whatever blade they held. It was all very Hollywood.

My wakeful moments were as fitful. My awareness of the policeman sitting outside my door put me off balance. The creak of his chair as he fidgeted to get comfortable, the snap of a match as he lit a cigarette, then the long, slow plume of smoke that filtered through the crack of my double door. Which of course I couldn't see and could only imagine.

In my distress, I might have invented it all, the dreams, the policeman at my door, the smoke, which I had greeted thankfully as a sign of his presence. Because when I woke, showered, dressed, and opened the door to greet him, no one was there. Instead a mother hen, her adolescent brood chirping and kicking up dirt, greeted me.

I had no one to cling to in my distress. No handsome policeman—I had fantasized sitting and having a cup of tea with him. No Wayan Tyo, Tyo who was a complication. Nothing. No rejection, if a rejection was needed, no acceptance, if one was desired. I needed to ride my bike. I needed to get away from my fear and away from this town.

The policeman, the same policeman, was in the lobby. He looked startled when I came through with my bike. "No, you cannot go."

"Ah, but I am. You're welcome to follow." I put on my helmet. I knew that Wayan Tyo would be angry, but I could ride as fast as the wind. That bullet hadn't hit me. I would be safe on my bike.

"Wait, wait." He turned and spoke urgently to the receptionist, who hesitantly handed him some keys. Smart boy. Following me on a motorbike would be a lot easier than following me in a car or on foot. We set off.

On one of the steep inclines outside of Ubud, he roared ahead. When I caught up, I saw that he was texting. Probably Wayan Tyo. I turned in the direction of Goa Gajah, and once again he trailed behind.

In the parking lot of the ancient site we locked my bike to his motorcycle and I paid for my ticket. As a local he was admitted free. He walked a few steps behind me, watchful, embarrassed. "Have you been here before?" I asked him, slowing, trying to get in step.

"No."

"What's your name again? I seem to have misplaced it during the night."

"Ketut Putra."

"Okay, Putra, you're in for a treat."

There were other sites that I hadn't yet visited, sites farther away from Ubud and probably a better ride. But they were for other days. I said, "I like this cave. It has a fierce face that swallows you up as you enter. And the atmosphere inside is dark and dank and smells like bats."

He nodded, though he looked uncertain and spooked once we were inside.

I took pity on him. "C'mon," I said. "I'll show you something even better." We walked across the ravine to the Buddhist temple, where a fragment of a Buddha, armless, headless, and covered with a checkered cloth so that you couldn't see his lower torso or his legs, sat in a small, thatched shrine in a lush tropical setting. From that temple we walked to the pond that lay between Hindu and Buddhist sites, and I circumambulated it seven times. He stopped following me after the second time, which surprised me, as the Balinese like odd numbers: roofs of seven or five or eleven levels, cremation towers the same.

Walking around the ancient site did what a lengthier ride would have done, soothed me, and I walked back up the slight hill, Putra trailing me, away from the tropical temple, the waterfall, the pond, to my hotel and breakfast, then back to Flip's for more cataloguing.

WHEN we came into the compound of Flip's house, Putra seemed to know one of the women. They joked and smiled shyly. Maybe he was smitten.

"You're going to help me," I told him as the girl unlocked the door. I was becoming used to his distress at any new suggestion. He had his orders, and I kept defying the regularity that he expected and desired. "You're going to help me catalogue these paintings." I gestured toward the larger paintings.

"Yes?" he said uncertainly.

"I'll show you what to do. Do you know anything about Balinese painting?"

"A little. I studied . . ."

"*Ya, ya.*" Okay, okay. So he was an art historian, too. "Who was your teacher?"

"My father."

"Okay. Not the same as Made or Wayan Tyo?"

"Yes, the same."

"I Nyoman Anariksa is your father?" I was astonished at the long arm of nepotism, of these linked painting students. "Wayan Tyo hired you?"

He nodded.

"Well, good. I met your father last night, and he was very kind."

"Thank you."

"I'll show you what you need to do."

He was good. He could pull a painting halfway out and tell me who had painted it. Still, I made him pull them all the way so that he could read the signature and be entirely certain and so that we could take a quick snapshot. When a painting was good, he would say, "*Bagus sekali*," and I would get up and we'd examine it. If it wasn't, he would assign a title. Some of his titles were rather hilarious, I thought, though he didn't understand why I was laughing. *Strange Fishing, Bad Women, Worse Men, Strange Happenings in the Forest.* He seemed to like the word "strange." There weren't as many good paintings as a collector or scholar would hope for, but enough to make it an interesting morning. And we weren't seeing any oak leaves.

"Bu, your lunch is ready," the young woman Putra liked said from the door.

I looked at the time on the computer. "Gosh, the morning flew."

They both frowned, trying to decipher what I meant.

"We've gotten a lot done, thanks to you, Putra."

The girl looked at him proudly.

He slid the last painting back into the stack of canvases and rubbed his upper arms. The girls had been very attentive that morning, visiting us to see if we wanted tea, water, or anything else they could bring. Clearly they all liked Putra, and why not? He was nice-looking, bright, employed, from a good family, and obviously unmarried. A real catch.

As we stepped outside, I heard a bird squawk, then cry, "Hell yes, hell yes, hell yes." Ah, Flip's bird. I'd have to have the girl show it to me when we came back after lunch. It bothered me that I didn't remember it clearly from the day of Flip's death.

"Hell yes, hell yes," it cried again. I don't know what it is about talking birds that inspires their owners to teach them to say stupid things.

Putra went in the kitchen door, while the girl led me around the house to the living room. It had been acceptable to bring me through the kitchen when I was alone, but with another present she seemed to feel she should lead me through a proper door. As we neared the living room, I saw why. Wayan Tyo stood looking at the Spies painting. The servants didn't want to do anything that might anger him, and maybe they thought taking me through the kitchen would.

"I thought you were going to move these to the storage room."

"Nice to see you, too."

He scowled.

"We plan to do it this afternoon. If Putra doesn't collapse before then. He must be exhausted."

"You look tired as well."

I softened. "We all do."

Tyo led the way to the table. Today they had brought a larger pitcher of fresh lime soda as well as a pitcher of water. There was *mie goreng*, the noodles handmade, and *kangkung*, the water spinach I liked. Both dishes were laden with bright red chilies. A bowl of Balinese *sambal* lay between us. Tyo served me, an apology of sorts.

"Tell me," I said.

"We didn't find him in time. I think that we were close. We got to the bodies not long after they were killed, maybe an hour or less. I haven't yet heard the time of death from the doctor." He took a bite of the noodles, then added more *sambal*. My mouth burned to watch.

"It was not like Flip. He had fought. The girl had fought. I knew her. She was the younger sister of a friend. I think he stabbed her first, judging by how the bodies lay and the fact that the kris was next to Eric's body, which suggested the killer finished with him."

"I don't need details."

"No. It was very disturbing. We found the other paintings in the house. The ones that he took from Flip's."

"I'm glad I didn't find Eric and the girl."

"I am glad too. I imagine if you had, you would have been in the thick of it. Practicing some martial art on the murderer."

I laughed. "Probably."

"You know *pencak silat*, martial arts?" he asked, surprised.

I didn't answer, placing a small amount of *sambal* next to my noodles.

"Anything interesting in the paintings?" he asked.

"Not particularly. You've given me a good assistant. Putra knows a great deal. But nepotism is rampant, isn't it?"

He ignored the jibe. "Yes, he does know a good bit from his father. I understand you met Nyoman last night."

Who did he understand that from? More and more I realized that though this town had thousands of residents and even more tourists, everyone knew what Anak Ani was up to. "Yes, he was very kind, and he introduced me to collectors whom I will visit with him. Very nice for my education."

"Good." He served me more *kangkung*, ignoring my objections. "My mother expects you for dinner tonight."

"*Ya.* I might not last long. Not much sleep."

"We are planning on your sleeping at our home, so that we do not need a guard on you at the hotel. They were not happy at having a policeman hanging around all night. I gather one of the other residents asked who he was."

"I really would like to sleep in my own bed." I blocked my plate as he tried to pile on more noodles.

"I know, but it cannot be helped. I will come to get you about six."

We ate in silence for a while, each absorbed in our separate thoughts. "What does this mean, Tyo? Eric provided the link between Flip's death and the paintings. Or rather, Eric provided a link. Without him, what do we have?"

"Nothing," said Tyo unhappily. "This leaves the mystery open. Could be an angry husband. Could be someone else involved in paintings. Could be something or someone we hadn't considered."

"Oh, that reminds me. A thought I had. Whoever tried to kill Ulih used a kitchen knife. Flip's, and now these murders, were with traditional weapons. I'm thinking maybe there are two different murderers."

"That seems unlikely."

"Yes, it does, but . . . Or maybe he hadn't planned to hurt Ulih, but when he got there something happened."

"But it looked as if the person who stabbed her had sneaked up on her."

"True. Maybe they argued downstairs. She thought he'd left and went up to change. Something like that?"

"I'll think about it," he said. "I don't want two murderers."

"No. What else haven't we considered?"

"We haven't considered that maybe someone just wandered in and killed him." Tyo took more *kangkung* for himself and offered some to me.

"Wandered in and violently fought with and killed Eric and his girlfriend? Stabbed Ulih? I don't think so. It seems more likely that the murder was planned. I doubt there are too many people running around Ubud with a spear or kris in hand. Have you had any luck finding out who the third person coming to lunch might have been?"

"No. And we haven't seriously considered Flip's staff, though we did interview them all."

"You spoke with the one husband I mentioned to you?"

"Yes. It is not him," he said impatiently. "In general, the staff was content working for him, with the usual grumbles. He paid well and on time and gave them holidays for family gatherings and festivals and a day off each week. He also gave them good recommendations if they wanted to go to another job. He seems to have been a good boss."

"A surprise." I took a single long noodle from the platter, held it high, and let it slither into my mouth.

"Yes. He insisted on complete discretion, and if he discovered they had said anything about him behind his back, spread any rumors, judged his guests—meaning the women who came to his house—he fired them immediately. He made that clear from the moment they joined his staff."

"Okay. Anyone he owed money?"

"No. He had one of his staff paying bills so that he didn't have to worry, and she is very good. She has a degree in accounting."

"Wow."

"So I honestly don't think it was any of them."

"They did have access to his weapons, didn't they?"

"Yes, but not easy access. His housekeeper seems to hold on to those keys rather tightly. Except, of course, that she couldn't find them the day of the murder."

I hesitated. "There's the amulet. The small sculpture that he wore."

"There is."

"Did you find it?"

"Yes, I did."

"And?"

"Nothing to say about that."

"Why is that?"

"It belonged to the temple." He looked off into the distance, clearly not wanting to meet my eyes.

"It belonged to the temple where I left it?" I asked incredulously. "You're joking, aren't you?"

"No, I am not."

"That was the sculpture that was stolen?"

"Yes, it was."

"Uh, isn't that a motive? Someone at the temple knew he had stolen it or had it stolen and wanted to get it back?" I would have to talk with Ani about the amulet. Esa, too, forbidding as he was. His insights might be instructive.

"That doesn't explain Eric's death. That's what's confusing. I'm hoping when Ulih wakes up, we will find out what the connection is. That she can tell us who the killer is."

"Or at least who her attacker was." Again making the point that there might be two different murderers involved. "When do they think she might wake up?"

"They don't know. She is not coming around as quickly as they thought. They are wondering if she went without oxygen for too long. Or if there is internal bleeding."

"So, are you waiting for her? On the off chance that she saw who attacked her?"

A flicker of anger crossed his face. "No, I am not." He put down his napkin and stood. "I will see you tonight."

To try to divert him, I said, "Maybe the bird is involved."

"What bird?"

I pointed at the cage. "Remember? He was here. His favorite phrase seems to be 'Hell, yes.'"

"Very helpful," he said ruefully. "I will see you this evening."

47

Putra angled the painting to get better light. "Flip has a few works by Spies. They are valuable, but they are not the best of Spies."

"That's my impression, too. Was Spies this prolific?"

"I don't know. I don't know of that many of his paintings. They are not easy to find. Flip must have searched Bali for these. Or he had," he hesitated, "joggers out seeking them."

"Runners," I laughed.

"Runners."

"That's possible. Or maybe he found someone who owned a collection of his works. Wayan Tyo hasn't found records of Flip's holdings. Otherwise you and I probably wouldn't be doing this."

"No." He frowned as he looked at the painting.

"You don't think it is wrong, do you?"

"No, I do not. I'm just looking. I have never held a Spies in my hands, and all of the paintings by him that I have seen have been behind glass. I was looking at his brushwork. Very flat."

"Do you still paint?"

"I have to."

"Your father insists?"

"Not with his words."

I waited.

"With his eyes. I do not want him to be sad, so I continue to paint."

"Ah."

"Also, I earn extra money for when I marry."

"Are you engaged?"

He glanced toward the door. "No."

"Not yet."

"Not yet." He flushed.

I changed the subject. "What do you think of these painters? Spies, Bonnet, the Western painters who are given so much credit for revolutionizing Balinese painting. Do you think that they're the ones responsible for the changes that occurred in painting here?"

He slid the Spies painting back into its slot along the wall. "Spies and Bonnet were here in the thirties. Much had changed since the royal families were eliminated." He stopped to think.

"Yes?"

"They introduced Balinese painting to the West. The Pita-maha were active in marketing Balinese work." He pulled the Spies painting back out and turned it around so I could see it. A landscape, with Walter Spies's unusual split horizon, two landscapes piled one on top of the other. "This painting does not relate to paintings done by Balinese in the 1930s. Yes, Balinese painted jungle and crowded landscapes like this. However, the scale and composition are different. Spies chooses this split landscape, this double horizon. Our paintings differ because they include multiple points of view of the landscape." He paused. "I think he and the others helped open minds to alternate ways of looking at the world."

I nodded. "But not exact stylistic influence. Is that what you're saying?"

"Yes, his painting is too different from any of the Balinese painters of that time. His figures are larger, his landscapes are busy, but not with the dense activity of many of our painters.

Dreamlike, but not our dreams. Not Lempad's dreams, which grow out of our belief in demonic forces."

"Yes, that seems right."

"Did he influence us? Or did we influence him?" he asked.

"That's an interesting question. Has anyone written about or explored it?"

"Probably." Again he put the painting away. "Who will ever be able to say?" He smiled wryly.

"It's one more instance of Europeans claiming to change the course of a region's history. They say they influence the local art, always in a positive way. Comparatively little is said about the cultural influences going to the West from the 'primitives.'" I made quotes in the air. "But there are scholars who address those issues."

"Yes, probably." He pulled out another painting and looked abstractedly in the lower corner for a signature. "Not much has changed. The Westerners still come, still consider themselves superior, try to change us."

"Does it anger you?" Though I could hear it in his voice, I was curious what else he might say.

"It angers all of us." He changed the subject. "This is another of Flip's paintings." I added it to our list.

BY three we were weary and getting slap-happy. "I think we'd better stop," I said.

"Yes. I will take you back to your hotel."

"I'll just straighten up here. I think we'll be able to finish tomorrow. That is, if you're still working with me."

"I will ask Wayan Tyo to let me continue. It would be difficult for one person to do this alone. We still have the paintings on the upper shelf to finish. Many of those frames are heavy."

"They certainly are." I turned off my computer. "Oh, damn. We were supposed to bring the paintings from the living room in here. We'd better do that before we leave. We can catalogue them tomorrow."

He grabbed a pile of acid-free paper, and we walked together to the living room.

"I can take a few of the small ones stacked, and maybe you could carry one or two of the larger paintings. Does that sound about right?"

Putra nodded as he took the Spies off the wall. "This is the best one in the collection." He picked up another painting and headed back to the storage.

"Yes, it's lovely." It took us multiple trips, and when we had finished and I was leaving the living room one of the servants came running out of the kitchen with a painting in her hands.

"What's that?" I asked as I took it from her.

"The ground," she said, pointing.

"The floor?"

"When he dead."

"Oh, I see. But it wasn't on the floor when we hung the paintings back on the wall."

The girl looked sheepish. "We cleaned. It had blood."

I remembered that on the day when Wayan Tyo and I hung the paintings on the wall, the easel had been upright and the painting that had lain next to it the day of the murder was no longer there. "When?"

She looked confused.

"When did you clean?"

"Every day."

So much for preserving the crime scene.

"Mr. Flip made us to clean every day."

Tyo was not going to like this. "So this is definitely the painting that was on his easel?"

She nodded, her head down.

Putra was walking toward us.

"Thank you." A thought occurred to me. "Just a minute, Putra. I want to see something."

"What are you doing?" he asked.

I hung the painting in the empty spot on the wall. "I'm wondering if this is the painting that was missing from this wall. It was lying next to the easel the day of the murder, so we assumed it had fallen off. But look, it's the same size as the painting that was here. Maybe his easel was empty and we were fooled because the painting didn't have a frame." I thought for a moment. "Though a number of them didn't have frames."

"What does it mean?" he asked as he took it off the wall.

"It means that we followed a false trail."

"A false trail?"

"Yes. We all got the impression that Flip was painting in Balinese style, which made us suspicious. Because of our suspicions we looked closely at his paintings and drawings."

"But you discovered that he had been making fakes."

"True. However, we discovered that for a wrong reason. It doesn't alter the fact that he was doing it. It just means that we came at the solution for the murder from a false direction."

"It's good that you discovered this."

"Most definitely. Most definitely." I looked at the painting. "I'm glad that we did. It just makes me realize how one misstep in the beginning . . ." I took a step back and looked at the blank wall, as final and dead as Flip. "Let's put this away. Then both of us need to get some sleep. Can you get Wayan Tyo to assign someone else to guard me for a few hours so you can go home?"

"I will stay with you. You go to his home at six. I am fine until then."

If I nap, it's usually a brief power nap. My brain was in overdrive, and I doubted I would even be able to sleep for ten minutes.

The same false trail that had led us to Flip as a forger was the exact trail that we had been following in the investigation. Yes, we'd discussed other possibilities, and I knew that Wayan Tyo had followed up on some of those, but . . . Even P.P. had questioned our methodology. Yet we had always veered back to Flip the forger. Wayan Tyo and I needed a serious conversation.

48

I told Ani and Tyo that I wanted to take them to dinner, and, after much wrangling, they agreed. The little girls, who hadn't eaten out often, were admonished by their grandmother to be good, and they barely wiggled, sitting wide-eyed and polite. Wayan Tyo accepted every dish readily, much to his mother's consternation. Ani frowned at most of the food placed in front of her, though she was polite enough to eat and not complain. She was right. Home-cooked food—especially from her kitchen—was always better.

"You are telling me that the missing painting from the wall is the one that lay near the easel?" Wayan Tyo spooned prawns onto his plate, then served his older daughter. "Try some of this."

"Exactly. I hung it, and it fit the dark spot on the wall perfectly. We've been following a false trail all along."

For a moment he didn't speak. "I have been following other leads. I have not found a cheated husband angry enough to kill him."

"Have you found any husbands that link Eric and Flip?"

"That's more problematic. I spoke to some of the husbands before Eric was killed, when we suspected him. We need to go back and interview those people again."

"How many cheated husbands are there?" Ani asked.

"A lot."

"Let's think clearly about any other possibilities. Let's look at what has happened." I had ordered too much food and now couldn't decide what to eat.

Tyo chewed on a spare rib, apparently disinclined to encourage or discourage me.

"Flip is murdered. Some of his paintings are thrown on the floor. Someone shoots at me, tries to run me over."

"Forgot. Someone stole Flip's amulet." He set down the rib.

I glared at him. "Someone took Flip's amulet. Eric stole paintings from Flip's. Someone shot at me. Someone returned the amulet to the temple where it came from."

"Impulsively."

"Subconsciously aware that the temple was where it belonged."

His jaw dropped open. Luckily he didn't have any food in his mouth. "You have to be joking."

Ani's lips turned up, but she didn't say a thing.

"Sort of yes, sort of no. I was there, and it was as if I had no choice but to leave it there."

"You are unbelievable."

"Children," said Ani.

We both glared at her.

"What's next? There's an attempt on Ulih's life."

"The theft at Ulih's before that," Ani interrupted.

"Yes, put that in. Maybe we should also add the resistance to Flip's funeral, which may be related to the theft. Do you think?"

"I don't see how that could have anything to do with Flip's murder."

That stopped me. "You know . . ." My brain was scrambling.

"We may be talking about two murderers, as you suggested," Tyo said, giving credit where credit was due.

"Yes, maybe we are. Could Eric's murder be a revenge murder? But wait, we're getting ahead of ourselves chronologically. We should be writing this down." I got my notebook out of my purse, and wrote down the list, point by point, as Ani reeled it off.

"So now. The attempt on Ulih's life. Eric and his girlfriend's murders. Those are the facts. Thus far."

"Why are people murdering people?" asked Tyo's older daughter.

"That is what we are trying to figure out," he said.

"Frankly, when I look at it listed this way," I said, "if we are looking at a single killer, I can't really see how the jealous husband gets into it. Unless it is the husband of the young woman who was murdered with Eric."

"We discovered that Eric was married. Wife and kids in Perth."

"Bastard," I muttered. The younger girl began to play with the word. To distract her, Ani asked if she wanted another prawn. "I don't see how that could have anything to do with the murders, unless she flew here to kill them."

"No, she's at home. Going to work. Didn't get on a plane."

He *had* been investigating multiple avenues. "And you've said the servants are all in the clear."

"Yes."

"Where does that leave us? What links these two? Because I think the girlfriend was just in the wrong place at the wrong time. Unless you have suspicions about her husband. Did she have a husband?"

"Used to. Not now. He lives in Sanur and has remarried. He's very unlikely."

"Not uncommon, is it?"

"What?"

"Divorce. Women having affairs with foreigners? Husbands moving off to the beach towns."

Tyo flushed.

"I'm sorry. I wasn't thinking." I was probably redder than he. I'd put my foot in it. I veered back to our discussion.

"Then we're left with Flip's work, his paintings. Dealers and gallery owners. Collectors? Could both Eric and Flip have offended some collector? You know, a deal where Flip sold Eric a fake and Eric sold the fake to a collector. Something like that?" I thought of the affluent collector who had established Made's museum. He would have the wherewithal to hire a hit man.

"Or curators." Tyo looked at me innocently.

"Curators?"

"You seem willing enough to consider wealthy collectors."

"Then why not poverty-stricken curators? You don't mean Made?" I was incredulous. "Or me?"

"Doesn't seem like it could be Made. He has been too busy and too calm throughout. He hated knives when we were kids."

"I remember him crying as a teenager when his father made him dress traditionally and carry a kris for his grandmother's funeral," added Ani.

"So it would not be his weapon of choice."

"No, The pen maybe," said Tyo. "Then there is the amulet."

I wanted to glide by that one. I didn't want the amulet to be the key.

"You know, Made told me that he recently suggested to his museum founder that a couple of the paintings might be fakes."

"How did he react?"

"Angry. Took it out on Made, then apologized. He insisted on looking at the paintings. Asked Made who he thought might have painted them."

"What did Made tell him?" Tyo aimed a spoonful of the chicken dish at my plate.

I covered the plate with my hands. "He didn't know, though he said as they discussed the question Flip's name came up. Along with one or two Balinese painters."

"I will go to talk with him tomorrow. I can't imagine a man of his stature running a spear through Flip."

"What is 'running through'?" his daughter asked.

That silenced the three adults, until Ani said, "Running through the garden."

The child looked confused.

"The fact that both Flip and Eric were foreigners. Is that significant?"

"Let's talk about the amulet."

"Okay." I hadn't managed to break his train of thought.

"It didn't look old to me."

"Nor to me," I said. "What on earth could that mean?"

"That it was recently made."

"Thank you for that clarification. I've been trying to find a good bronze-caster here in town, without any success."

"I thought that you went to see Esa?" Ani said.

"I did, but he only makes weapons. Not sculpture. He did give me a name, but I haven't gotten to that person."

"He makes sculptures," said Ani. "Not often, but he is one of the finest artists in Ubud."

"But," I said at the same moment that Tyo said, "He rarely makes sculptures because he feels that they should only be made when they have meaning, ritual significance."

My mind reeled. Esa was a sculptor. He had lied to me. Finally I said, "Maybe the fact that they were both foreigners is significant. Maybe that is something to explore, though I'm not sure how or why or what."

Tyo pushed a prawn around his plate. "No, the killer can't kill off every foreigner who comes to town."

"They were expats—in Flip's case, at least. Eric had been coming to Bali yearly, multiple times a year, for decades and almost counted as an expat. Expats, rather than foreigners? People who alter life here in bigger ways?"

"Yes. Maybe I should investigate their circle of acquaintances." He was slumping as he spoke. The task was bigger than the resources he had.

"You could narrow it down to just those who the two knew."

"That's a large group."

"Would anyone care for dessert?" asked the waitress.

"Yes," squealed the girls in unison.

Ani asked what the desserts were, and I insisted that we order one of each, so that we all had choices.

"There is a very vocal group of locals who are against allowing expats to buy property and to own businesses," Wayan Tyo said.

"That might be a good place to start." I reached for the teapot.

"Esa knows them. I'll speak to him tomorrow." Wayan Tyo took his younger daughter onto his lap. "She's fading now, but once that dessert is put in front of us she will be up all night."

"I could go with you. He told me . . ."

"No, you could not," he snapped.

His daughters looked at him in surprise. I apparently brought out the worst in the man.

"You need to do what you need to do, which is to look at paintings. I need to investigate these crimes. You've already created enough problems."

"A minute ago—"

"We were talking. Talking differs from acting for most people, though they seem to be the same for you, words veering from your mouth to your feet. You never consider the effect of your actions on others. You have created—"

"I heard you say that the first time." I leaned back in my chair. "I may or may not have created one problem. I have not created a mass of problems."

The dessert arrived, but I'd lost interest. The girls had not.

He softened. "I appreciate why you are interested. You did find the body."

"Body?" The little one frowned as she shoveled a huge bite of fried banana into her mouth and aimed her spoon at the bowl of ice cream.

We both ignored her.

"Yes, and when you see fit—like when you need someone to do your work for you and catalogue the paintings—you call on me. That's very convenient, but not very considerate. You don't seem to be taking account of the fact that I have met a finite number of people since coming here and that a number of them have been murdered or attacked. And if they were not, then the other people I know are trying to figure out who did the murdering. This involves me."

"Yes, it does," he acknowledged wearily. "You are right in that. But it does not mean that you are intended to investigate it. That is my job. It is not your job."

We glared at each other.

"Do you understand that, Jenna? I am very serious about this."

"Don't patronize me."

"Girls, leave some for Jenna and your father." Ani turned to us. "These girls are tired. Jenna, what are you doing tomorrow?"

"I have a date with I Nyoman Anariksa to visit two of the collectors I met at the museum opening." I wasn't sure I appreciated her attempt to divert Wayan Tyo and me. All of our conversations and interactions felt incomplete.

"That sounds interesting. If it isn't too early, you could join me in the morning to go to the temple. Because of the festival, many women will be coming with their offerings. You could help me make *porosan.*"

"I want to help," chorused the girls.

"I'm afraid that I can't. We're meeting before eight a.m. An odd time, but that's what the collectors requested. So I'll have to go back to the hotel tonight." I looked at Tyo as I said this. In fact, I wasn't meeting the collectors until 10:30, late enough for me to go see Esa first thing in the morning. Why had he lied to me about whether he made sculptures?

Tyo opened his mouth to object, but decided not to fight that battle and instead pulled out his cell phone to make a call.

"Putra. Did I wake you? Good, I'm glad you got some sleep. I need you to spend the night on Jenna's doorstep again."

I had questions for Esa. I probably had more questions than Tyo. It bothered me that Esa had lied. It was a lie I should have seen through. I'd looked at the tools on his shelf and seen the wax that one uses to fabricate lost-wax bronze sculptures, to fabricate an image like the amulet. Still, I hadn't put two and two together.

Flip's amulet had been stolen from the temple. As a priest at the temple, Esa had the perfect opportunity to steal it. Why had he done it? I needed to talk with him.

Another question. Why was the amulet new? Ani had told me it was an ancient treasure. The old man in Java had said it was new. I thought he was right. Tyo, too. Why steal a new sculpture from the temple? It didn't make any sense, but maybe Esa could clear it up.

"Jenna, are you listening?" Tyo tapped my arm.

"Oh, sorry. Started thinking about something. Unrelated." I looked at Ani rather than Tyo. She raised one eyebrow.

Tyo, who was trying to wrestle his cell phone from his younger daughter, wasn't paying attention to either of us.

Ani looked like she wanted to say something, but didn't.

Tyo sensed the silence and looked from one to the other of us. "What?"

"Nothing." I said, a little too brightly.

"You are a terrible liar."

"Jenna's not a liar," his daughters said in unison.

"There you have it," I said, and reached for the bill that the waitress was about to hand to Tyo.

"I'm serious, Jenna."

"I know. I got it." I concentrated on the bill. I knew Tyo wouldn't hear any suspicions about Esa. Not suspicions, really, questions.

I thought about how I would sneak past Putra in the morning and get to Esa very early.

49

I heard Putra step off the porch and edged my legs over the side of the bed, avoiding the creaks as best I could. I stopped and listened to his retreating steps. I eased the door open a crack and saw him turn the corner, headed for the restroom adjacent to the lobby.

I looked down at my wrinkled T-shirt, my leggings. I'd slept in them so that I would be ready to escape at the opportune moment. I turned the lock on the inside of the doorknob and pulled the door shut.

In the lobby I could hear two of the receptionists laughing in the office and hurried to get past before they saw me. I didn't want them to tell Putra that I had gone out. I didn't want to get him into trouble. I would go to Esa's, ask my questions, and when I returned, Putra would be chagrined, but that was better than him being in trouble. Esa wasn't likely to talk with me with a cop in tow.

I pulled my shawl more tightly around my shoulders as I got to the road; the morning chill hadn't yet burned off. As I walked, I could hear voices in the houses, the small hotels, the temples that I passed. The occasional scooter overtook me, but the streets were otherwise quiet.

Three women walked out of a courtyard, offering baskets on their heads, and I said, "*Selamat pagi.*"

"*Pagi*," they answered, the one laughing as she teetered under her load, her friend raising an arm to balance the heavy pyramid of fruit. They walked in the opposite direction or I might have tried to engage them in conversation. Find out about today's ceremony, for they were gaily dressed and their offerings were piled higher than the usual daily offerings.

A few houses further on, an old woman swept, bent over her short broom. Without looking up from her task, she nodded as I passed. Ubud smelled like frangipani. The dust of the roads, the exhaust of the cars, the breath of thousands hadn't yet diluted the flowers' fragrance, and I breathed it in.

This was what Bali was about, this calm, this peaceful gentleness. Not murder and pain. I wished myself back on the plane, arriving. I wished Flip awake, though I knew it couldn't be. I hoped that Esa would help me resolve the questions I had so that I could get on with this quiet loveliness, with moments like these.

As I came up to Esa's street, an ox cart rounded the corner. The farmer, withered and mahogany tanned, clicked at his ox as he gently tapped his back with a switch. Our eyes locked for an instant, and he nodded. I smiled and gave him a wave, stopping to watch him go down the street, two scooters slowing to pass the huge animal.

I could see smoke rising from the blacksmith's forge. Esa was already at work. I'd been framing what to say to him all night. I waited, took a deep breath before entering. He wasn't in the outer shop, but the doors were open, and I moved past the counter where the boy had sat during my last visit, toward the pounding I heard from the forge. I stopped in the doorway.

Esa knelt at his anvil, a red-hot piece of metal gripped in his tongs. He raised his mallet and struck the metal in short rhythmic strokes. He could be a drummer, I thought, each downward stroke so perfectly timed. I didn't step in, but watched him, his relaxed body, his concentration, the ancient task he was undertaking and that he so intently practiced.

He rose to dip the curved piece of metal back in the flaming fire, white hot. In the small space, I could see the waves of heat radiating from the furnace. Sweat covered his face and would coat his body soon enough. He glanced at me and stopped, then pulled the metal from the furnace and lay it on the anvil.

I entered and sat on the single chair to watch. He didn't look up as he held the tongs to the fire, nor did he pay me any mind as he struck the blade on the anvil, repeating the task three times before he lay it on the anvil to cool. Then he walked across the room, picked up a bottle of water, took a long drink, and came back to stand in front of me.

He didn't speak, but his antipathy toward me was obvious. I finally said, "The amulet. The small sculpture." Then I waited.

"What about it?"

"You made it, didn't you?"

He walked back to his anvil, looked down at the blade he'd been pounding. "I make tools, blades."

He was a lousy liar. "Yes, but everyone has been telling me that you also make sculpture. That you are the best bronze sculptor in Ubud." That was a slight exaggeration, but I hoped that if I complimented him, pride might urge him to speak.

He looked up. "They are mistaken."

"Tyo is mistaken?"

He looked toward the door. "Where is Tyo?"

I hesitated before saying, "He'll be here."

Esa gave me a long look, uncertainty grazing his brow. "You're lying."

"Why would I lie?"

He nodded and began to pace.

"What I don't understand is why you made it. I don't understand that."

He squatted in front of the anvil, held his hand above the blade, feeling the heat.

"You Westerners," he said.

It seemed an odd response to my question, but I guessed that it pointed to Flip, for Flip was linked to that amulet. Flip was the man who had been murdered. "We aren't all like Flip," I said defensively.

He began to pace, each step kicking up a little more of the ash that had settled over the workshop from the furnace, though his feet seemed to barely graze the earth. His face gave away nothing, though the tension in his body said plenty.

I'd finally considered the amulet as a possible motive for killing Flip. A motive I hadn't wanted to consider because by taking it I'd hindered any inquiry in that particular direction. As I'd lain in bed, my thoughts kept going to Esa. Esa who lied about making sculptures. Esa who knew about ancient weapons. Esa who made krises and spears. Esa, the insider who knew details of Tyo's investigation. Like the fact that Eric Shelley had stolen paintings after Flip's death.

I said, "That amulet had no patina, no evidence of burial. It hadn't been handled, and the quality of the metal was brassier than I would have expected an old sculpture to be."

He stopped his pacing and looked at me.

I went on, "So, when Wayan Tyo told me that it was the missing sculpture from your temple, that didn't ring true. Yet Ani said it was definitely the sculpture that had gone missing, and no one else seemed to question it, no other priest. Or, at least, neither of them mentioned that anyone questioned it."

"They are mistaken. I saw it. It was the sculpture that was stolen." But as he said it he looked away from me.

"My guess is that you are the one who has the best visual memory. Better than Tyo, better than Ani. You would know if it was the sculpture that was stolen. And I can't believe—"

"No." He said forcefully, "You Westerners. You've ruined Bali." He waved his arm in an expansive gesture that encompassed the entire town, the island, the fields and temples.

"I know that Bali has changed, but the Balinese have adapted to new ideas throughout their history."

"Be quiet," he snapped. He pointed his finger to the ground in a gesture that didn't allow dissent. "You Westerners, you use up our water, change the way we eat, what we wear. You invade our temples and turn them into tourist destinations."

I couldn't argue with anything he said. We had done all that. "The Balinese have made choices throughout history to change, to add, to alter your way of living, not to remain stagnant." The look he gave me was so malevolent it stopped me in my tracks. I looked toward the door, but his pacing placed him between me and any possibility of escape.

In the course of my fitful night, I had come to certain conclusions. It was Esa who wouldn't shake my hand. Esa who hated and was wary of foreigners. And hadn't Flip and Eric been the worst of foreigners? Forging Balinese art, screwing Balinese women, buying local land. Still, I hadn't been able to figure out what the amulet being new could mean.

"You say you don't make sculptures." Why couldn't I keep my mouth shut?

"Not anymore." He picked up a kris from an open drawer and continued his pacing.

Shit, I thought, but instead of doing the sane thing and getting up and saying, nice to see you, I'll be on my way, I persisted. "You saw that amulet. Tyo told me you verified it was the one that was stolen. It looked new to me, didn't it to you?"

He observed me sadly. "It looked like the sculpture from the temple."

I heard a shift in his voice, defeat rather than the forceful anger I had sensed up to this point. I began to stand, but he moved toward me, signaled for me to sit back down.

"We must maintain the old ways. Flip destroyed tradition in every way he could. He took pleasure in this destruction, our women, our art. Even in death he destroyed tradition. Flip.

Buried as a Balinese. Unspeakable." His anger surged back, and his pacing took on new intensity as he circled my chair, a panther observing its prey. "People are fools. They make the wrong choices."

I continued talking, hoping someone would show up if I talked for long enough. "Outsiders have been coming here from time immemorial. Java, Bali didn't exist in isolation before the arrival of the Dutch. Traders from other islands, merchants from far away—China, Vietnam, Thailand—came and traded ideas and goods. You know about the excavations of ancient ports on both the north and the south sides of the island. The people who arrived at those ports brought new ideas. Some of those ideas were embraced, some were ignored, and others disdained."

He leaned in to me, so close his breath dried my eyes as he spoke. "Have you walked down Monkey Forest Road? Have you seen the trash that the shops sell as art? Have you seen those young men drunk and stumbling? The young girls dressed in nothing and throwing themselves at men they barely know? Why are you here? You Westerners. First the Dutch came. What did they do? They decided to sell my home, my island, as a tourists' paradise. Now the tourists outnumber us." He stopped, then spit out, "They have no respect." He stepped back, moved away.

"Yes, and before them the eastern Javanese came and married your rulers, eventually taking over control of the island."

He moved back toward me, menacingly holding up the kris. "That is what the Dutch said when they decided it was time for them to take Bali. They claimed to be saving us from the Javanese. But really they wanted control of the slave trade. They ignored us for centuries, since we had no land for their plantations. Then their greed and desire for power extended across the strait from Java."

That was pretty accurate, I knew, but what caught my attention was the kris hilt he gripped with such ferocity in his left hand. He had drawn it, and I could see it all, blade, hilt, and sheath. The hilt was classic Balinese-style, gold and silver encrusted with jewels, the figure in the shape of Barong. The dagger was old, the pattern of the metal, the *pamor*, the most elegant that I had ever seen.

Had we been acting in a B movie, the power pulsating from the blade would have been visible. It raised the hair on my arms. At least I would die from a venerable weapon. The thought dried my mouth and made my heart beat faster.

I wondered what happened when that wavy blade passed into one's insides. I shook off the thought and concentrated on the kris hilt. One of the stones was gone. It had probably been missing for decades. I guessed he had preserved the weapon as it had come down to him, an heirloom. The details of Barong's body were smooth from handling. It was old, but how old?

I must be nuts. I was trying to date the weapon that would kill me if Wayan Tyo didn't hurry up. That was what was supposed to happen. The detective to the rescue. If only I'd told him my worries. If only I hadn't been so damn rash.

I would have shaken my head at the absurdity of my thoughts, but Esa stuck the point of the kris against my neck. I had to keep him talking. If I kept him talking, I hoped he would back away and resume his pacing.

"Not very nice of them, I agree."

He held the blade up, touched the point to his forehead, and looked at me in disgust. "Not very nice. They forced our royal families to kill themselves. They promoted us as an island for their entertainment. A tourist spot—a destination, as you say now."

I tried to divert him from the evil European theme. "Your royal families were largely of Javanese descent through marriage to Balinese."

He leaned into me again, his anger so dense I could barely breathe. "They were our rulers and our kin, our patrons. We danced in their courtyards and created art, weapons, and ritual items. Those patrons kept the artists alive. The Dutch destroyed their palaces and took home all we had made, *oleh-oleh*, souvenirs." He stomped away, and I judged the distance between me and the door. Too far. He spun back to look at me.

"Nothing has changed. Now who are our patrons? Fat Americans in their shorts stuck up their asses. Tanned Germans with their blond children as scornful as their parents. Brits, with their pompous talk and colonial sneers. And Australians with their beer mugs in hand whether it's morning or night. They wander the shops, buying garbage that looks like all the other garbage for sale in all the other shops along the streets of Kuta, the beaches of Sanur."

"It's true. But you walk ten feet off those roads and there is Bali. The Bali of forest and paddy, of women weaving offerings and children playing with toys made of palm fronds and whatever else they find."

"You mean poverty. That's what you like?" he sneered.

"No, I don't mean poverty. I mean the little things that make up the culture of this island, the little things that tie all of us to the past. The rituals and practices without which we would be soulless. I mean the basic, perfect flow of life."

I hesitated, uncertain whether to continue in this vein, but I'd gotten myself in this deep. "I get up in the morning and with my Balinese mother I make offerings. We walk to the temple— your temple that you so love—and we give the ancestors offerings that will dry and warp and be discarded and burned within the day. They are as impermanent as the lives we venerate. The act is as ephemeral as the offering."

He was behind me now, dizzying me with his circular path. His voice rose. "And who are you to join these Balinese women? Anak Ani." He said it with a sneer and I felt myself shrink.

"I—"

"Anak Ani." He leaned over me, his words spitting out with all the venom he felt toward Westerners. "A girl who visited twenty years ago, stole a family's love, a boy's love. A woman who comes back now, so many years later to claim . . . To claim what? That she is Balinese? That she belongs here?"

"I lay no claim." I realized that I now embodied the enemy. I was the Westerner.

He slapped his hand hard on the back of my chair, and I jumped.

I looked down at my hands and saw that my knuckles were white. I was afraid. But I was also pissed, and I glared at him as he passed in front of me. Then I ducked my head. I didn't want him to see either my anger or my fear. I breathed in, counting my breaths, until I thought I could speak without my voice wavering.

He circled and circled again, moving further from me with each round, until he was a distance that felt safer. I hoped the drone of my voice might calm him. "That action—of weaving, walking together, presenting a small gift—perpetuates the past and everything that's been Bali before. That small act and a thousand others like it set Bali apart from everywhere else on this planet. The tourists are here, yes. They probably will always be here, and they probably will change Bali in ways that you won't like. That I won't like.

"There are differences, but traditional Bali coexists with tourist Bali. The traditions, the rituals and dance and art, continue side by side with the new. It's unfortunate that there are people like Flip, corrupt people whose greed dominates their lives, whose karma spills over into ours."

Esa stopped abruptly, the dust rising around him, and said, "He stole our temple's most sacred image. He stole it and sold it, and we will never again be able to reach our ancestors. We will never again be able to care for them as we should." Pain filled his words, and his voice came from a constricted place. The anger was there, pulsing in his forehead, but his pain was palpable.

Unconsciously I raised my hand toward him, and he winced. I said, "So you did make the sculpture that he wore?"

He nodded miserably. "Yes. That is the one that I made him, but he wasn't content with a copy. He stole the original, had the original stolen."

"You're a brilliant artist." I took a breath. "If he did steal it, he was wrong. His karma has proven that. Yet we can do all that's in our power to get back the image." I spoke of the future, hoping he wouldn't think I knew.

He shook his head, began to walk away. I moved my leg to sprint to the door, but he turned suddenly and glared at me, all his hatred for Westerners focused in that look.

I blurted, "You can't kill all of us." His eyes hooded over, and I realized I had just said the wrong thing.

"No, but I can kill you. You are the only one who knows my shame." He looked at me closely. "Who are you to speak of yourself as Balinese? To take a place in our daily life. Who are you to weave offerings along with our women? Your doing these things is as bad as Ulih's creating a traditional *kremasi* for Flip."

I had to answer this as best I could, even though I didn't know the answer. "When my car drove into Ubud, I knew that I was home. It's not the home where I'll live, work, raise my children. It's not the home where my mother and father live. It's the home of my heart. I can't explain it, but I think I felt it as a child. I think that Ani and Tyo recognize it in me, and because they do, they welcome me, no, they invite me to participate in Balinese life. I can only partake as a visitor. A visitor who feels one foot tentatively reaching into your culture while the other is firmly placed in Marin, California."

My right calf had begun to cramp from my bracing it to run. I reached down to squeeze the muscle, never taking my eyes off him. "You're a man who embodies all that's Bali. Born here, living here, a priest and a blacksmith, an ancient and venerated profession with much power. I envy you this," I said.

I pressed down with the ball of my foot, trying to release the knot.

He looked down at my feet.

If I spoke as a person who would live, maybe I would. "To see your way of life shaken by men like Flip, by the thousands who arrive to 'eat, pray, and love' must be terribly, horribly unsettling. I can't stem the tide of tourists. I can only offer you my help in trying to find the original sculpture. I give you my promise that I'll do this."

He was thoughtful. "How would you help to get the sculpture back?"

This was good, concrete. "I would contact Interpol and IFAR, a group that registers stolen objects. I would contact museums and serious collectors of Balinese art—there aren't that many—to be on the lookout for the piece. I would circulate the photograph. We could try to discover Flip's contacts here. I have some ideas already who might have helped him."

"Who?"

"I don't know his name, but there was a foreigner who suddenly vanished at the time of the theft."

He shook his head. "No. I have followed this lead and it went nowhere."

I wondered what he had done. Had he killed the foreigner? Did that mean that he had killed Wayan Tyo's wife? Had he murdered Eric and tried to kill Ulih? I didn't understand why he would have done that, unless he felt so strongly about the funeral. "Did you steal Ulih's textiles?"

He was insulted. "I am not a thief."

Just a murderer, I thought. "Well, who could have done that?"

"That has nothing to do with Flip. That is only greed. Shelley's greed. He stole and tried to kill Ulih, whose only wrong was to see Flip for more than he was. To love the wrong person. And to trust Eric when he offered her a painting as payment."

That made sense, and it followed that he'd killed Eric. I kneaded my calf. But how to dissuade him from killing me? "You do this for honor?"

"What else?" He collapsed onto a stool and gazed out the window. "What have I begun? No man can stem this tide."

"No."

"My people are giddy with the money brought by the tourists. Bigger houses, cars, motorbikes, new foods. Their lives improved, they think, by wealth." He ran the blade of the kris along his palm, drawing blood as he did.

"Be careful," I said, thinking of the feeding frenzy of sharks.

He looked down at his palm, clenched his fist, then shrugged. "I no longer know why I have done what I've done. My anger at Flip overcame me. My guilt."

I stared at his hand. I didn't want this confession. I wanted to walk out of here, and a confession was not going to get me out the door.

He sighed and drew the blade again, a parallel line of blood. "He was a greedy man and a curious one. He wanted to understand what a priest did in our temples. I was naive. He questioned me, and I spoke to him about practices that he had no right to hear about. Not at first." He paused.

No. I shook my head, my eyes on those lines, the droplets of blood oozing up from his flesh, the droplets falling to the floor. He watched, too.

"I didn't tell him these stories at first. But I knew him for years. And little by little I told him about the chants, the meanings of different offerings. I told him what the rituals meant. He was obsessed by death and wanted to know what went on in the ancestor temples."

He clenched and unclenched his fist, the blood forming a tiny puddle on the floor. This was not good. Would he rise to the smell of blood to kill more? Was this self-cutting a prelude to what was to become of me? Nicks and cuts, one at a time, rather than a clean thrust of the blade. A knot began to form in my other leg.

"I was flattered by his interest in Bali life, in my culture, in my temple. I told him about the sacred objects in the temple, and he asked me to make a copy for him. He would pay me handsomely. I needed money, and it wasn't the original." He left the words hanging, watching the blood move from his wrist to his hand, to the floor.

"I knew that I could make a copy different enough from the original that it wouldn't matter." He looked up. I stopped wriggling my leg, and the knot just tightened more. "He repaid my generosity in telling him and making the sculpture for him by stealing the most important ritual object from our temple. He stole it and offered me money to be quiet when I told him he must give it back.

"When I refused and said I would turn him in, he said that he would say that I had worked with him to steal this sculpture. He said, how could he have even known that it was there if I hadn't told him. If I hadn't made him the copy. He said that he would say that I had come to him to get him to steal it. He would reveal me." Esa looked down at his kris. Glistening blood pooled on the rippling metal, and a thin, viscous stream moved down his thumb.

"I didn't tell Tyo, though maybe he would have understood the cunning of that man. I acted with Flip as if nothing had happened. After many months, long past the time when he would be suspicious of me and he thought that we were friends, I told him that I had come across a spear used in the defense of Buleleng by one of Jelantik's soldiers."

"Jelantik?"

He shook his head impatiently. "He was the general who led the resistance to the Dutch in north Bali, in the kingdom of Buleleng at Jagaraja. I told him that the spear had come to me from a family living in that region who claim to be descendants of the royal family and whose ancestors had died in the battles. I told him I would sell him the spear since I needed money and he liked old things." Esa laughed an ironic laugh.

"He invited me for lunch. Told me a woman interested in old Bali was coming. She would like to see the spear. I arrived early.

He thought my early arrival very funny, making jokes about *jam karet*, rubber time, and how *jam karet* was never early but always late. I arrived early because I knew that his people would be busy in the kitchen cooking and would not see me come. He had a Balinese painting on his easel. I'm sure that he made it to sell."

"You knew he did that? Sold fake paintings?" It surprised me, not that he knew, but that he would have stayed friends with him once he knew.

"Of course. He was a deceitful man who took pleasure in fooling others. I saw that, but ignored it for years. When I met him, I was young. I was flattered by his friendship. When I finally saw the extent of his evil, the real meaning of it, it was too late." He started to stand and I braced myself. Then he sank back down. "He told me that you came from a museum that owned one of his paintings. He liked that he had fooled the experts."

That resolved that question.

"His eyes turned greedy when he saw the spear. I held it up for him, the blade to the ceiling, and spoke of the *pamor*, how lovely, how refined. He said he couldn't see it well, so I held down the spear, the blade toward him. As he approached I drove it through him." He shrugged.

The knot had resolved, but I was frozen in place, Flip and the spear as vivid in my imagining as they'd been when I found him. It was as I'd suggested to Tyo. Flip had been reaching for the spear.

"You arrived. I heard the servant bringing you to the room. I ran outside and watched you as you stood over the body. I saw you bend over it and take something. I thought it was the sculpture and waited for you to tell Tyo." He looked at me with disgust. "You didn't. You stole it, and I was only certain when your boyfriend asked where he could find one like it."

I looked down in shame, shifting as I did, ready to take my chances and spring for the door.

"I watched and saw Tyo's look of surprise, and later learned from him that you were the sister that we met as children. The sister he thought one day he would wed. I heard Ulih screaming at the gate and knew it was time to leave." He watched me and I realized that he knew I was tensing to flee. The heat in his eyes died. "Is Tyo coming?"

"Yes," I lied.

He shook his head, then he raised his kris and drew it hard across his throat.

The moment stretched, the blood spurting from the severed artery. I watched, fascinated and shocked. I thought that he had intended to draw that lovely thing across my throat, sever my artery, bring me my death.

Now I found that death was a spectacle and I its witness. I screamed.

"IF ONLY I'd told you about the amulet. If only—"

"You should not have come here." Tyo's eyes flashed.

"Yes."

"Yes, what? Yes, you should have come?"

"I should not have. I suspected him, but thought you wouldn't believe me."

"And?"

"I was angry at you for trying to keep me from the investigation. I thought if I found something . . ."

"You would walk into the arms of Rangda to make a point."

I looked at him. "Yes, I suppose I would. I should have talked with you." I bent my head down contritely, a position I found difficult. "I should have tried to run."

"Yes, then maybe you would have died rather than Esa." His look was both speculative and sad. He started to reach for me but pulled back. "Did he speak? Did he confess?"

"Yes. He told me how it happened. That he was the third person coming for lunch. That he had brought the spear pretending he would sell it to Flip." I told him all that Esa had said.

"He'd been angry since the theft, but was biding his time. He knew all the servants would be preparing the meal and snuck in. He came early and Flip joked about rubber time."

"And the textiles and Ulih?"

"He said he wasn't a thief. He wasn't the one who tried to kill Ulih. Look, Ulih's killing was different. She was stabbed with a kitchen knife. Although he didn't admit it in so many words, I feel pretty certain he killed Eric."

"But why would Esa have killed Eric? How did he even know him?"

"He didn't tell me. But when you were young, was he in love with Ulih?"

"Yes, when we were very young. But it ended." Wayan Tyo looked thoughtful. "He said it ended, and I believed him."

"Well, he felt some loyalty to her. We can only speculate. I was trying to drag out the conversation so that I could live longer. I hoped if I kept talking . . . I hoped I had time to ask everything before I died. At one point he said, 'the girl.' I think he regretted the death of the girl. Maybe some evidence will turn up here." I looked at Esa, now lying on the floor in a pool of blood.

"Ulih has told me it was Eric who attacked her."

"She's awake? She's all right?"

"Yes. She didn't actually see him. She thought it was one of the servants coming up the stairs. He crept up behind her and drove the blade into her back. She did smell him, a smell of cologne she recognized mixed with cigarettes, a smell he carried with him everywhere. Whether that would have been enough to convict him, I do not know. He did know her house, as he had bought textiles from her in the past. But I still do not understand what Esa had to do with Eric."

"Did you tell him that Eric had stolen the paintings?" I asked, reaching for my calf that was knotting again.

"Yes, I did."

"Maybe the link to Flip was enough. He might have been afraid that Eric would reveal his connection to Flip. Or that Eric would continue where Flip left off."

"Possible. Or maybe he knew Eric tried to kill Ulih."

"There are many possible reasons. His former feelings for Ulih. His hatred of foreigners."

Tyo scowled. "I don't think so. I know he was angry at the changes brought about by all the foreigners here. But hate all the foreigners? No."

"I felt it. And, really, what else was this about? Esa hated the changes we foreigners bring. He hated that he'd been taken in by Flip."

Wayan Tyo didn't answer.

"We talked about the theft. I told him I would help him find the sculpture."

Tyo reached for my elbow to steer me out of the forge. He'd seen that I was mesmerized by Esa, the blood, that I had begun to shake. "What did you say?"

"I told him the steps that I would take. I told him that I knew another possibility, a foreigner who had been in contact with Flip and who vanished at the time of the theft." I didn't add, at the time your wife vanished.

He stopped in his tracks. "And?"

"He said that he had followed that lead and that it led no-where. He was very dismissive."

"Did you get the sense that he'd harmed that man?" Wayan Tyo's brow furrowed.

"I wondered. I thought of it as he spoke. But I don't think so. I don't think that he did. I think he knew that the man had left and that was it. Maybe he asked Flip. Maybe there was more. I didn't get the information. I'm sorry."

He looked away. "I am sorry, too."

"I'm so grateful that you came to look for me."

Surprised, he said, "I wasn't looking for you. I came to ask Esa about the sculpture in the temple. It didn't seem old to me.

I had no idea that you were here. Like you, I had switched the direction of my inquiries."

So much for my abilities with mental telepathy. I looked back over my shoulder.

"Ani, too." He didn't continue.

"Ani, too, what?"

"She suspected him. I think she could see the direction your suspicions were moving. Last night as we went home, she told me that I had to talk with him. She encouraged me to go last night." He shook his head. "I should have listened."

Vehicles were arriving. We watched in silence as men carrying cases and cameras piled out of the vans.

"The blood does spurt, you know."

He looked at me incredulously. "This is what strikes you? A man, my oldest and best friend, is dead and this is what is in your mind?"

I shut my eyes. "It's the visual. It's what I see that's in my mind. Esa pacing. The kris dangling from his fingertips. The parallel lines of blood across his palm. Barong, grinning its golden grin. Esa's sad eyes on me. The brief, refined motion as he raised the kris, then drew it across his neck."

Wayan Tyo gathered me in his arms, and, with my face pressed into his damp shirt, I said, "I see Flip and how he lay. I could lie exactly as Flip lay on that bamboo floor."

He squeezed me tighter.

"But, I have no feeling for Flip. He wasn't a nice man, was he?" I pulled back and looked up at him. "But Esa was different. He was your friend, accepted into your family. I saw their warmth toward him that first night. You two with your shoulders together as you sat. Your daughter leaning against his knee as she spoke with you."

"Yes," he said, his voice tight.

"He hoped to deliver Bali from the horde of tourists that descend upon his home every year. A completely unrealistic hope, which he went about trying to achieve in the most primitive manner."

"Flip was blackmailing him. He pushed him into a corner," Tyo said sadly.

"He felt duty."

We both thought about that for a few minutes.

"Yes, he was a dutiful man," said Tyo.

"Yes." I hesitated to say more, but finished by saying, "He murdered him. A primal act. Was he a primitive man? He was a man of learning, a man of power, a blacksmith. Ani told me that one day he would be an important man in your community. He ignored all that. He felt at a loss to control his way of life. He saw all this slipping away." I waved my free arm and stepped away from him.

"No, the seeing is how I absorb it. I look, I see the scene, the object, I observe the details, I take it in. I fit it into my mind through the visual. Murder is not right, but you can almost understand."

Tyo squeezed my hand.

50

"I'm so tense, my shoulders are practically in my ears." I was sitting with Ani under her tree in the familiar courtyard, but I could barely recall getting there. We were side by side, her proximity a comfort. I put a *porosan* on the pile of *porosans* and rolled my shoulders.

"No wonder," said Ani. "You have had a difficult week."

"You could call it that. I hope next week I can fall into a routine of research, paintings, collectors. The simple things of a curator's life."

"Maybe. Then you will go home."

"Yes."

"Are you anxious to get away?"

"No, I'm not. Now that I'm here, I could stay. But my life is there, you know. My career. My other family." I looked at her out of the corner of my eye as I folded another *porosan*. "I'm happy that I've found you and Tyo again. I'll have to talk my parents into coming here with me. My mother is thrilled that we've met."

"Did you tell her what has been happening during your time here?"

"No, she'd have a heart attack. I'll tell her when I get home. After it's over."

Wayan Tyo's daughters came in and hung on me. "I'll miss these two."

"We will all miss you. In the meantime, you should come to our home as often as possible while you are here, so that we renew our friendship to the fullest."

I didn't answer. My relationship with Wayan Tyo felt so confused, so filled with ups and downs, so intense, that I wasn't sure how much time I wanted to spend around him.

Sensing my hesitation, Ani said, "It is fine. He is your brother. There have been moments that he has not known that. He knows now and it is a bit of a disappointment. I can see it in him. A disappointment and a relief."

I nodded, uncertain if she was correct. She certainly knew more than I.

"YOU are very tense," Tyo said as he walked toward me.

"You look relaxed. Sad, but relaxed."

"I am sad. Esa and I were very close for many years. Recently it has been more difficult. I have worried about the loss of my wife, and that distanced us, as he never liked her and thought her leaving good. Also, he had become more and more rigid, so that often I could not talk with him about important things. He would get too angry. He had become anger."

Ani patted his arm and he sat down heavily.

We sat for a long time, each of us in our thoughts. I tried to frame what had happened that morning and how I felt. But, instead I framed a series of scenes culminating in Esa, kris sliding across his throat.

I felt that my life would never be the same. The phrase "a defining moment" marched like a banner across my mind.

"I've just come from Flip's house." He ran his hand through his hair. "I went to tell them what happened. I found most of them at the servants' quarters, talking with the bird. When the bird saw me, he said, 'Hell yes, Hell yes.'"

I smiled. "That's what it said to me."

"Yes. When I said to them that it was foolish of Flip to teach him to say 'Hell, yes,' they all laughed at me and said that was not what he said."

"What did they think he said?"

"They said that he was saying "Hello, Esa." He said hello to many of Flip's friends. He learned their names over the years. He was telling us the name of the killer."

"That would have been one for the books."

He reached across Ani and touched my shoulder and squeezed. "Like a rock. I'm going to give you a massage."

"Good idea," said Ani, who had begun weaving small boxes for offerings. We were each trying to move from the morning's events in our own way.

I thought of the few moments he'd massaged me the other day. "That's okay. I don't need a massage."

"Yes, you do."

"Don't. I'm fine."

"He is a very good masseur," Ani said. "Trained."

"When did you have time for that? Between being a painter and a policeman? Were you a Bali cowboy on the beach?"

"Very funny. Come to the massage table. This will help relax me, too."

"You have a massage table?"

"My brother gives massage here. Did you not know? He has a large foreign clientele."

"No, I didn't know. Really, I'm fine."

He grabbed my hand and pulled me out of my seat. I followed, uncertain how I felt about his hands on me.

"It's okay. I know your body."

"What are you talking about, you know my body?"

"From all our past lives. You have been my wife before."

"Ah, I see. You mean I've had this body many times? Seems unlikely."

"Yes, it does. If I had described it before you arrived last week, I would have described exactly you, down to the mole next to your belly button."

This startled me. "That must have been there when I was eight."

He shrugged. "Take off your clothes."

"This isn't appropriate."

"Shall my mother come to join us, so that you feel safe? You are so stubborn."

"All right, all right." I turned modestly away, stripped down to my underwear, wrapped a sarong around me, then lay face down on the table.

He began with my feet, gently tapping the pressure points, testing what needed work. Then he slowly, languorously swept his hands up my leg. His gentle touch caressed me from the tips of my toes to my upper thigh. When he kneaded the flesh from thigh to knee, I felt the thrill of pure touch, not sexual, and as he continued over my legs, my back, my arms I could feel myself relax and fall into the sensations of my body.

I fell asleep and woke only briefly when he rolled me over, then fell back into a peaceful slumber and a dream of voluptuous, sensual contentment. In my dream I felt him run his hands up the length of my body. Then with the lightest of touches he swept his fingers over my face, like the hint of a feather. I could have sworn that he kissed me on the forehead and said, "I'll always love you, Mimpi." But that may have been part of my dream.

Acknowledgments

There are so many people who have been supportive throughout the writing of this manuscript that I hardly know where to begin. Elizabeth Fuller Collins, my number one reader, comments brilliantly on everything she reads. The weekly support of my writing group—Nina Schuyler, Eliza Harding Turner, Elizabeth Rieke, John Philipp, Amy Torgeson—helps keep me going. The people who have recently traveled with me in Bali— Tracy Power, Ken Seeger, Fawn Yacker, Hisako Takahashi, Lynn Roy, Marie-Helene Yalom, Barbara Wood—tolerated my endless questions with grace, and I thank them. Badung, who answered many of my questions, was helpful above and beyond the call of duty. I couldn't ask for a more patient and helpful group of people than the staff of Swallow Press. Special thanks to Gillian Berchowitz, director and editor in chief, who is always available, thoughtful, and insightful. And, of course, my thanks to my family, who always cheer me on.